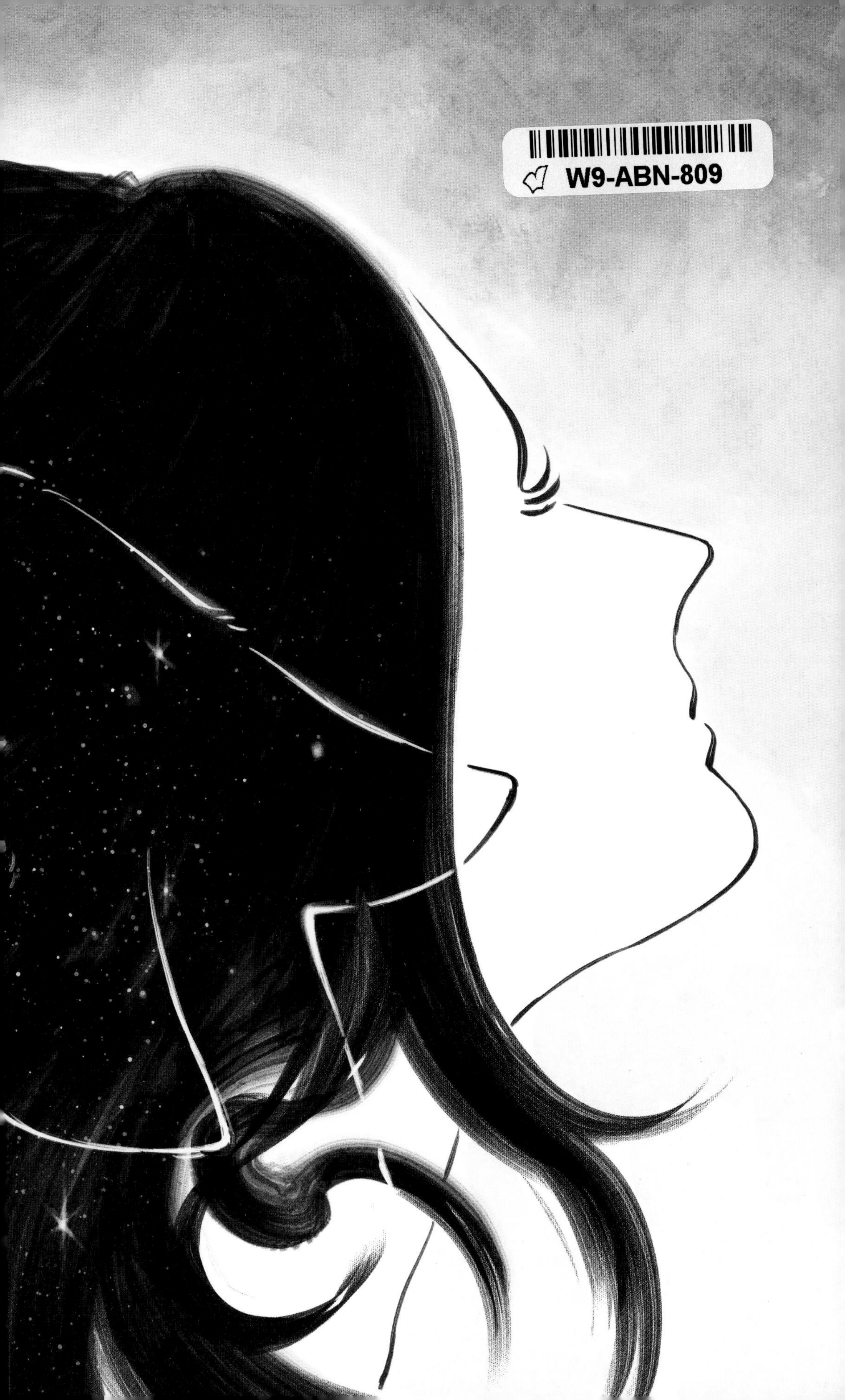

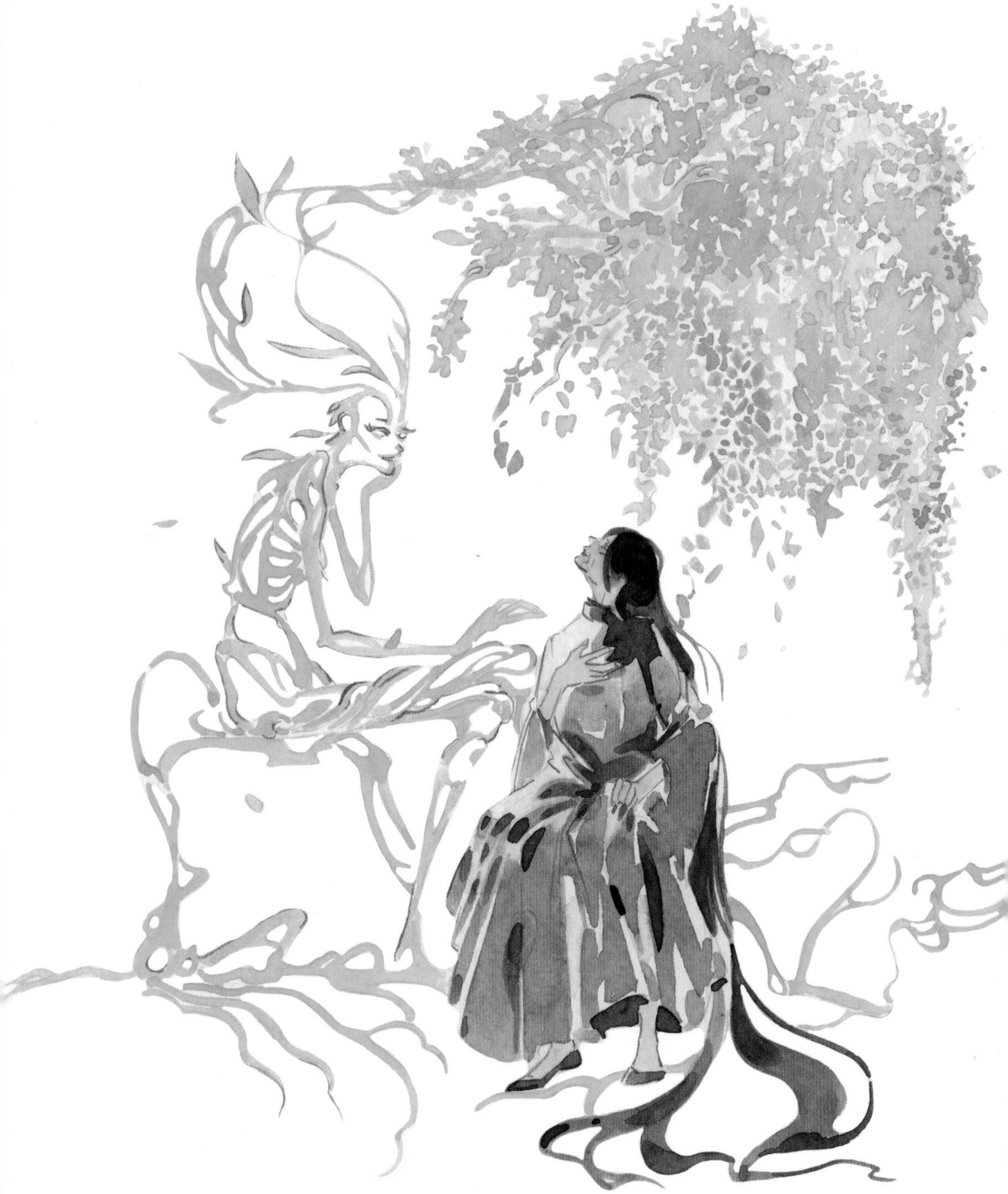

MIRROR
THE NEST

*Special thanks to Tricia Ramos, Carey Hall,
Eric Stephenson, and Jeff Boison.*

HWEI LIM . EMMA RÍOS

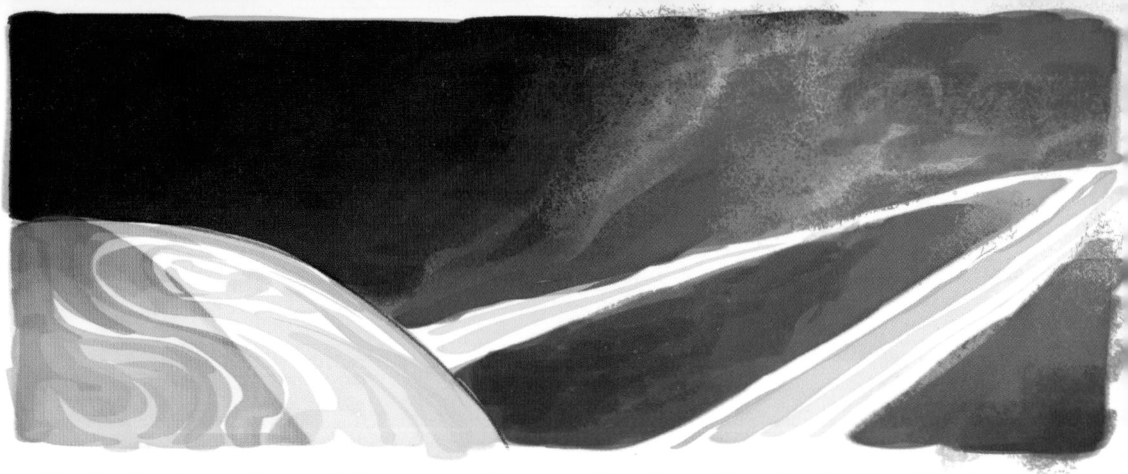

The Synchronia - a collective of planets, centrally governed by a Council based on the planet Temple.
On Temple is located one of the few portals to the *span*, an inter-dimensional space filled with a mysterious substance given the simple name of *ether*, whose exact nature and composition remains a mystery to the scientists and mages of the Synchronia even today.

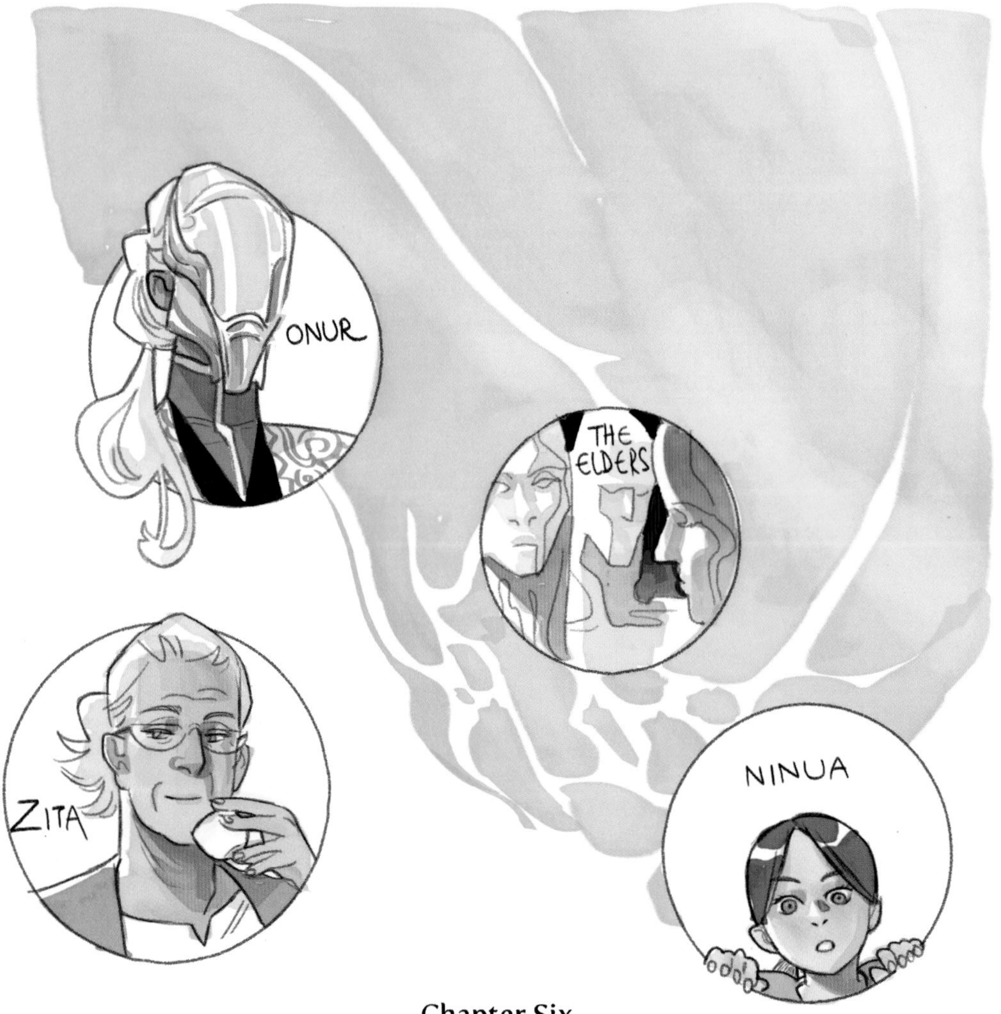
ONUR
THE ELDERS
ZITA
NINUA

Chapter Six

The survivors of the colony leave the Irzah asteroid for good and retrace their steps home, and their memory kindles the history behind their first departure.

In the utopian dreamlands of the Synchronia, half a century ago, a young artist awakens something from its long, deep sleep, in the stones of a primitive ruin.

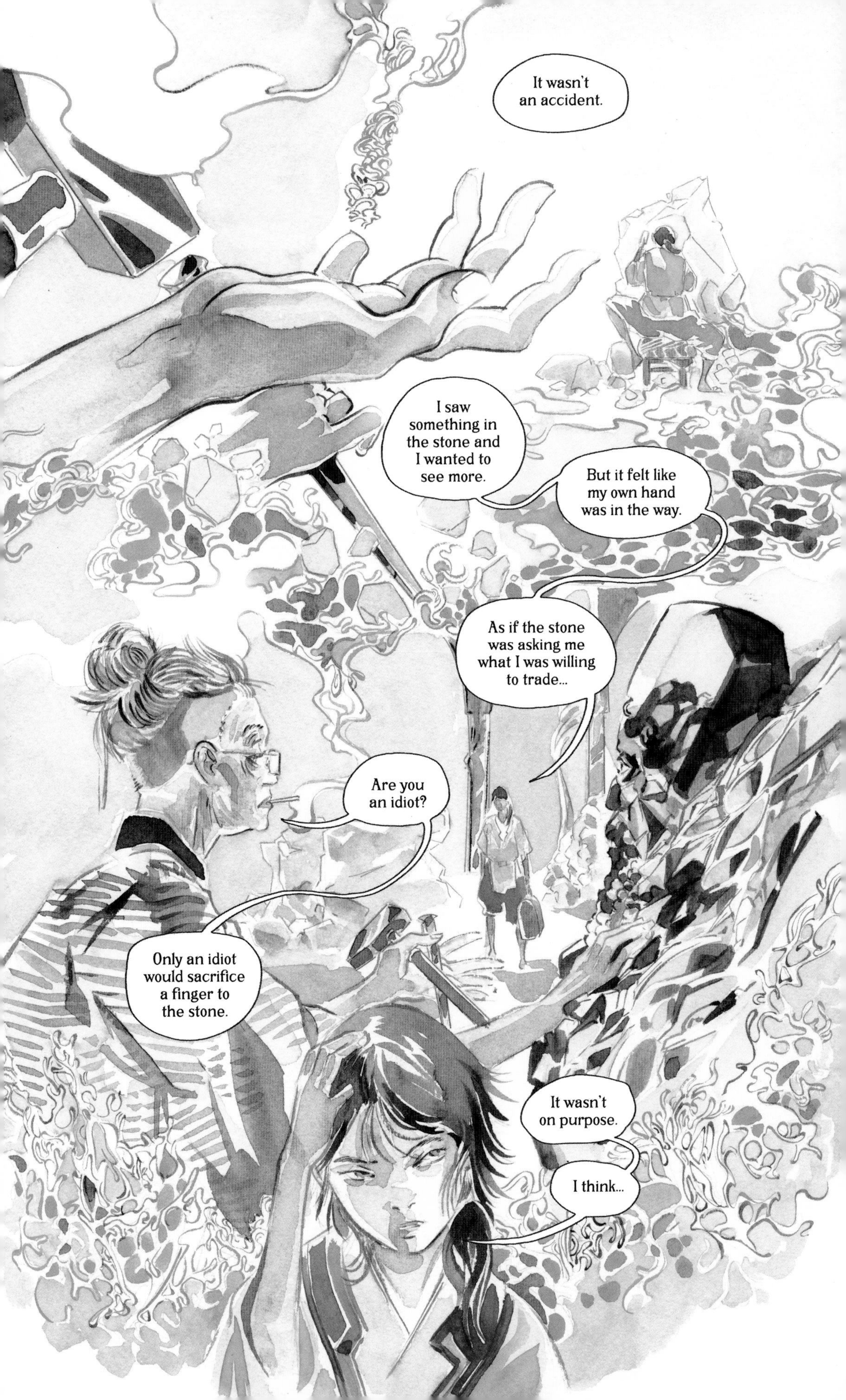
It wasn't an accident.
I saw something in the stone and I wanted to see more.
But it felt like my own hand was in the way.
As if the stone was asking me what I was willing to trade...
Are you an idiot?
Only an idiot would sacrifice a finger to the stone.
It wasn't on purpose.
I think...

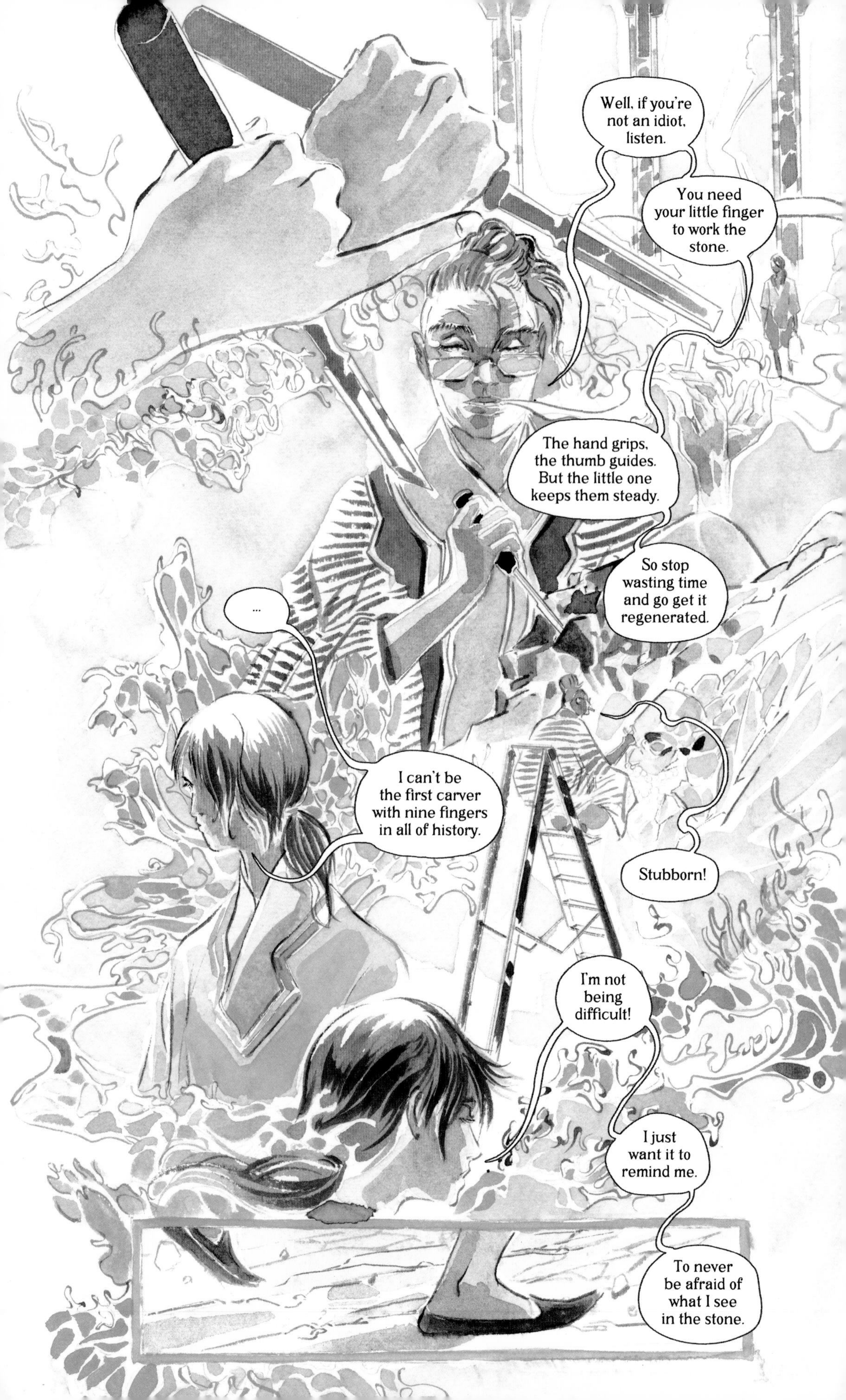

Well, if you're not an idiot, listen.
You need your little finger to work the stone.
The hand grips, the thumb guides. But the little one keeps them steady.
So stop wasting time and go get it regenerated.
...
I can't be the first carver with nine fingers in all of history.
Stubborn!
I'm not being difficult!
I just want it to remind me.
To never be afraid of what I see in the stone.

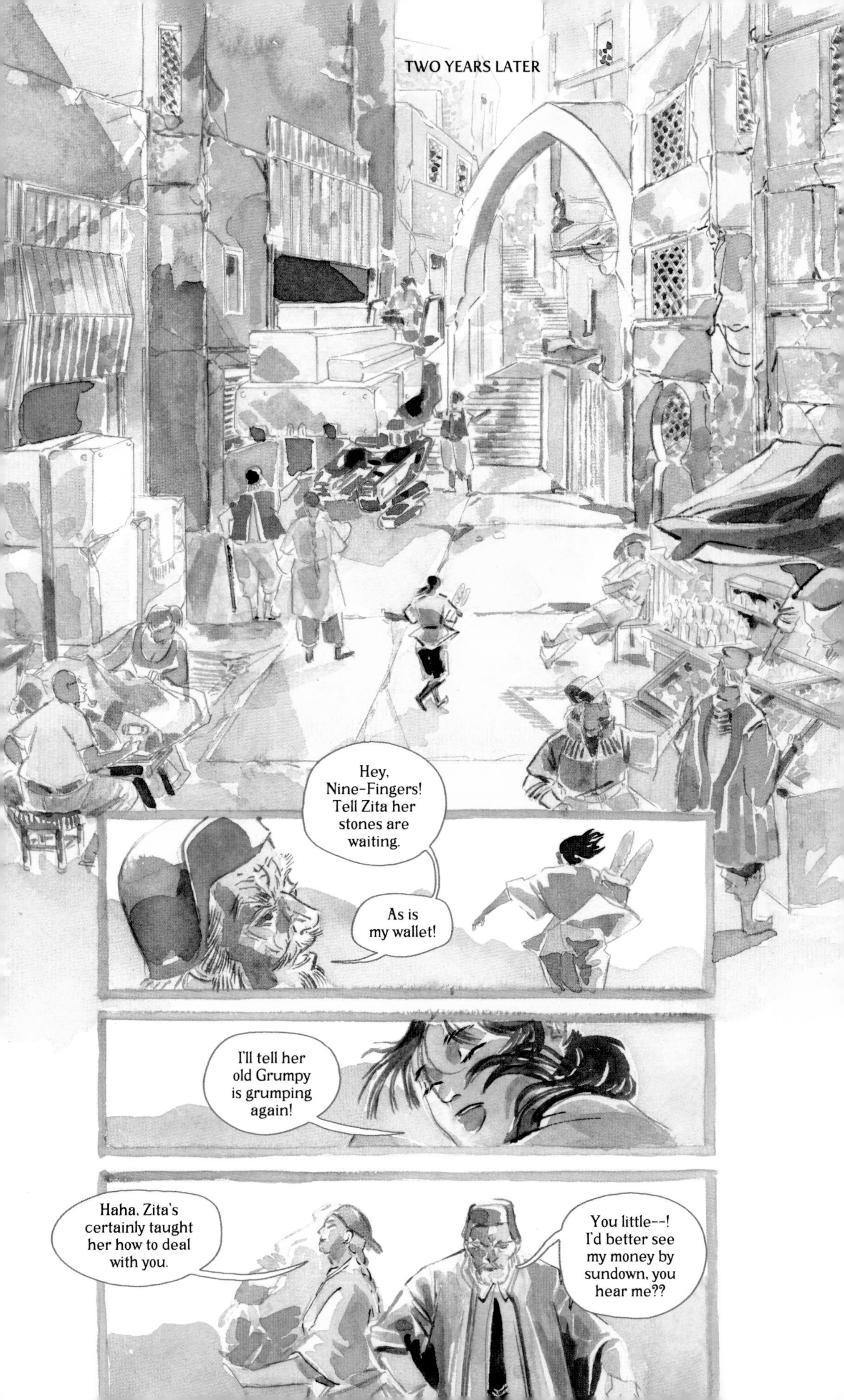
TWO YEARS LATER
Hey, Nine-Fingers! Tell Zita her stones are waiting.
As is my wallet!
I'll tell her old Grumpy is grumping again!
Haha, Zita's certainly taught her how to deal with you.
You little--! I'd better see my money by sundown, you hear me??

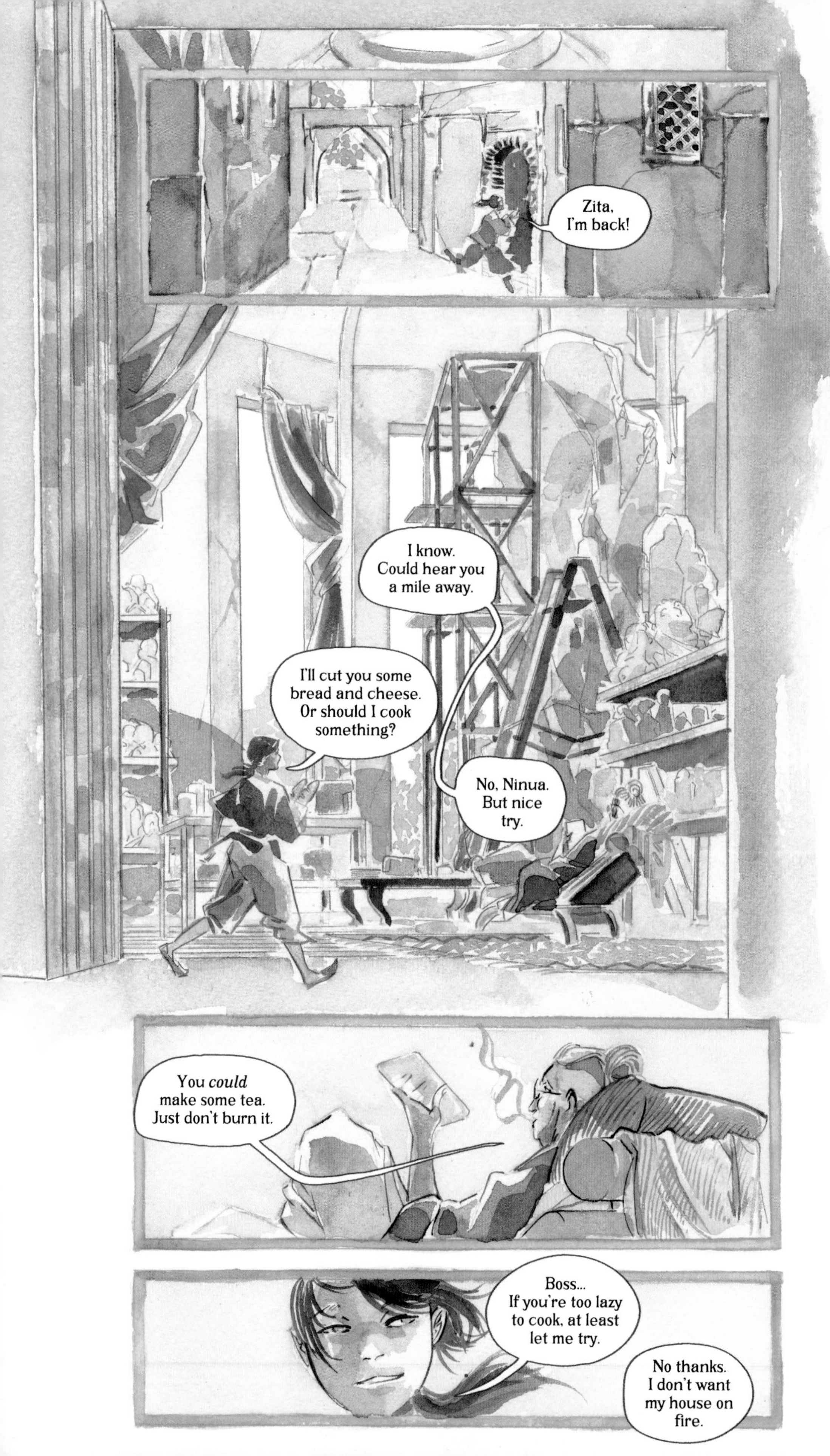
Zita, I'm back!
I know. Could hear you a mile away.
I'll cut you some bread and cheese. Or should I cook something?
No, Ninua. But nice try.
You *could* make some tea. Just don't burn it.
Boss... If you're too lazy to cook, at least let me try.
No thanks. I don't want my house on fire.

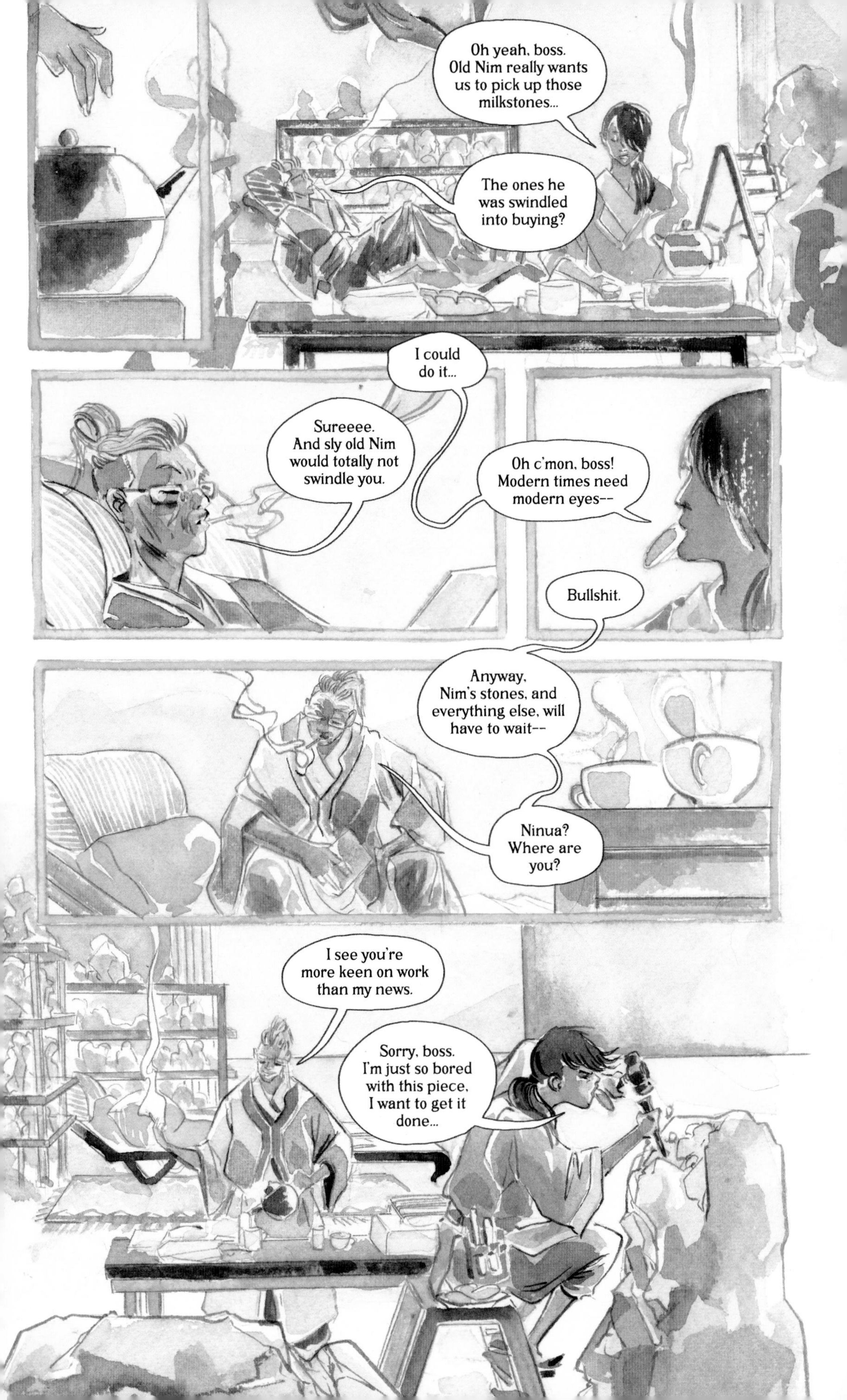
Oh yeah, boss. Old Nim really wants us to pick up those milkstones...
The ones he was swindled into buying?
I could do it...
Sureeee. And sly old Nim would totally not swindle you.
Oh c'mon, boss! Modern times need modern eyes--
Bullshit.
Anyway, Nim's stones, and everything else, will have to wait--
Ninua? Where are you?
I see you're more keen on work than my news.
Sorry, boss. I'm just so bored with this piece, I want to get it done...

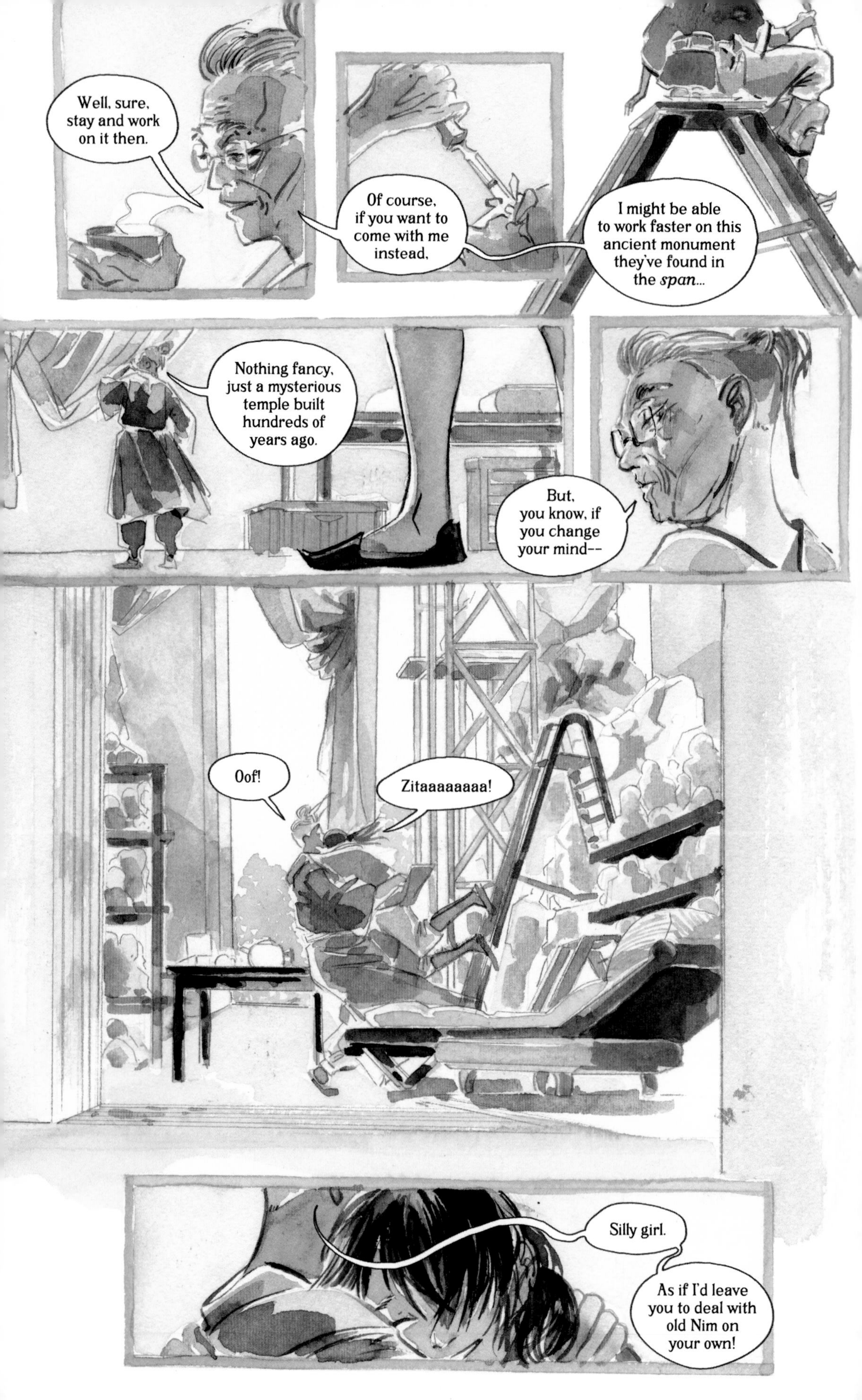
Well, sure, stay and work on it then.
Of course, if you want to come with me instead,
I might be able to work faster on this ancient monument they've found in the *span*...
Nothing fancy, just a mysterious temple built hundreds of years ago.
But, you know, if you change your mind--
Oof!
Zitaaaaaaaa!
Silly girl.
As if I'd leave you to deal with old Nim on your own!

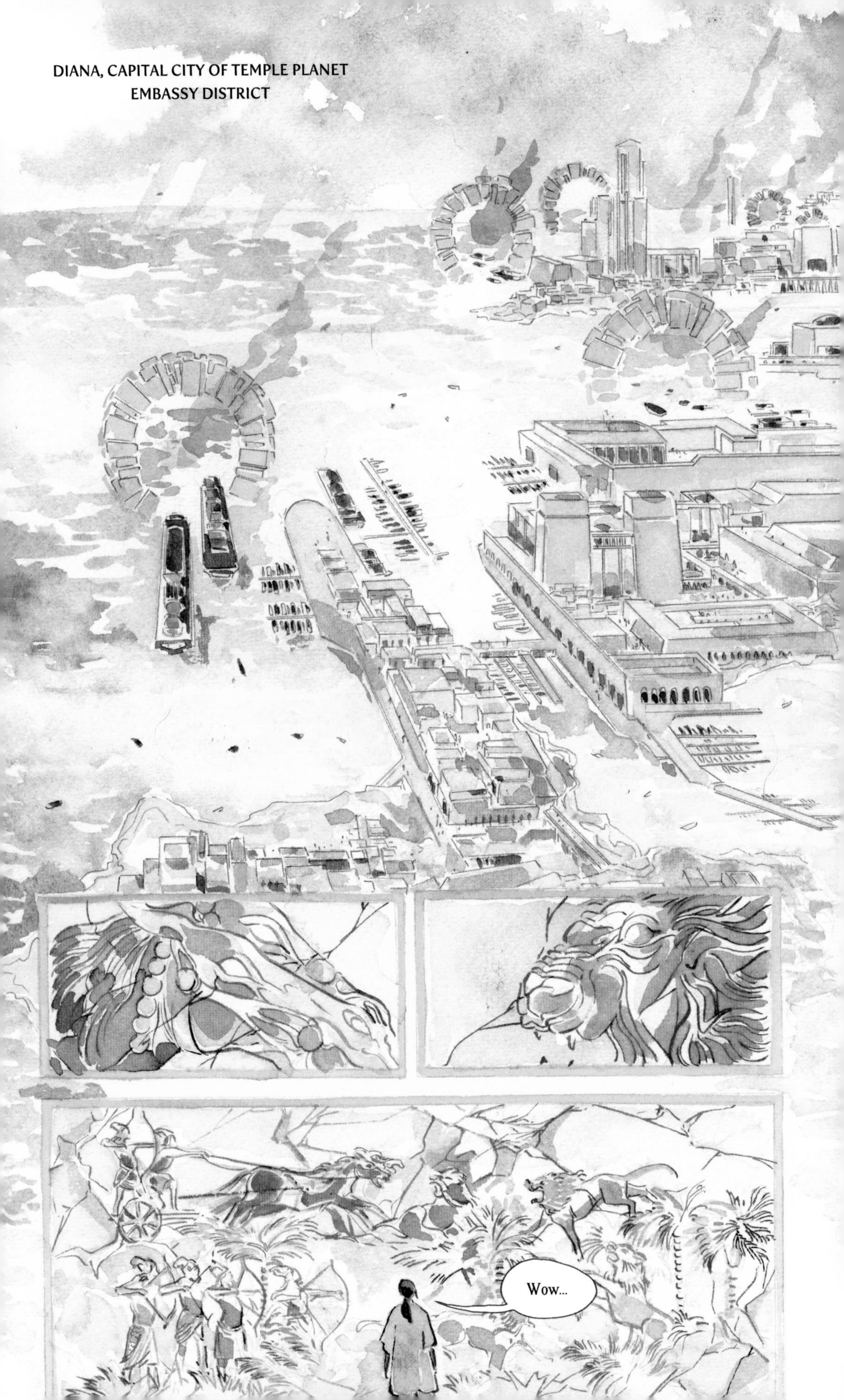
DIANA, CAPITAL CITY OF TEMPLE PLANET
EMBASSY DISTRICT
Wow...

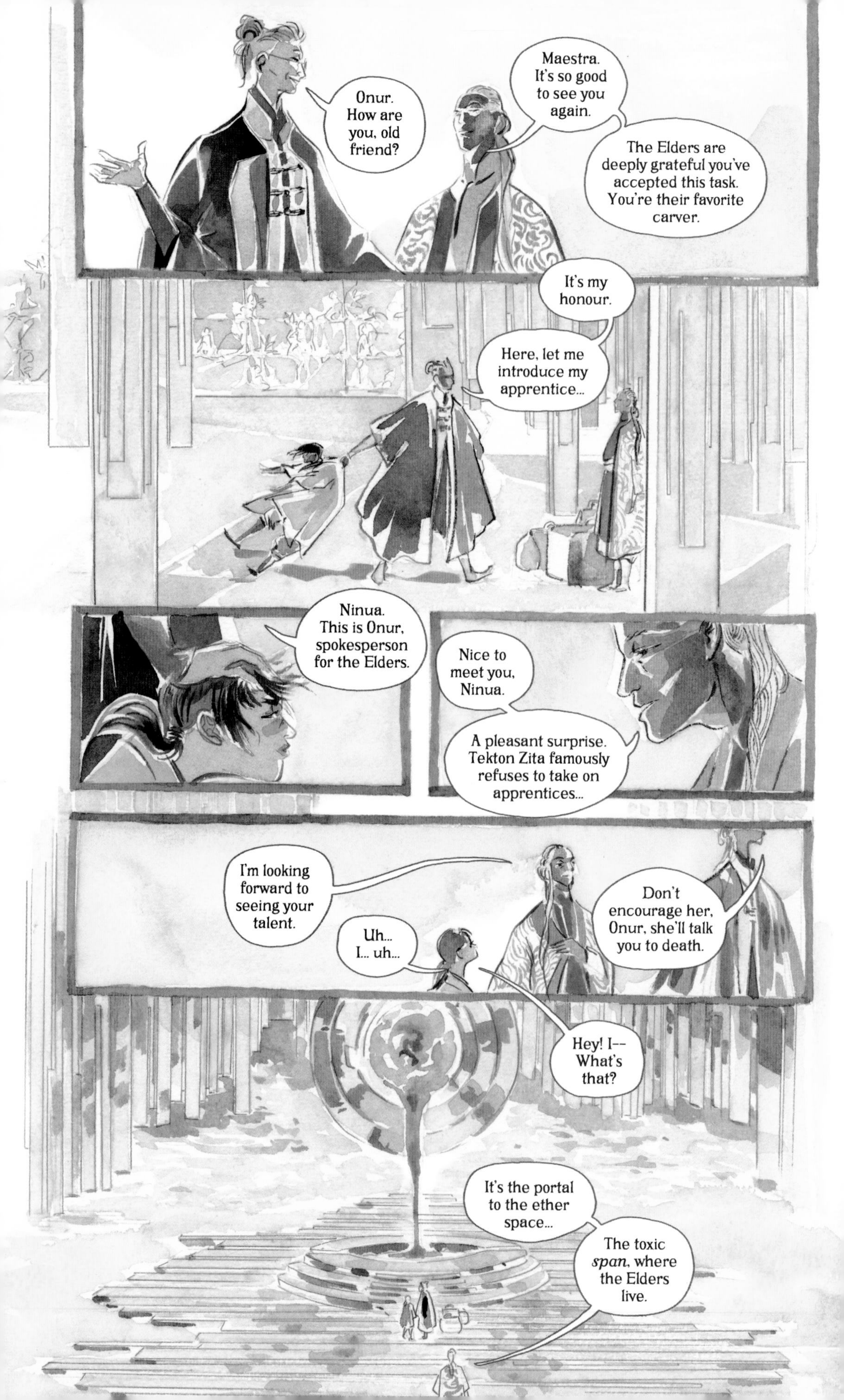
Onur. How are you, old friend?
Maestra. It's so good to see you again.
The Elders are deeply grateful you've accepted this task. You're their favorite carver.
It's my honour.
Here, let me introduce my apprentice...
Ninua. This is Onur, spokesperson for the Elders.
Nice to meet you, Ninua.
A pleasant surprise. Tekton Zita famously refuses to take on apprentices...
I'm looking forward to seeing your talent.
Uh... I... uh...
Don't encourage her, Onur, she'll talk you to death.
Hey! I-- What's that?
It's the portal to the ether space...
The toxic *span*, where the Elders live.

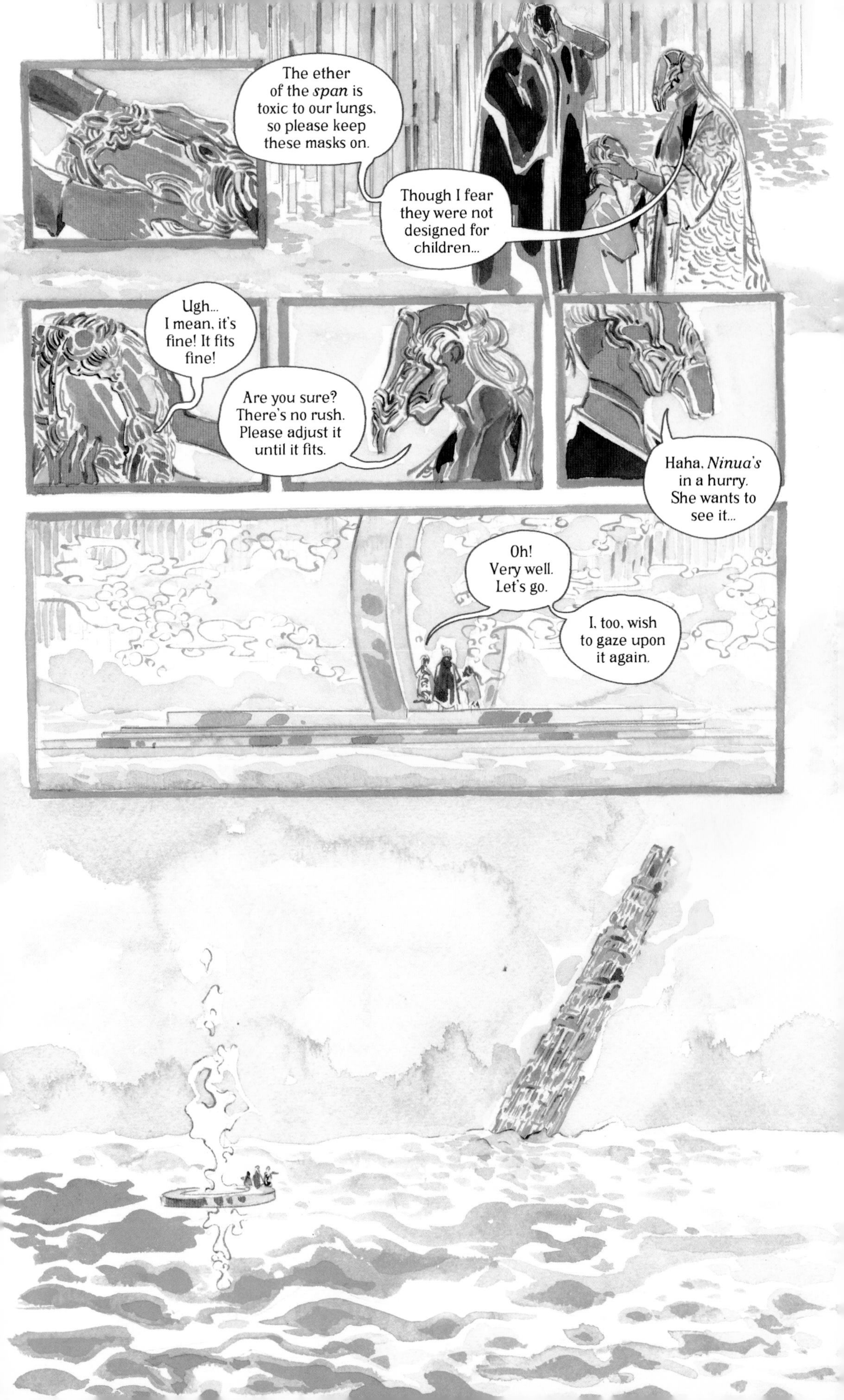

The ether of the *span* is toxic to our lungs, so please keep these masks on.
Though I fear they were not designed for children...
Ugh... I mean, it's fine! It fits fine!
Are you sure? There's no rush. Please adjust it until it fits.
Haha, *Ninua's* in a hurry. She wants to see it...
Oh! Very well. Let's go.
I, too, wish to gaze upon it again.

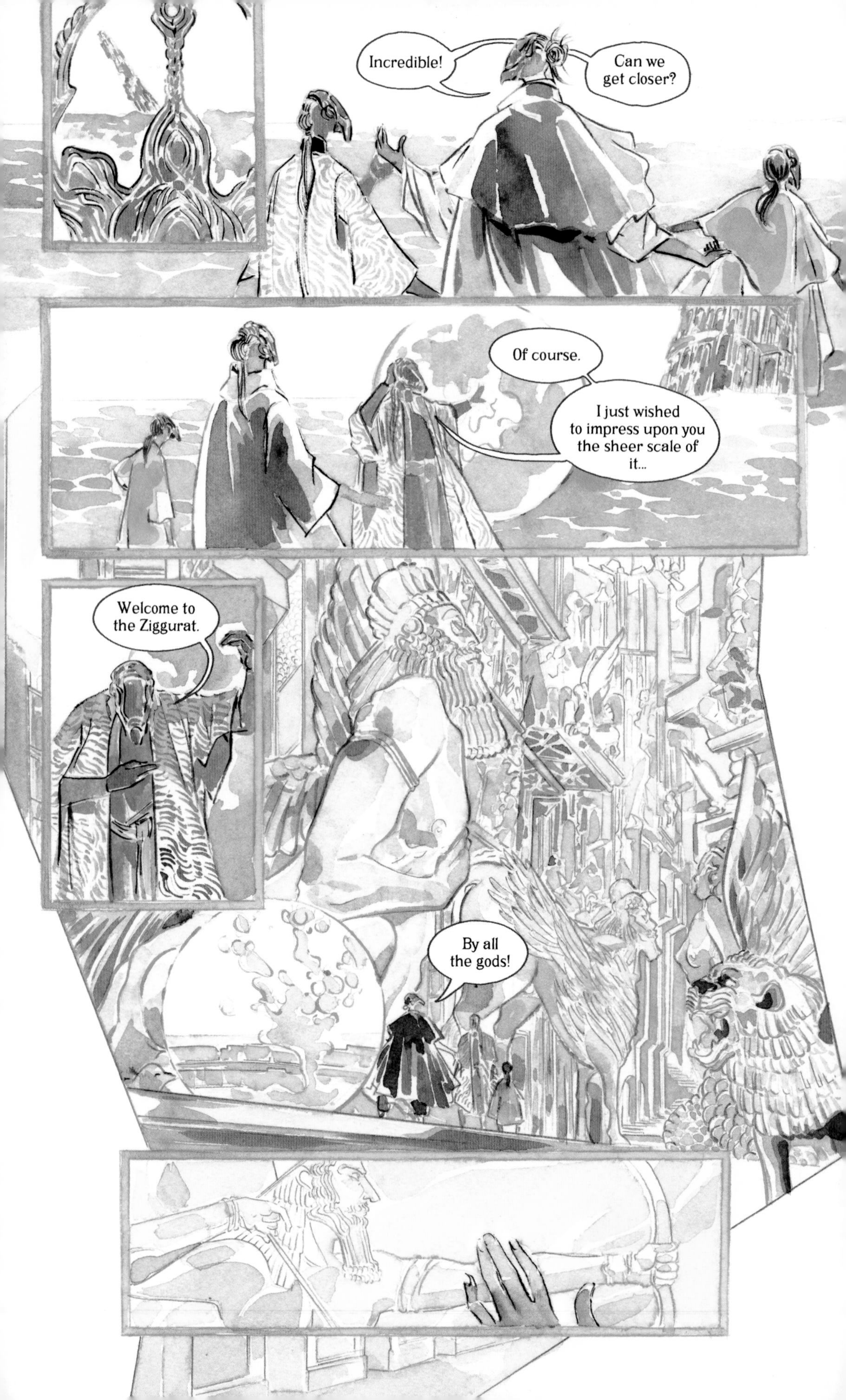
Incredible!
Can we get closer?
Of course.
I just wished to impress upon you the sheer scale of it...
Welcome to the Ziggurat.
By all the gods!

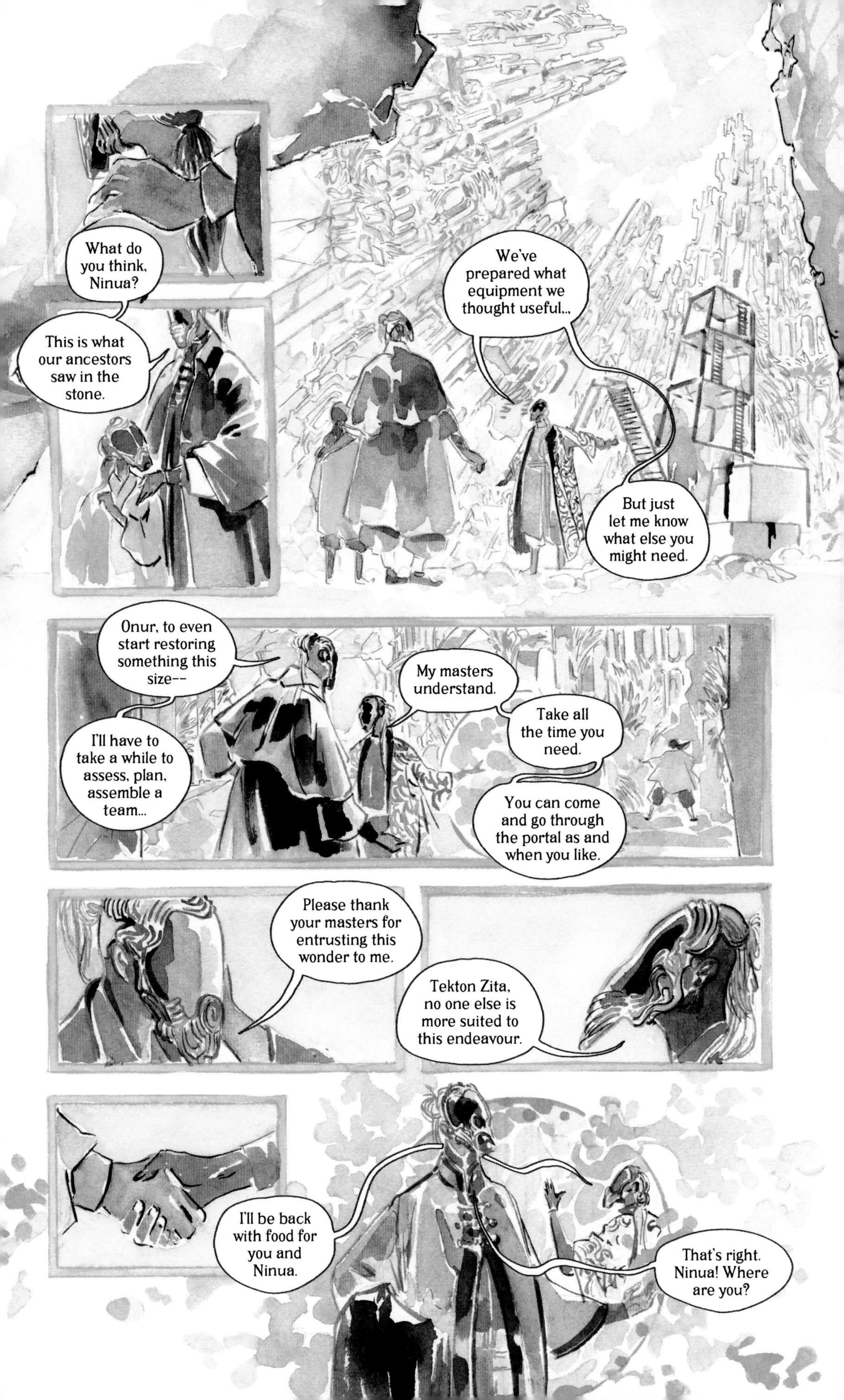
What do you think, Ninua?
This is what our ancestors saw in the stone.
We've prepared what equipment we thought useful...
But just let me know what else you might need.
Onur, to even start restoring something this size--
I'll have to take a while to assess, plan, assemble a team...
My masters understand.
Take all the time you need.
You can come and go through the portal as and when you like.
Please thank your masters for entrusting this wonder to me.
Tekton Zita, no one else is more suited to this endeavour.
I'll be back with food for you and Ninua.
That's right. Ninua! Where are you?

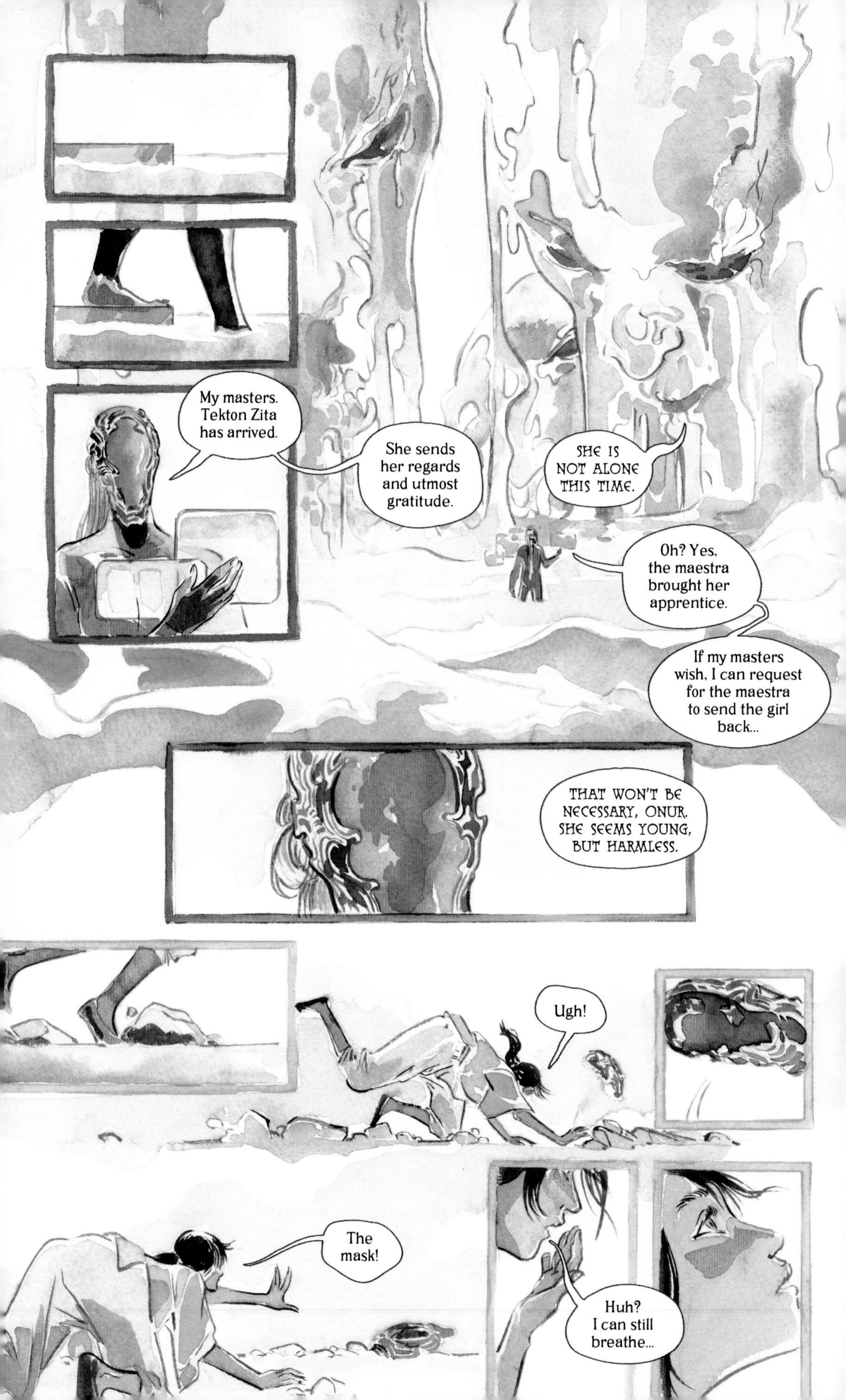
My masters. Tekton Zita has arrived.
She sends her regards and utmost gratitude.
SHE IS NOT ALONE THIS TIME.
Oh? Yes, the maestra brought her apprentice.
If my masters wish, I can request for the maestra to send the girl back...
THAT WON'T BE NECESSARY, ONUR. SHE SEEMS YOUNG, BUT HARMLESS.
Ugh!
The mask!
Huh? I can still breathe...

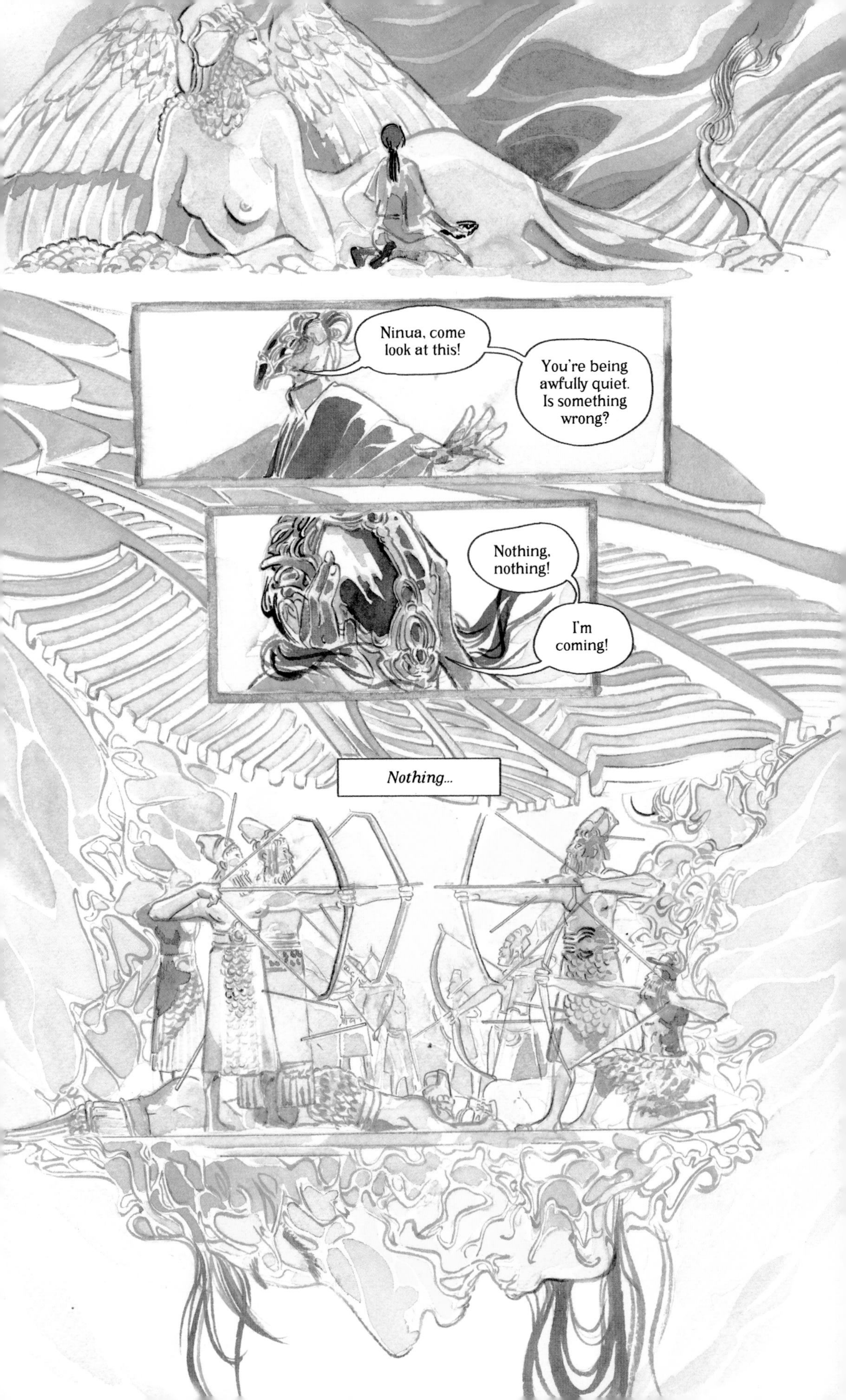
Ninua, come look at this!
You're being awfully quiet. Is something wrong?
Nothing, nothing!
I'm coming!
Nothing...

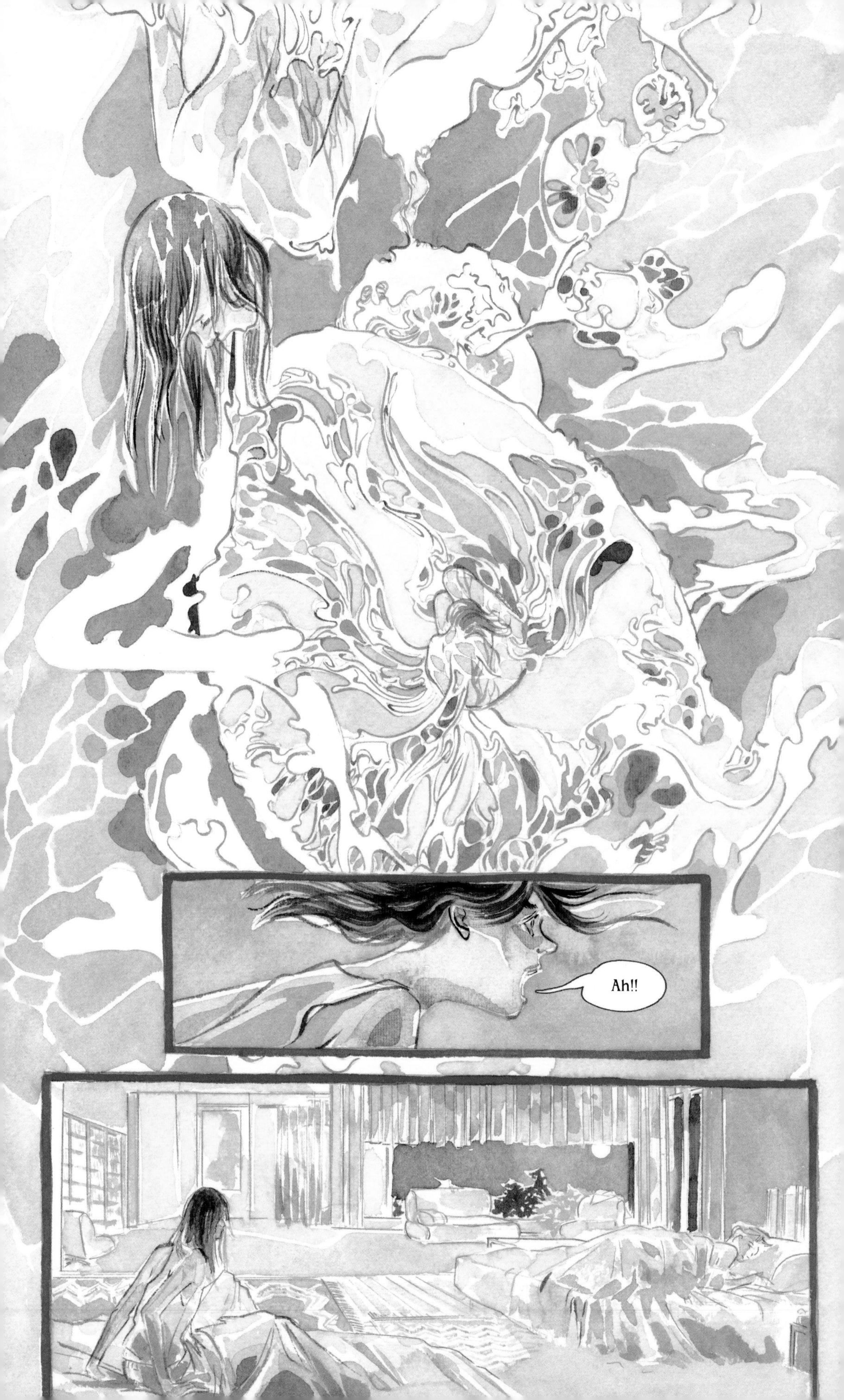
Ah!!

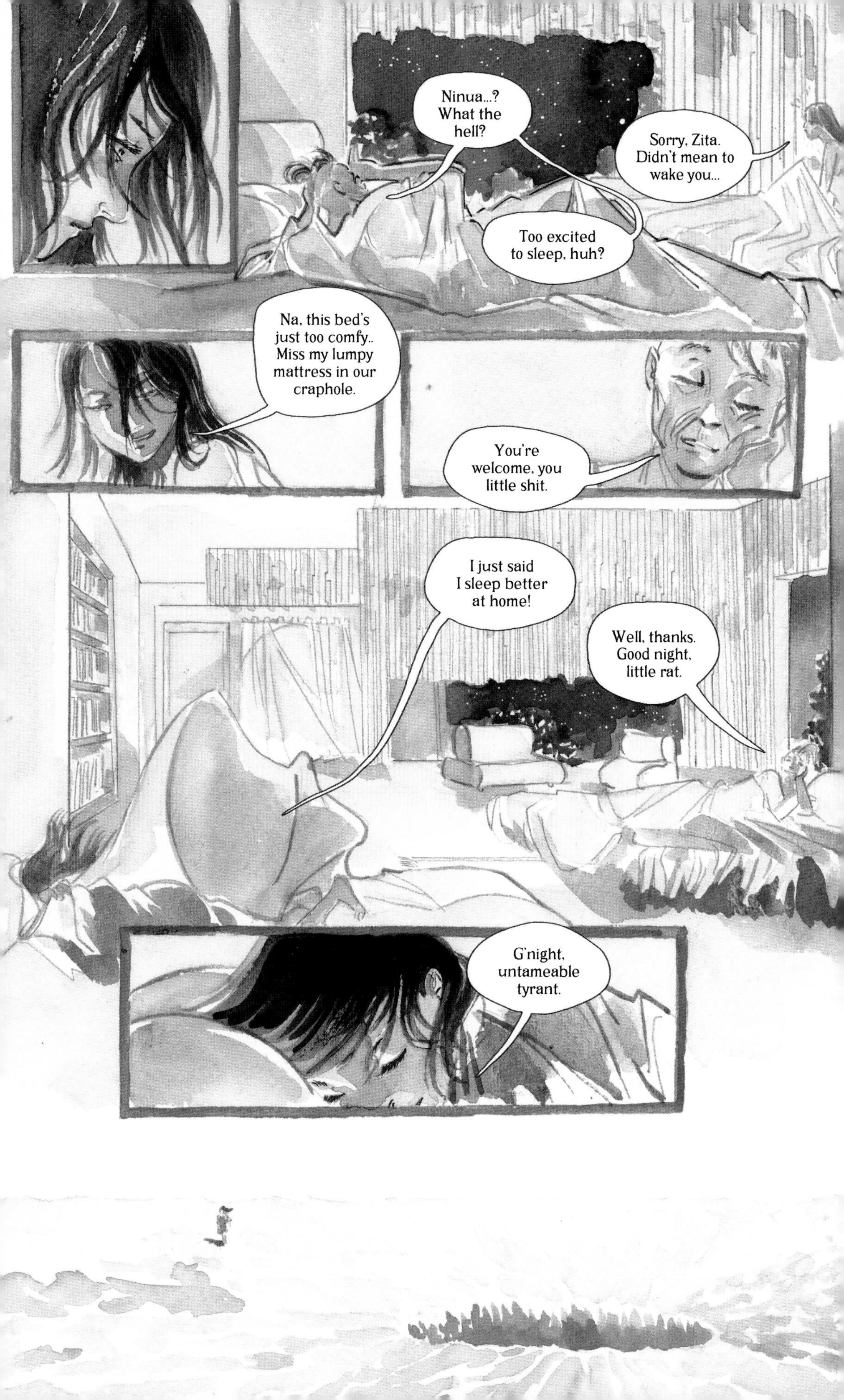
Ninua...? What the hell?
Sorry, Zita. Didn't mean to wake you...
Too excited to sleep, huh?
Na, this bed's just too comfy.. Miss my lumpy mattress in our craphole.
You're welcome, you little shit.
I just said I sleep better at home!
Well, thanks. Good night, little rat.
G'night, untameable tyrant.

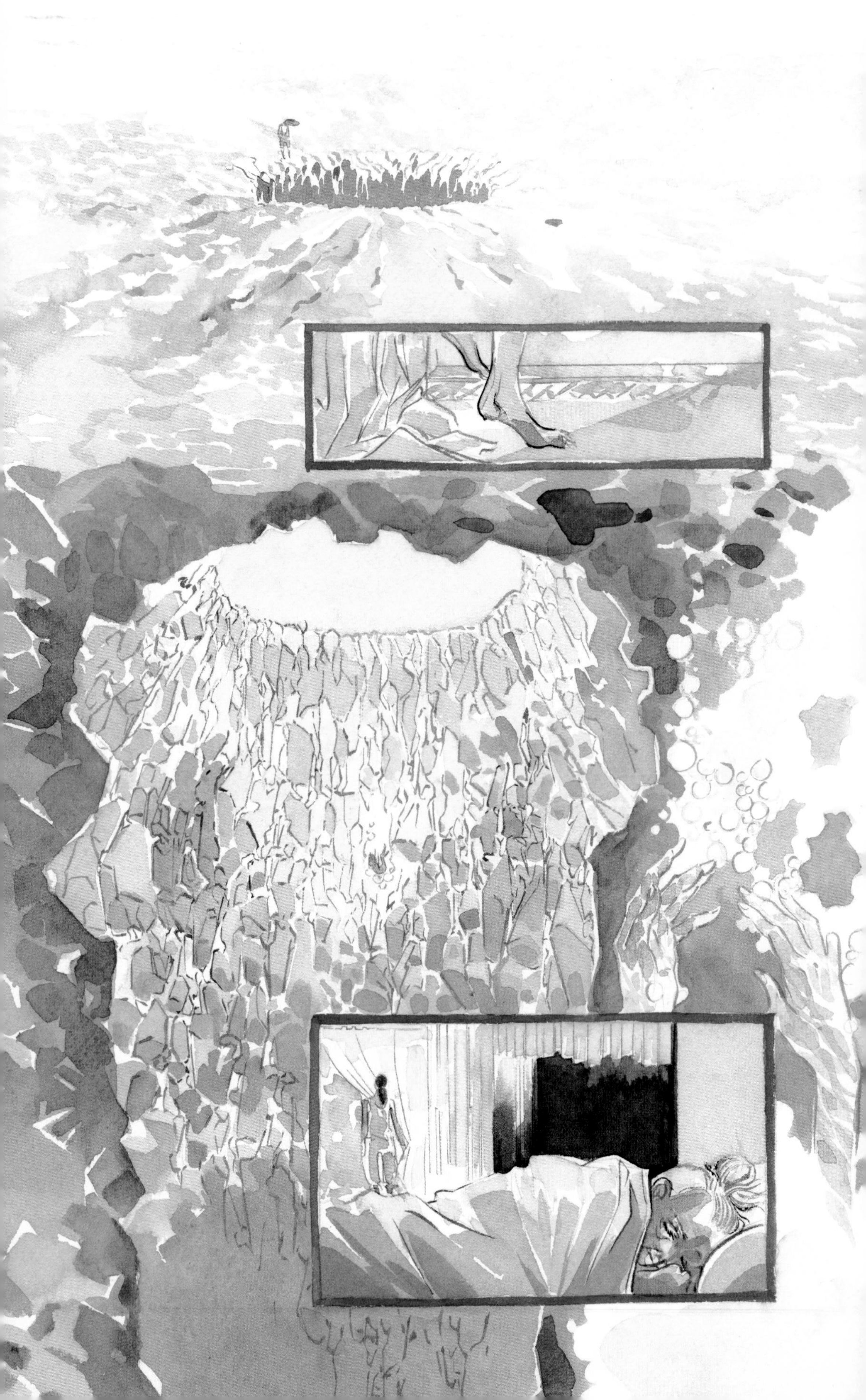

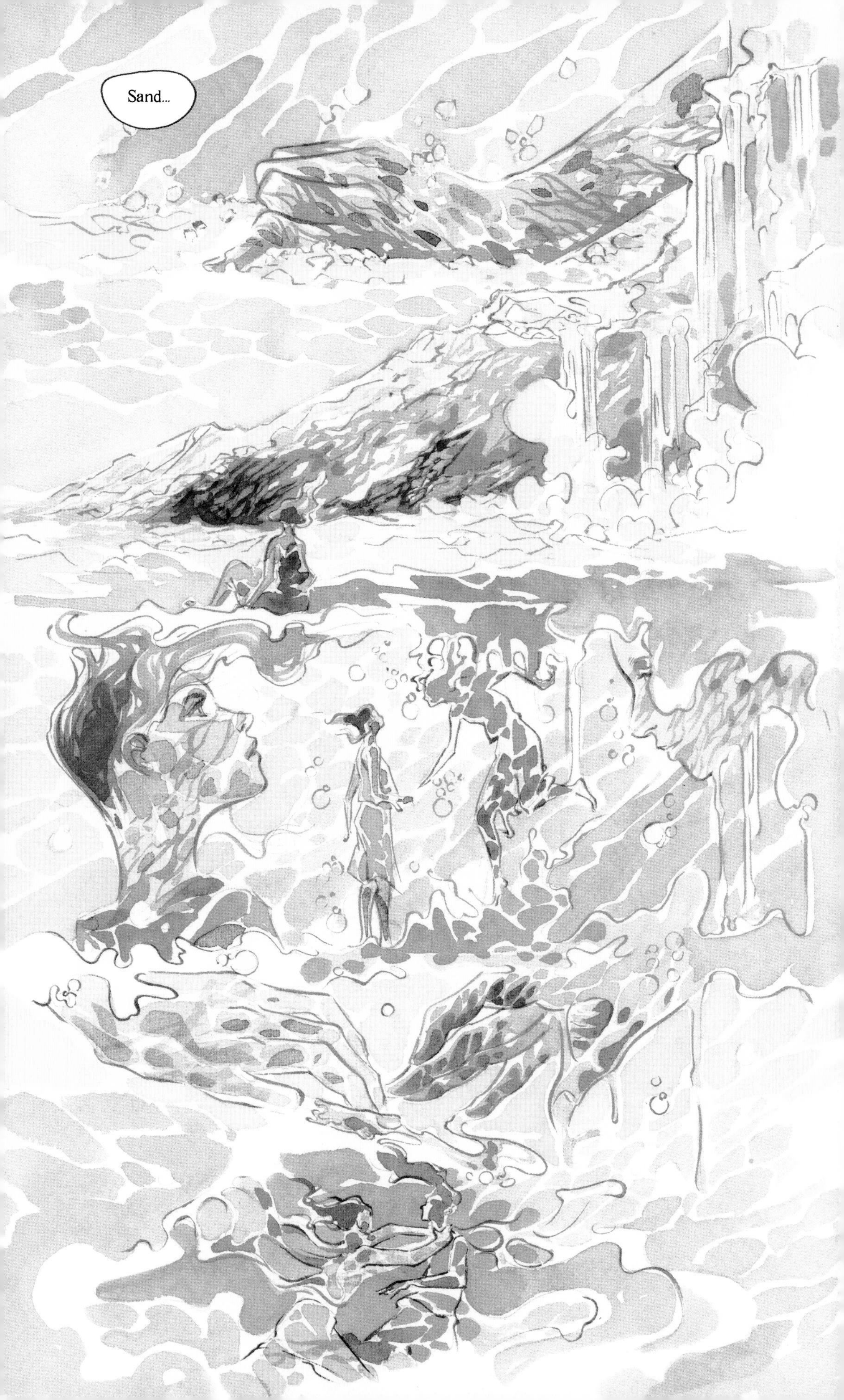
Sand...

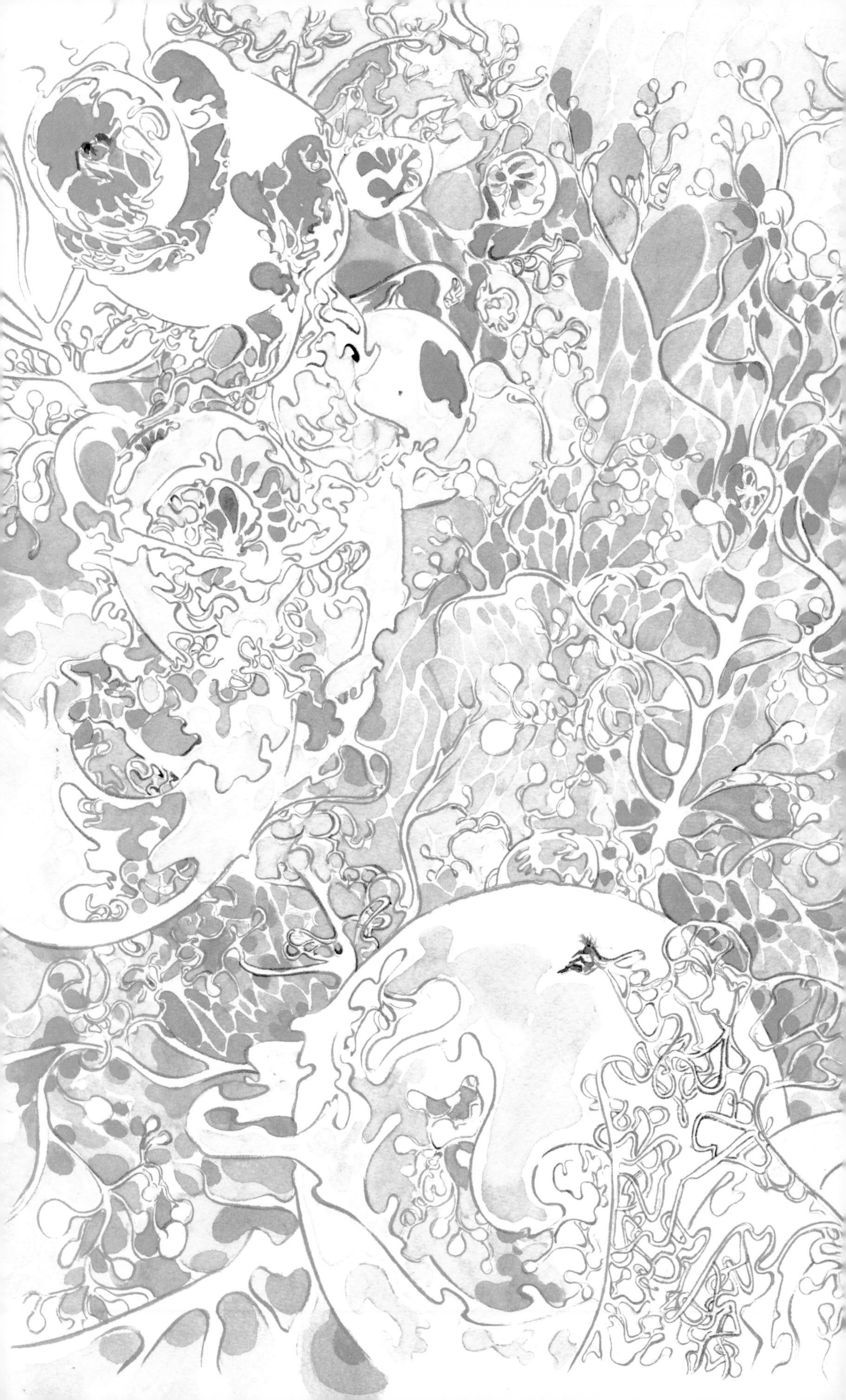

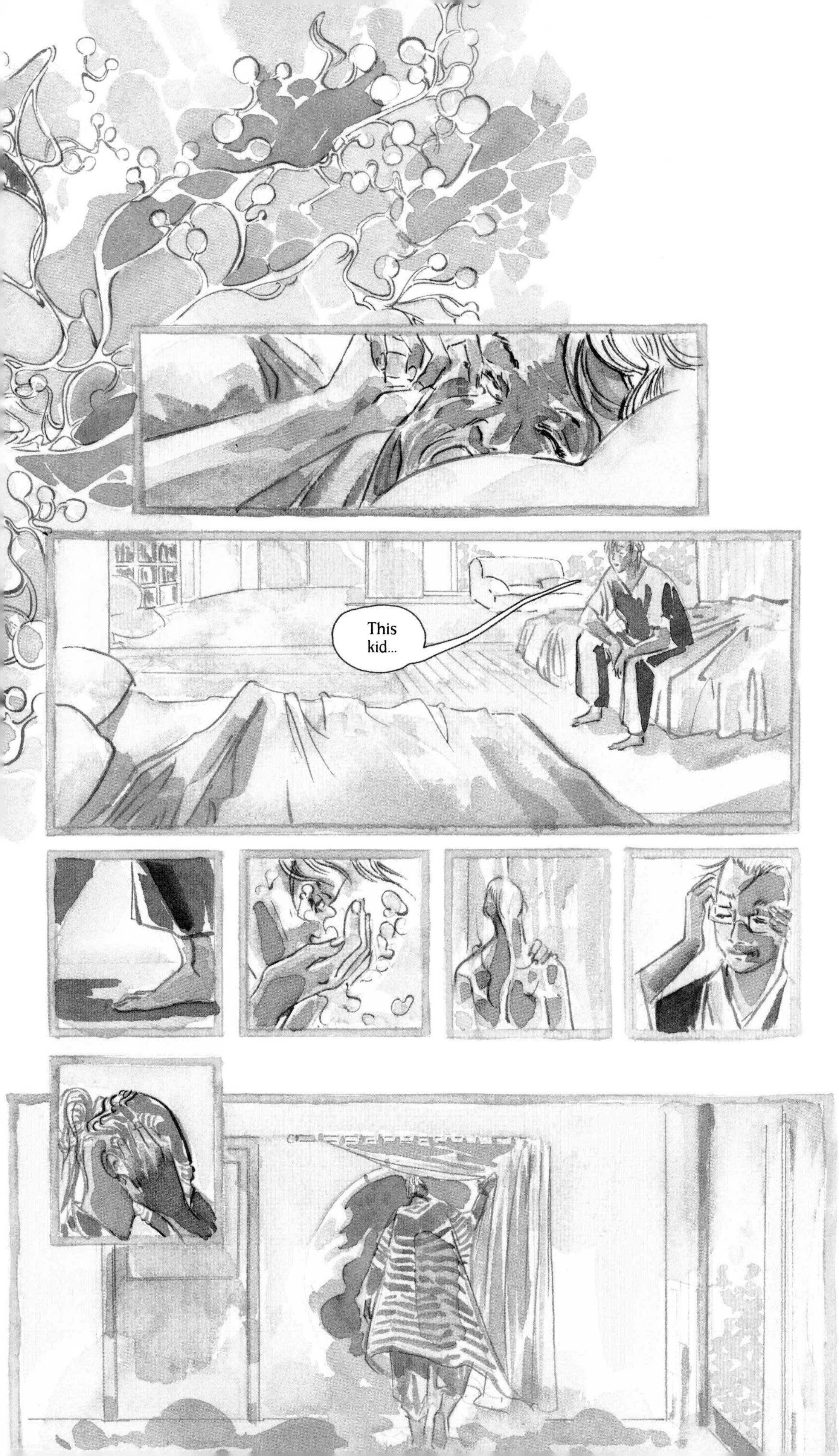
This kid...

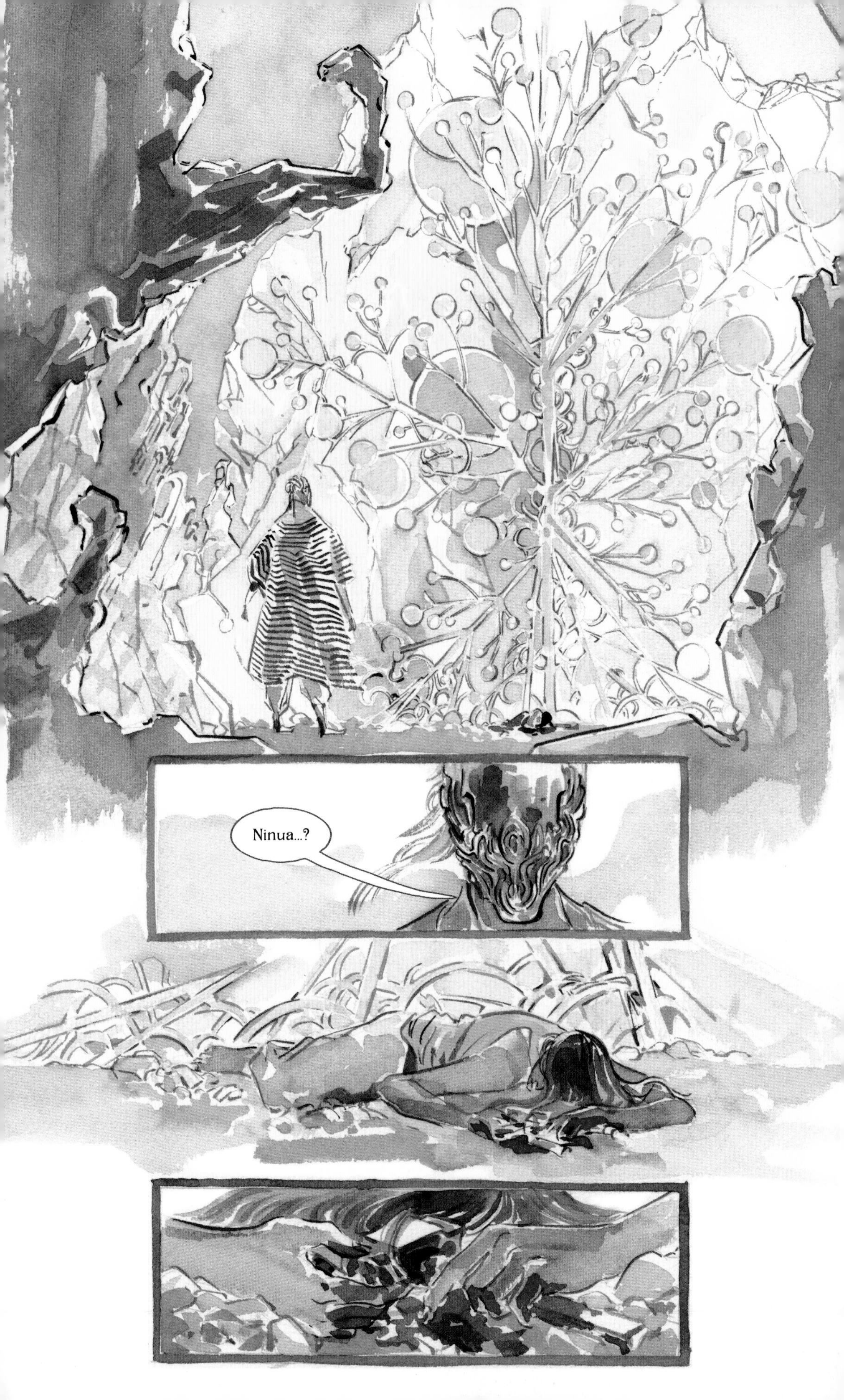
Ninua...?

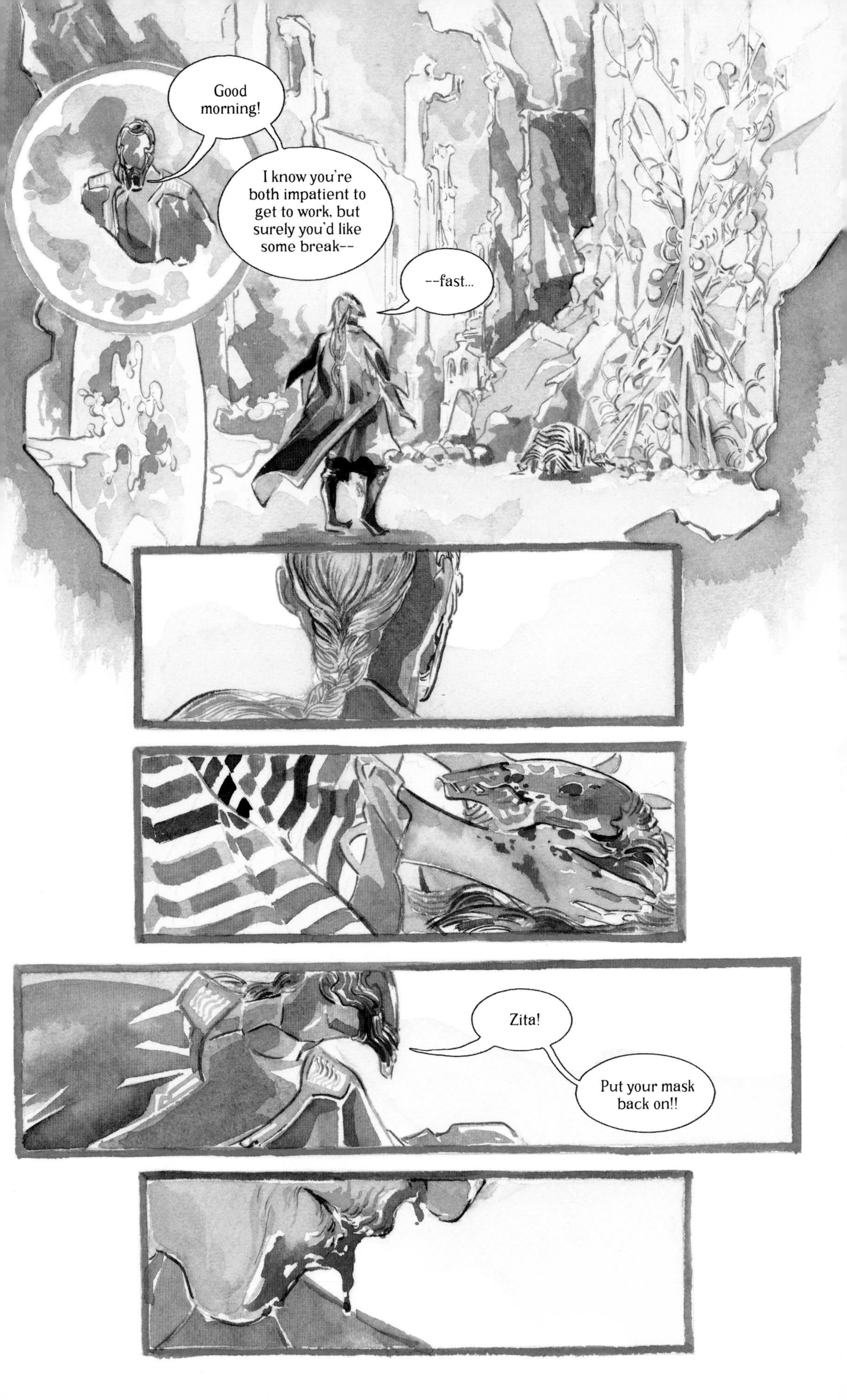
Good morning!
I know you're both impatient to get to work, but surely you'd like some break--
--fast...
Zita!
Put your mask back on!!

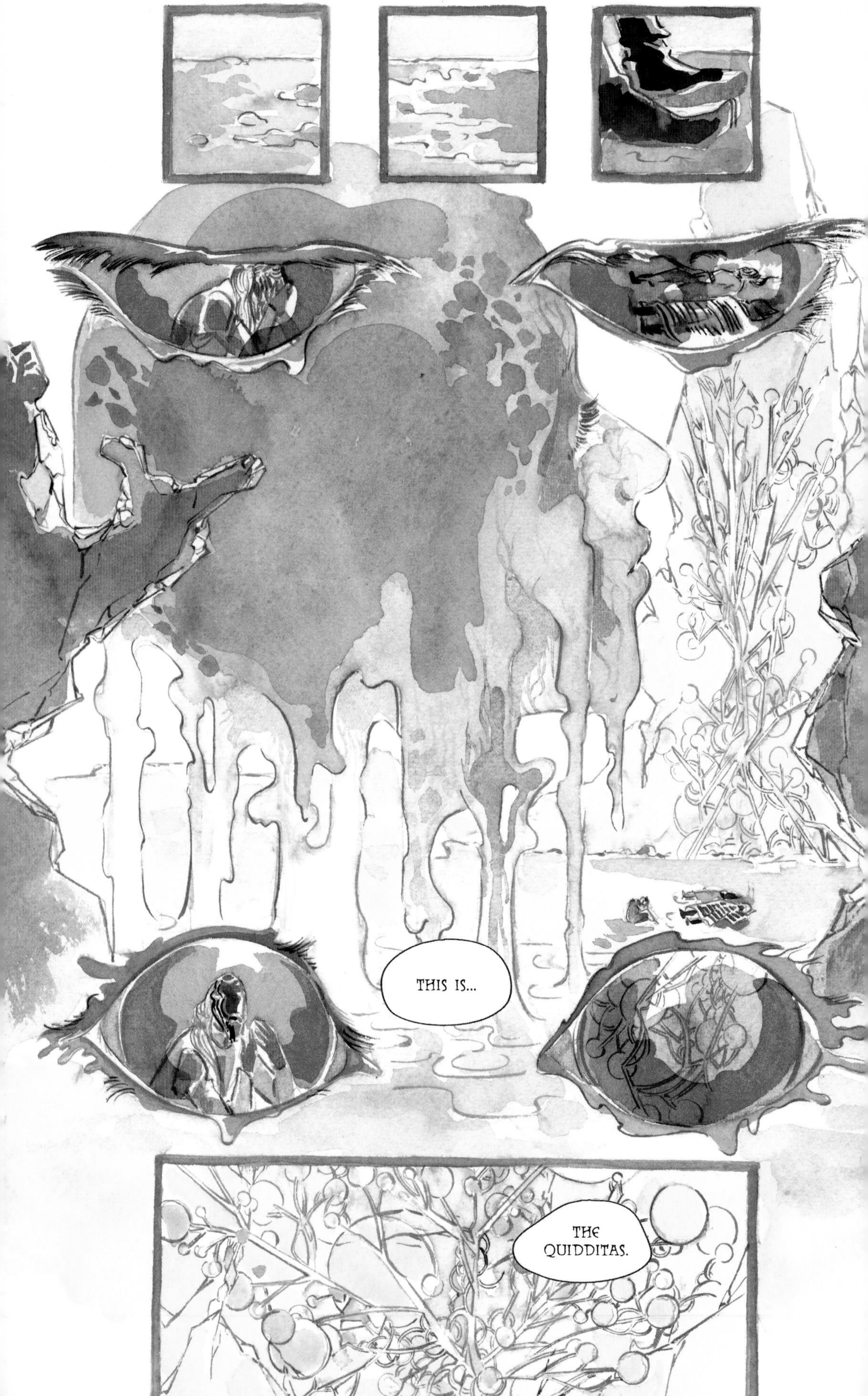
THIS IS...
THE QUIDDITAS.

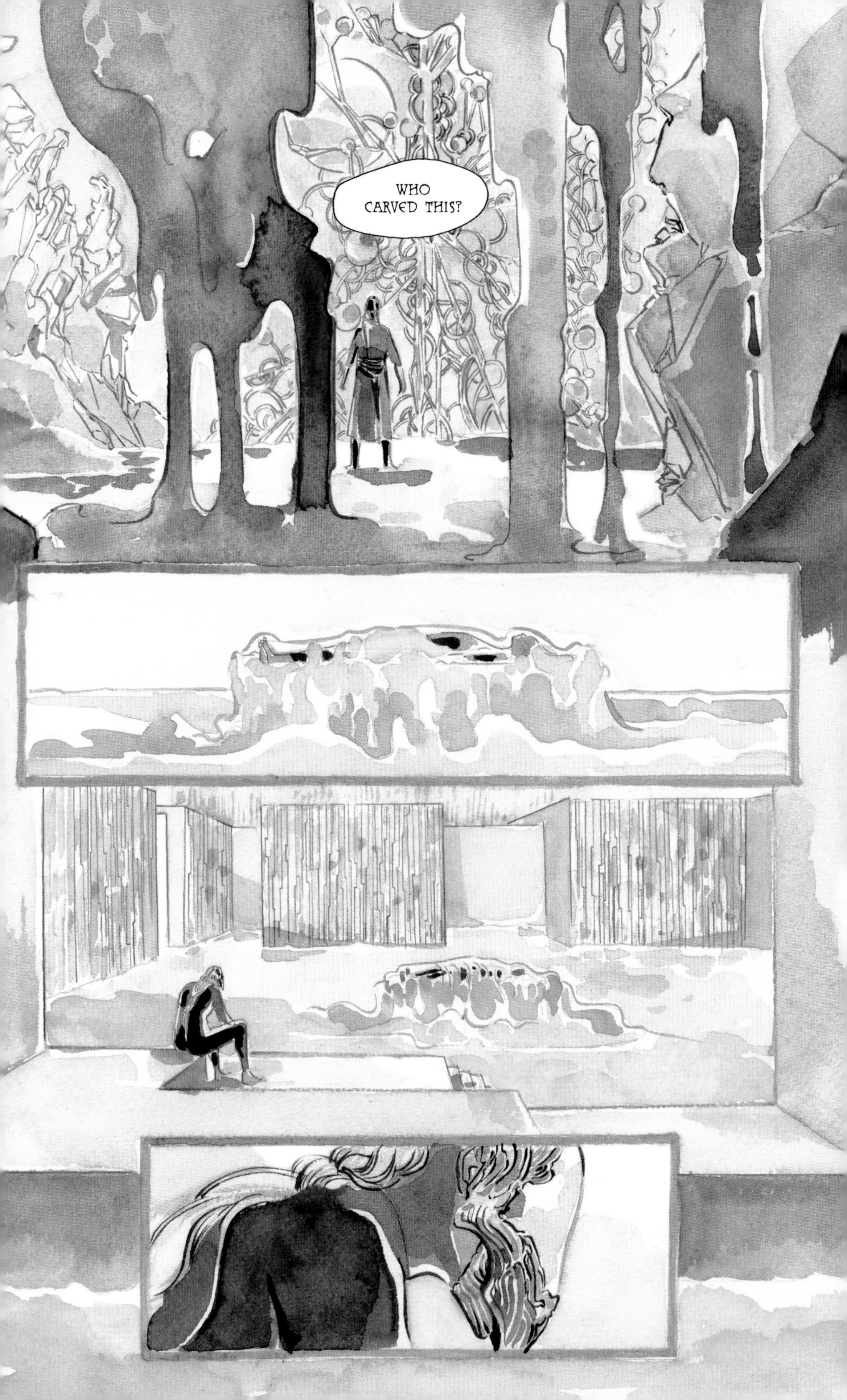
WHO CARVED THIS?

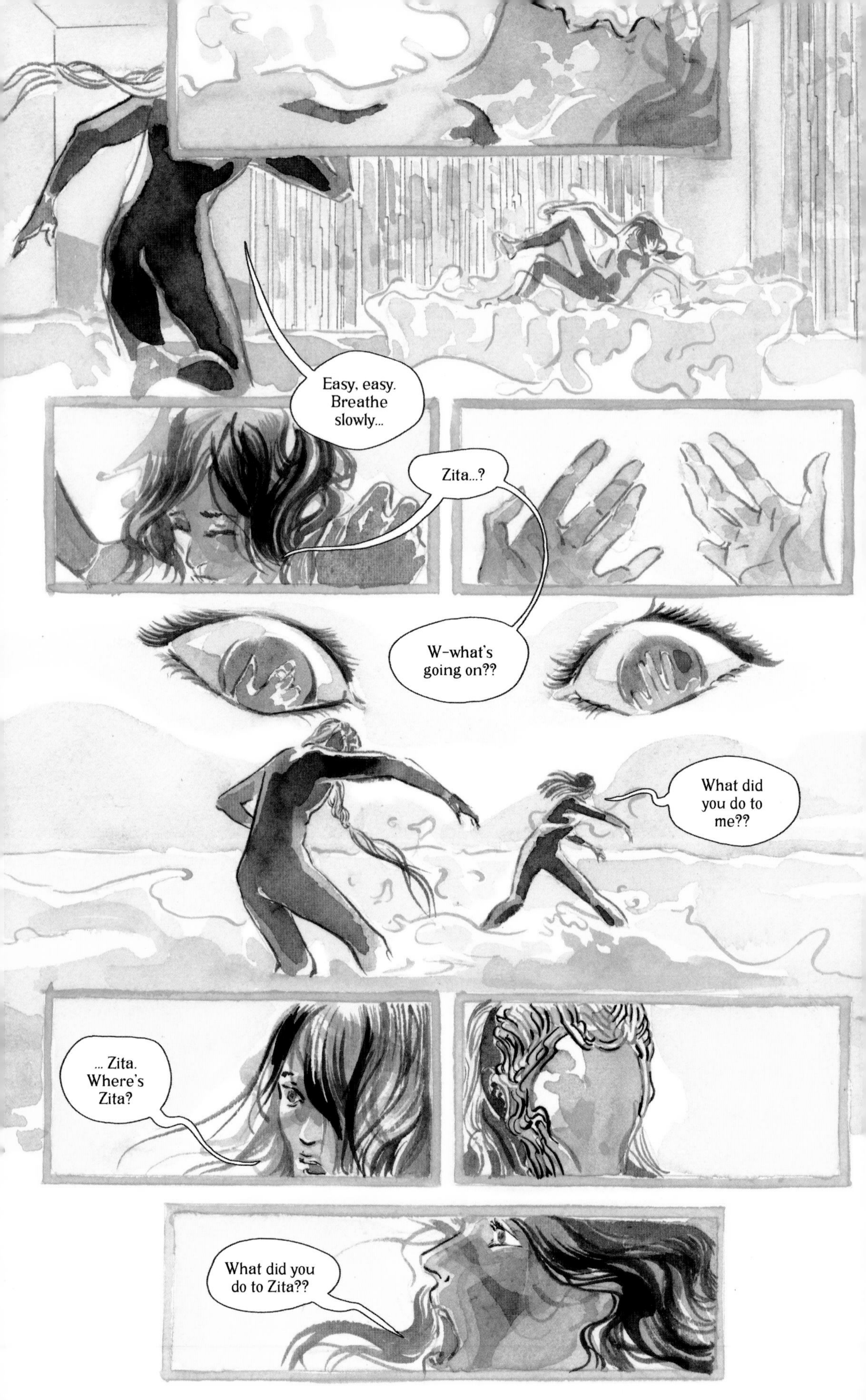

Easy, easy. Breathe slowly...
Zita...?
W-what's going on??
What did you do to me??
... Zita. Where's Zita?
What did you do to Zita??

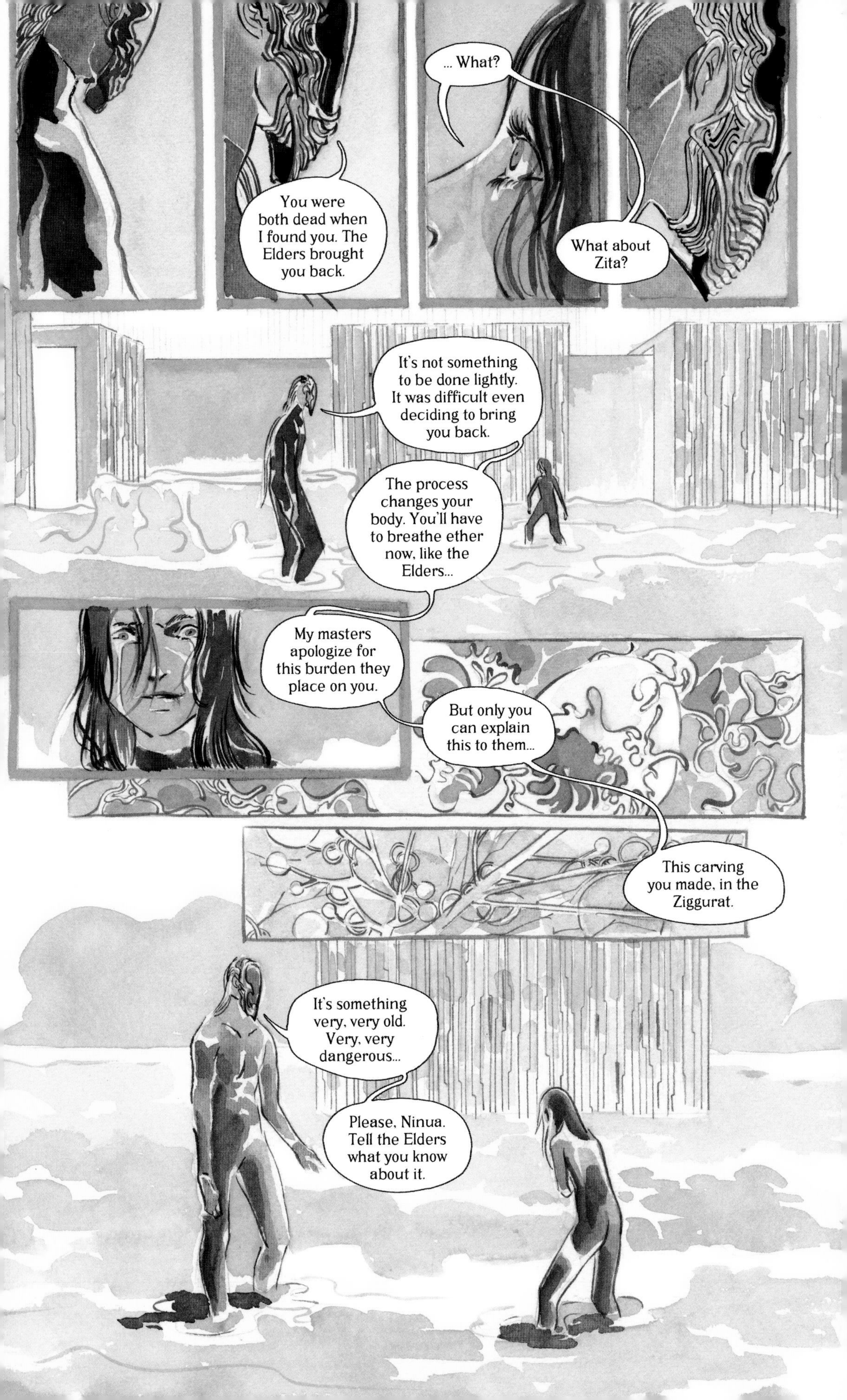

You were both dead when I found you. The Elders brought you back.
... What?
What about Zita?
It's not something to be done lightly. It was difficult even deciding to bring you back.
The process changes your body. You'll have to breathe ether now, like the Elders...
My masters apologize for this burden they place on you.
But only you can explain this to them...
This carving you made, in the Ziggurat.
It's something very, very old. Very, very dangerous...
Please, Ninua. Tell the Elders what you know about it.

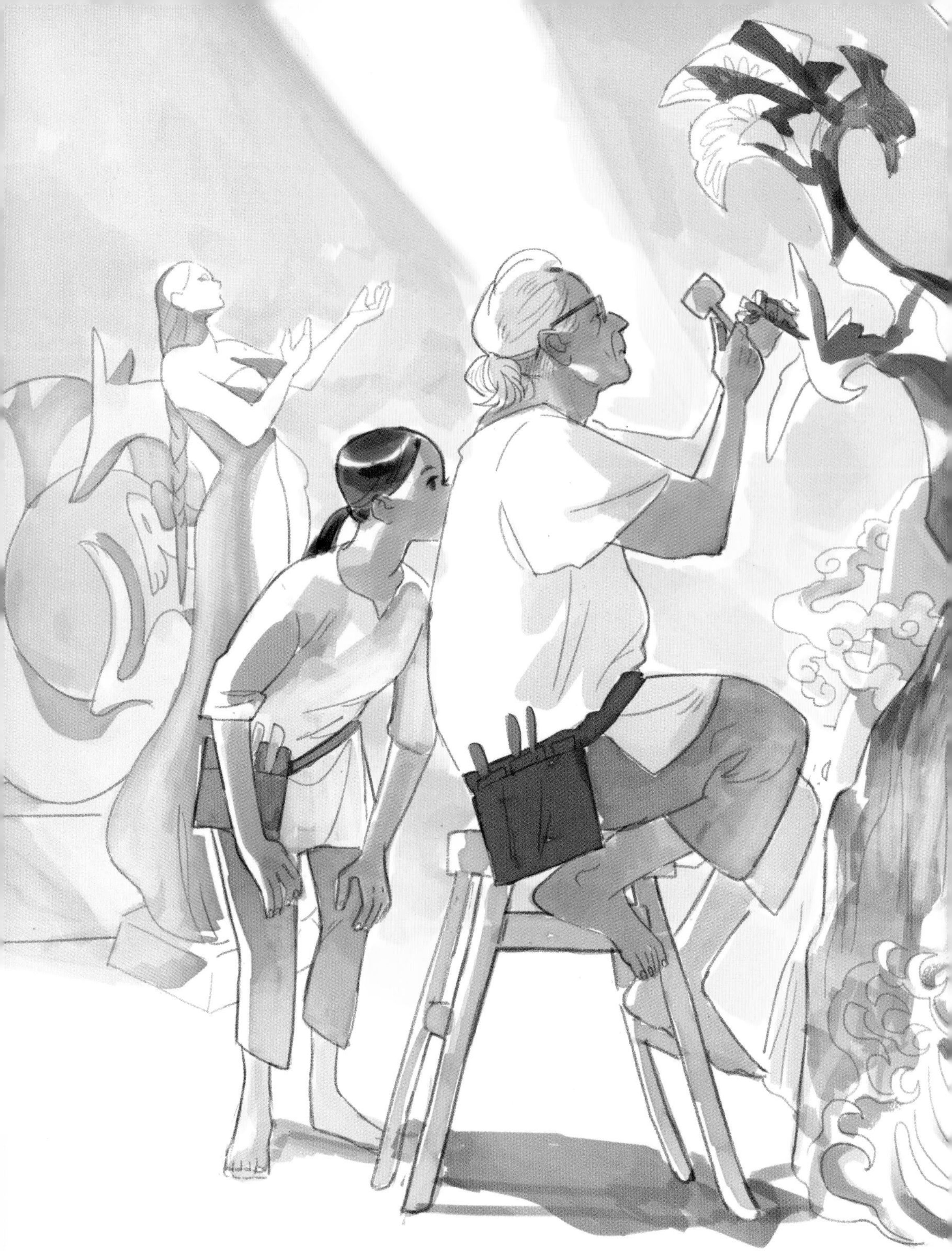

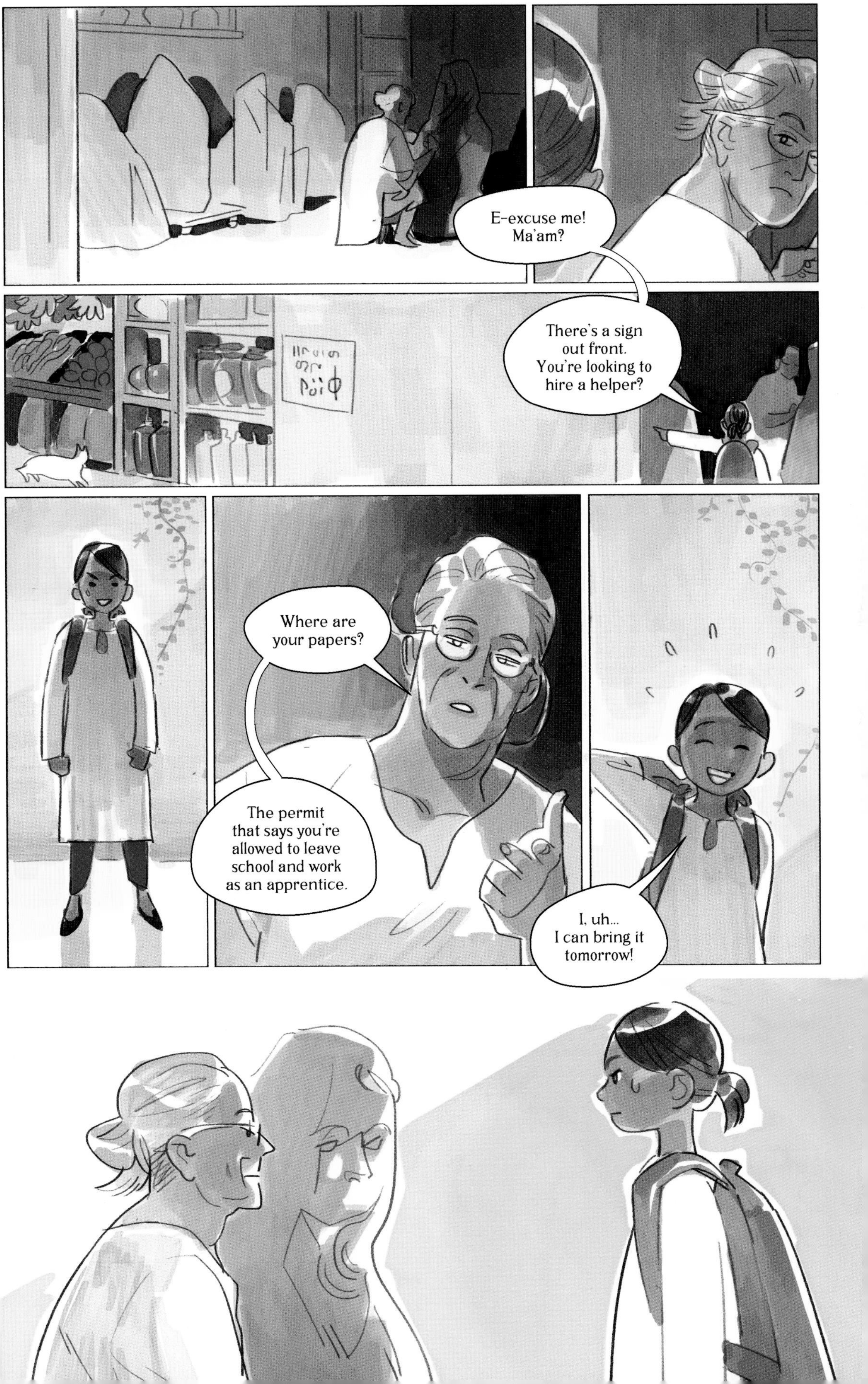
E-excuse me!
Ma'am?
There's a sign out front. You're looking to hire a helper?
Where are your papers?
The permit that says you're allowed to leave school and work as an apprentice.
I, uh... I can bring it tomorrow!

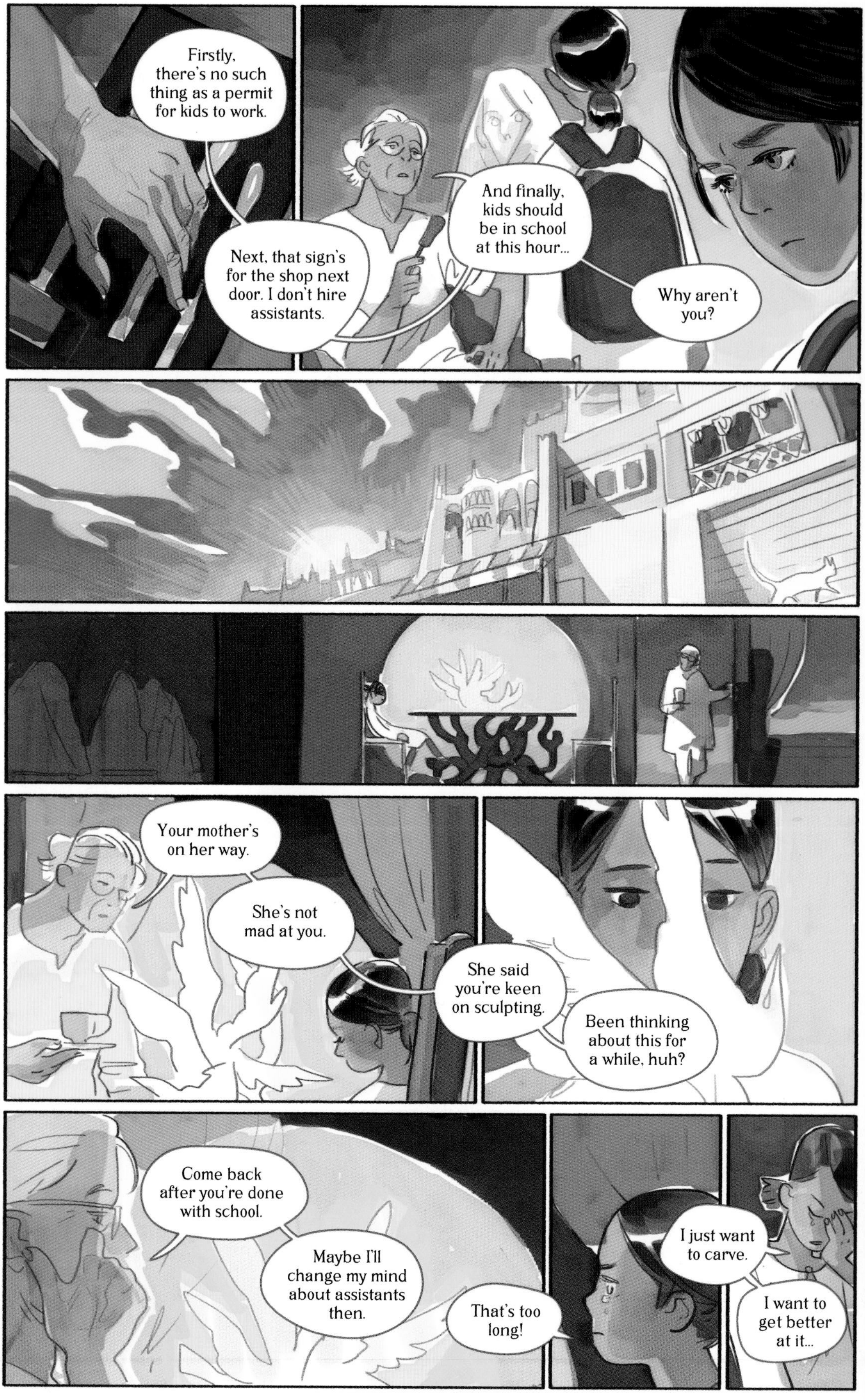
Firstly, there's no such thing as a permit for kids to work.
Next, that sign's for the shop next door. I don't hire assistants.
And finally, kids should be in school at this hour...
Why aren't you?
Your mother's on her way.
She's not mad at you.
She said you're keen on sculpting.
Been thinking about this for a while, huh?
Come back after you're done with school.
Maybe I'll change my mind about assistants then.
That's too long!
I just want to carve.
I want to get better at it...

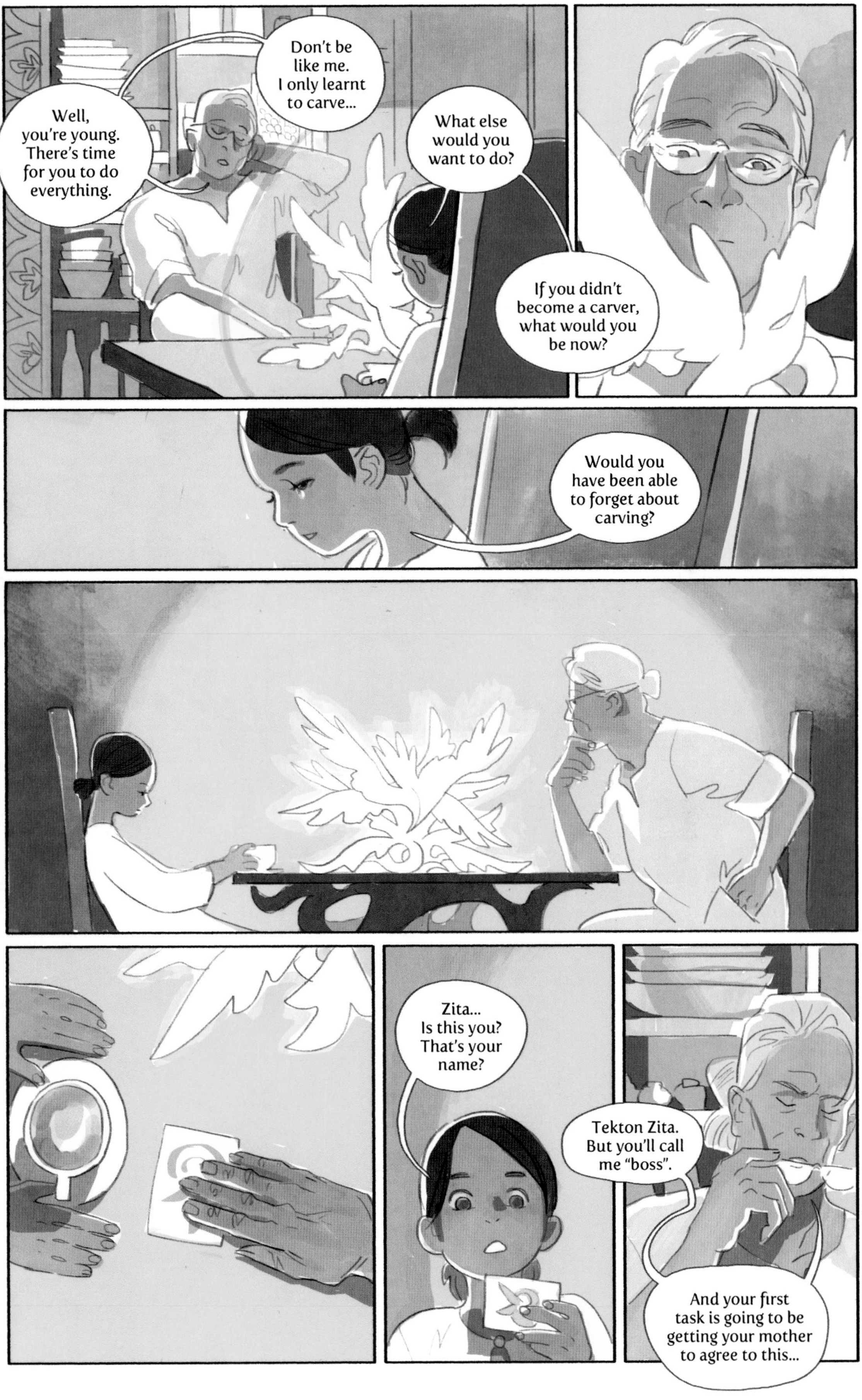
Well, you're young. There's time for you to do everything.
Don't be like me. I only learnt to carve...
What else would you want to do?
If you didn't become a carver, what would you be now?
Would you have been able to forget about carving?
Zita... Is this you? That's your name?
Tekton Zita. But you'll call me "boss".
And your first task is going to be getting your mother to agree to this...

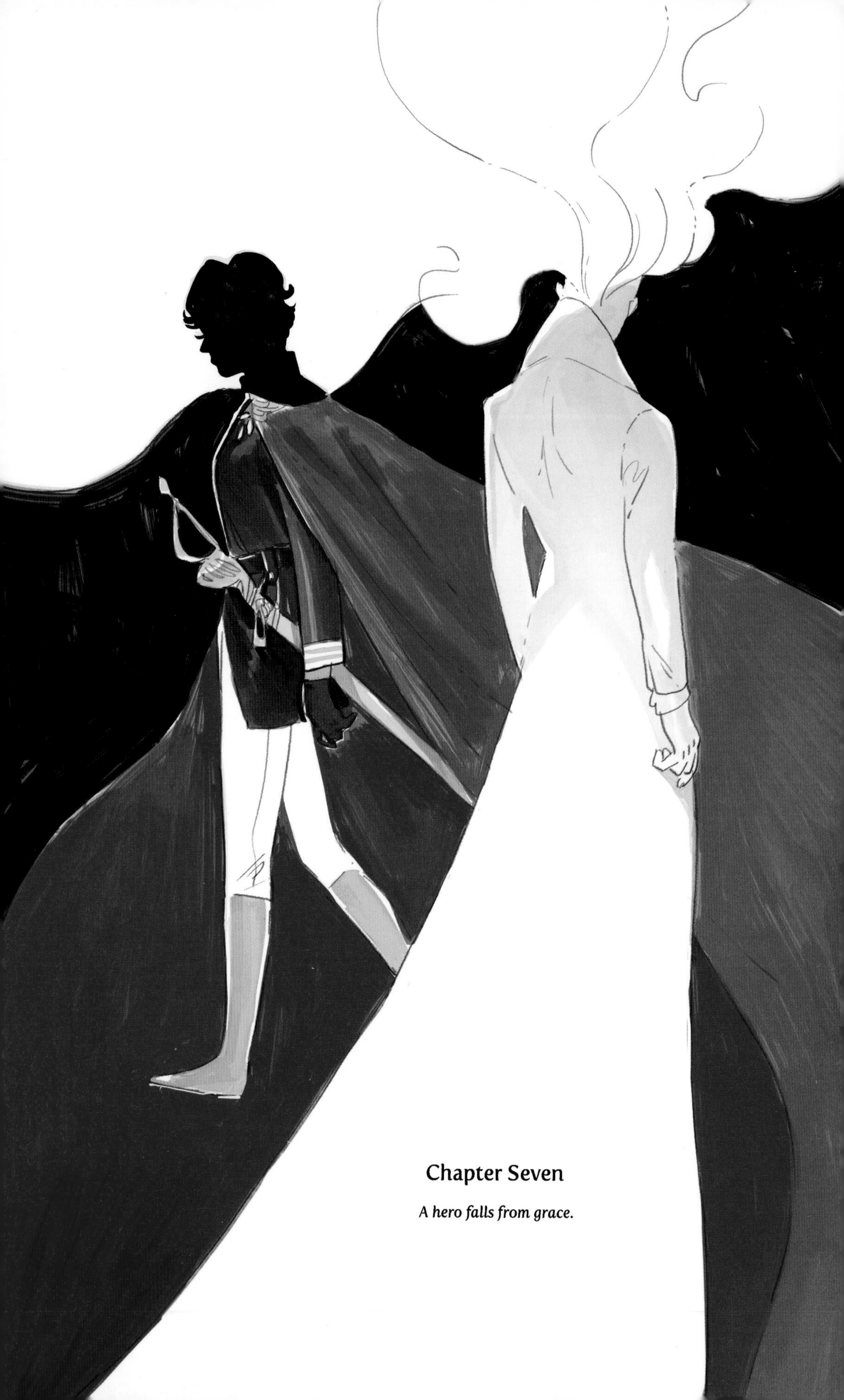

Chapter Seven

A hero falls from grace.

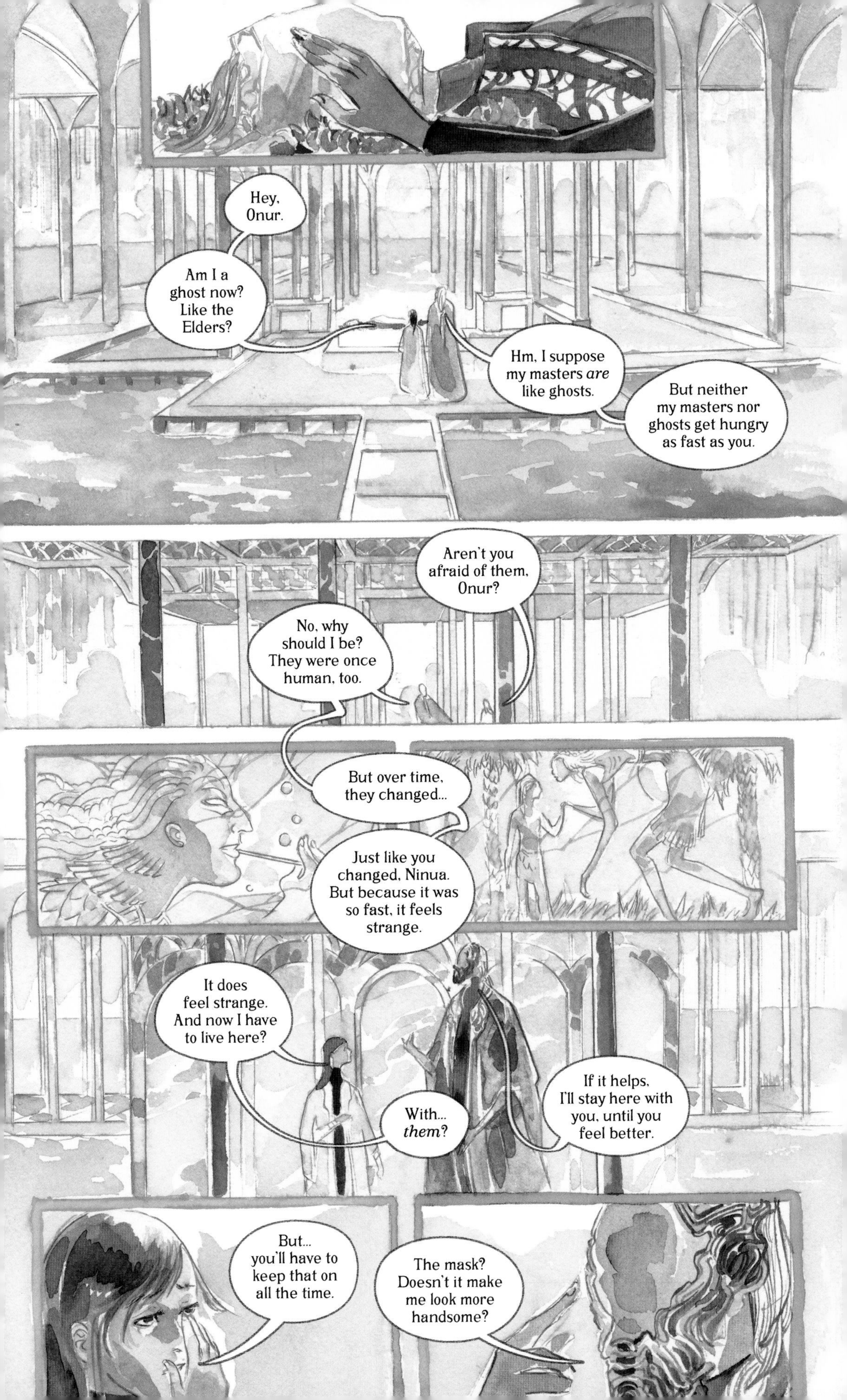

Hey, Onur.
Am I a ghost now? Like the Elders?
Hm, I suppose my masters *are* like ghosts.
But neither my masters nor ghosts get hungry as fast as you.
Aren't you afraid of them, Onur?
No, why should I be? They were once human, too.
But over time, they changed...
Just like you changed, Ninua. But because it was so fast, it feels strange.
It does feel strange. And now I have to live here?
With... *them*?
If it helps, I'll stay here with you, until you feel better.
But... you'll have to keep that on all the time.
The mask? Doesn't it make me look more handsome?

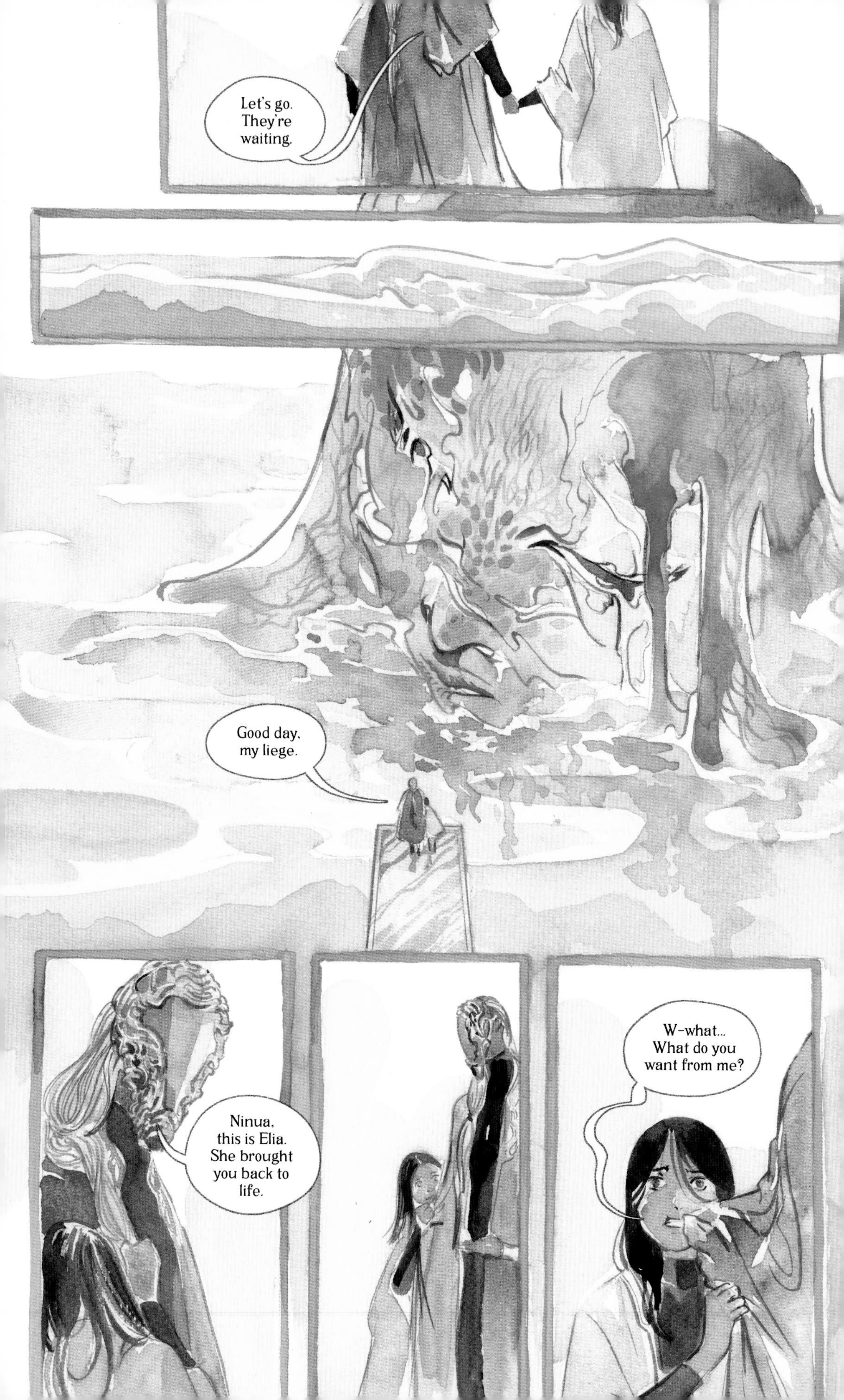
Let's go. They're waiting.
Good day, my liege.
Ninua, this is Elia. She brought you back to life.
W-what... What do you want from me?

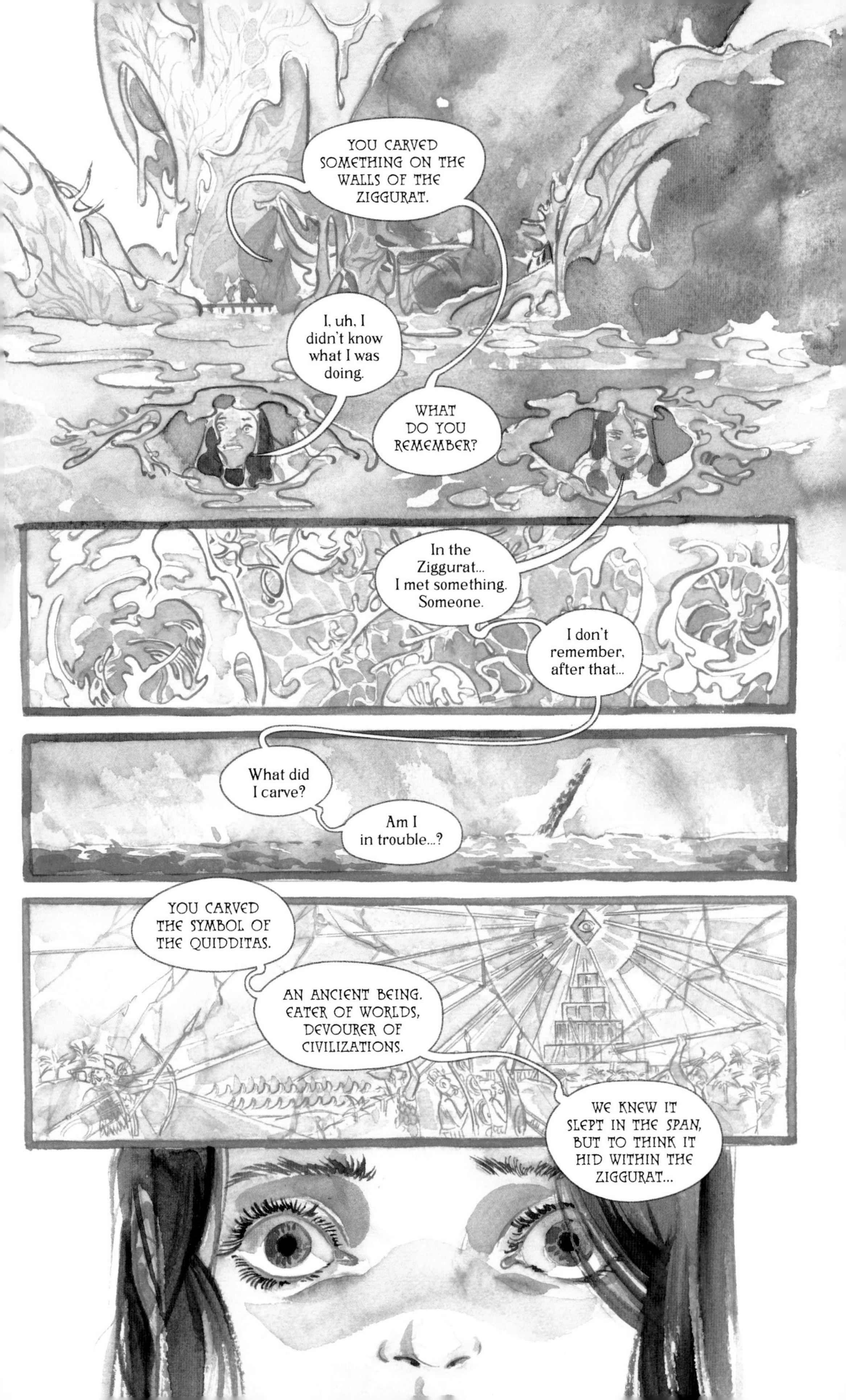
YOU CARVED SOMETHING ON THE WALLS OF THE ZIGGURAT.
I, uh, I didn't know what I was doing.
WHAT DO YOU REMEMBER?
In the Ziggurat... I met something. Someone.
I don't remember, after that...
What did I carve?
Am I in trouble...?
YOU CARVED THE SYMBOL OF THE QUIDDITAS.
AN ANCIENT BEING. EATER OF WORLDS, DEVOURER OF CIVILIZATIONS.
WE KNEW IT SLEPT IN THE *SPAN*, BUT TO THINK IT HID WITHIN THE ZIGGURAT...

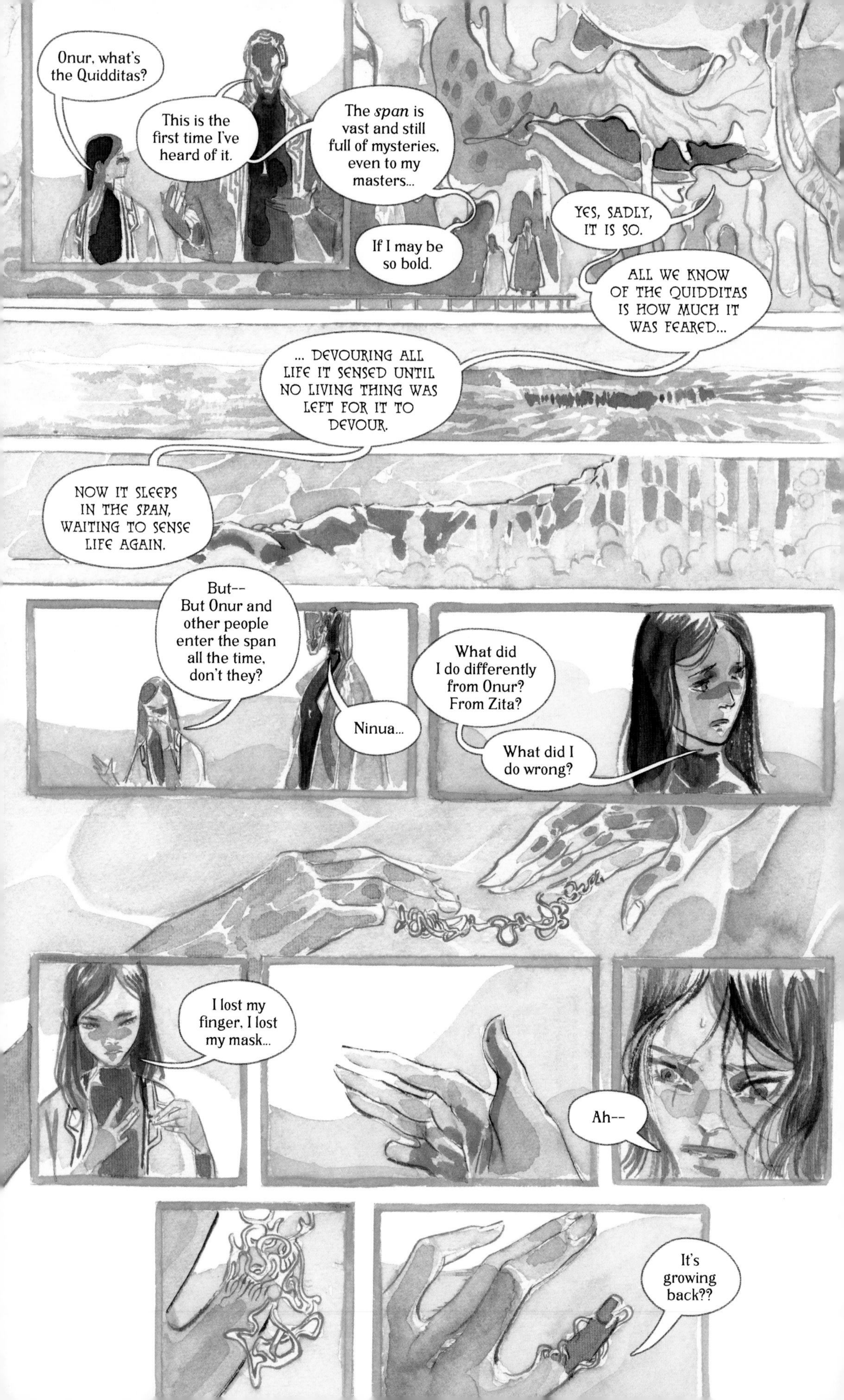
Onur, what's the Quidditas?
This is the first time I've heard of it.
The *span* is vast and still full of mysteries, even to my masters...
If I may be so bold.
YES, SADLY, IT IS SO.
ALL WE KNOW OF THE QUIDDITAS IS HOW MUCH IT WAS FEARED...
... DEVOURING ALL LIFE IT SENSED UNTIL NO LIVING THING WAS LEFT FOR IT TO DEVOUR.
NOW IT SLEEPS IN THE *SPAN*, WAITING TO SENSE LIFE AGAIN.
But-- But Onur and other people enter the span all the time, don't they?
Ninua...
What did I do differently from Onur? From Zita?
What did I do wrong?
I lost my finger, I lost my mask...
Ah--
It's growing back??

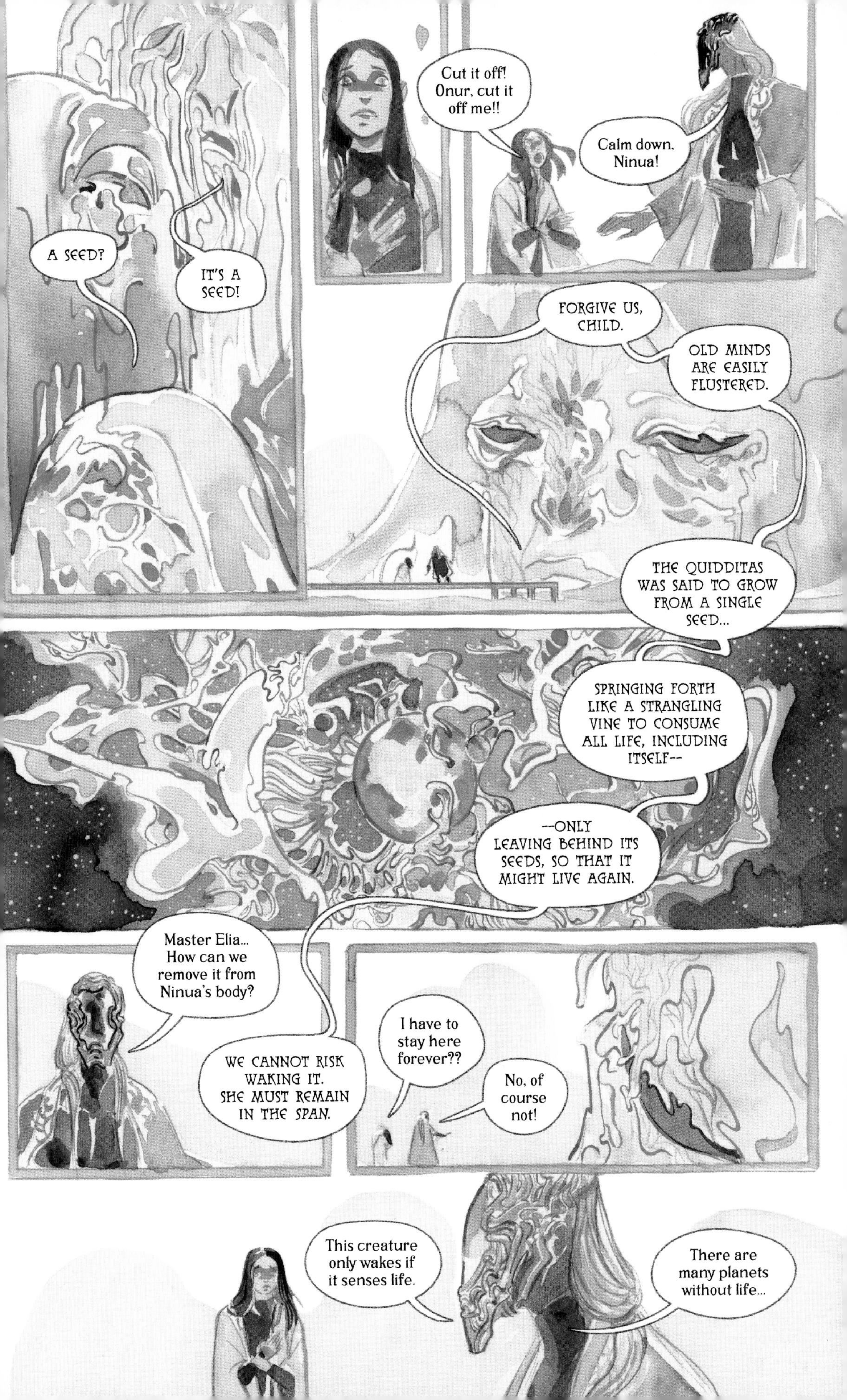
A SEED?
IT'S A SEED!
Cut it off! Onur, cut it off me!!
Calm down, Ninua!
FORGIVE US, CHILD.
OLD MINDS ARE EASILY FLUSTERED.
THE QUIDDITAS WAS SAID TO GROW FROM A SINGLE SEED...
SPRINGING FORTH LIKE A STRANGLING VINE TO CONSUME ALL LIFE, INCLUDING ITSELF--
--ONLY LEAVING BEHIND ITS SEEDS, SO THAT IT MIGHT LIVE AGAIN.
Master Elia... How can we remove it from Ninua's body?
WE CANNOT RISK WAKING IT. SHE MUST REMAIN IN THE SPAN.
I have to stay here forever??
No, of course not!
This creature only wakes if it senses life.
There are many planets without life...

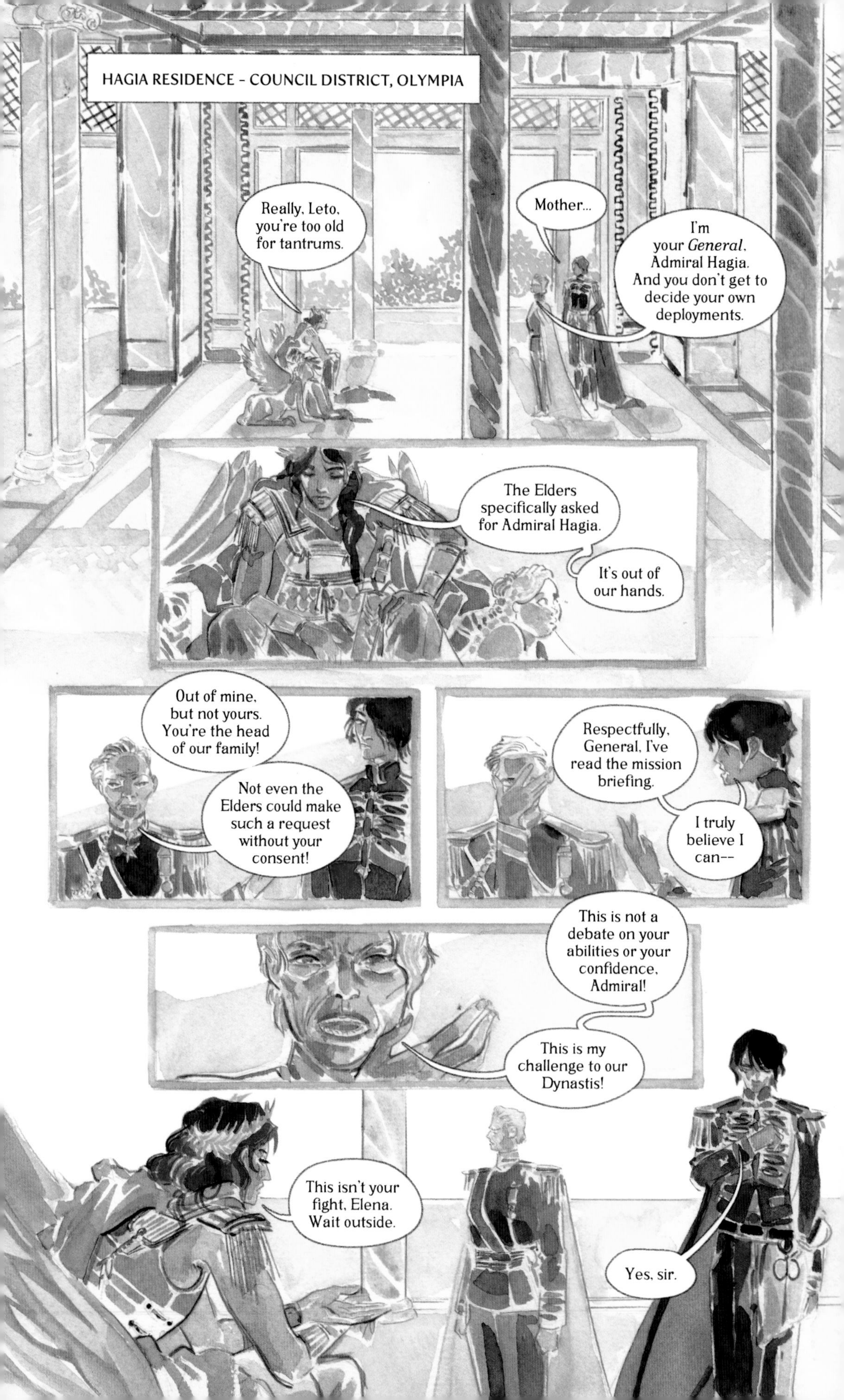
HAGIA RESIDENCE - COUNCIL DISTRICT, OLYMPIA
Really, Leto, you're too old for tantrums.
Mother...
I'm your *General*, Admiral Hagia. And you don't get to decide your own deployments.
The Elders specifically asked for Admiral Hagia.
It's out of our hands.
Out of mine, but not yours. You're the head of our family!
Not even the Elders could make such a request without your consent!
Respectfully, General, I've read the mission briefing.
I truly believe I can--
This is not a debate on your abilities or your confidence, Admiral!
This is my challenge to our Dynastis!
This isn't your fight, Elena. Wait outside.
Yes, sir.

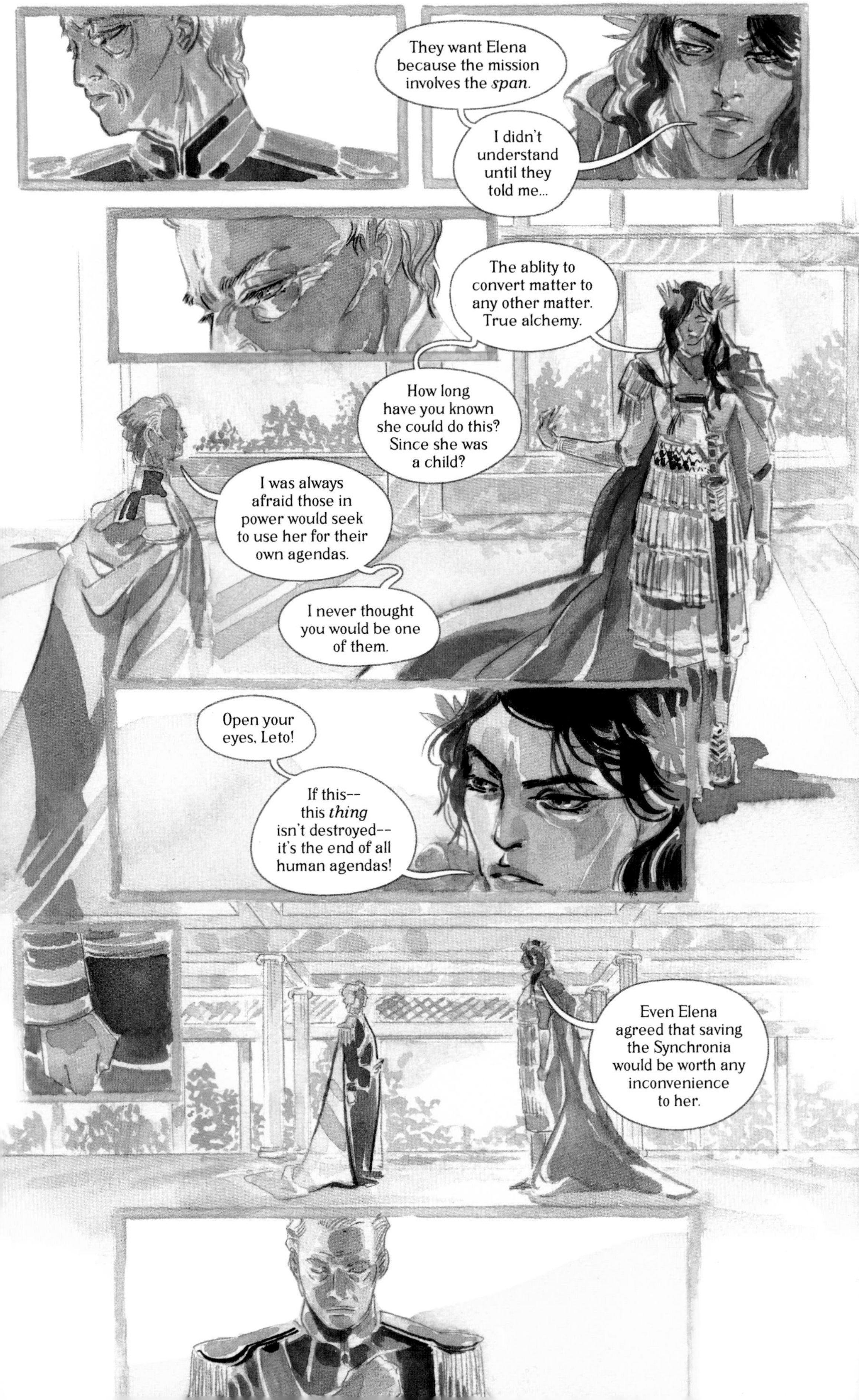
They want Elena because the mission involves the *span*.
I didn't understand until they told me...
The ablity to convert matter to any other matter. True alchemy.
How long have you known she could do this? Since she was a child?
I was always afraid those in power would seek to use her for their own agendas.
I never thought you would be one of them.
Open your eyes, Leto!
If this-- this *thing* isn't destroyed-- it's the end of all human agendas!
Even Elena agreed that saving the Synchronia would be worth any inconvenience to her.

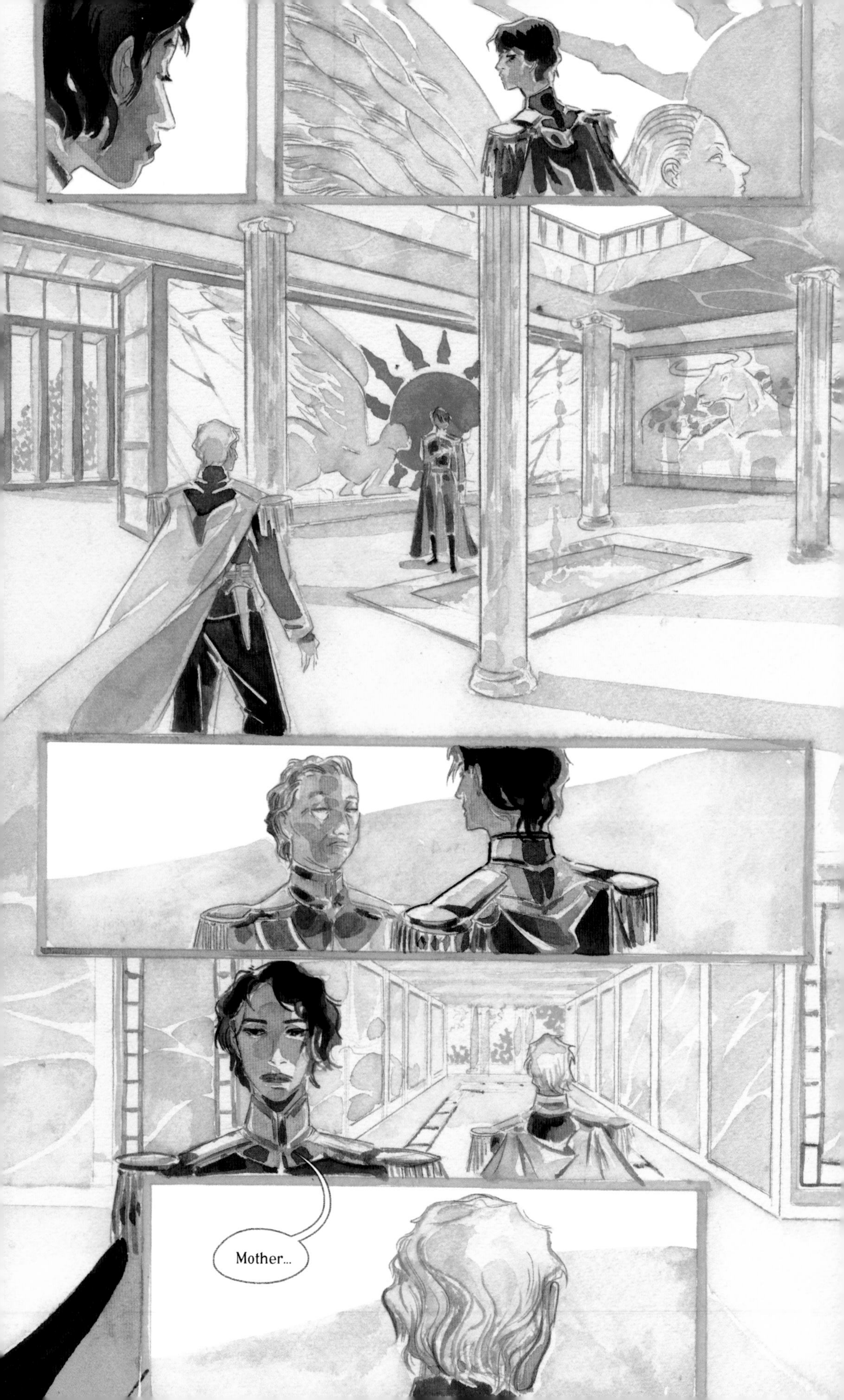
Mother...

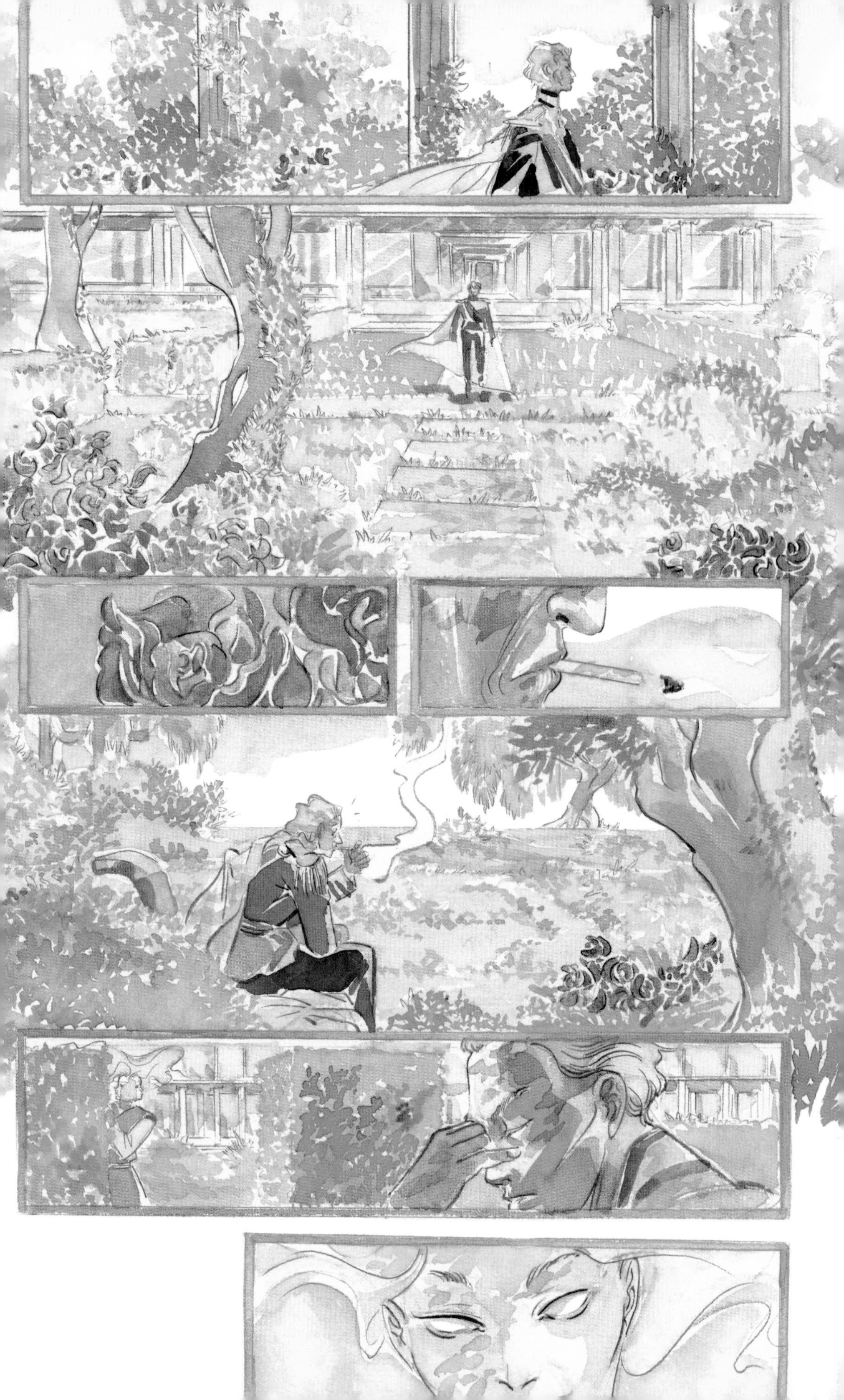

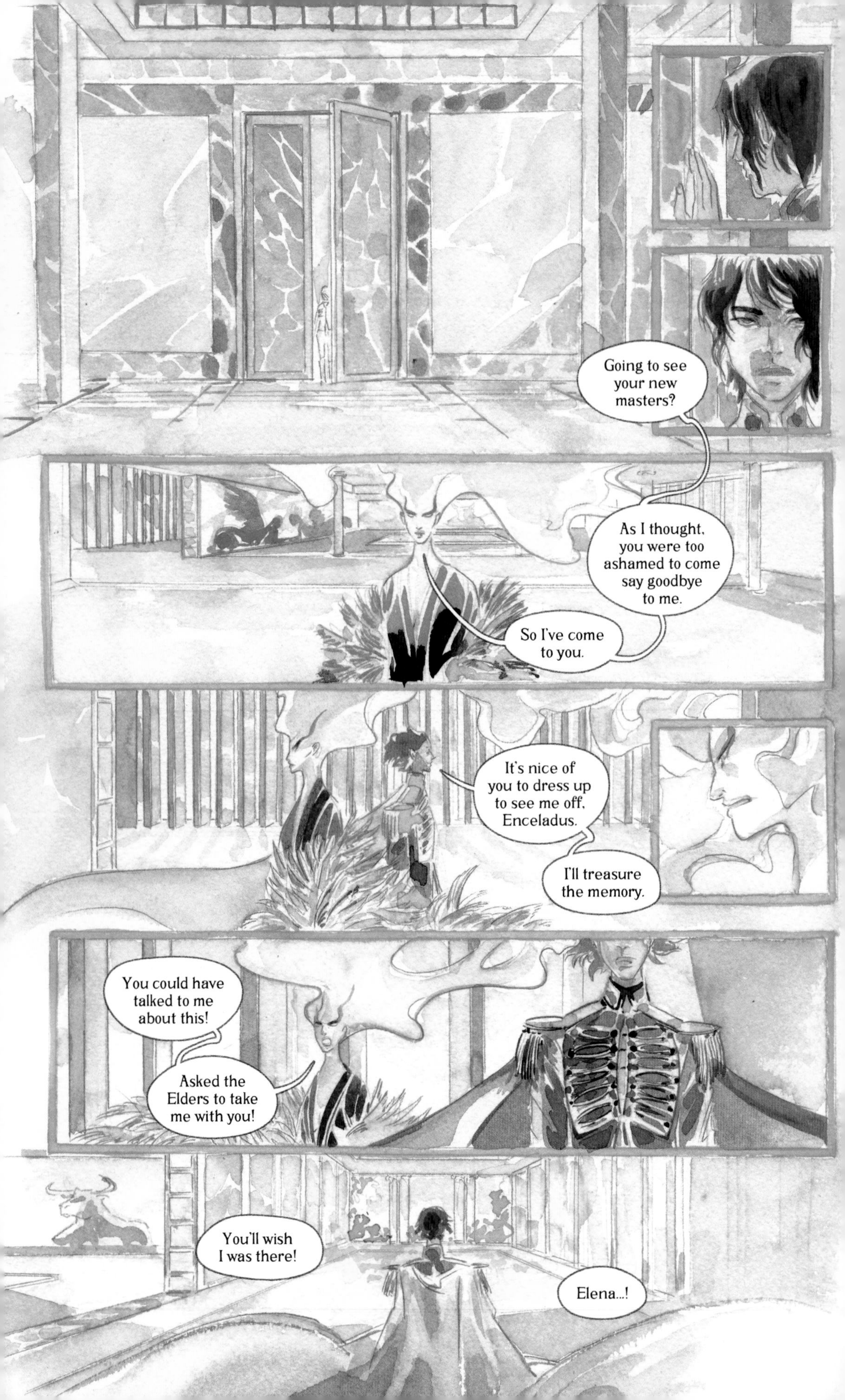
Going to see your new masters?
As I thought, you were too ashamed to come say goodbye to me.
So I've come to you.
It's nice of you to dress up to see me off, Enceladus.
I'll treasure the memory.
You could have talked to me about this!
Asked the Elders to take me with you!
You'll wish I was there!
Elena...!

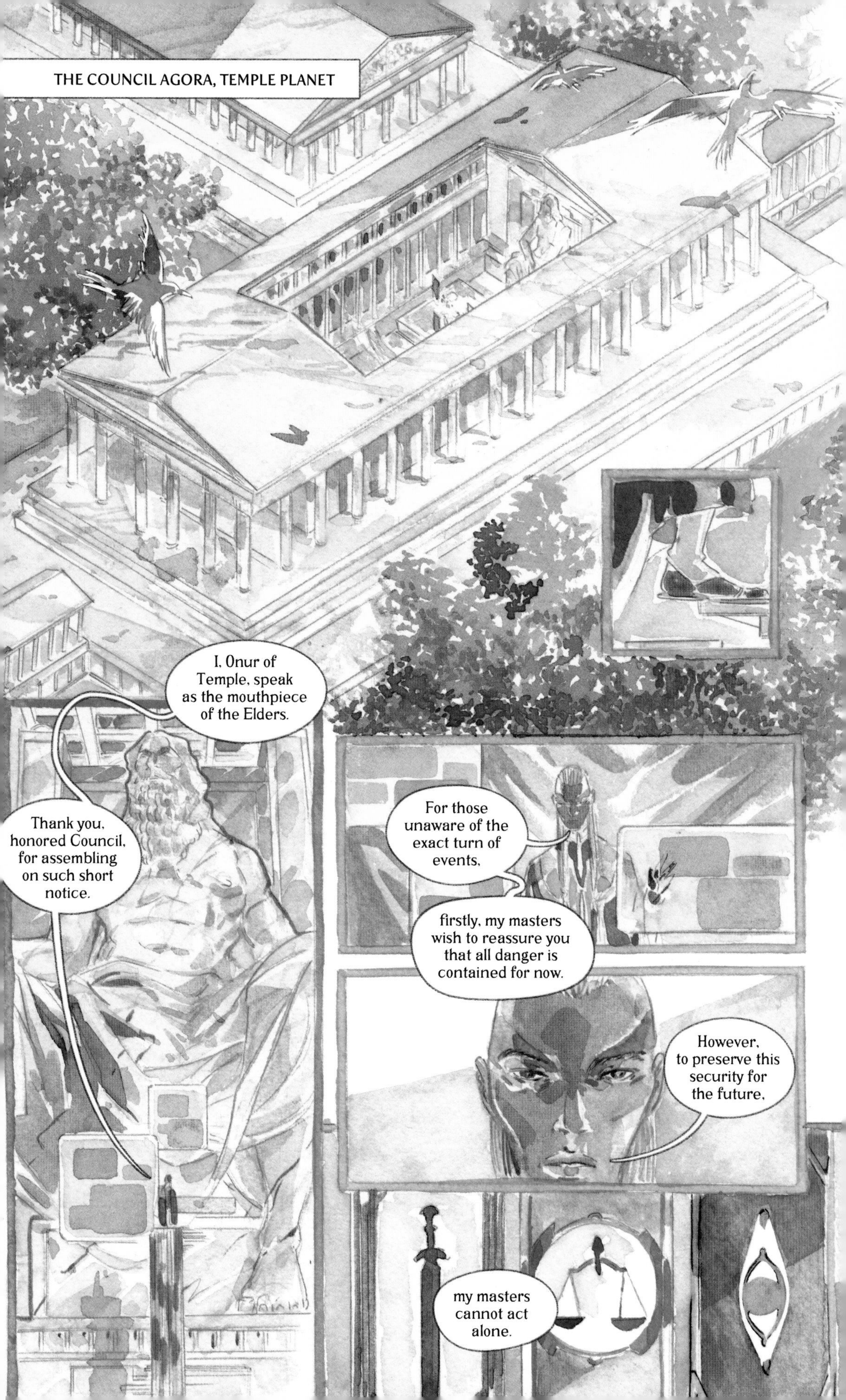
THE COUNCIL AGORA, TEMPLE PLANET
I, Onur of Temple, speak as the mouthpiece of the Elders.
Thank you, honored Council, for assembling on such short notice.
For those unaware of the exact turn of events,
firstly, my masters wish to reassure you that all danger is contained for now.
However, to preserve this security for the future,
my masters cannot act alone.

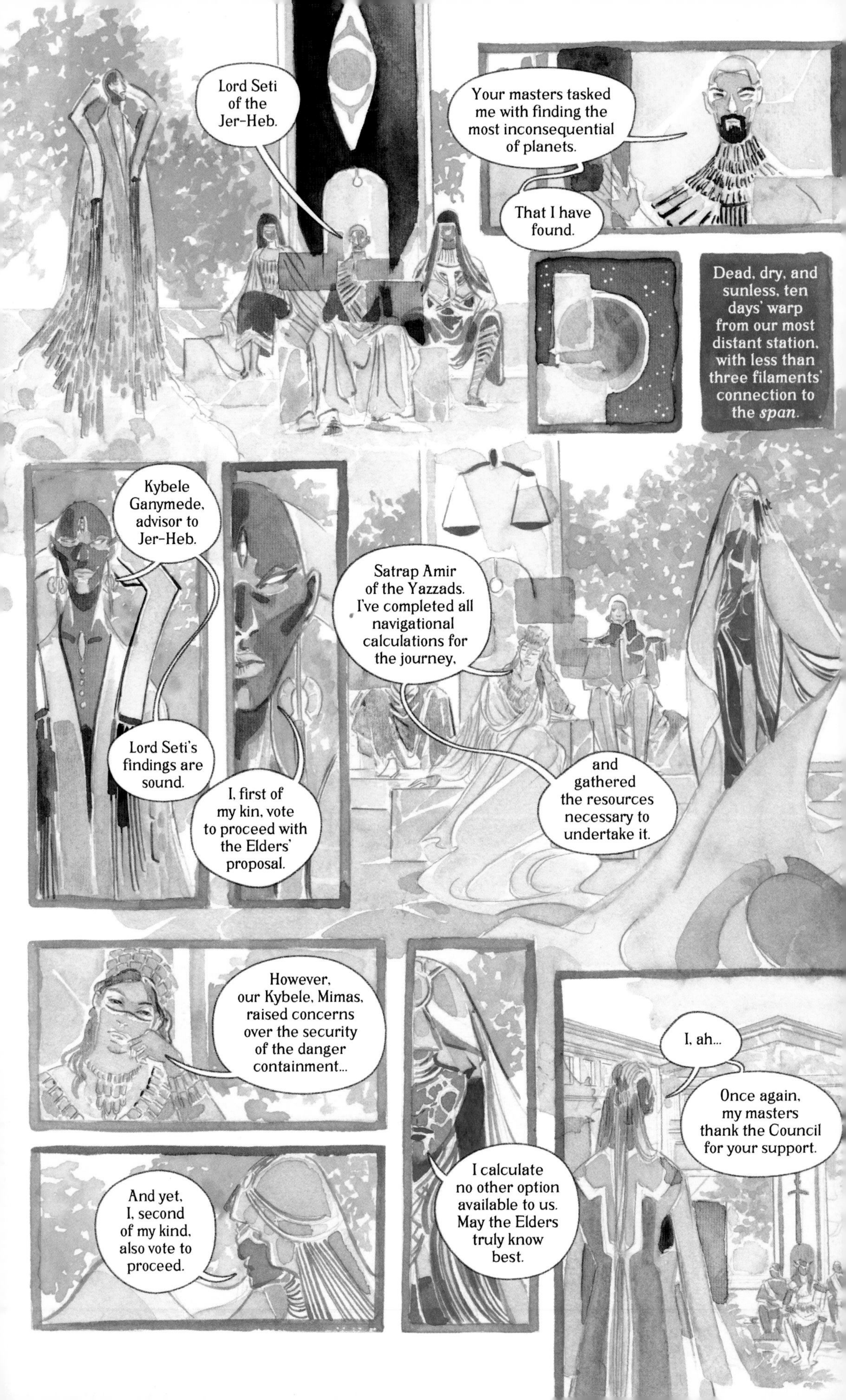
Lord Seti of the Jer-Heb.
Your masters tasked me with finding the most inconsequential of planets.
That I have found.
Dead, dry, and sunless, ten days' warp from our most distant station, with less than three filaments' connection to the *span*.
Kybele Ganymede, advisor to Jer-Heb.
Lord Seti's findings are sound.
I, first of my kin, vote to proceed with the Elders' proposal.
Satrap Amir of the Yazzads. I've completed all navigational calculations for the journey,
and gathered the resources necessary to undertake it.
However, our Kybele, Mimas, raised concerns over the security of the danger containment...
And yet, I, second of my kind, also vote to proceed.
I calculate no other option available to us. May the Elders truly know best.
I, ah...
Once again, my masters thank the Council for your support.

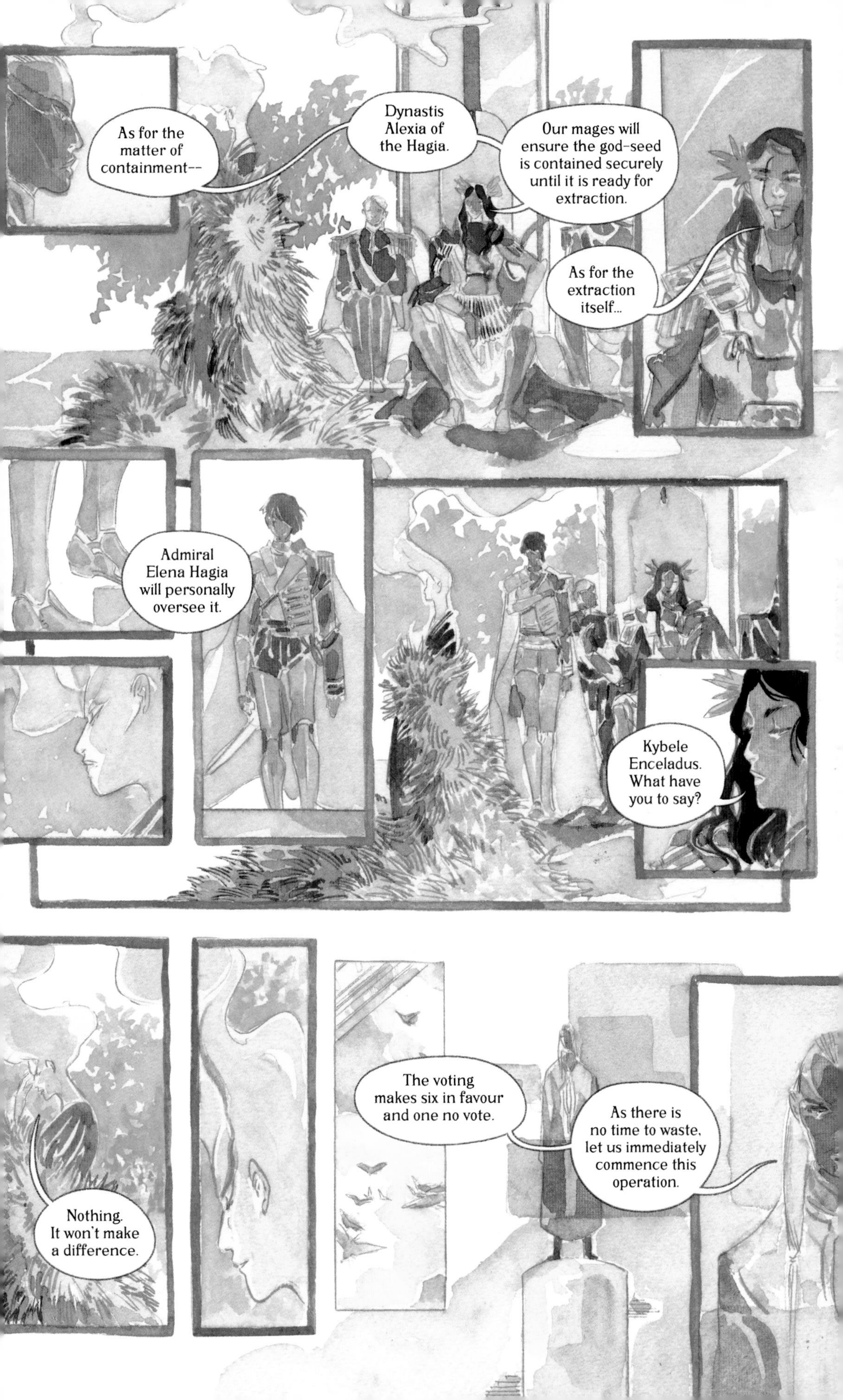
As for the matter of containment--
Dynastis Alexia of the Hagia.
Our mages will ensure the god-seed is contained securely until it is ready for extraction.
As for the extraction itself...
Admiral Elena Hagia will personally oversee it.
Kybele Enceladus. What have you to say?
Nothing. It won't make a difference.
The voting makes six in favour and one no vote.
As there is no time to waste, let us immediately commence this operation.

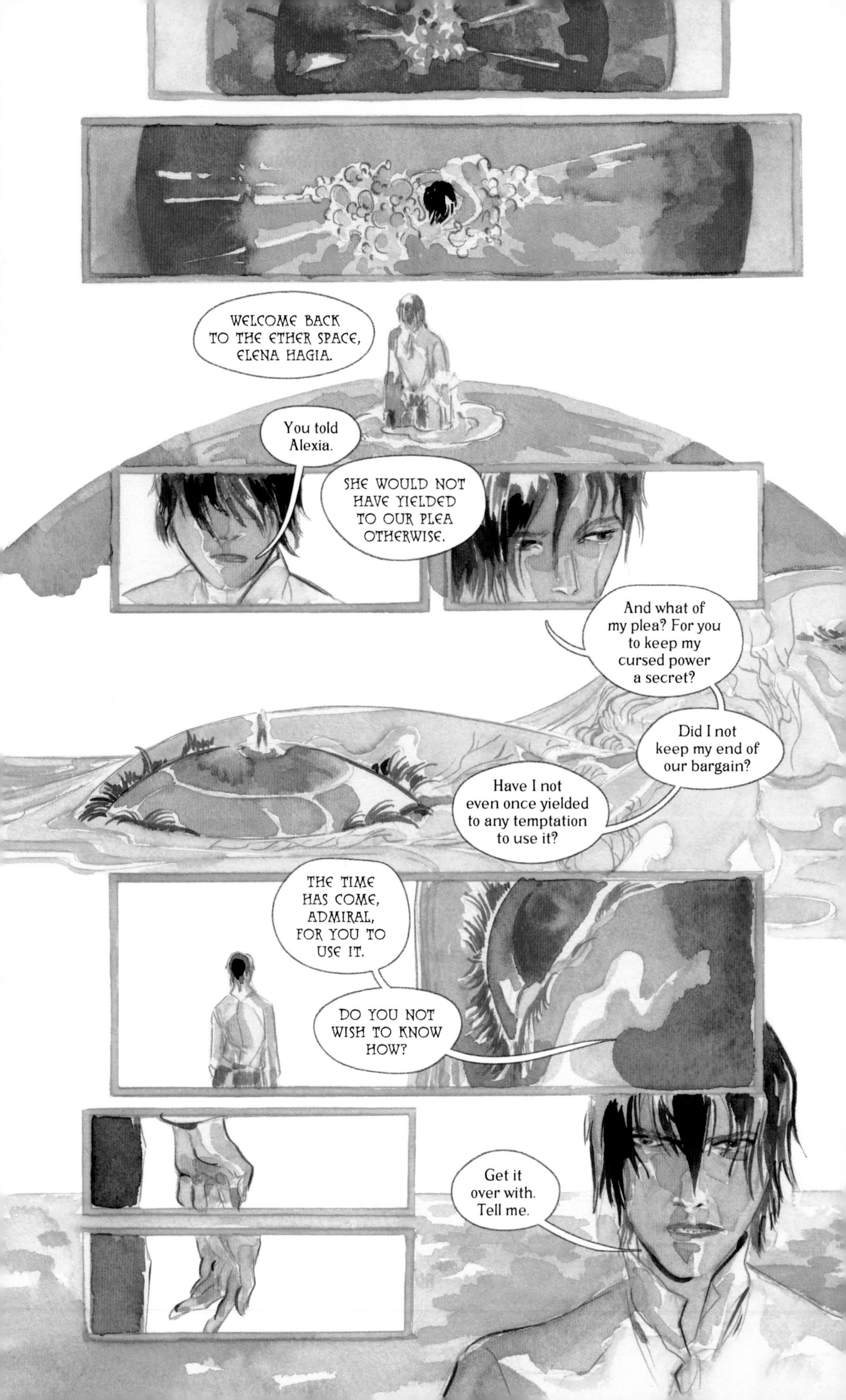
WELCOME BACK TO THE ETHER SPACE, ELENA HAGIA.
You told Alexia.
SHE WOULD NOT HAVE YIELDED TO OUR PLEA OTHERWISE.
And what of my plea? For you to keep my cursed power a secret?
Did I not keep my end of our bargain?
Have I not even once yielded to any temptation to use it?
THE TIME HAS COME, ADMIRAL, FOR YOU TO USE IT.
DO YOU NOT WISH TO KNOW HOW?
Get it over with. Tell me.

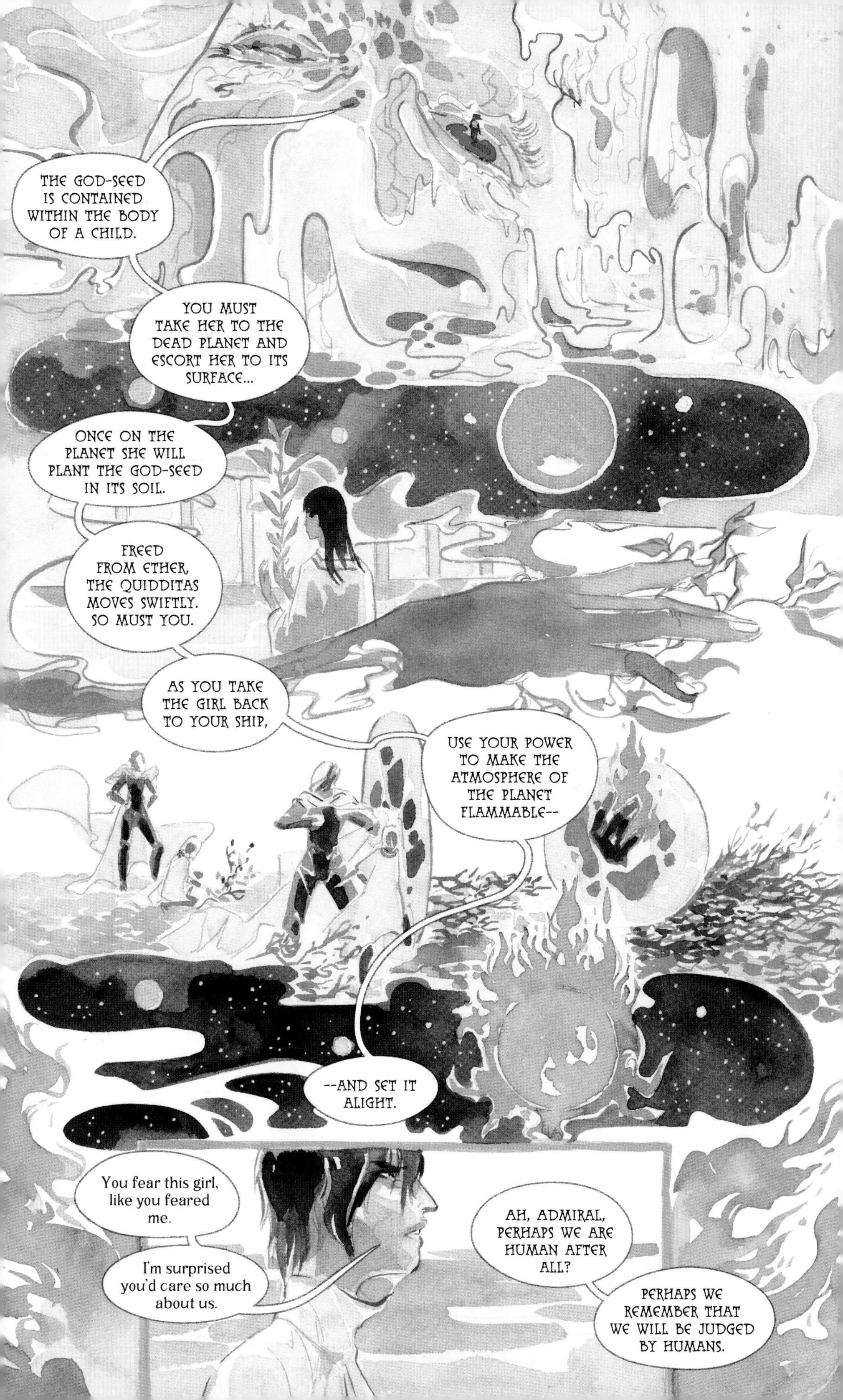
THE GOD-SEED IS CONTAINED WITHIN THE BODY OF A CHILD.
YOU MUST TAKE HER TO THE DEAD PLANET AND ESCORT HER TO ITS SURFACE...
ONCE ON THE PLANET SHE WILL PLANT THE GOD-SEED IN ITS SOIL.
FREED FROM ETHER, THE QUIDDITAS MOVES SWIFTLY. SO MUST YOU.
AS YOU TAKE THE GIRL BACK TO YOUR SHIP,
USE YOUR POWER TO MAKE THE ATMOSPHERE OF THE PLANET FLAMMABLE--
--AND SET IT ALIGHT.
You fear this girl, like you feared me.
I'm surprised you'd care so much about us.
AH, ADMIRAL, PERHAPS WE ARE HUMAN AFTER ALL?
PERHAPS WE REMEMBER THAT WE WILL BE JUDGED BY HUMANS.

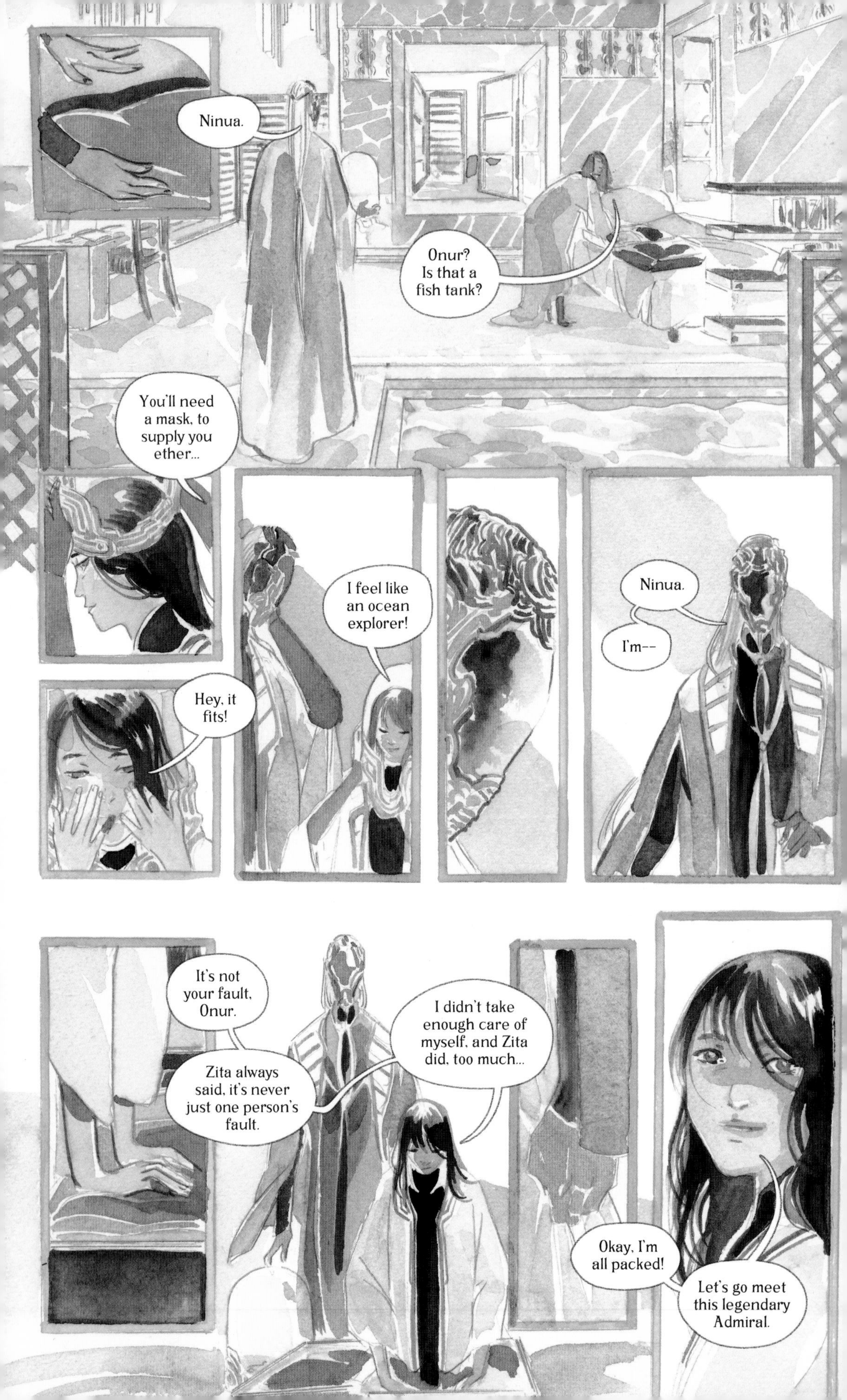
Ninua.
Onur? Is that a fish tank?
You'll need a mask, to supply you ether...
Hey, it fits!
I feel like an ocean explorer!
Ninua.
I'm--
It's not your fault, Onur.
Zita always said, it's never just one person's fault.
I didn't take enough care of myself, and Zita did, too much...
Okay, I'm all packed!
Let's go meet this legendary Admiral.

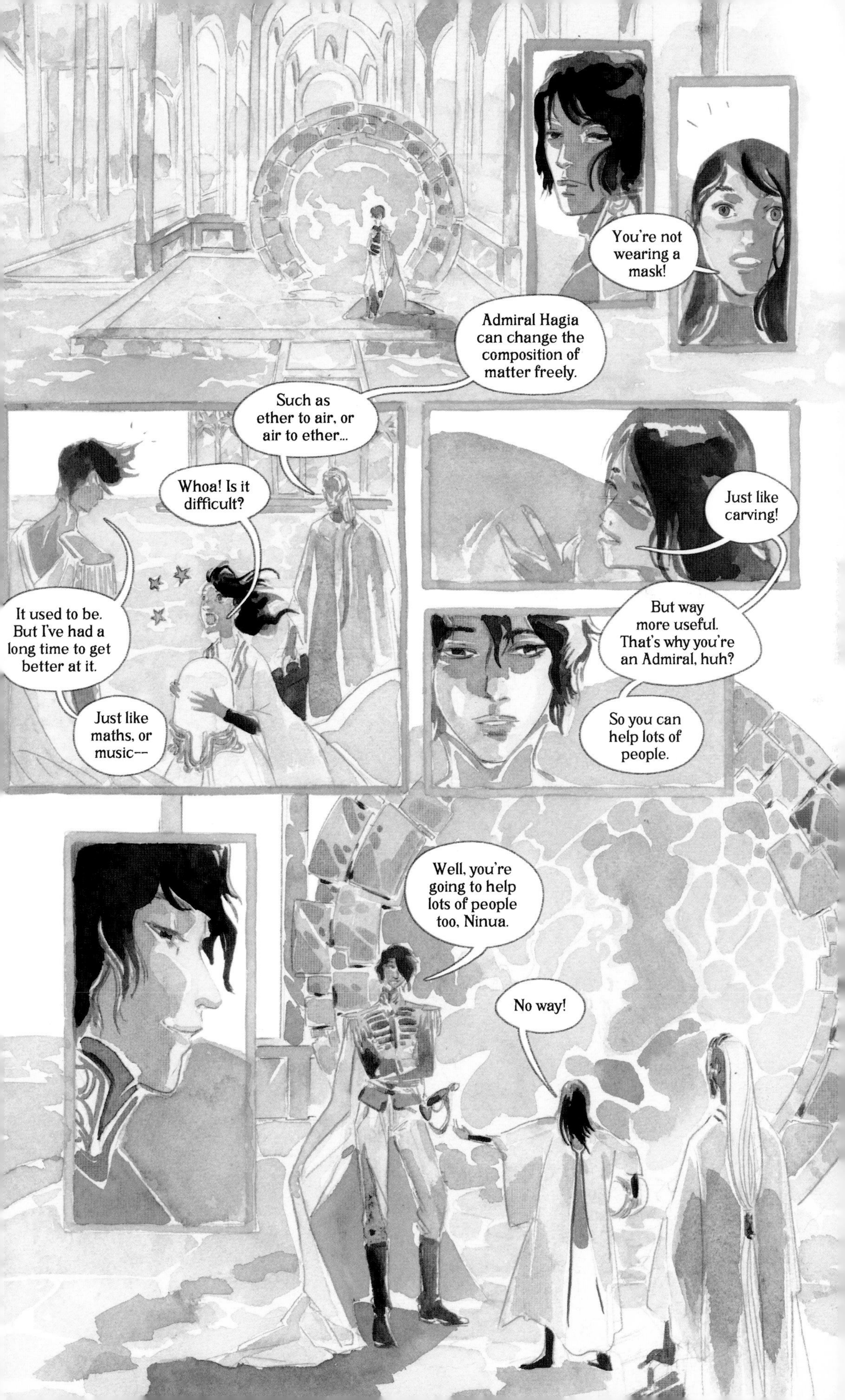
You're not wearing a mask!
Admiral Hagia can change the composition of matter freely.
Such as ether to air, or air to ether...
Whoa! Is it difficult?
It used to be. But I've had a long time to get better at it.
Just like maths, or music--
Just like carving!
But way more useful. That's why you're an Admiral, huh?
So you can help lots of people.
Well, you're going to help lots of people too, Ninua.
No way!

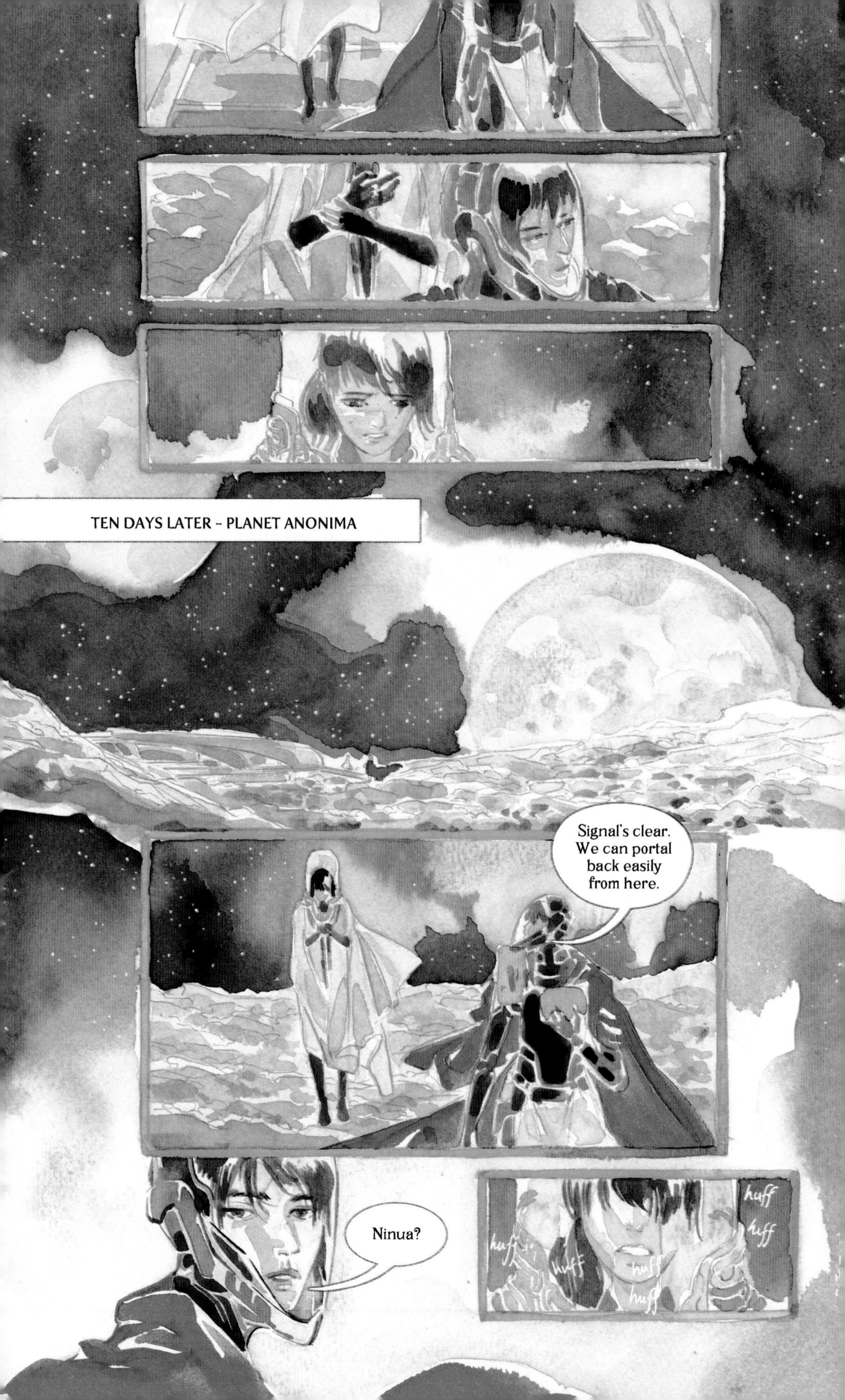
TEN DAYS LATER - PLANET ANONIMA
Signal's clear. We can portal back easily from here.
Ninua?
huff
huff
huff
huff
huff
huff

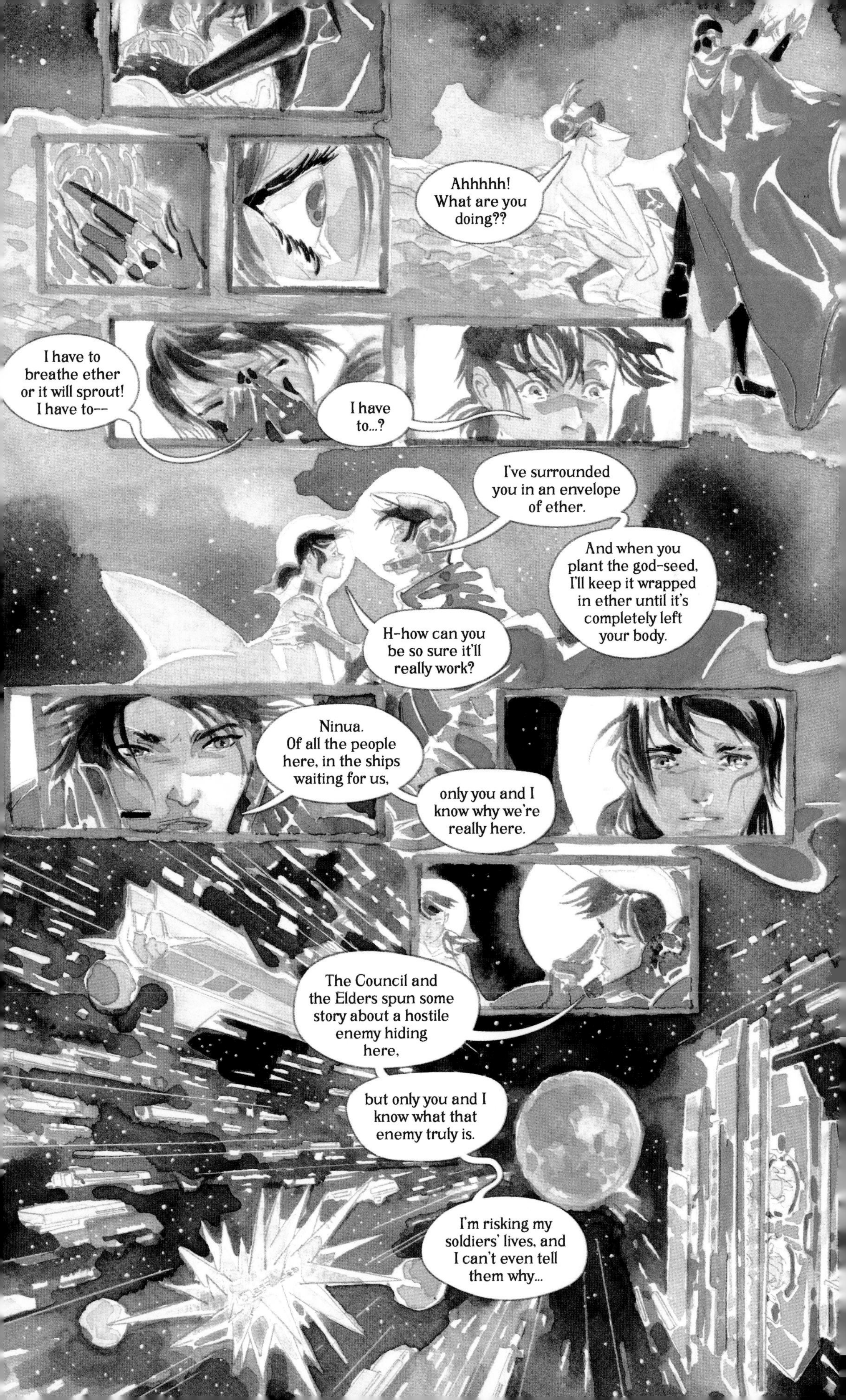
Ahhhhh!
What are you doing??
I have to breathe ether or it will sprout! I have to--
I have to...?
I've surrounded you in an envelope of ether.
And when you plant the god-seed, I'll keep it wrapped in ether until it's completely left your body.
H-how can you be so sure it'll really work?
Ninua.
Of all the people here, in the ships waiting for us,
only you and I know why we're really here.
The Council and the Elders spun some story about a hostile enemy hiding here,
but only you and I know what that enemy truly is.
I'm risking my soldiers' lives, and I can't even tell them why...

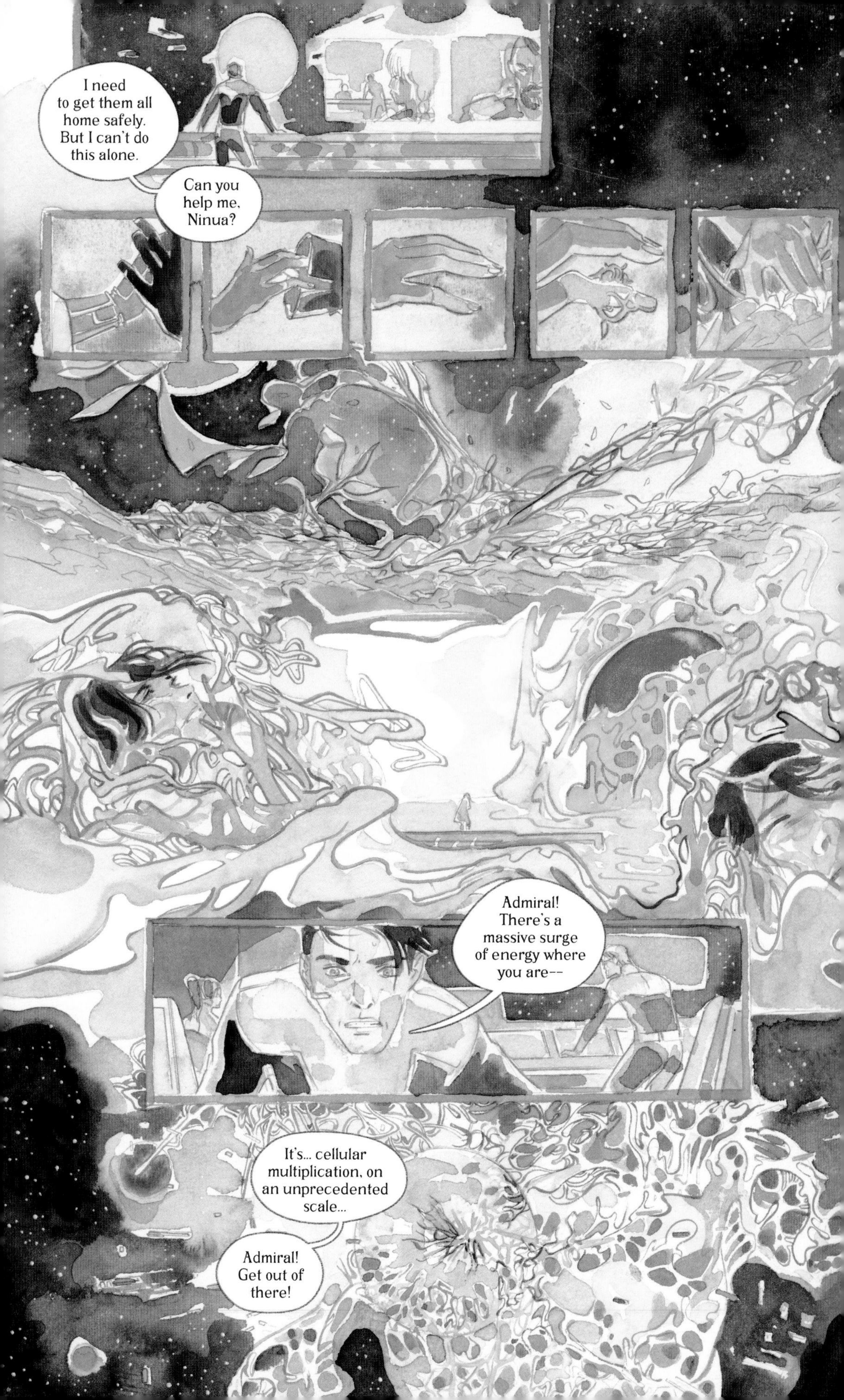
I need to get them all home safely. But I can't do this alone.
Can you help me, Ninua?
Admiral! There's a massive surge of energy where you are--
It's... cellular multiplication, on an unprecedented scale...
Admiral! Get out of there!

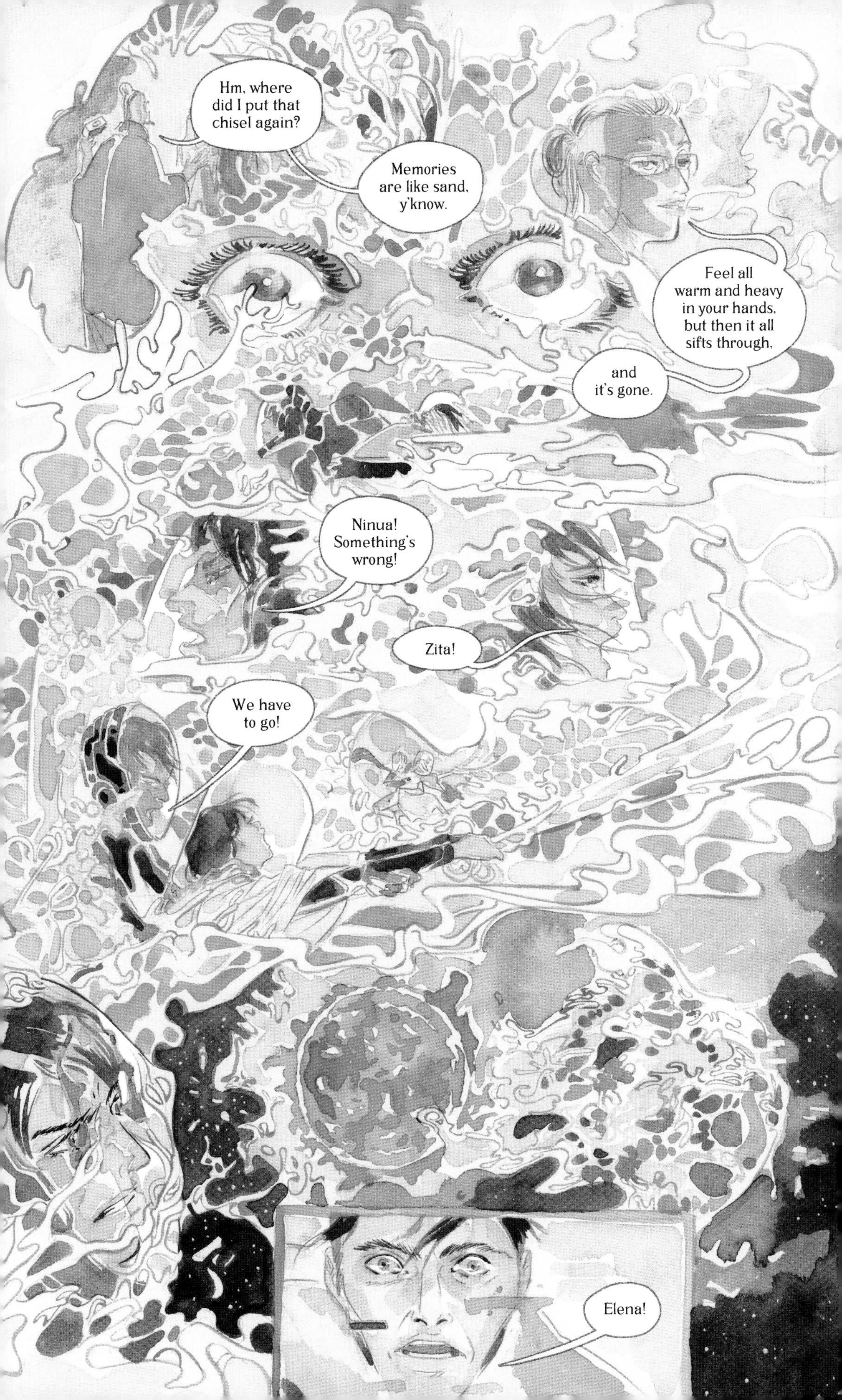
Hm, where did I put that chisel again?
Memories are like sand, y'know.
Feel all warm and heavy in your hands, but then it all sifts through,
and it's gone.
Ninua! Something's wrong!
Zita!
We have to go!
Elena!

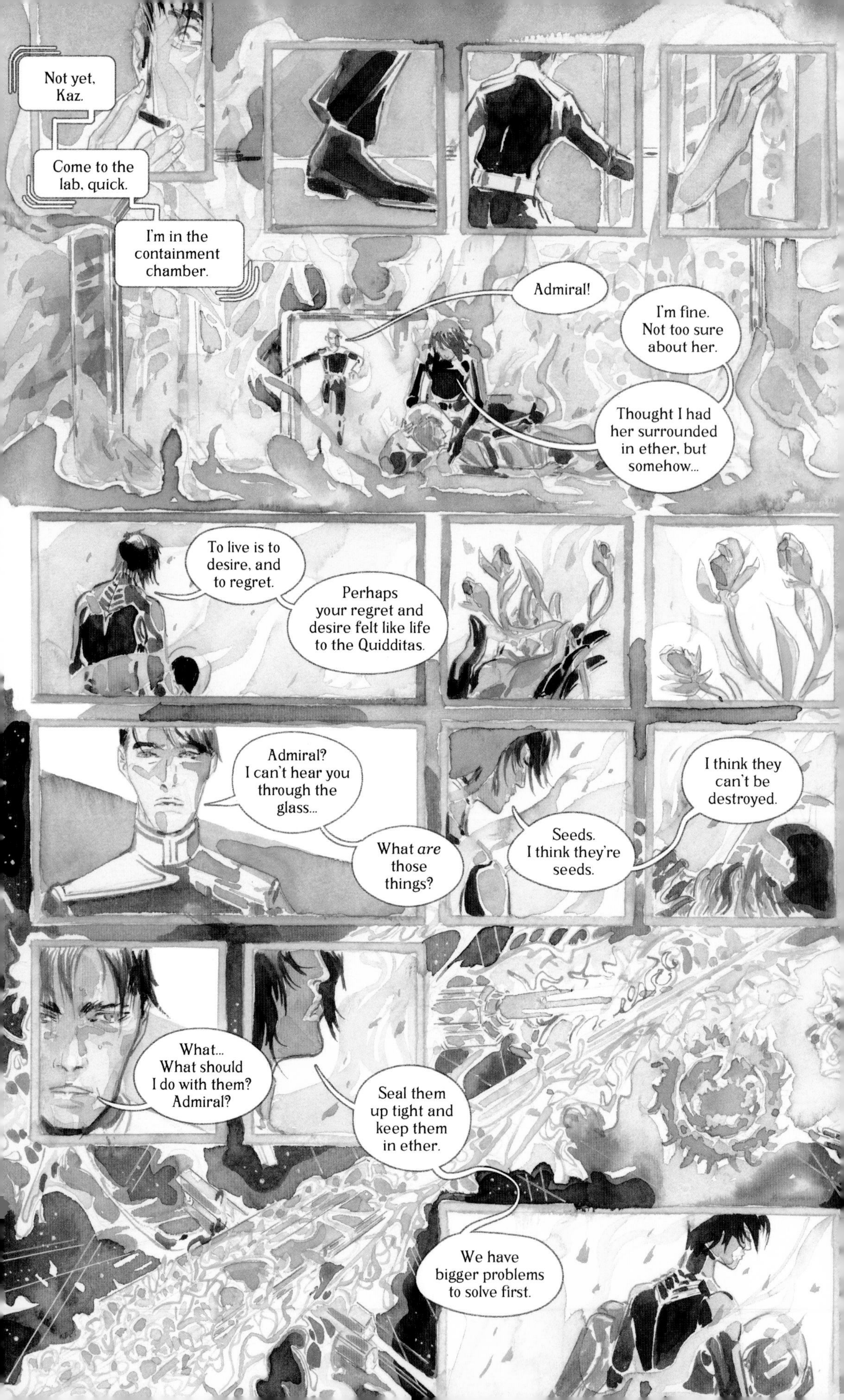

Not yet, Kaz.
Come to the lab, quick.
I'm in the containment chamber.
Admiral!
I'm fine. Not too sure about her.
Thought I had her surrounded in ether, but somehow...
To live is to desire, and to regret.
Perhaps your regret and desire felt like life to the Quidditas.
Admiral? I can't hear you through the glass...
What *are* those things?
Seeds. I think they're seeds.
I think they can't be destroyed.
What... What should I do with them? Admiral?
Seal them up tight and keep them in ether.
We have bigger problems to solve first.

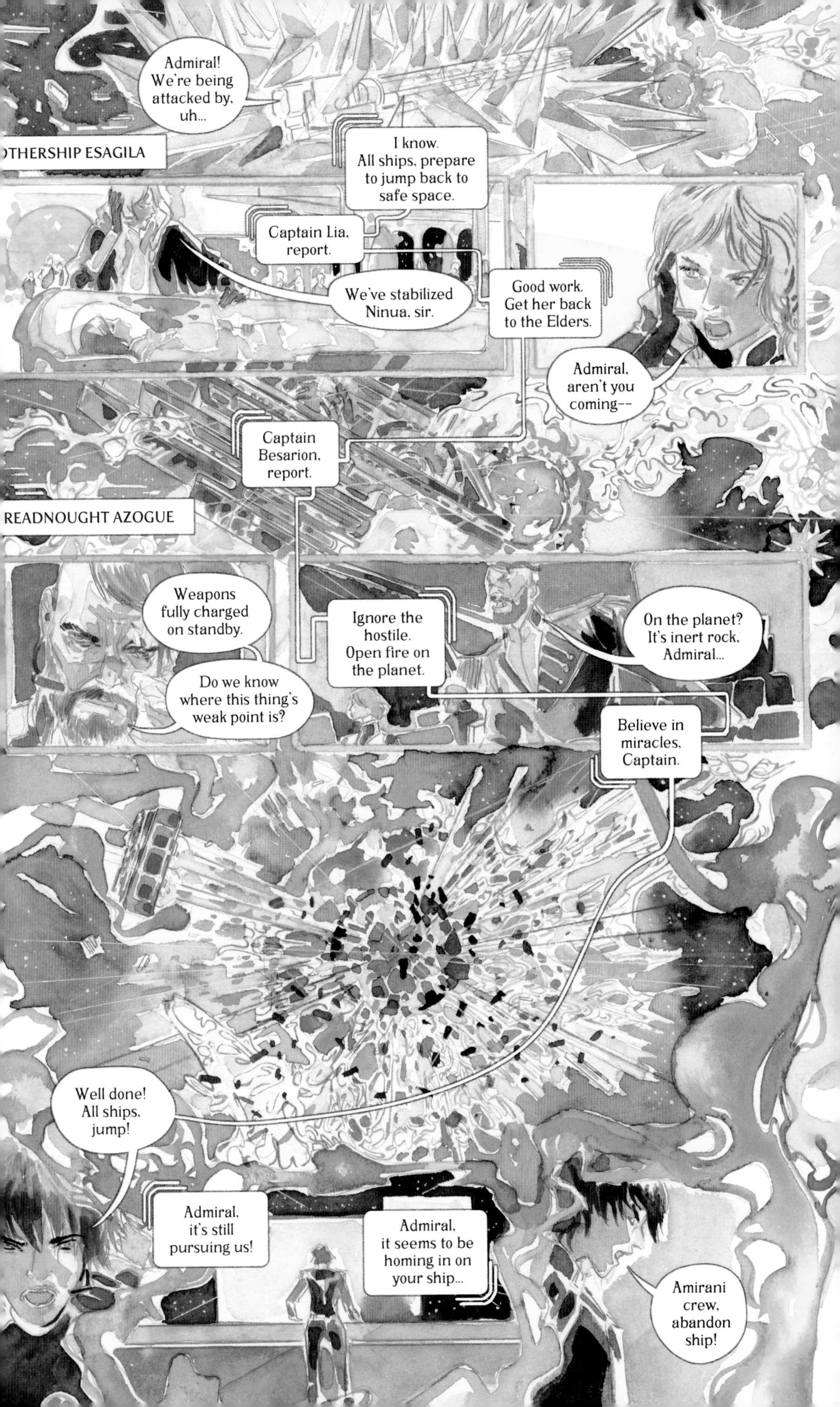
Admiral! We're being attacked by, uh...
OTHERSHIP ESAGILA
I know. All ships, prepare to jump back to safe space.
Captain Lia, report.
We've stabilized Ninua, sir.
Good work. Get her back to the Elders.
Admiral, aren't you coming--
Captain Besarion, report.
READNOUGHT AZOGUE
Weapons fully charged on standby.
Do we know where this thing's weak point is?
Ignore the hostile. Open fire on the planet.
On the planet? It's inert rock, Admiral...
Believe in miracles, Captain.
Well done! All ships, jump!
Admiral, it's still pursuing us!
Admiral, it seems to be homing in on your ship...
Amirani crew, abandon ship!

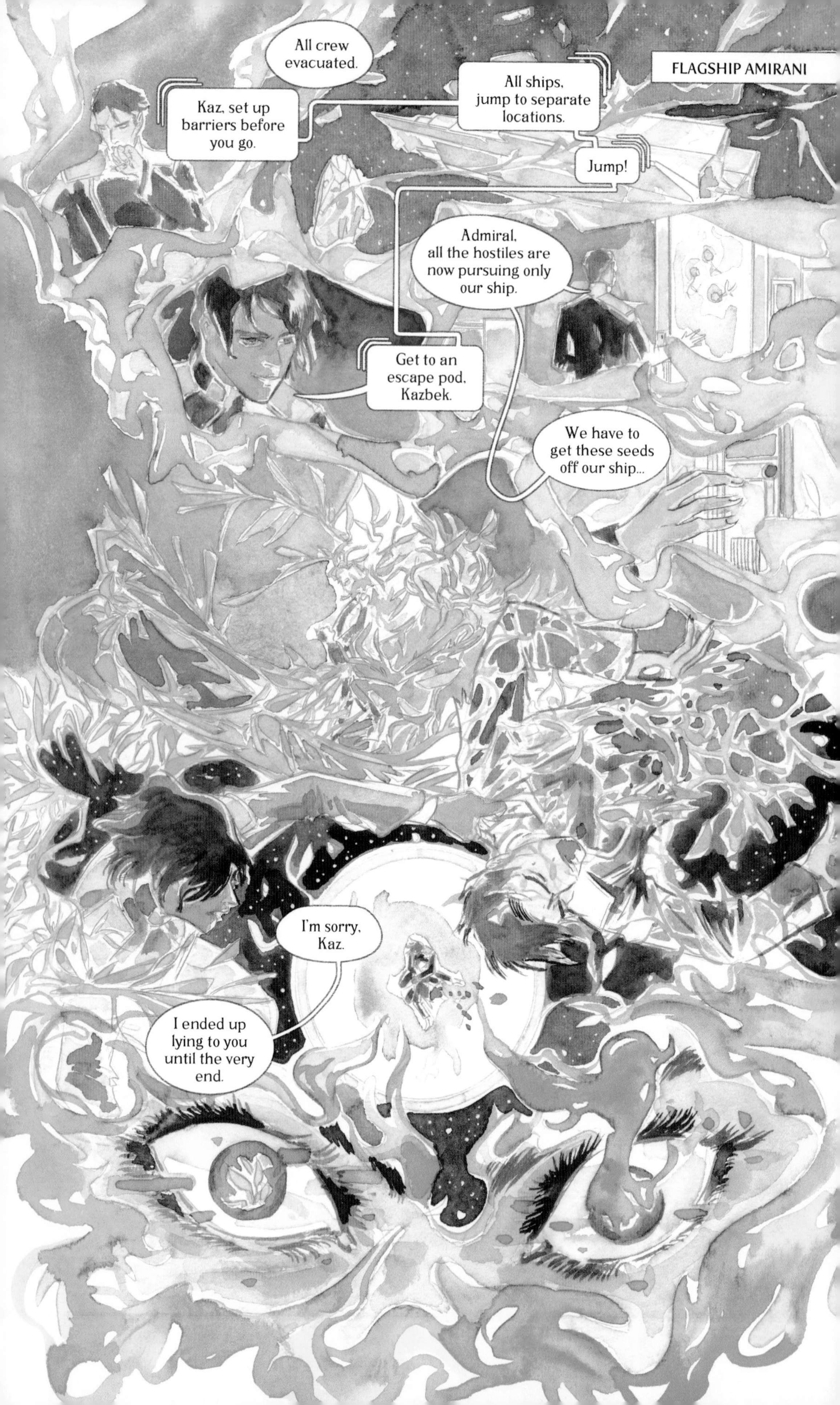
FLAGSHIP AMIRANI
All crew evacuated.
Kaz, set up barriers before you go.
All ships, jump to separate locations.
Jump!
Admiral, all the hostiles are now pursuing only our ship.
Get to an escape pod, Kazbek.
We have to get these seeds off our ship...
I'm sorry, Kaz.
I ended up lying to you until the very end.

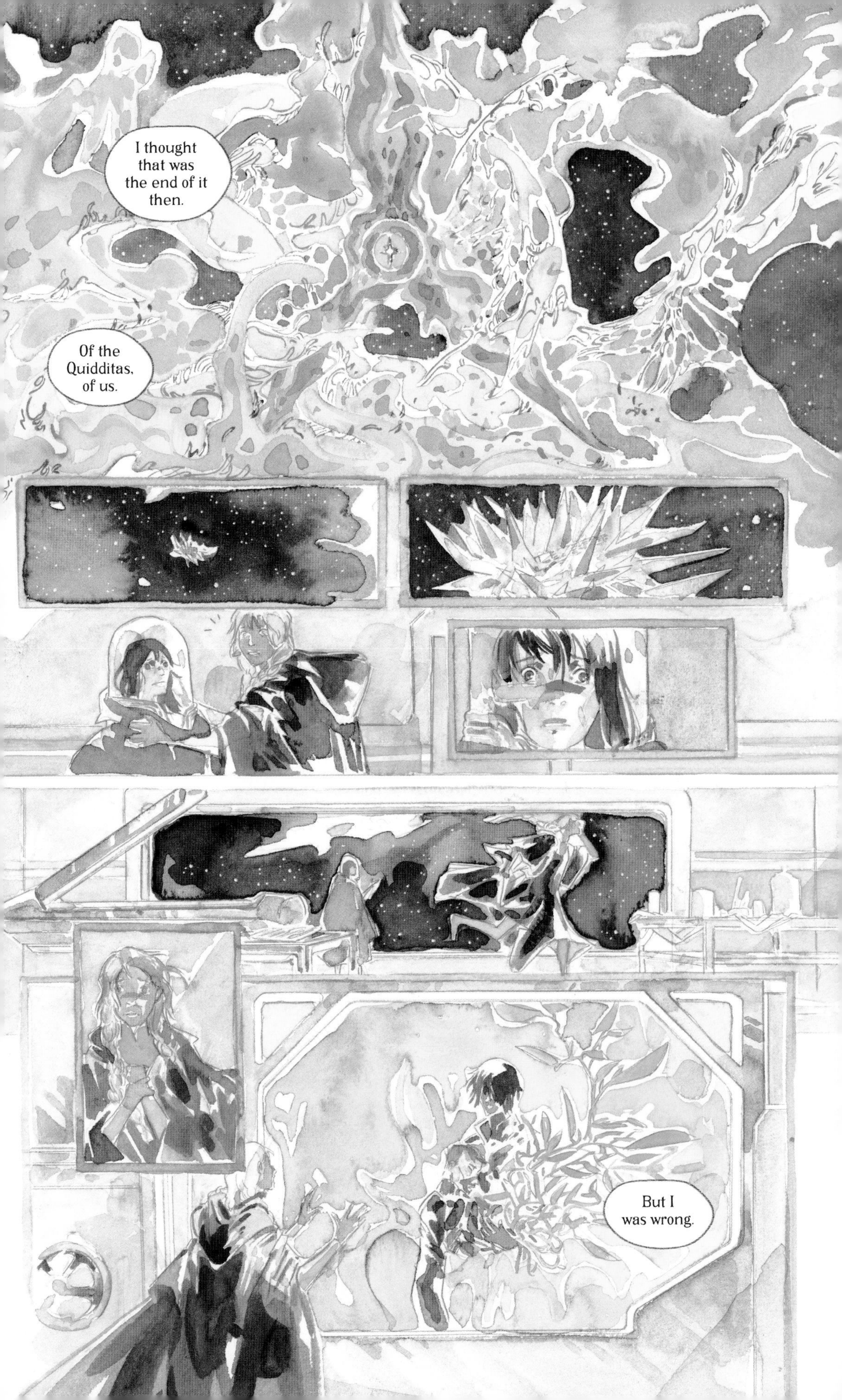
I thought that was the end of it then.
Of the Quidditas, of us.
But I was wrong.

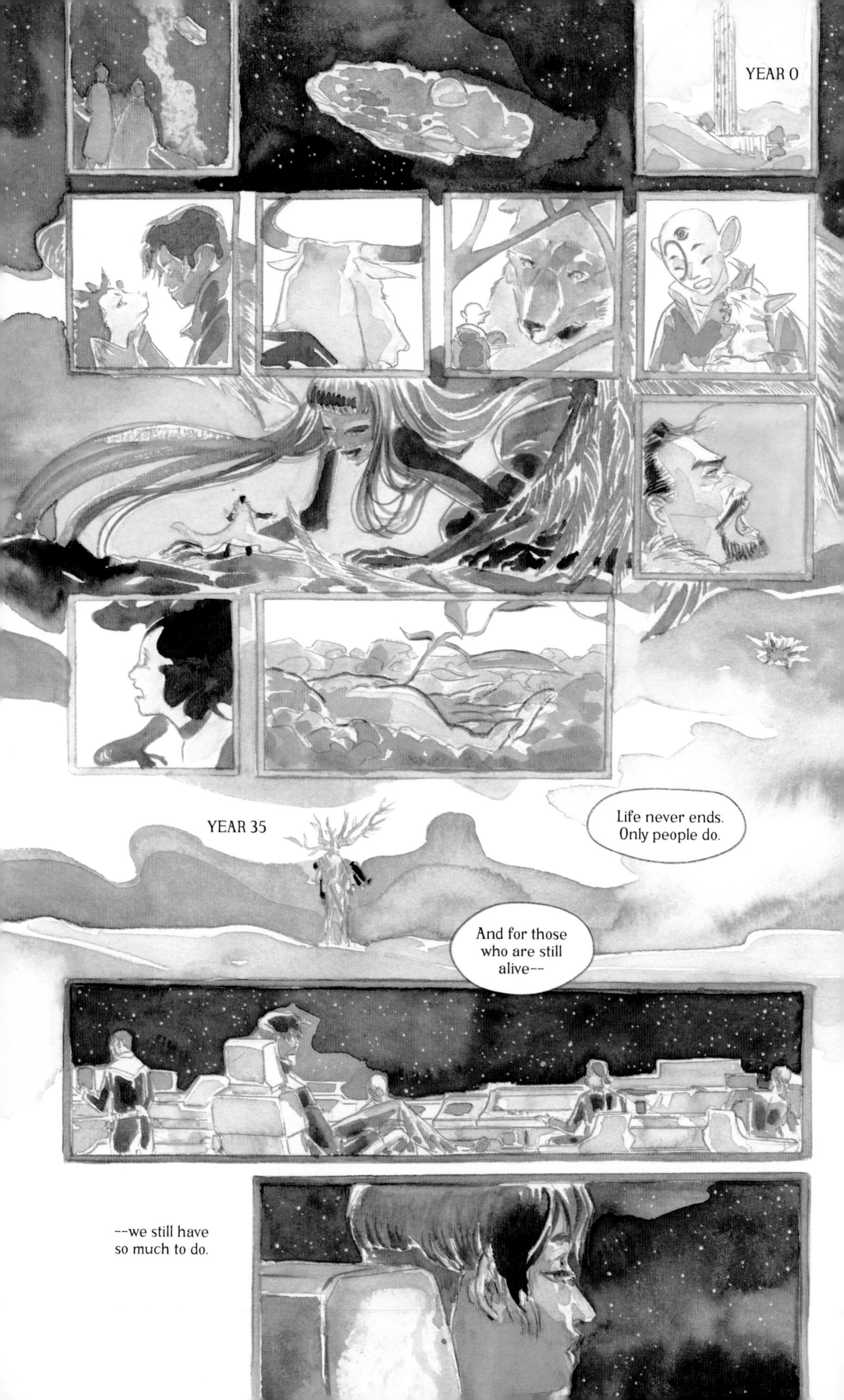
YEAR 0
YEAR 35
Life never ends. Only people do.
And for those who are still alive--
--we still have so much to do.

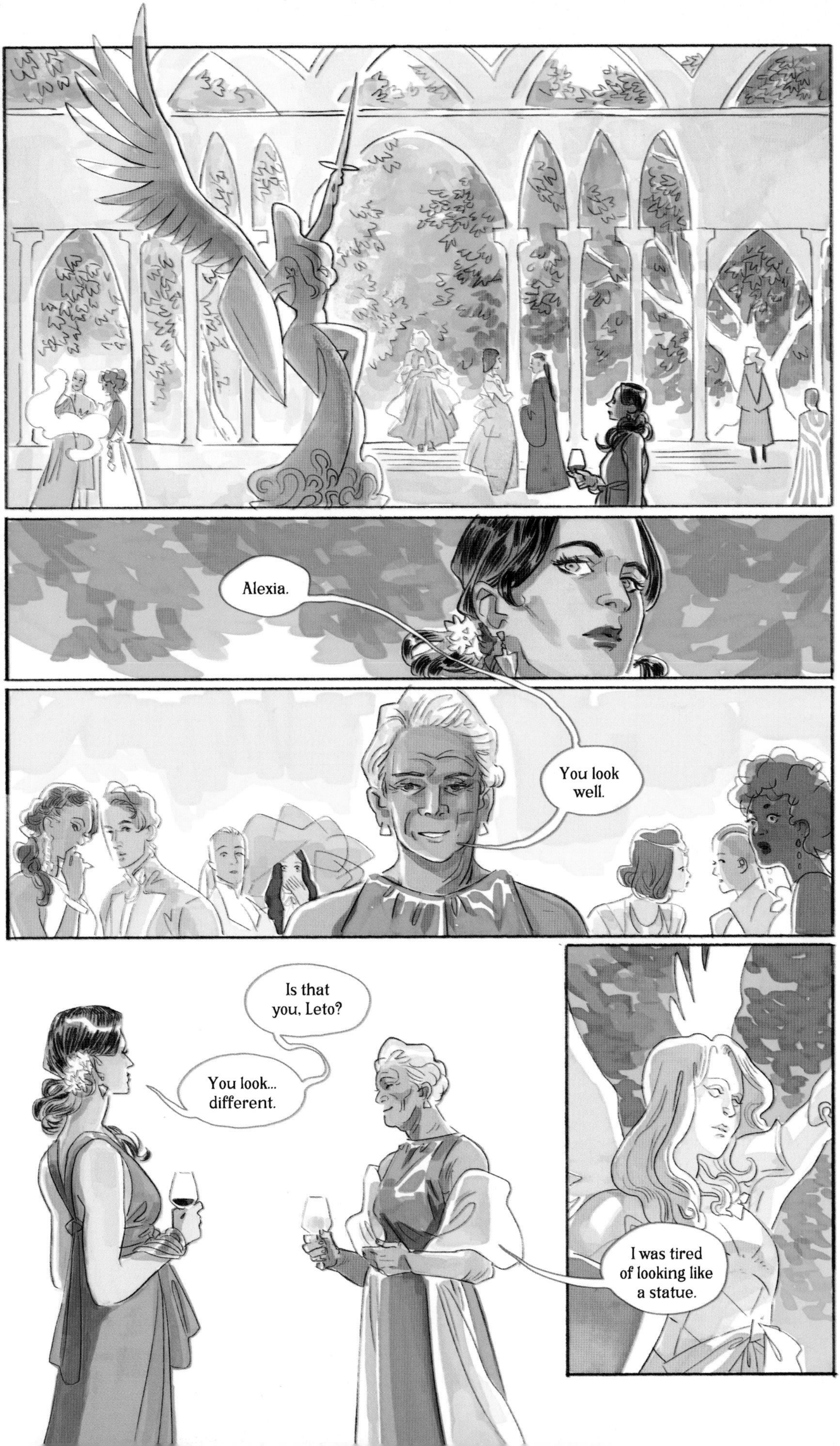
Alexia.
You look well.
Is that you, Leto?
You look... different.
I was tired of looking like a statue.

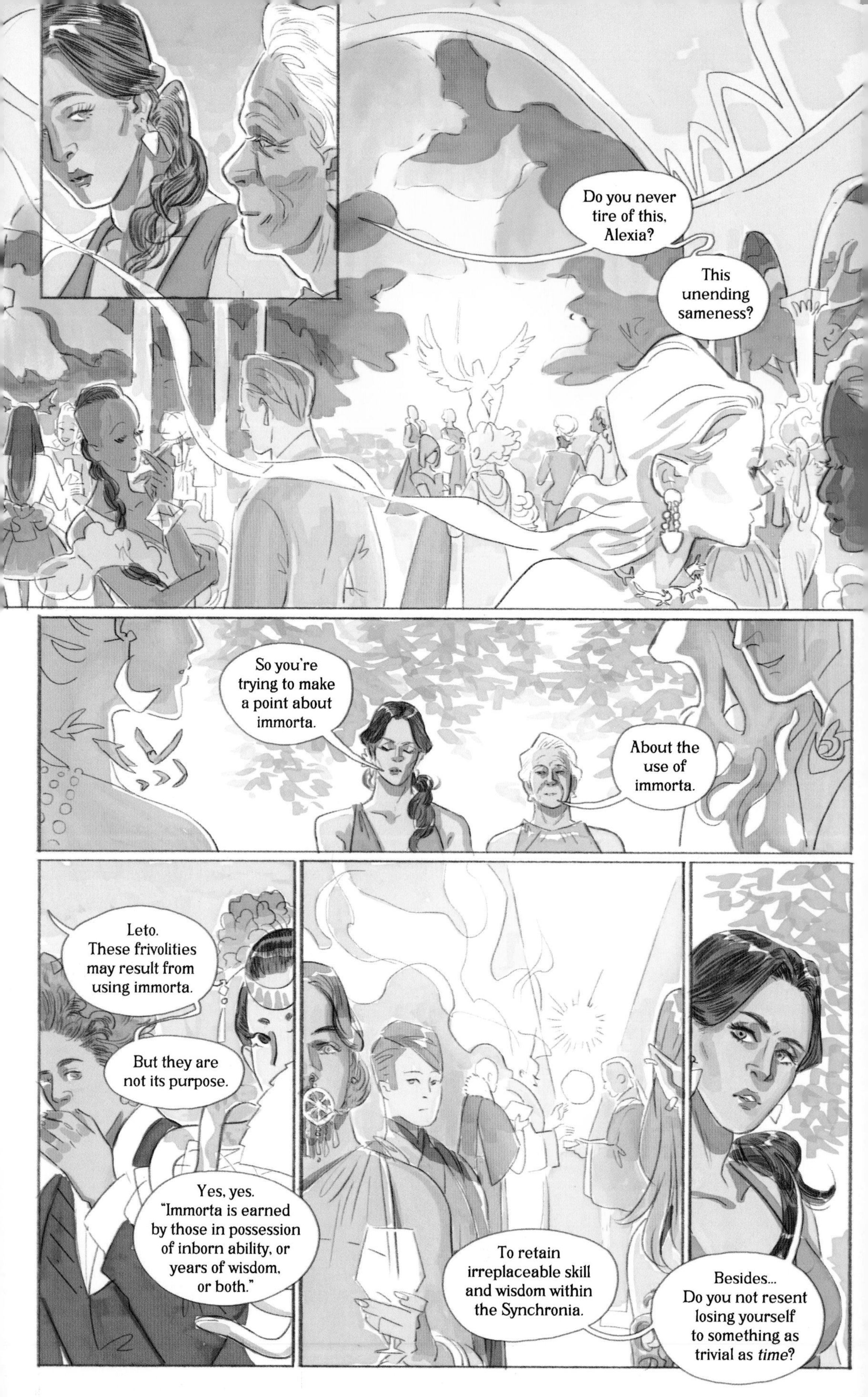
Do you never tire of this, Alexia?
This unending sameness?
So you're trying to make a point about immorta.
About the use of immorta.
Leto. These frivolities may result from using immorta.
But they are not its purpose.
Yes, yes. "Immorta is earned by those in possession of inborn ability, or years of wisdom, or both."
To retain irreplaceable skill and wisdom within the Synchronia.
Besides... Do you not resent losing yourself to something as trivial as *time*?

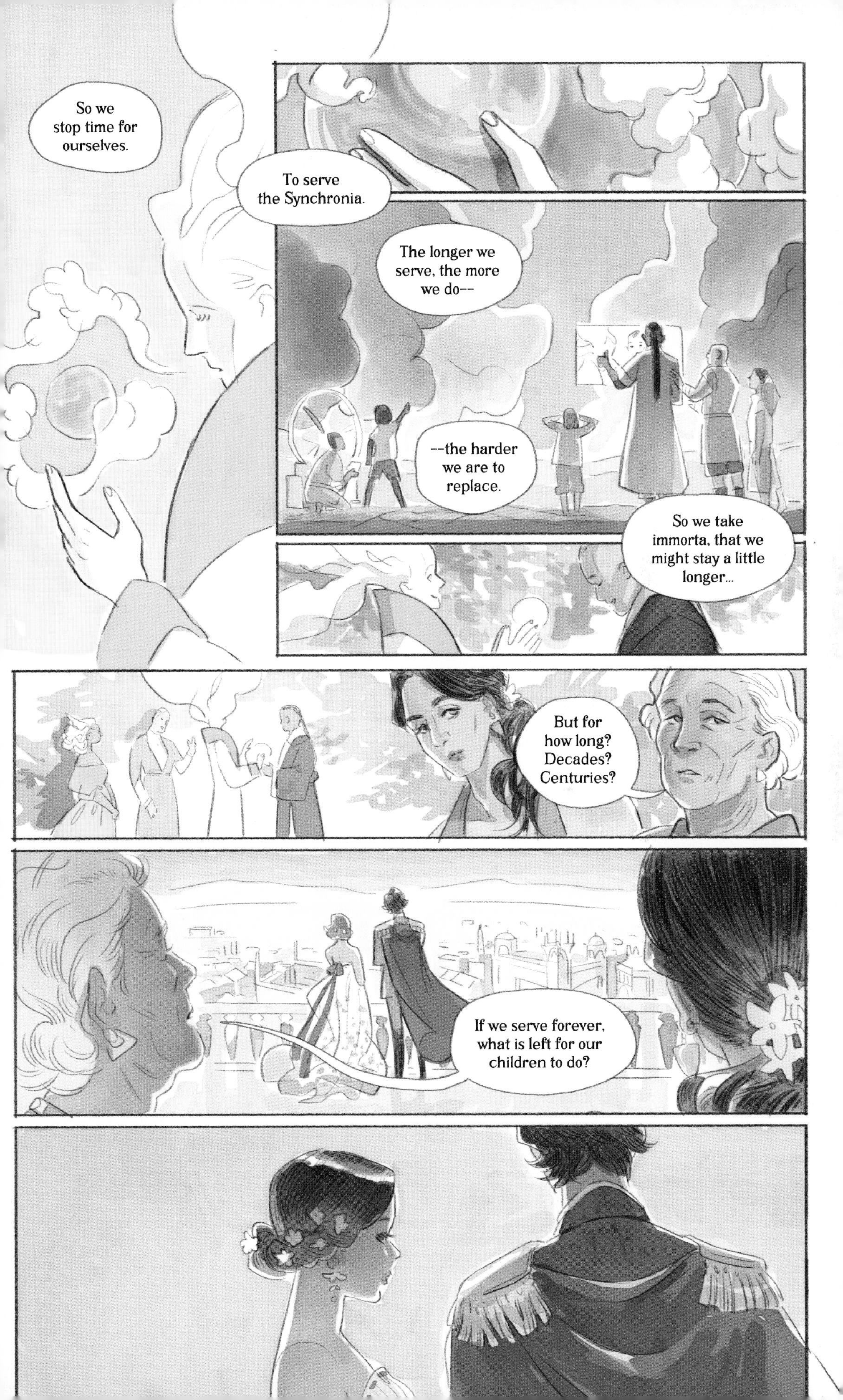
So we stop time for ourselves.
To serve the Synchronia.
The longer we serve, the more we do--
--the harder we are to replace.
So we take immorta, that we might stay a little longer...
But for how long? Decades? Centuries?
If we serve forever, what is left for our children to do?

Chapter Eight

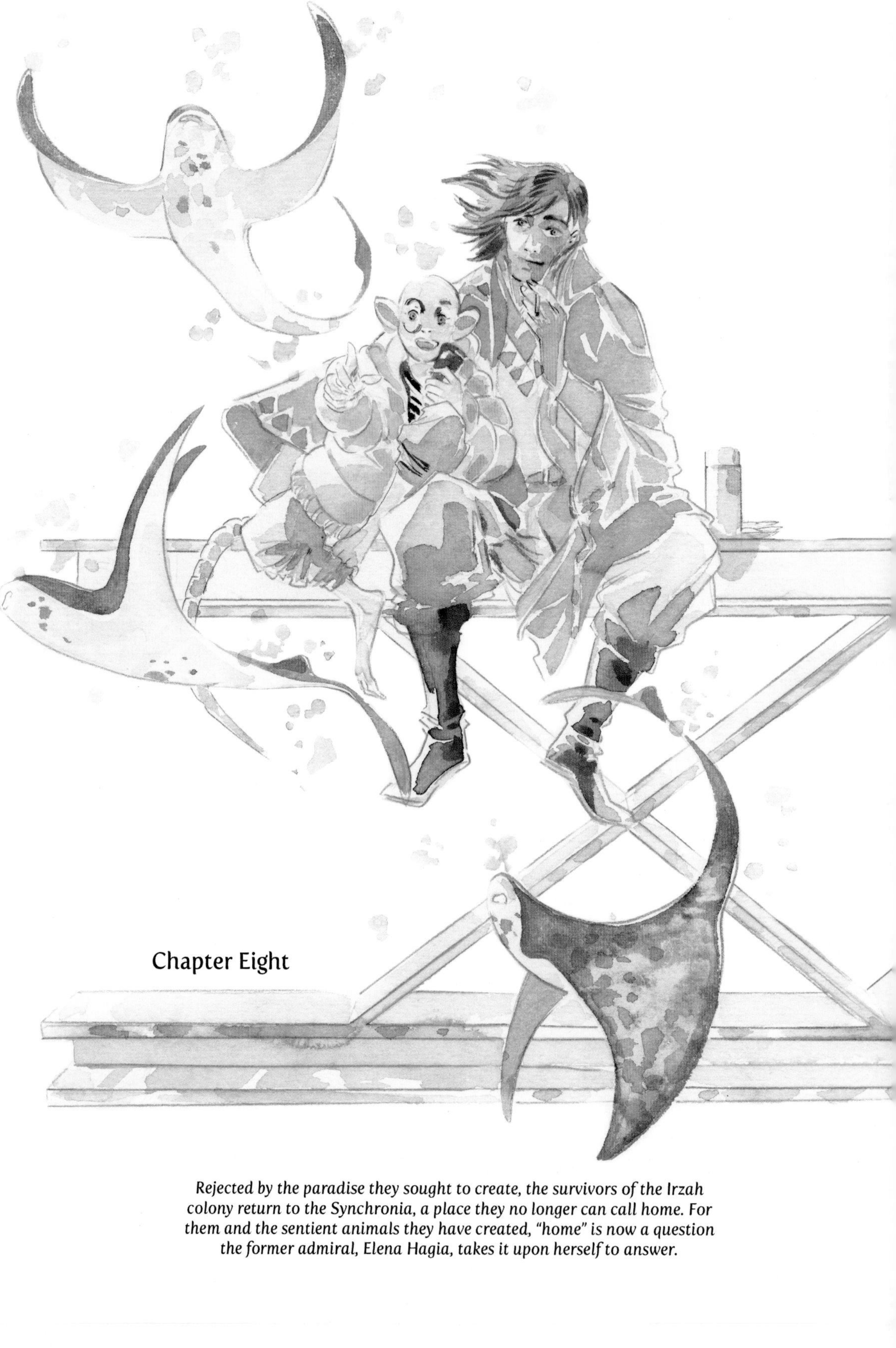

Rejected by the paradise they sought to create, the survivors of the Irzah colony return to the Synchronia, a place they no longer can call home. For them and the sentient animals they have created, "home" is now a question the former admiral, Elena Hagia, takes it upon herself to answer.

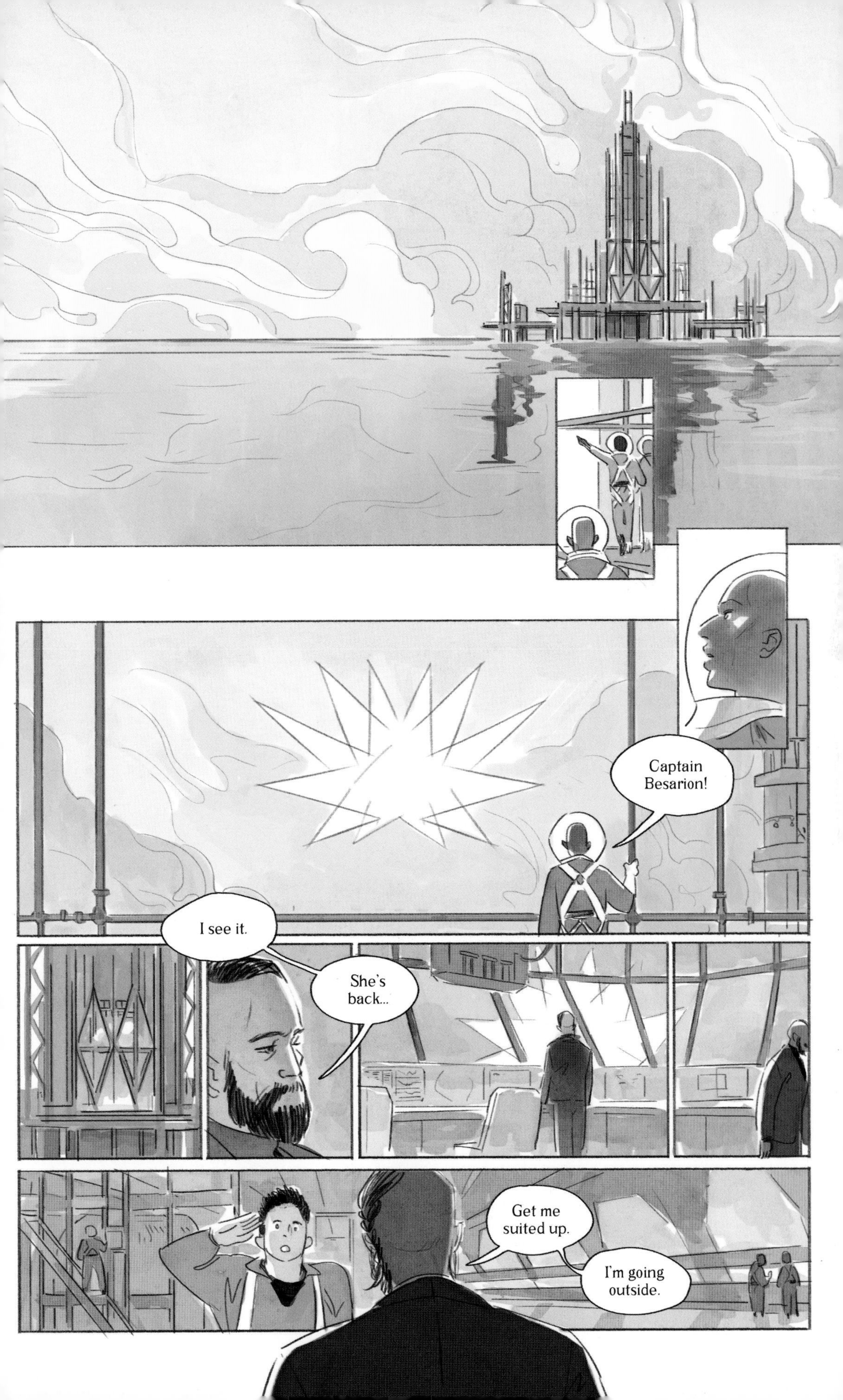
Captain Besarion!
I see it.
She's back...
Get me suited up.
I'm going outside.

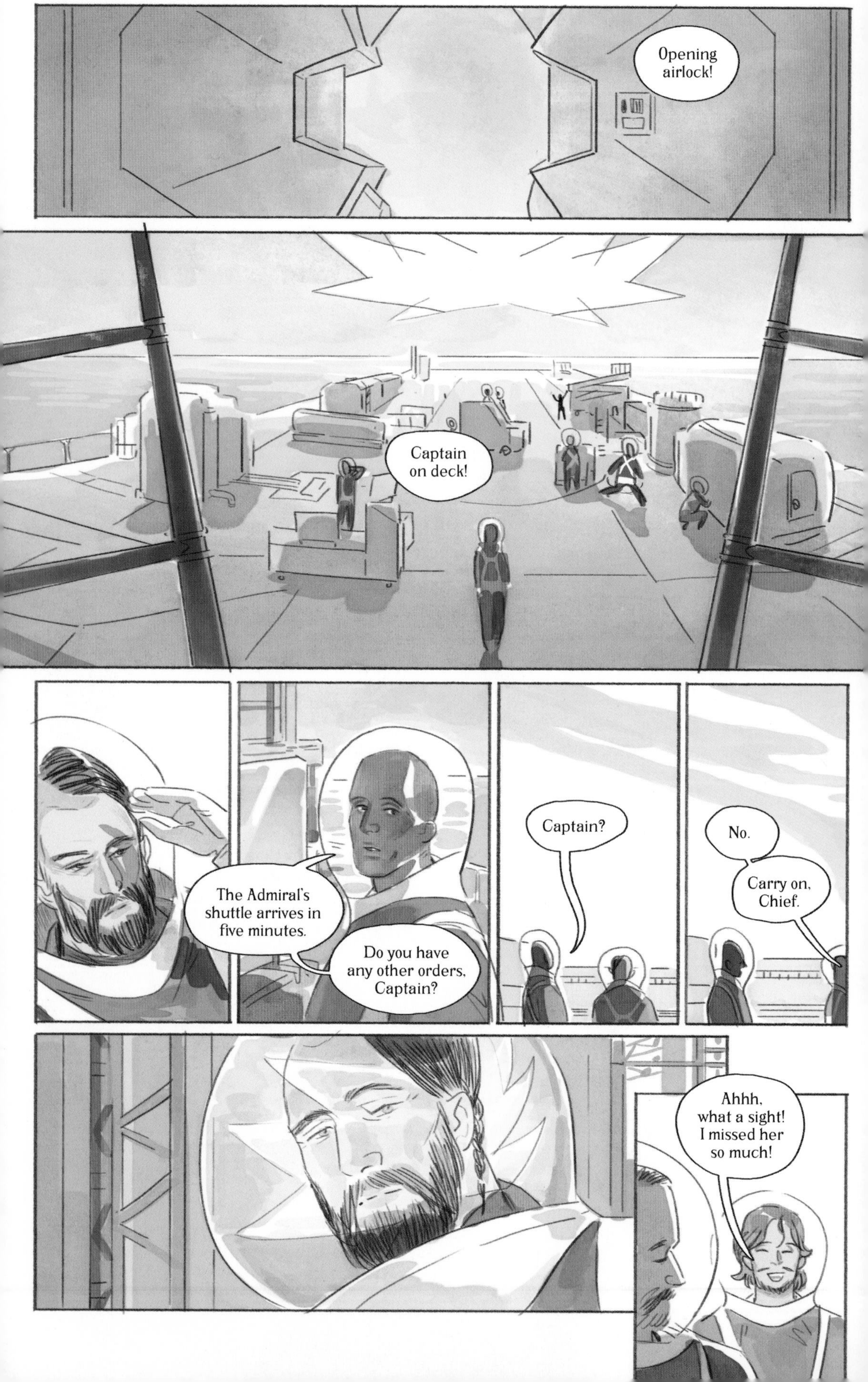
Opening airlock!
Captain on deck!
The Admiral's shuttle arrives in five minutes.
Do you have any other orders, Captain?
Captain?
No.
Carry on, Chief.
Ahhh, what a sight! I missed her so much!

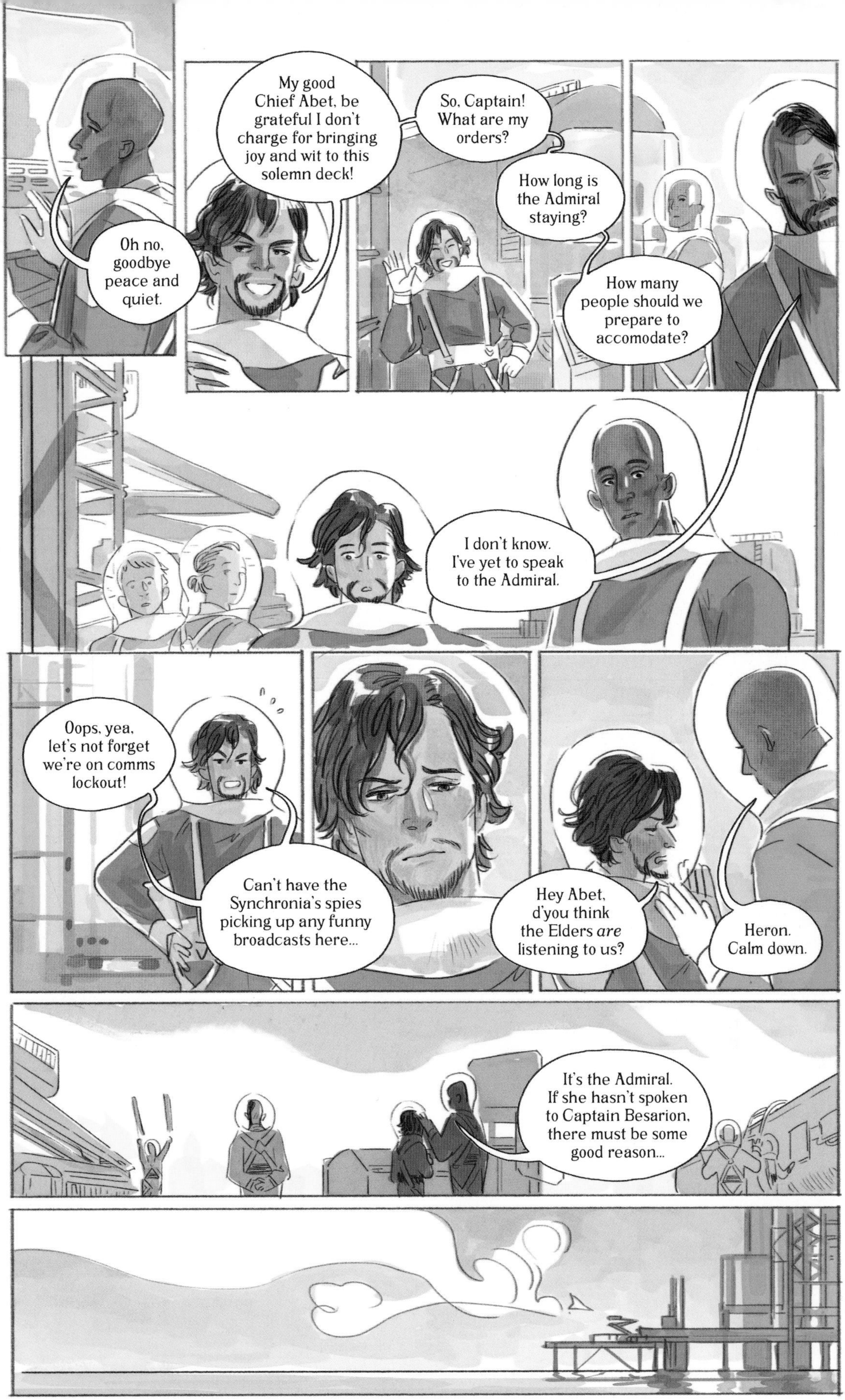
Oh no, goodbye peace and quiet.
My good Chief Abet, be grateful I don't charge for bringing joy and wit to this solemn deck!
So, Captain! What are my orders?
How long is the Admiral staying?
How many people should we prepare to accomodate?
I don't know. I've yet to speak to the Admiral.
Oops, yea, let's not forget we're on comms lockout!
Can't have the Synchronia's spies picking up any funny broadcasts here...
Hey Abet, d'you think the Elders *are* listening to us?
Heron. Calm down.
It's the Admiral. If she hasn't spoken to Captain Besarion, there must be some good reason...

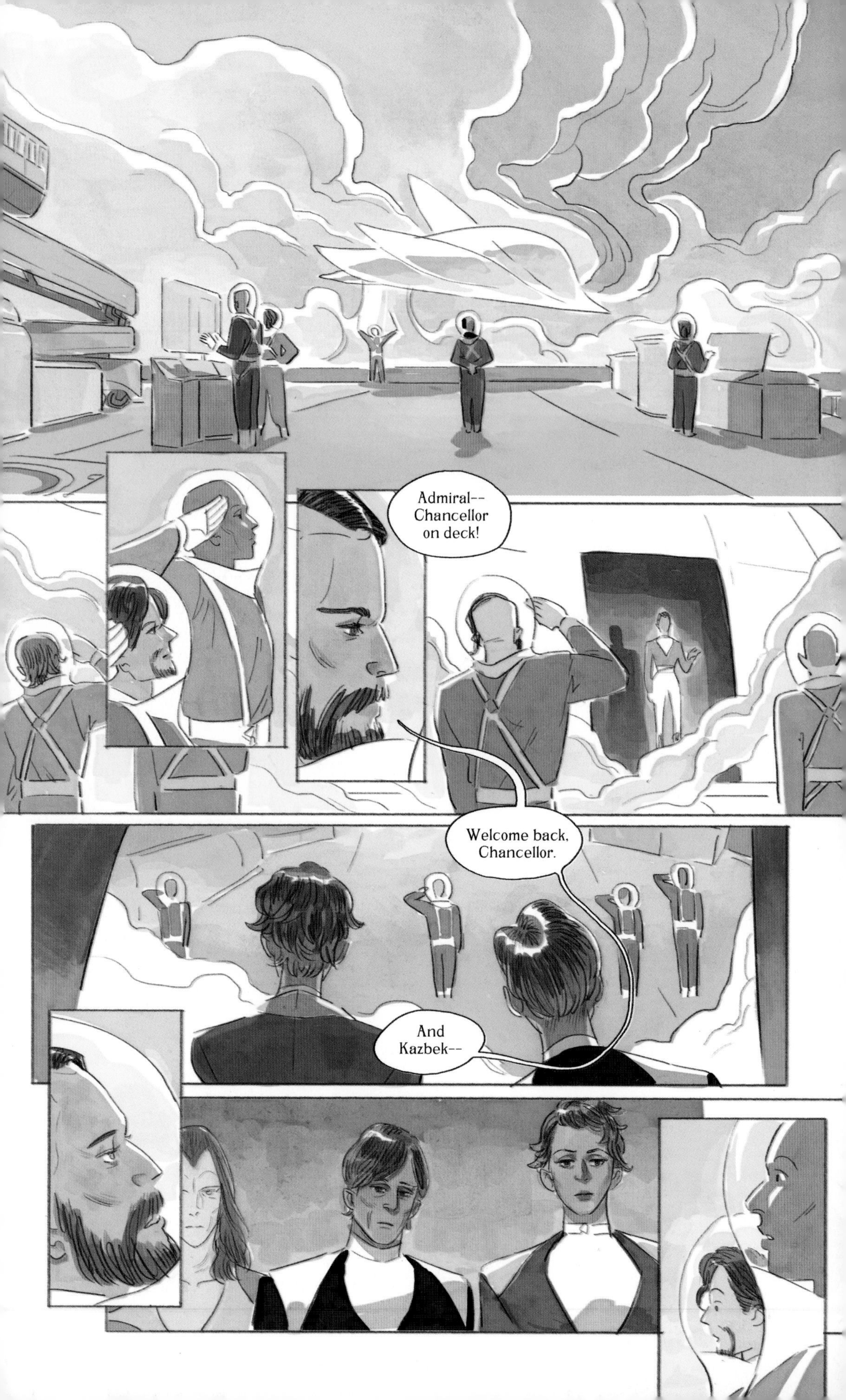
Admiral--
Chancellor on deck!
Welcome back, Chancellor.
And Kazbek--

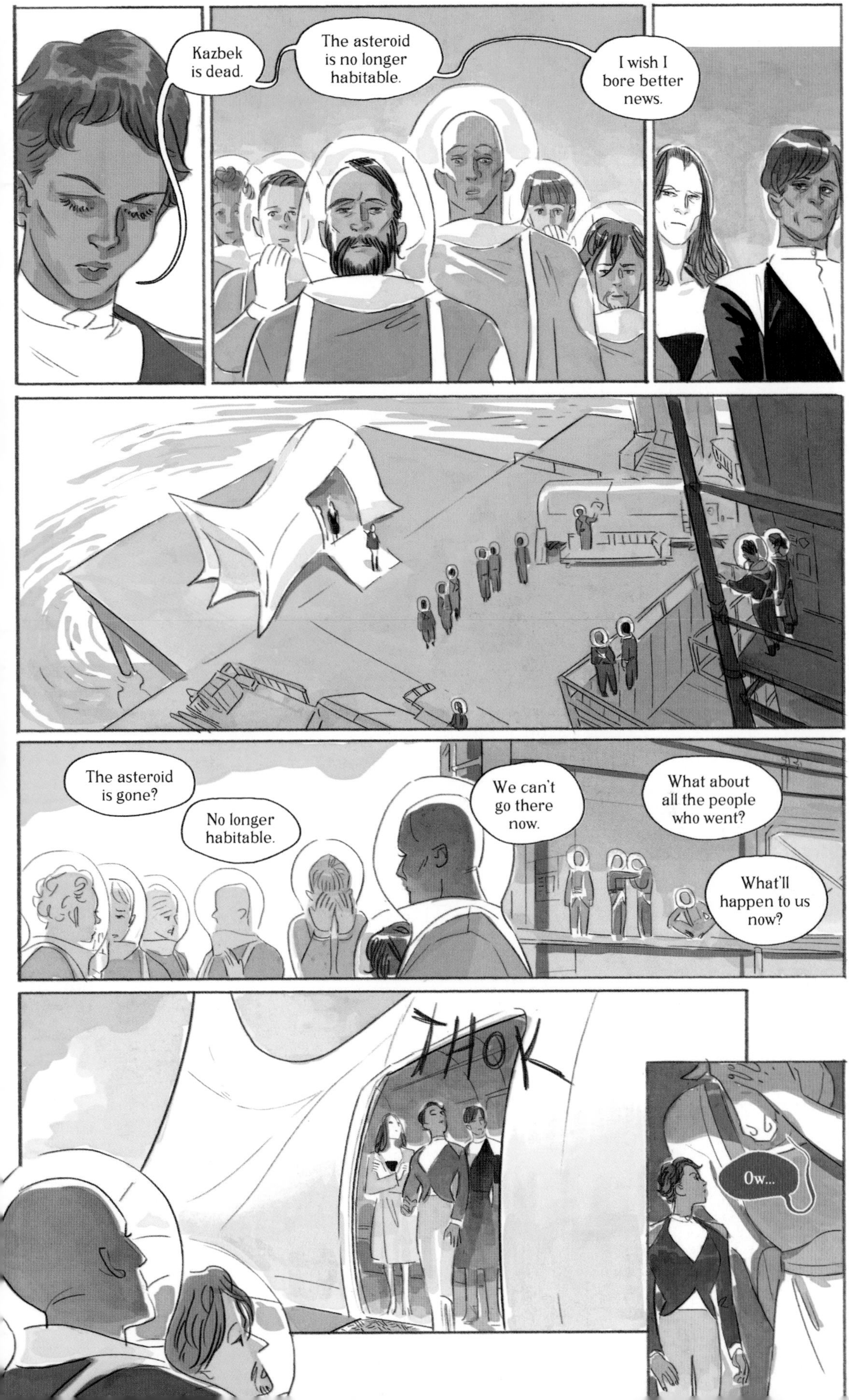
Kazbek is dead.
The asteroid is no longer habitable.
I wish I bore better news.
The asteroid is gone?
No longer habitable.
We can't go there now.
What about all the people who went?
What'll happen to us now?
THOK
Ow...

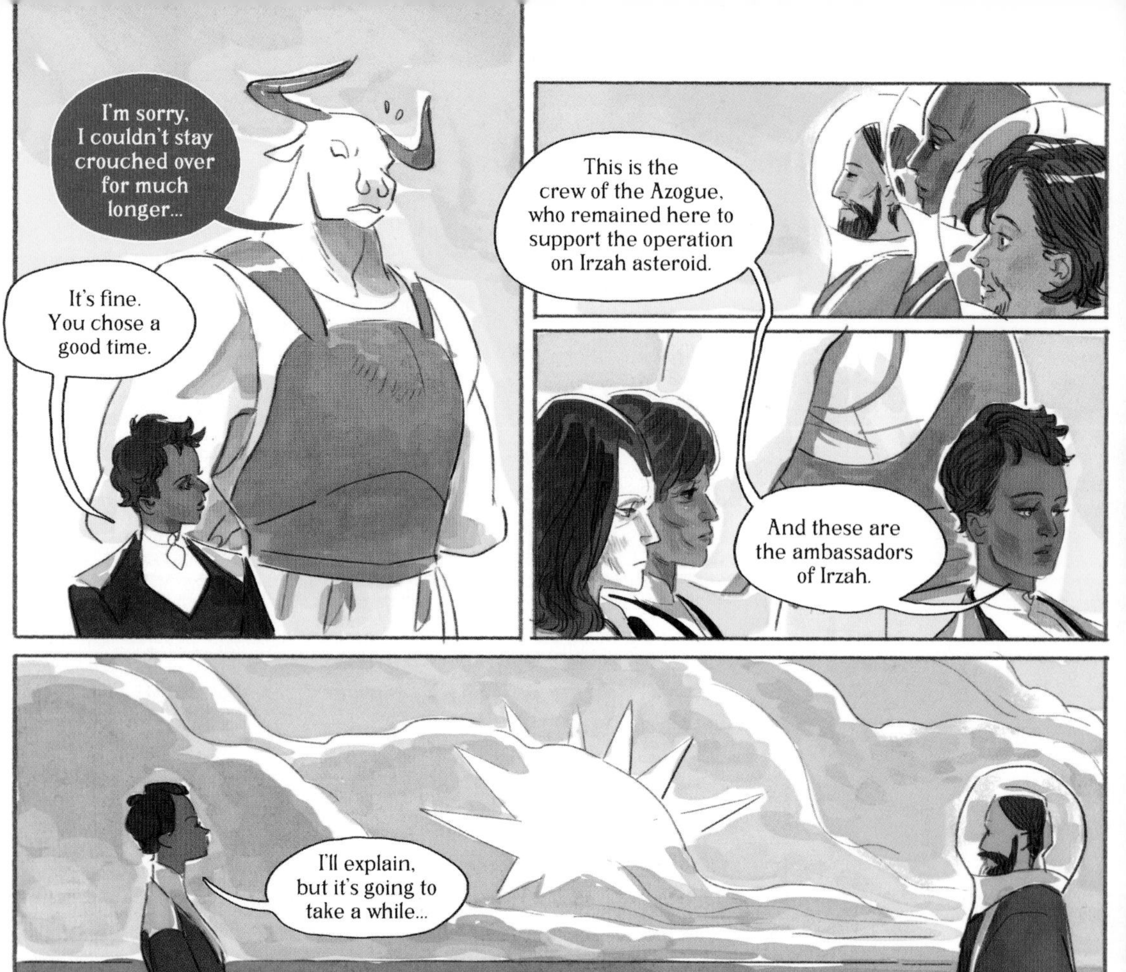
I'm sorry, I couldn't stay crouched over for much longer...
It's fine. You chose a good time.
This is the crew of the Azogue, who remained here to support the operation on Irzah asteroid.
And these are the ambassadors of Irzah.
I'll explain, but it's going to take a while...

MIRROR : EXODUS

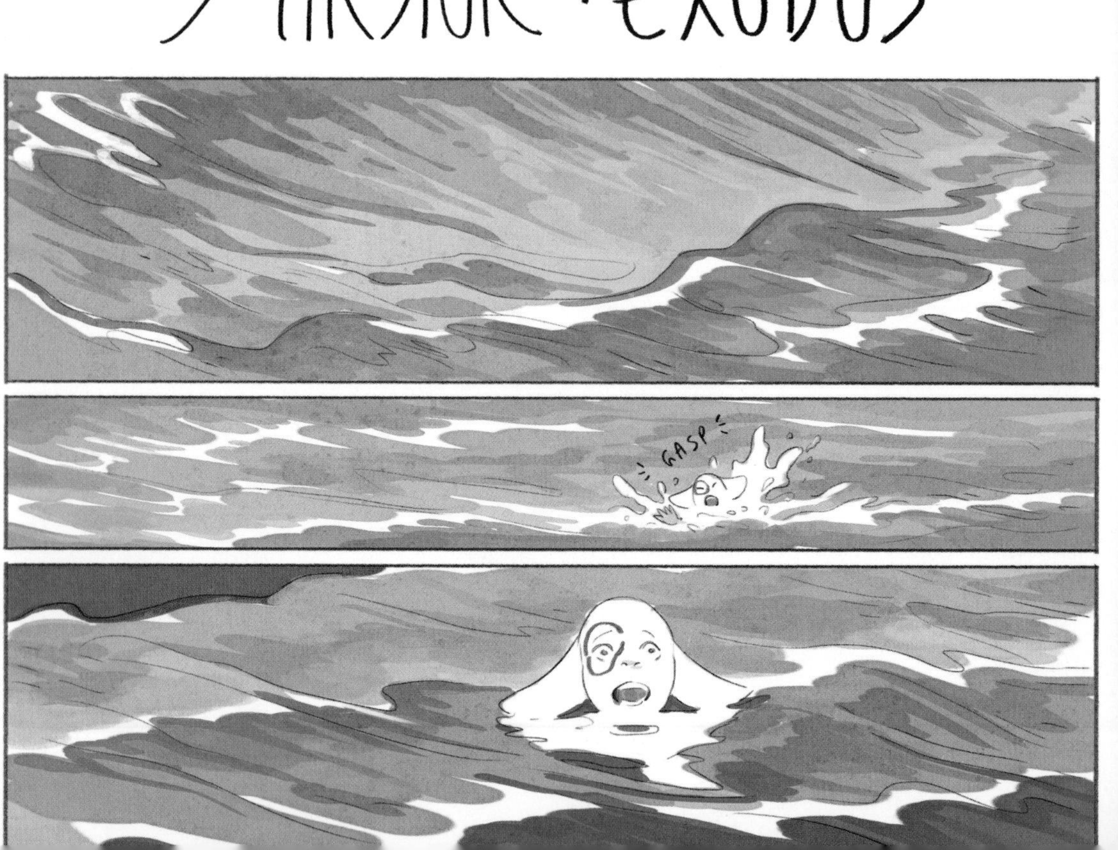
GASP

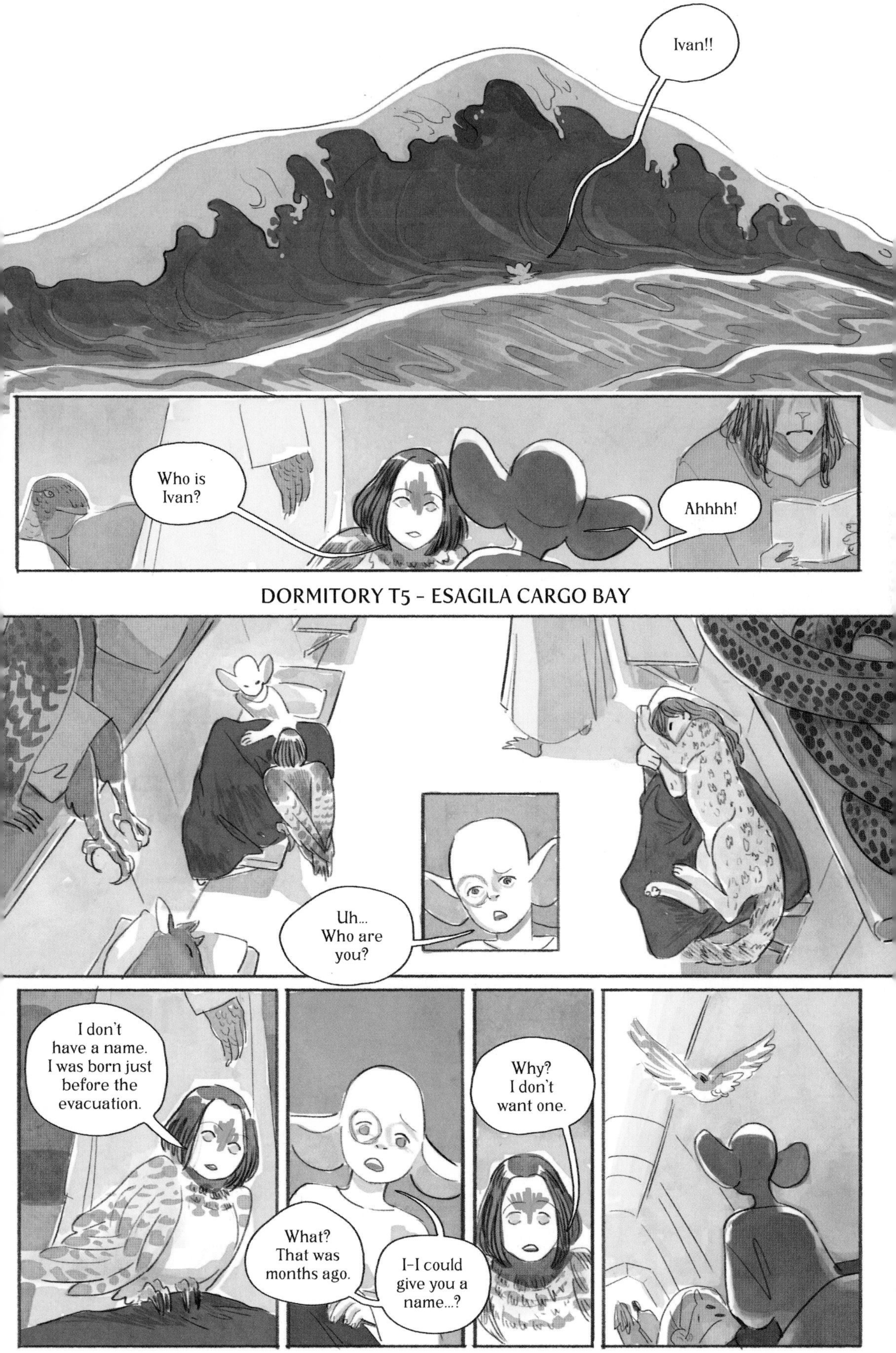
Ivan!!
Who is Ivan?
Ahhhh!
DORMITORY T5 – ESAGILA CARGO BAY
Uh... Who are you?
I don't have a name. I was born just before the evacuation.
What? That was months ago.
I-I could give you a name...?
Why? I don't want one.

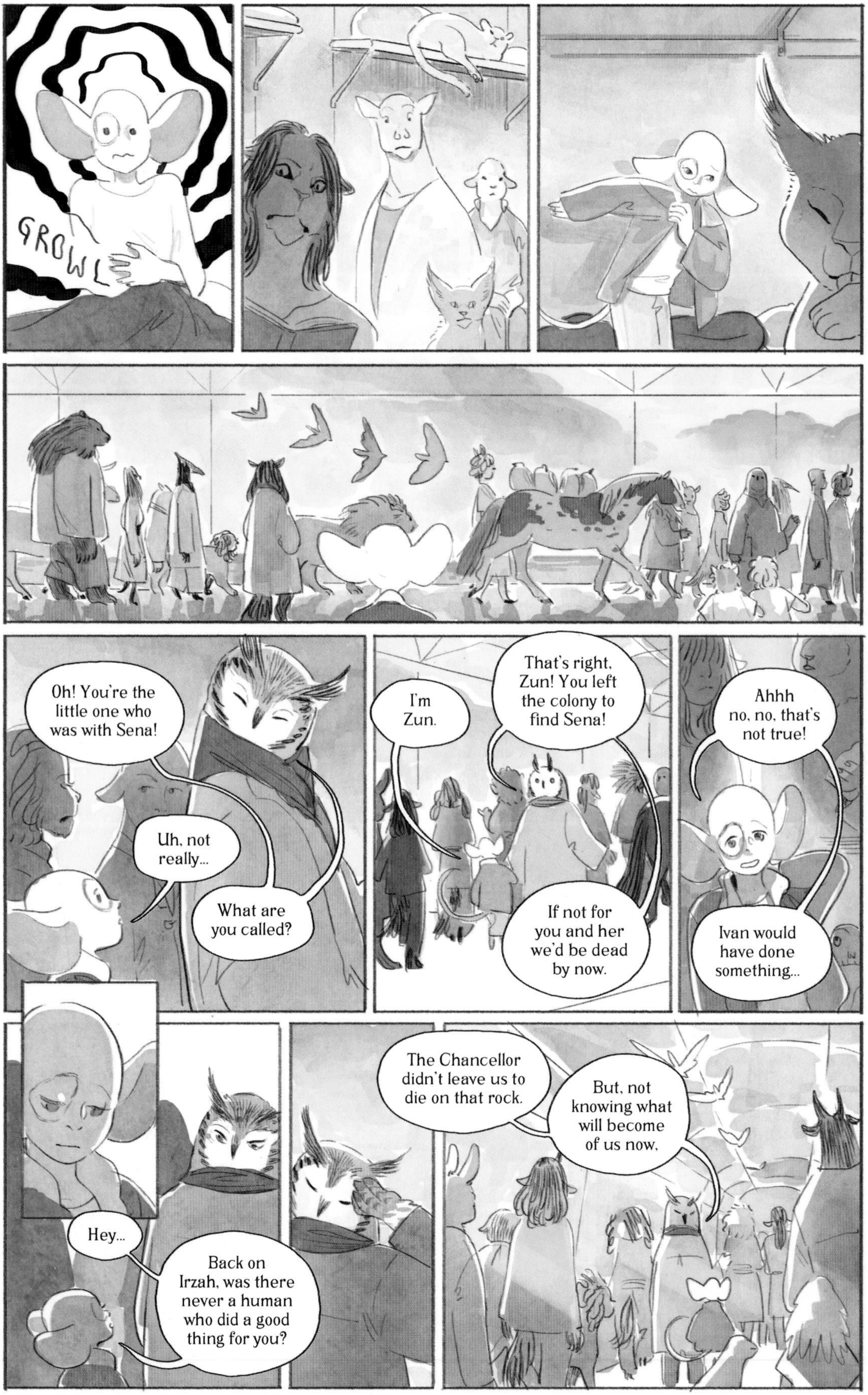
GROWL
Oh! You're the little one who was with Sena!
Uh, not really...
What are you called?
I'm Zun.
That's right, Zun! You left the colony to find Sena!
If not for you and her we'd be dead by now.
Ahhh no, no, that's not true!
Ivan would have done something...
Hey...
Back on Irzah, was there never a human who did a good thing for you?
The Chancellor didn't leave us to die on that rock.
But, not knowing what will become of us now,

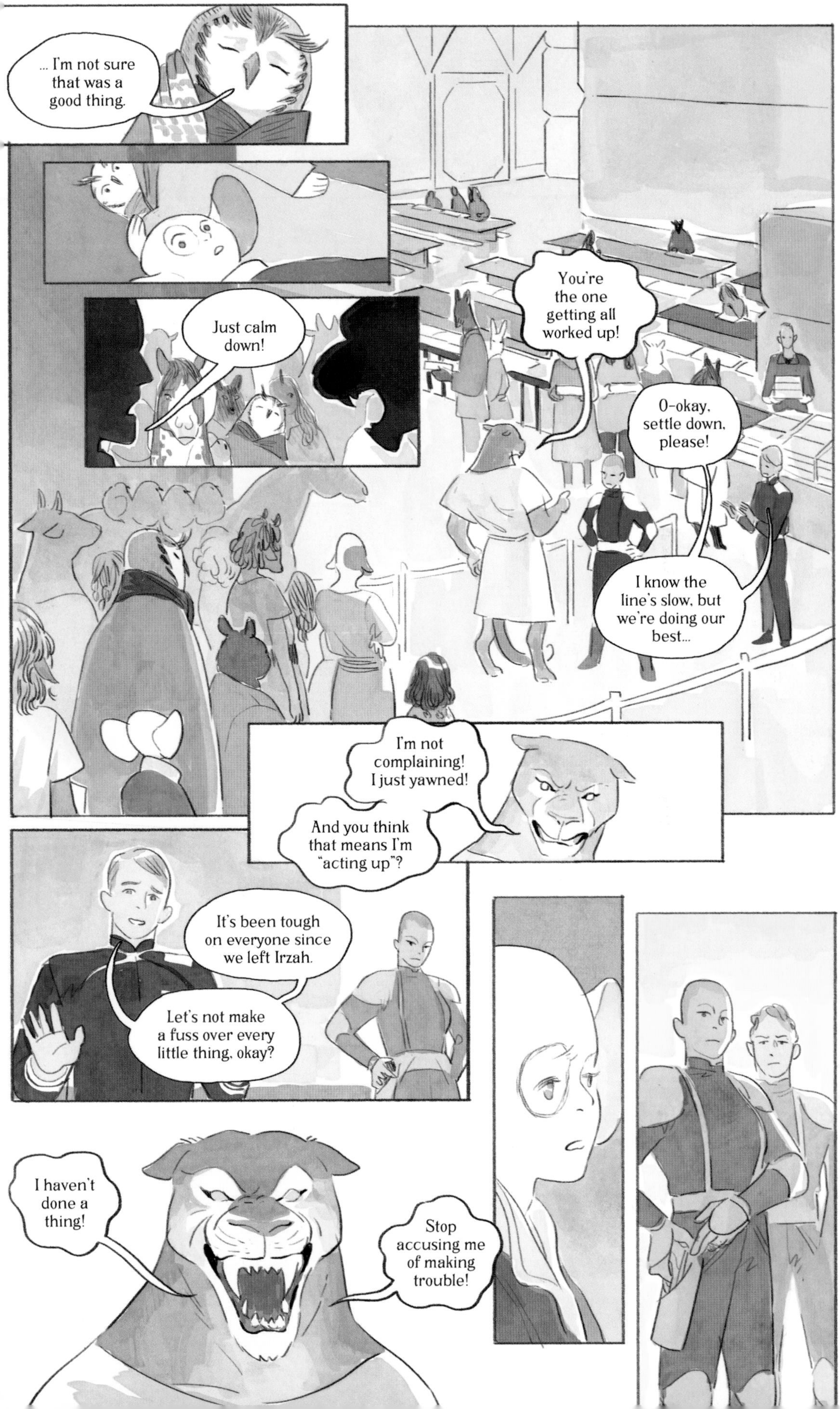
... I'm not sure that was a good thing.
Just calm down!
You're the one getting all worked up!
O-okay, settle down, please!
I know the line's slow, but we're doing our best...
I'm not complaining! I just yawned!
And you think that means I'm "acting up"?
It's been tough on everyone since we left Irzah.
Let's not make a fuss over every little thing, okay?
I haven't done a thing!
Stop accusing me of making trouble!

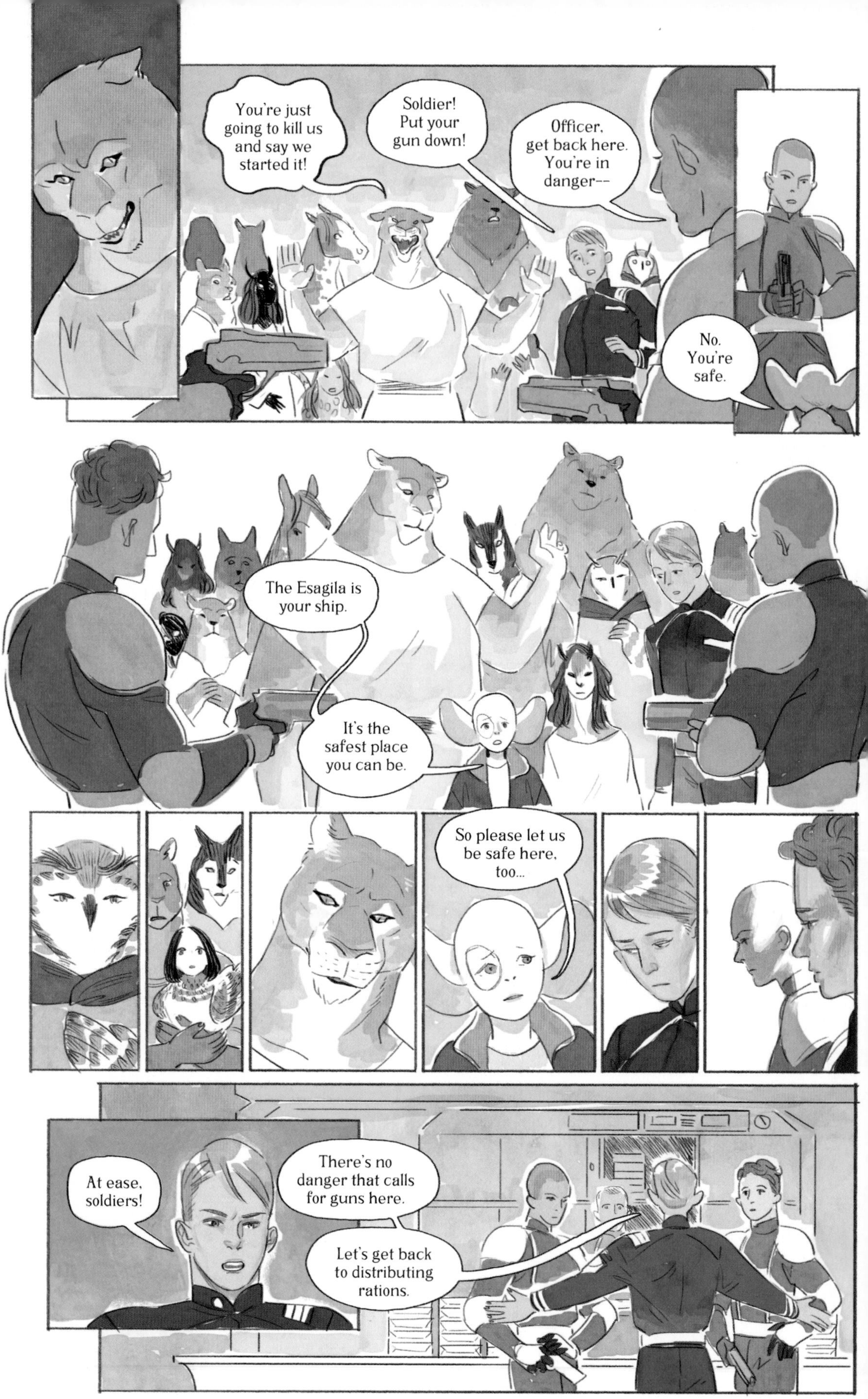
You're just going to kill us and say we started it!
Soldier! Put your gun down!
Officer, get back here. You're in danger--
No. You're safe.
The Esagila is your ship.
It's the safest place you can be.
So please let us be safe here, too...
At ease, soldiers!
There's no danger that calls for guns here.
Let's get back to distributing rations.

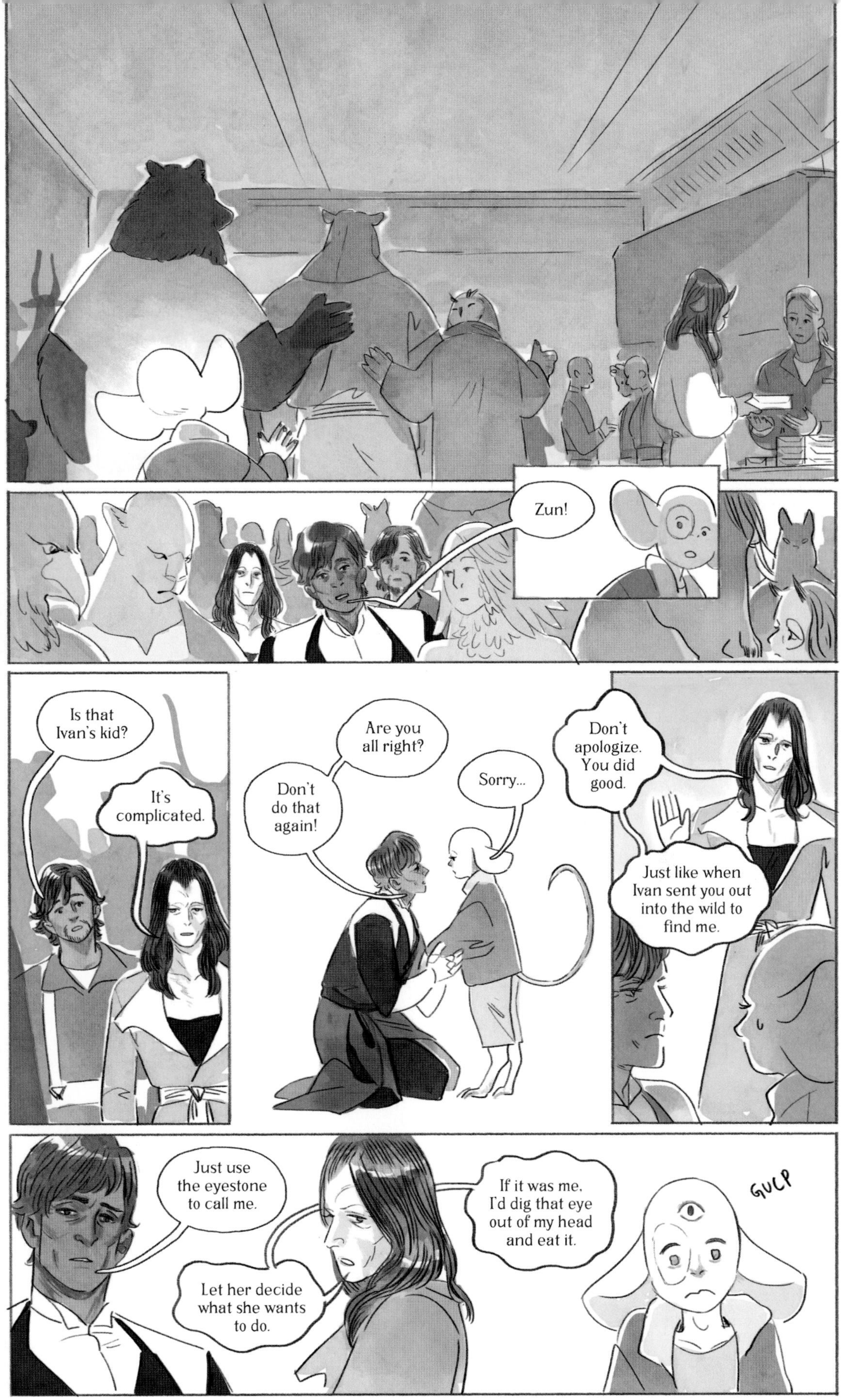
Zun!
Is that Ivan's kid?
It's complicated.
Don't do that again!
Are you all right?
Sorry...
Don't apologize. You did good.
Just like when Ivan sent you out into the wild to find me.
Just use the eyestone to call me.
Let her decide what she wants to do.
If it was me, I'd dig that eye out of my head and eat it.
GULP

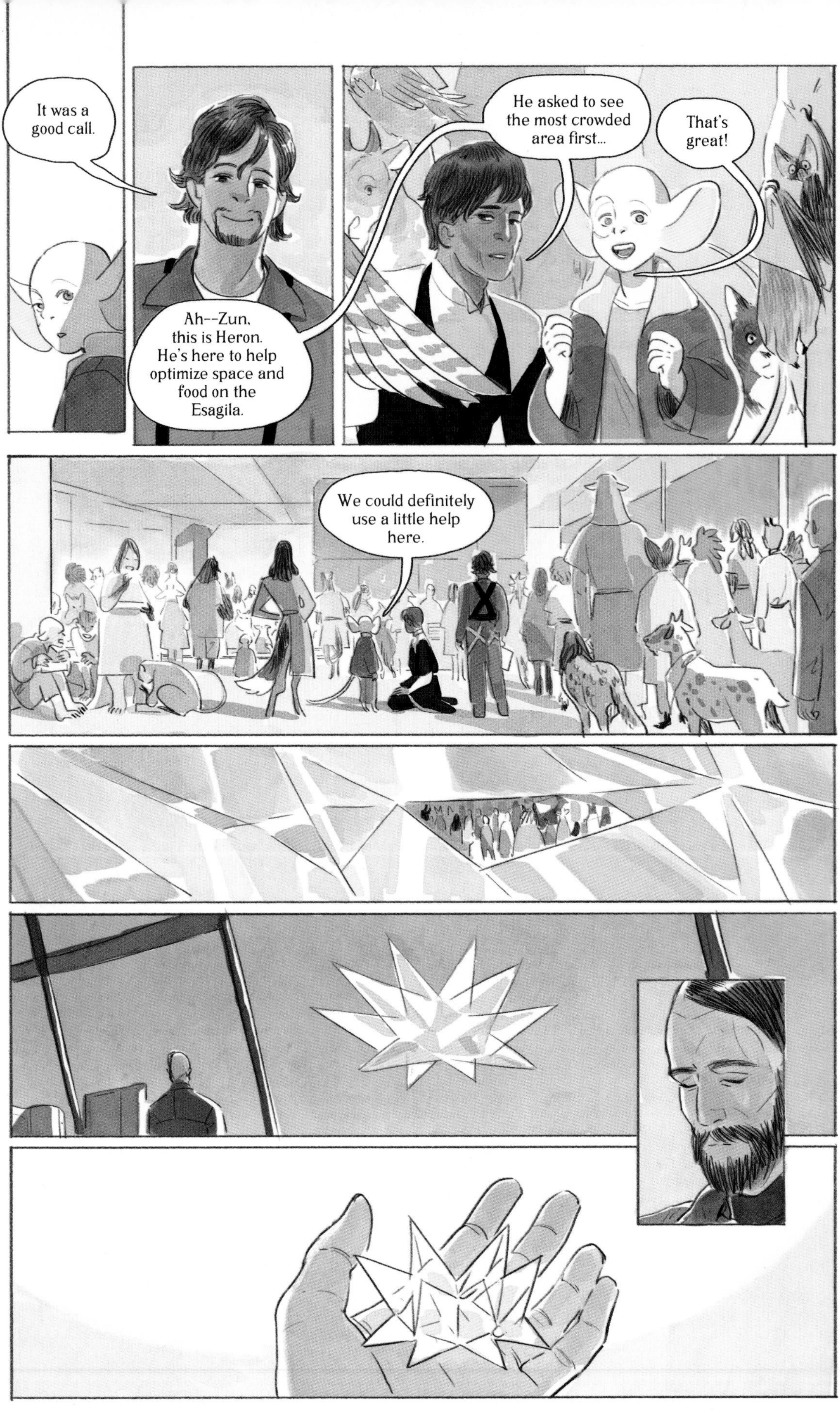
It was a good call.
Ah--Zun, this is Heron. He's here to help optimize space and food on the Esagila.
He asked to see the most crowded area first...
That's great!
We could definitely use a little help here.

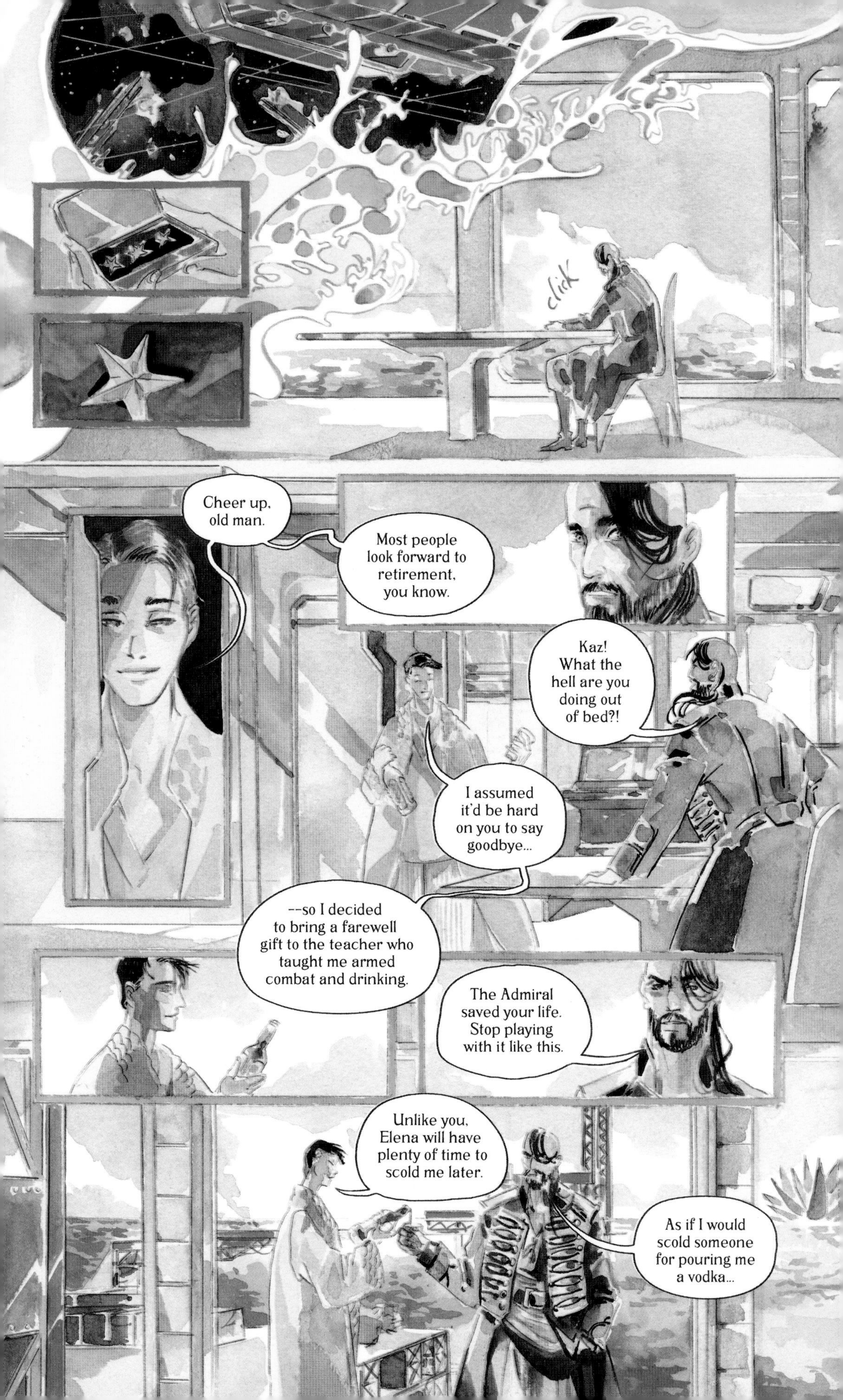
click
Cheer up, old man.
Most people look forward to retirement, you know.
Kaz! What the hell are you doing out of bed?!
I assumed it'd be hard on you to say goodbye...
--so I decided to bring a farewell gift to the teacher who taught me armed combat and drinking.
The Admiral saved your life. Stop playing with it like this.
Unlike you, Elena will have plenty of time to scold me later.
As if I would scold someone for pouring me a vodka...

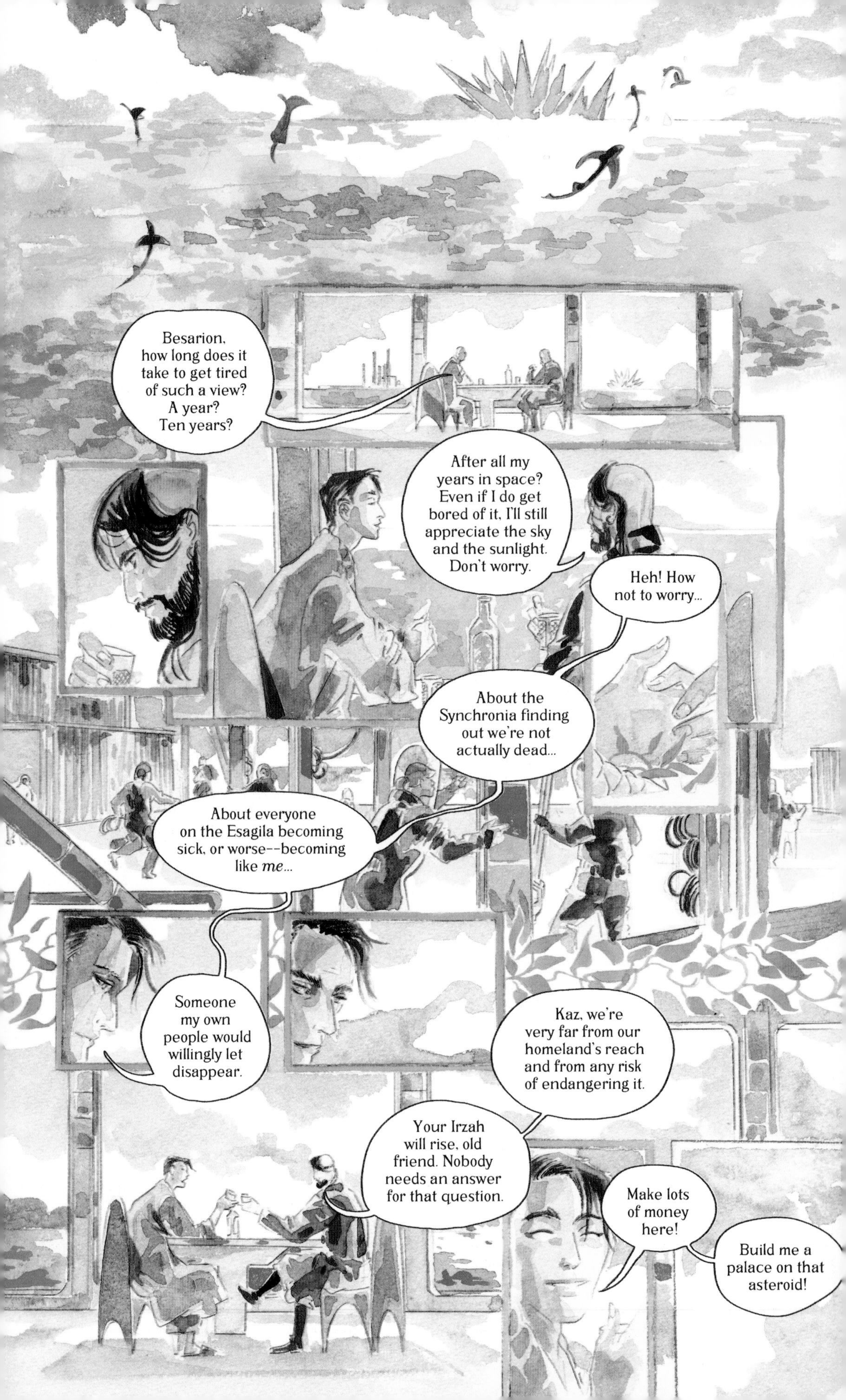

Besarion, how long does it take to get tired of such a view? A year? Ten years?
After all my years in space? Even if I do get bored of it, I'll still appreciate the sky and the sunlight. Don't worry.
Heh! How not to worry...
About the Synchronia finding out we're not actually dead...
About everyone on the Esagila becoming sick, or worse--becoming like *me*...
Someone my own people would willingly let disappear.
Kaz, we're very far from our homeland's reach and from any risk of endangering it.
Your Irzah will rise, old friend. Nobody needs an answer for that question.
Make lots of money here!
Build me a palace on that asteroid!

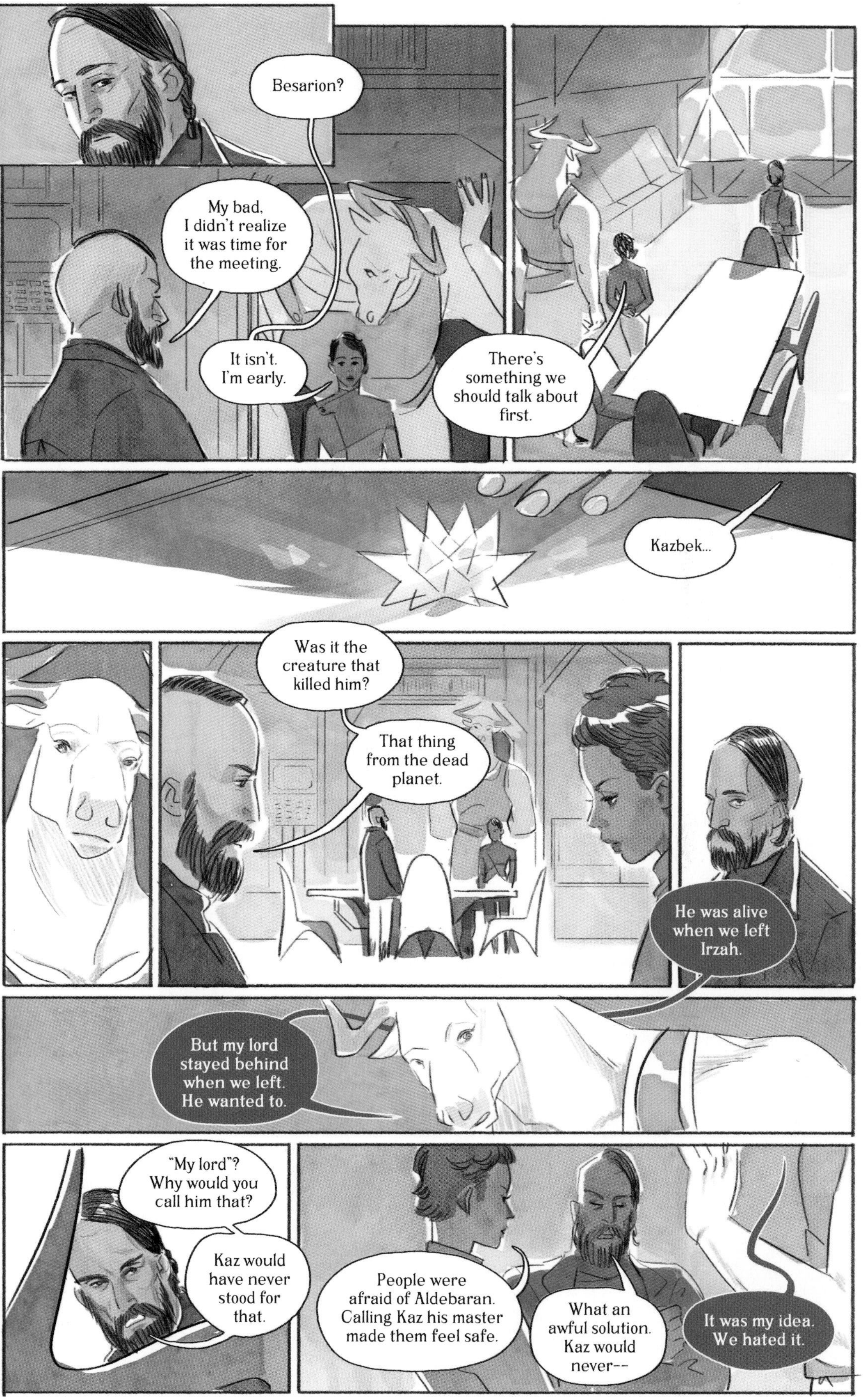
Besarion?
My bad, I didn't realize it was time for the meeting.
It isn't. I'm early.
There's something we should talk about first.
Kazbek...
Was it the creature that killed him?
That thing from the dead planet.
He was alive when we left Irzah.
But my lord stayed behind when we left. He wanted to.
"My lord"? Why would you call him that?
Kaz would have never stood for that.
People were afraid of Aldebaran. Calling Kaz his master made them feel safe.
What an awful solution. Kaz would never--
It was my idea. We hated it.

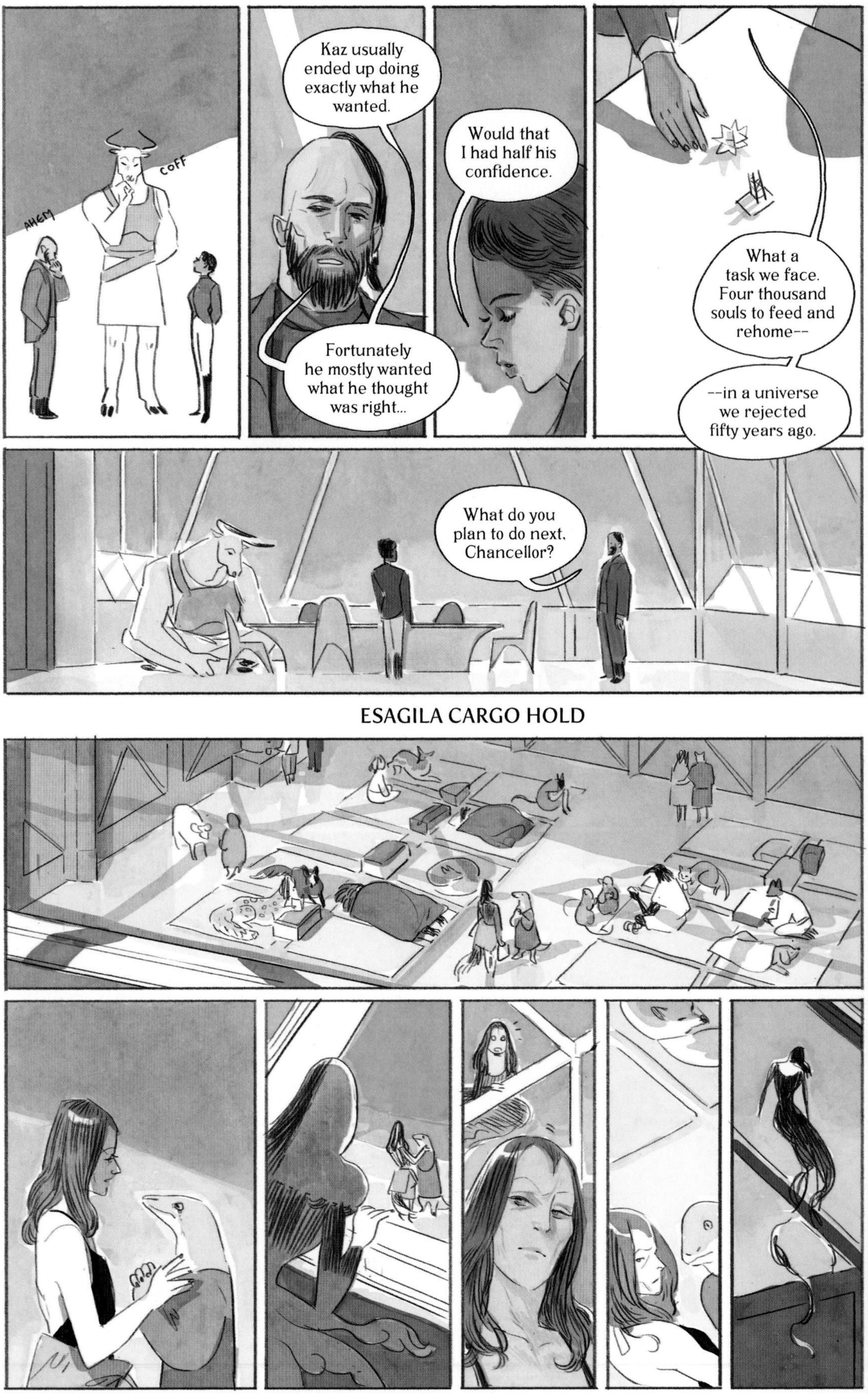
AHEM
COFF
Kaz usually ended up doing exactly what he wanted.
Fortunately he mostly wanted what he thought was right...
Would that I had half his confidence.
What a task we face. Four thousand souls to feed and rehome--
--in a universe we rejected fifty years ago.
What do you plan to do next, Chancellor?
ESAGILA CARGO HOLD

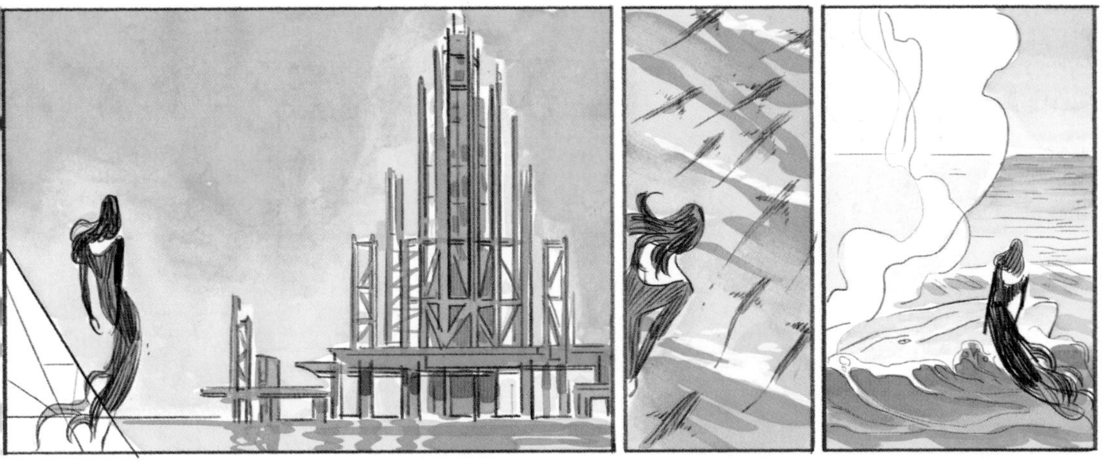

AZOGUE BASE – MAIN TOWER

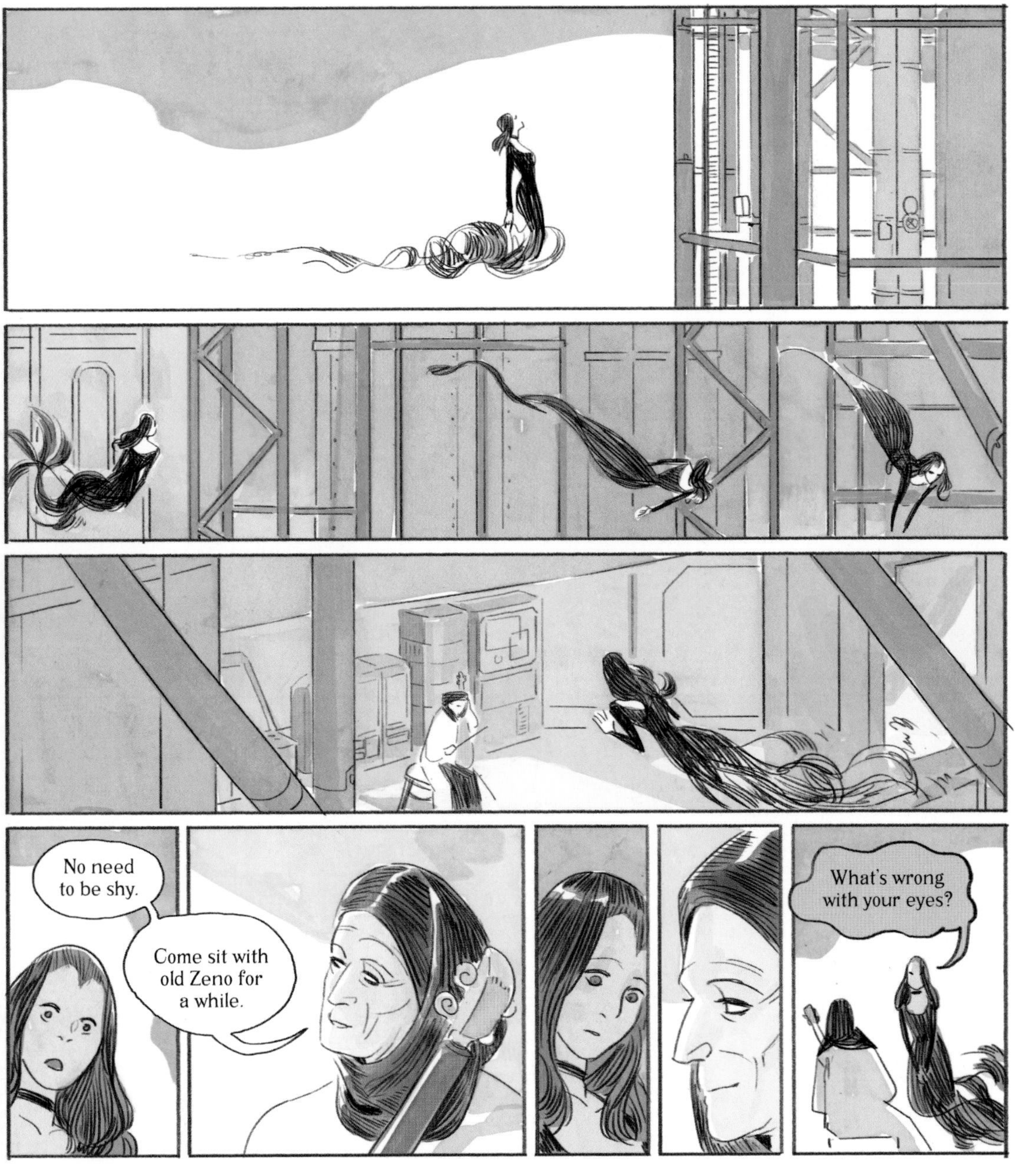
No need to be shy.
Come sit with old Zeno for a while.
What's wrong with your eyes?

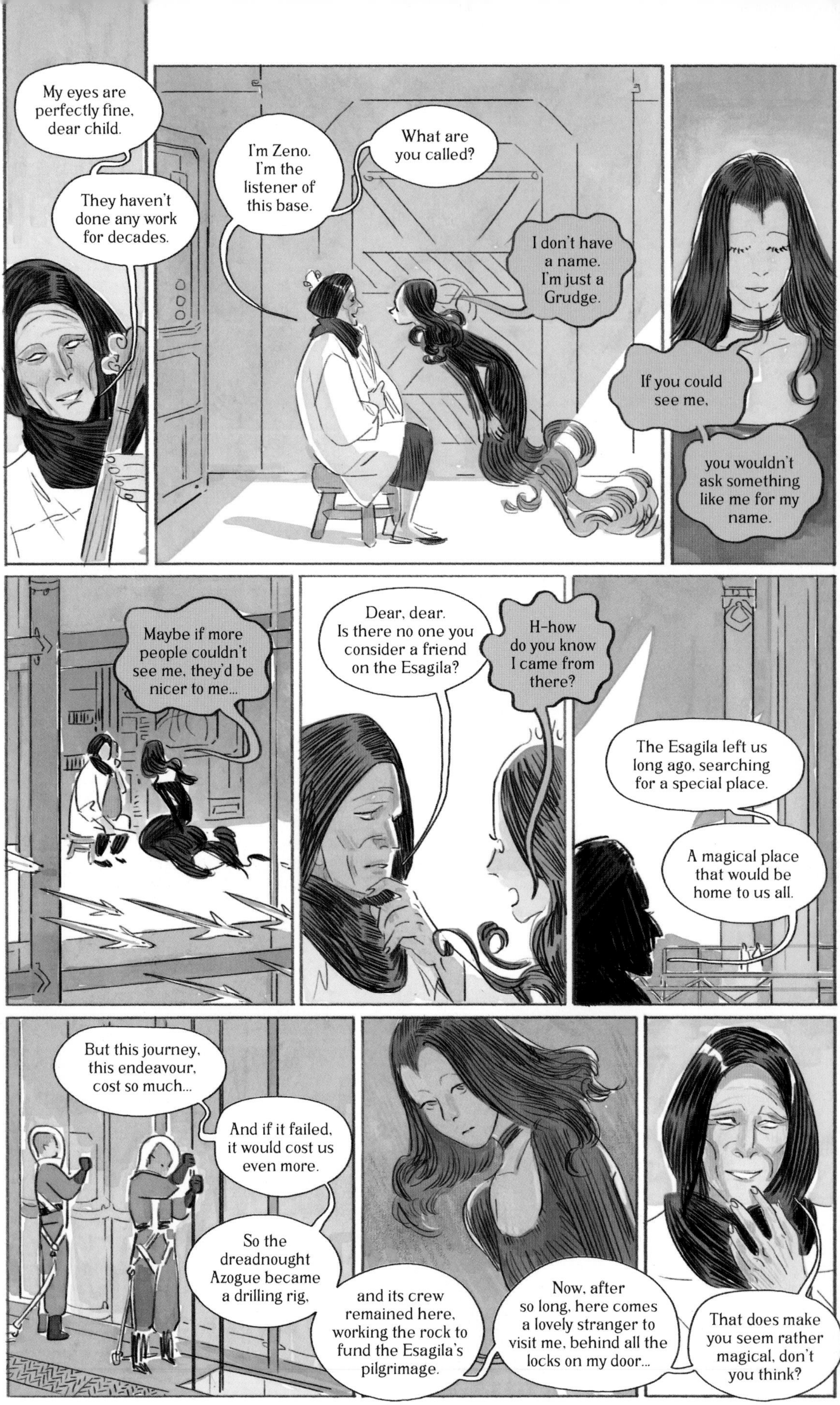
My eyes are perfectly fine, dear child.
They haven't done any work for decades.
I'm Zeno. I'm the listener of this base.
What are you called?
I don't have a name. I'm just a Grudge.
If you could see me,
you wouldn't ask something like me for my name.
Maybe if more people couldn't see me, they'd be nicer to me...
Dear, dear. Is there no one you consider a friend on the Esagila?
H-how do you know I came from there?
The Esagila left us long ago, searching for a special place.
A magical place that would be home to us all.
But this journey, this endeavour, cost so much...
And if it failed, it would cost us even more.
So the dreadnought Azogue became a drilling rig,
and its crew remained here, working the rock to fund the Esagila's pilgrimage.
Now, after so long, here comes a lovely stranger to visit me, behind all the locks on my door...
That does make you seem rather magical, don't you think?

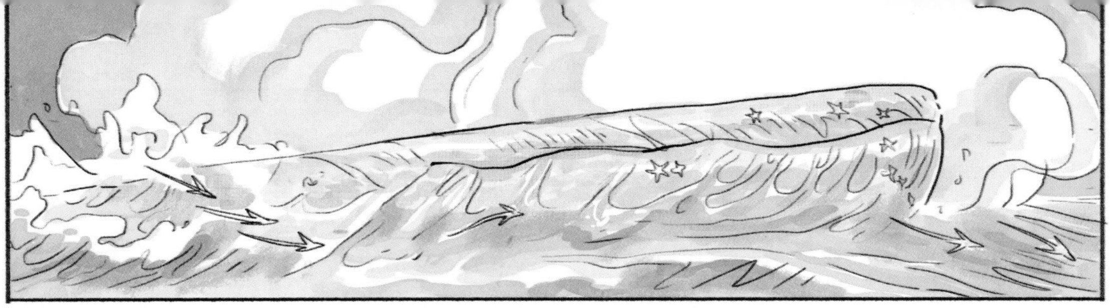

INFIRMARY 2 – ESAGILA WING 8

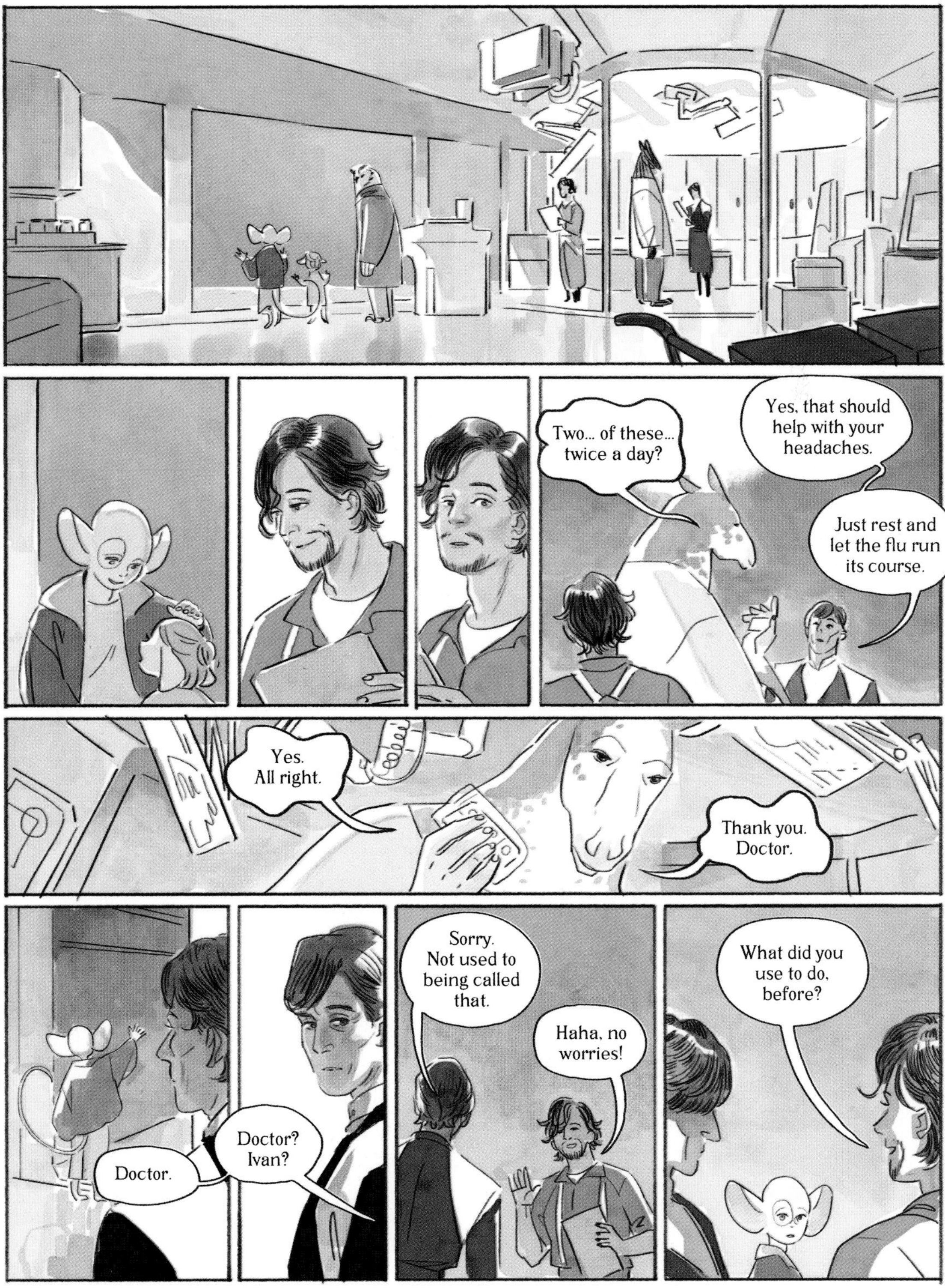

Two... of these... twice a day?
Yes, that should help with your headaches.
Just rest and let the flu run its course.
Yes. All right.
Thank you. Doctor.
Doctor.
Doctor? Ivan?
Sorry. Not used to being called that.
Haha, no worries!
What did you use to do, before?

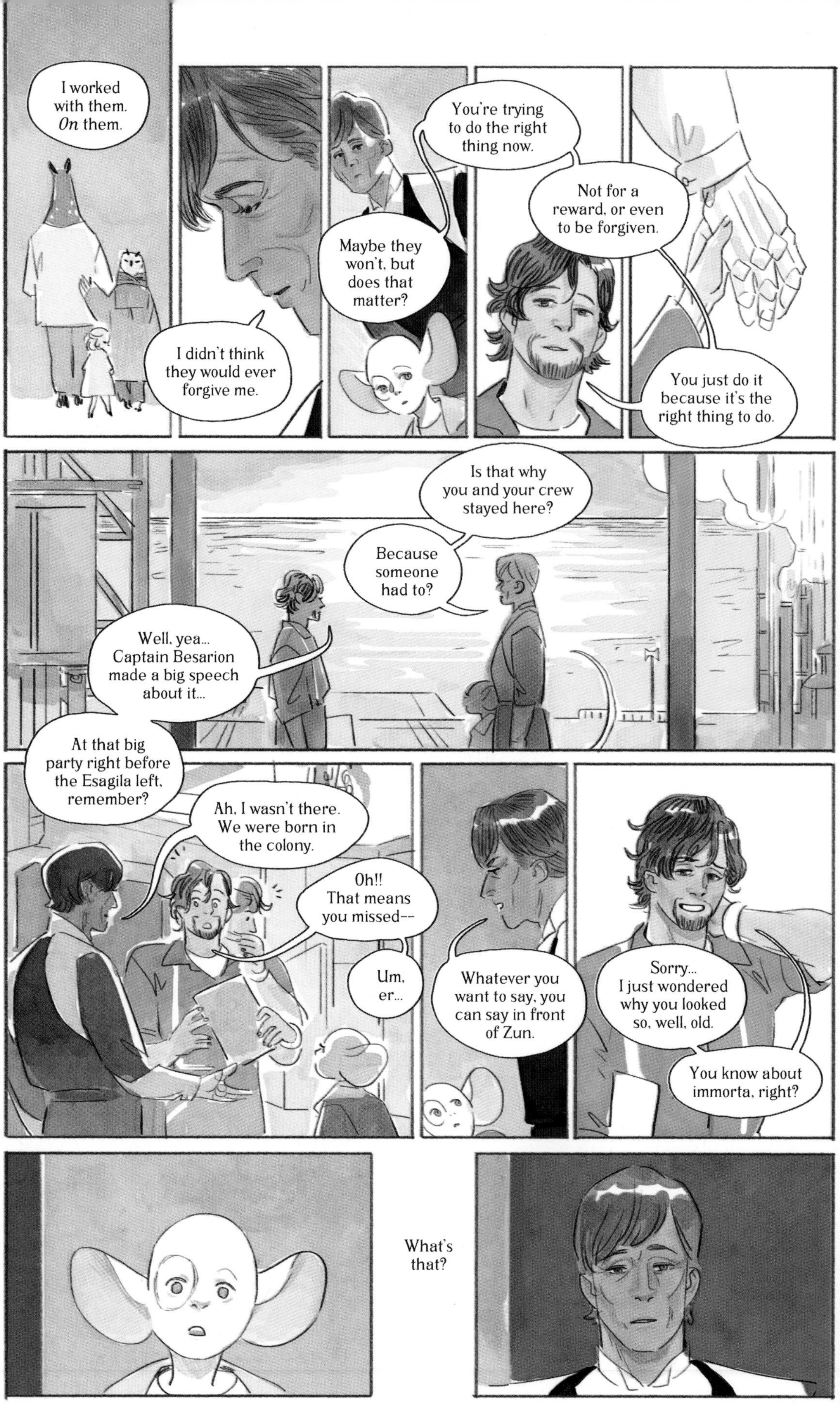

I worked with them. *On* them.
I didn't think they would ever forgive me.
You're trying to do the right thing now.
Maybe they won't, but does that matter?
Not for a reward, or even to be forgiven.
You just do it because it's the right thing to do.
Is that why you and your crew stayed here?
Because someone had to?
Well, yea... Captain Besarion made a big speech about it...
At that big party right before the Esagila left, remember?
Ah, I wasn't there. We were born in the colony.
Oh!! That means you missed--
Um, er...
Whatever you want to say, you can say in front of Zun.
Sorry... I just wondered why you looked so, well, old.
You know about immorta, right?
What's that?

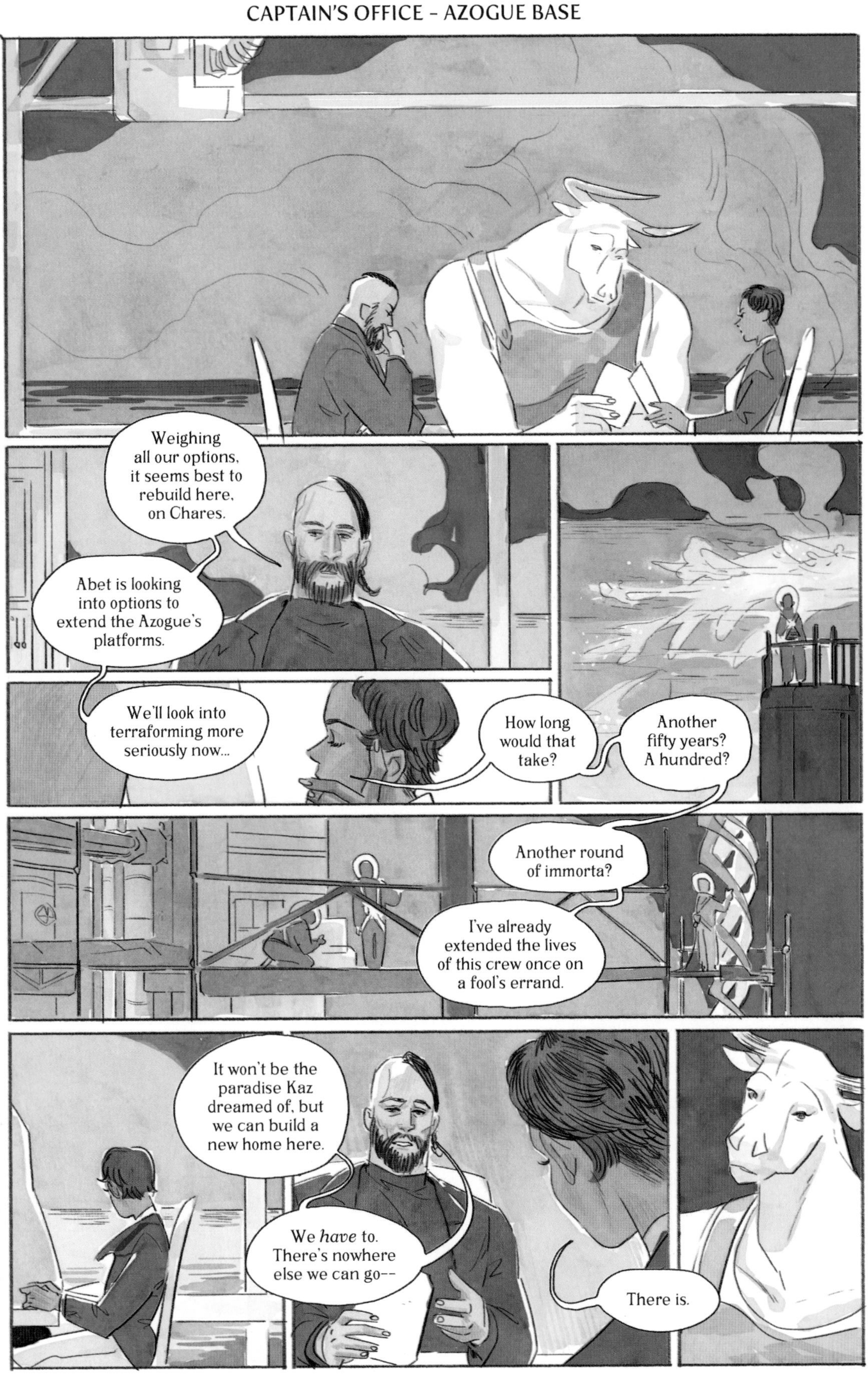
CAPTAIN'S OFFICE - AZOGUE BASE
Weighing all our options, it seems best to rebuild here, on Chares.
Abet is looking into options to extend the Azogue's platforms.
We'll look into terraforming more seriously now...
How long would that take?
Another fifty years? A hundred?
Another round of immorta?
I've already extended the lives of this crew once on a fool's errand.
It won't be the paradise Kaz dreamed of, but we can build a new home here.
We *have* to. There's nowhere else we can go--
There is.

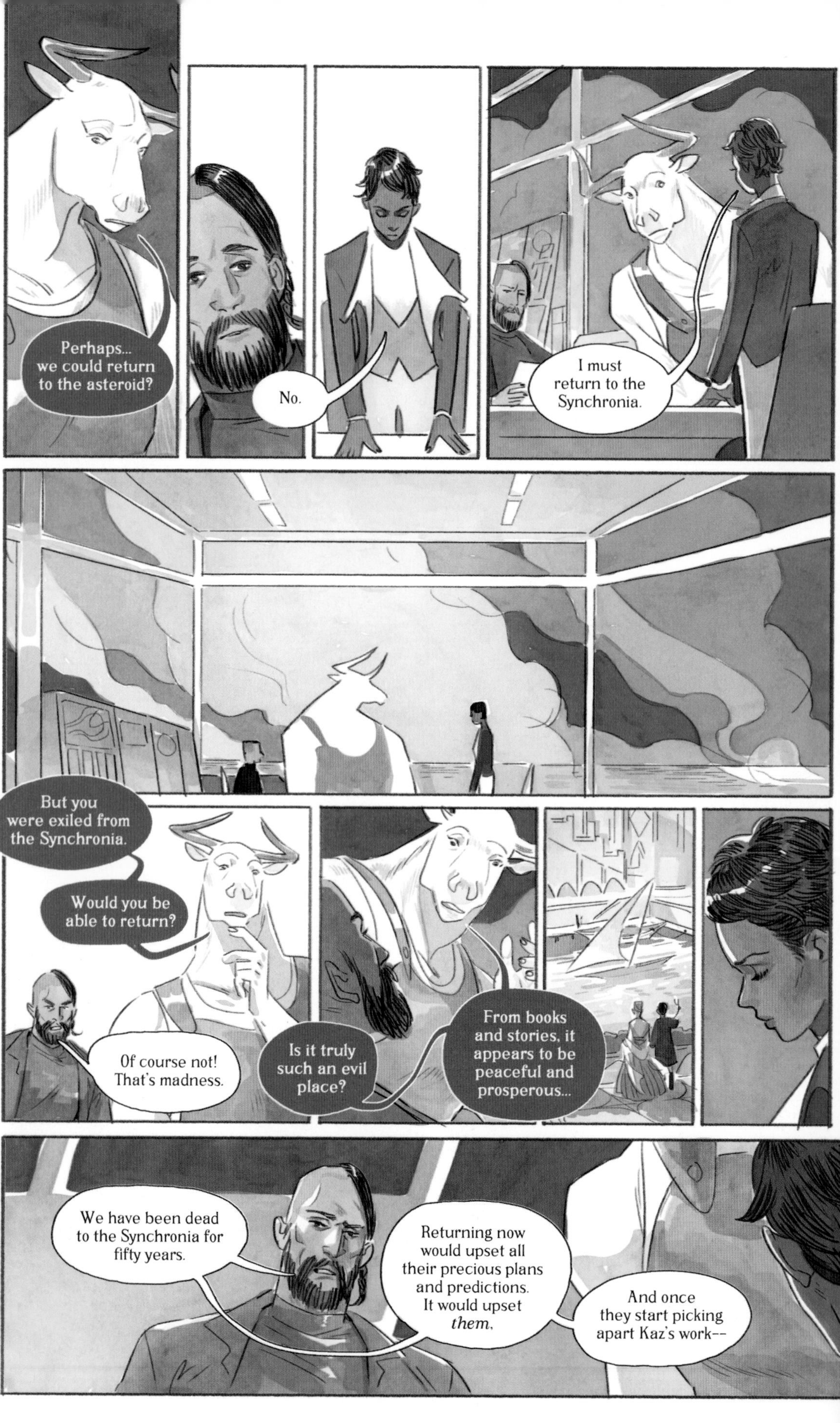
Perhaps...
we could return
to the asteroid?
No.
I must
return to the
Synchronia.
But you
were exiled from
the Synchronia.
Would you be
able to return?
Of course not!
That's madness.
Is it truly
such an evil
place?
From books
and stories, it
appears to be
peaceful and
prosperous...
We have been dead
to the Synchronia for
fifty years.
Returning now
would upset all
their precious plans
and predictions.
It would upset
them.
And once
they start picking
apart Kaz's work--

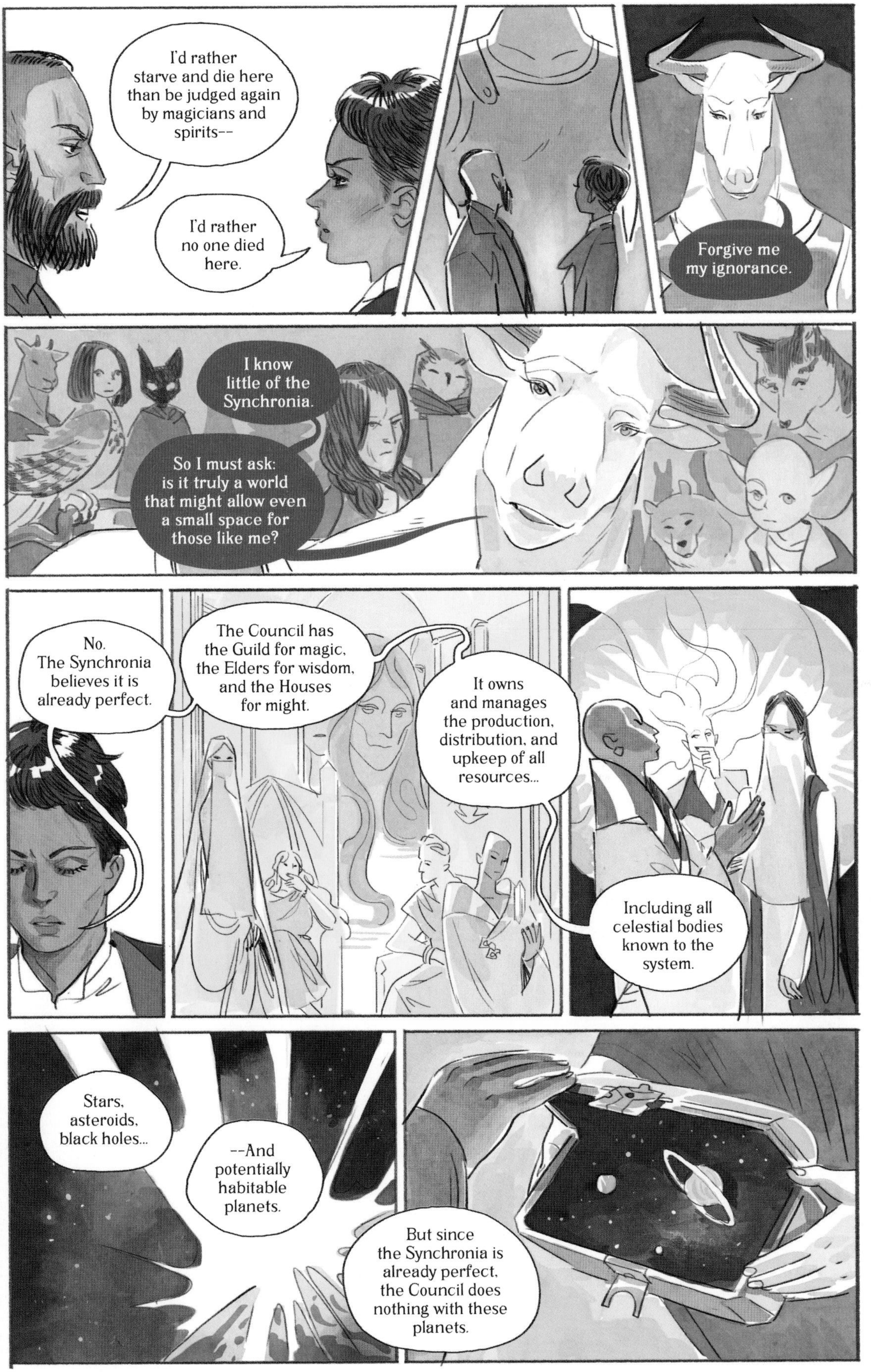
I'd rather starve and die here than be judged again by magicians and spirits--
I'd rather no one died here.
Forgive me my ignorance.
I know little of the Synchronia.
So I must ask: is it truly a world that might allow even a small space for those like me?
No. The Synchronia believes it is already perfect.
The Council has the Guild for magic, the Elders for wisdom, and the Houses for might.
It owns and manages the production, distribution, and upkeep of all resources...
Including all celestial bodies known to the system.
Stars, asteroids, black holes...
--And potentially habitable planets.
But since the Synchronia is already perfect, the Council does nothing with these planets.

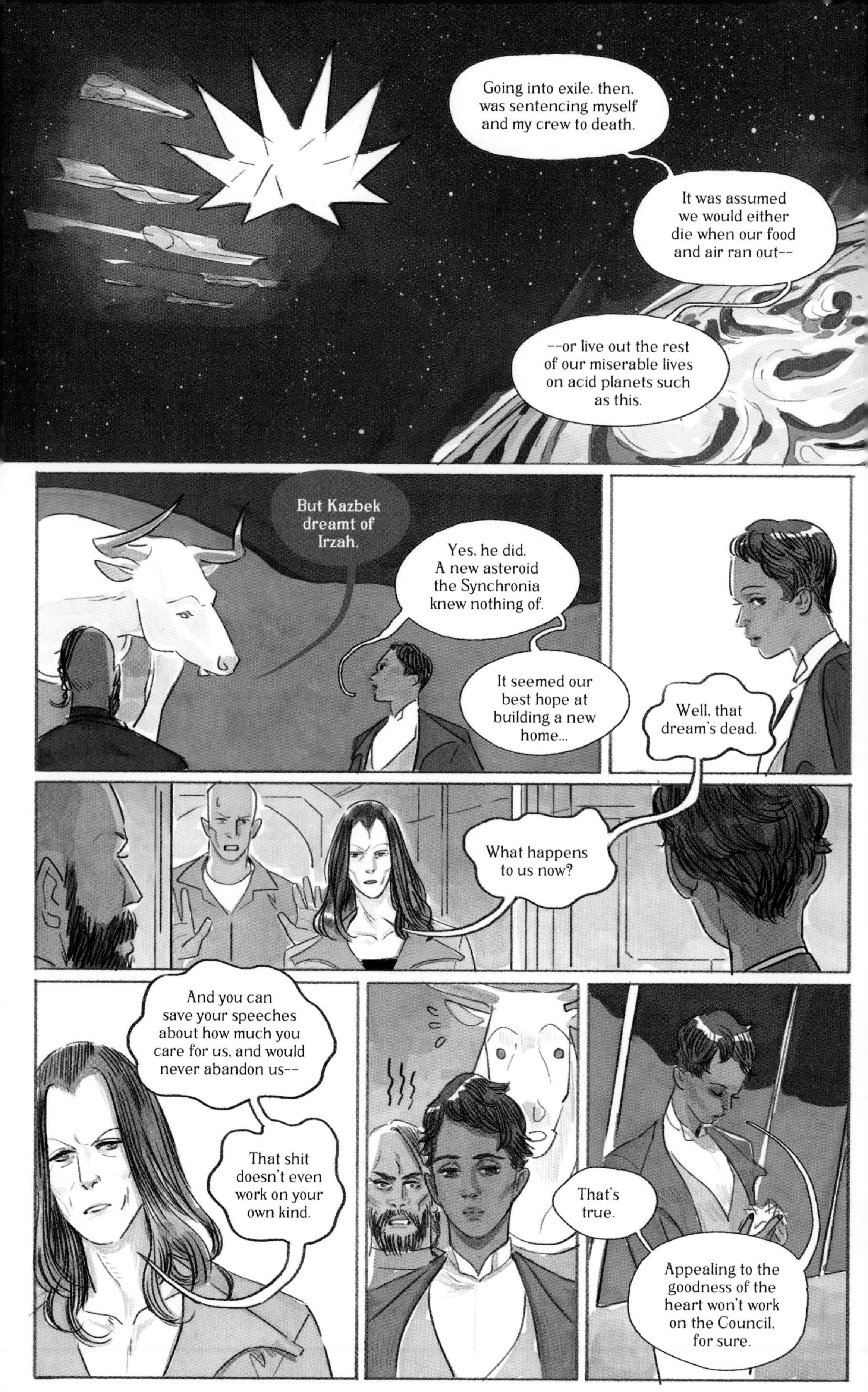
Going into exile. then, was sentencing myself and my crew to death.
It was assumed we would either die when our food and air ran out--
--or live out the rest of our miserable lives on acid planets such as this.
But Kazbek dreamt of Irzah.
Yes, he did. A new asteroid the Synchronia knew nothing of.
It seemed our best hope at building a new home...
Well, that dream's dead.
What happens to us now?
And you can save your speeches about how much you care for us, and would never abandon us--
That shit doesn't even work on your own kind.
That's true.
Appealing to the goodness of the heart won't work on the Council, for sure.

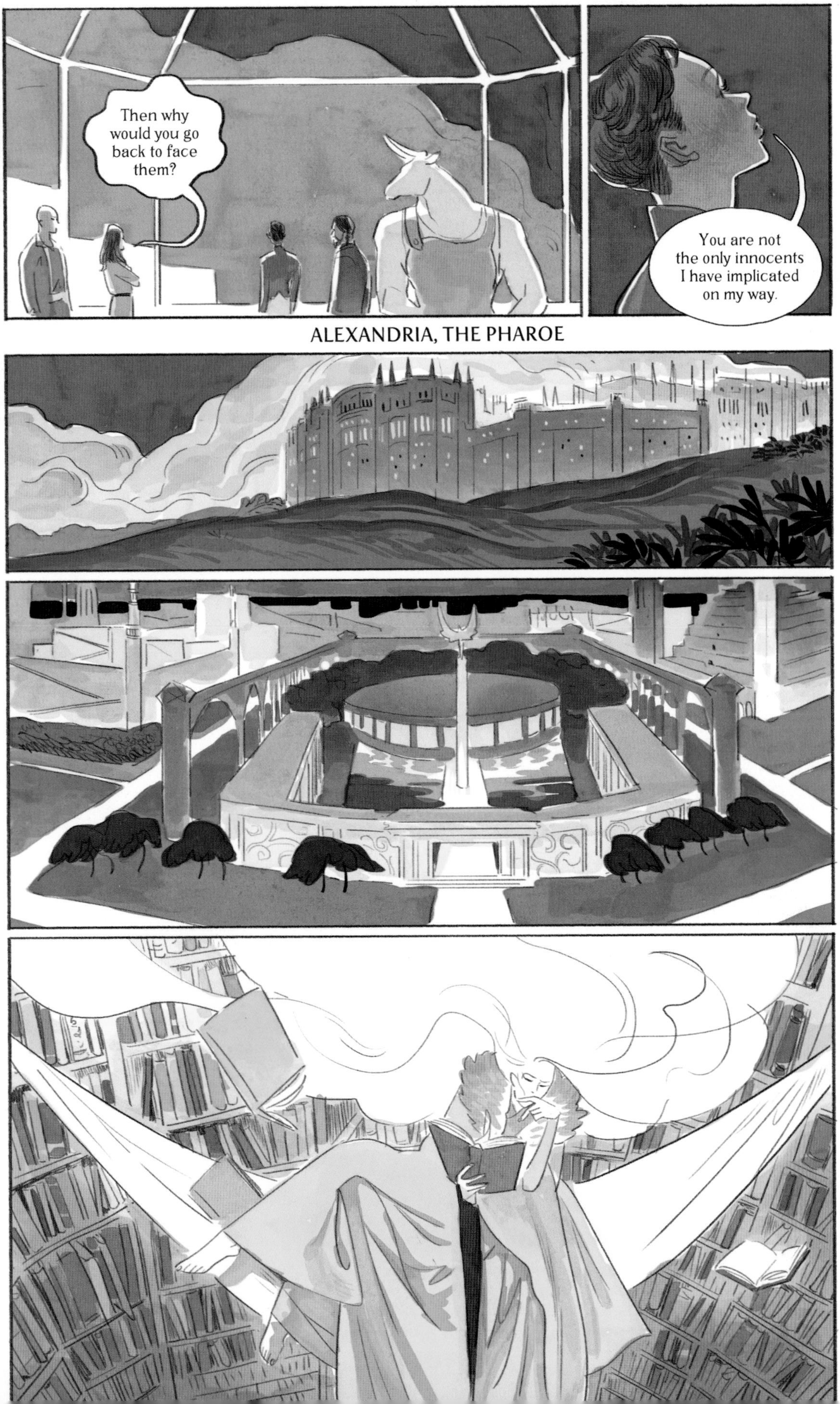
Then why would you go back to face them?
You are not the only innocents I have implicated on my way.
ALEXANDRIA, THE PHAROE

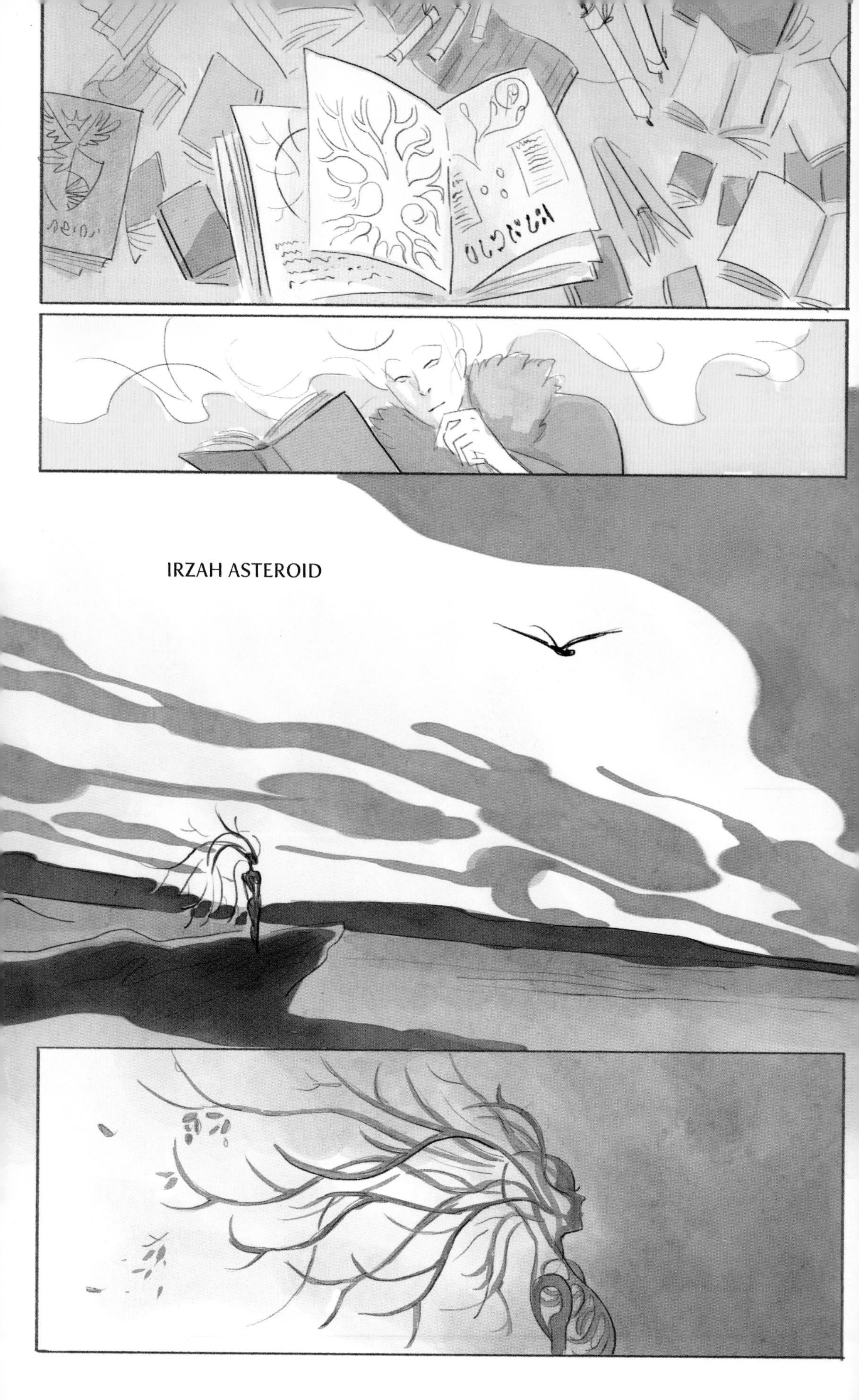
IRZAH ASTEROID

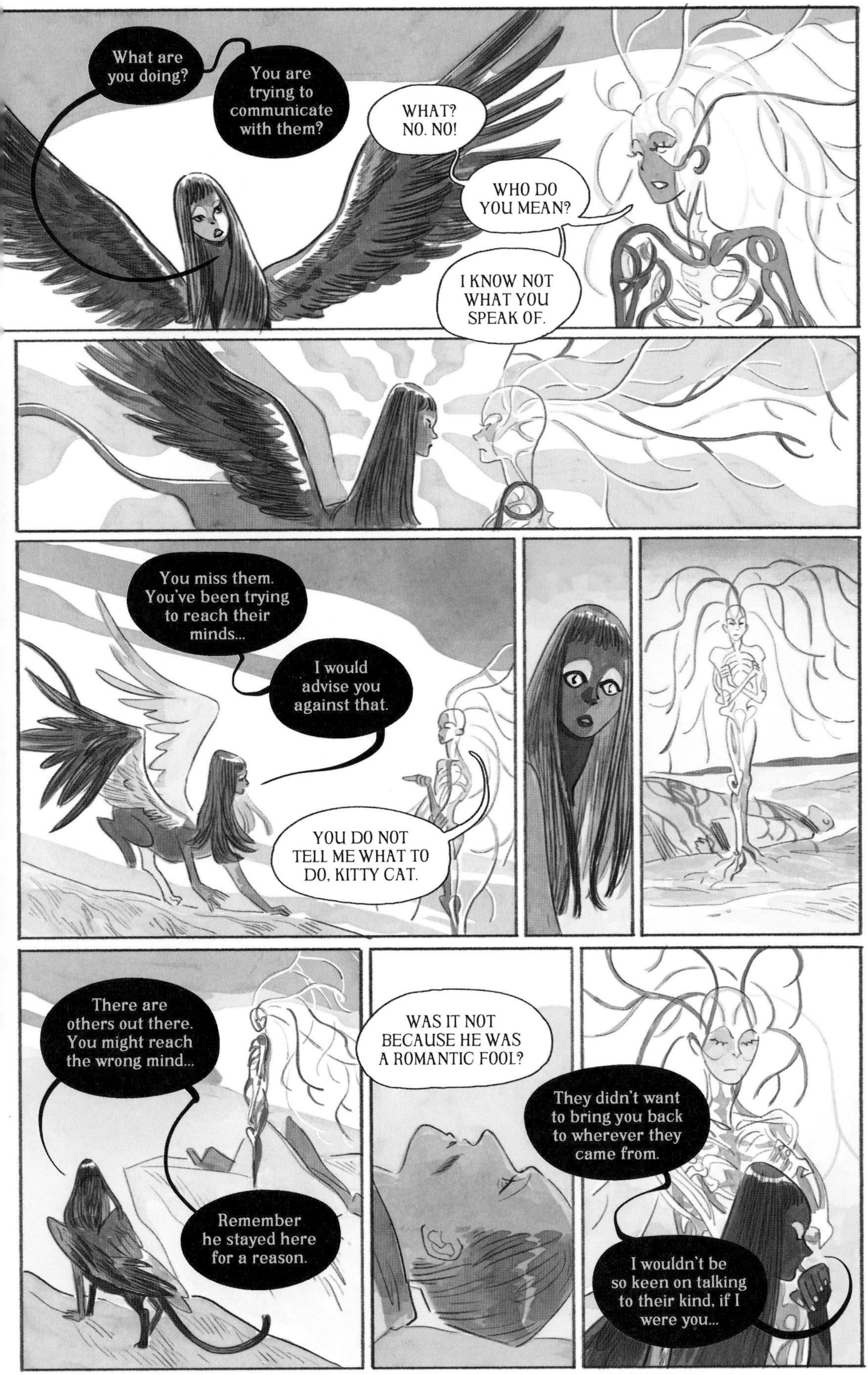
What are you doing?
You are trying to communicate with them?
WHAT? NO. NO!
WHO DO YOU MEAN?
I KNOW NOT WHAT YOU SPEAK OF.
You miss them. You've been trying to reach their minds...
I would advise you against that.
YOU DO NOT TELL ME WHAT TO DO, KITTY CAT.
There are others out there. You might reach the wrong mind...
Remember he stayed here for a reason.
WAS IT NOT BECAUSE HE WAS A ROMANTIC FOOL?
They didn't want to bring you back to wherever they came from.
I wouldn't be so keen on talking to their kind, if I were you...

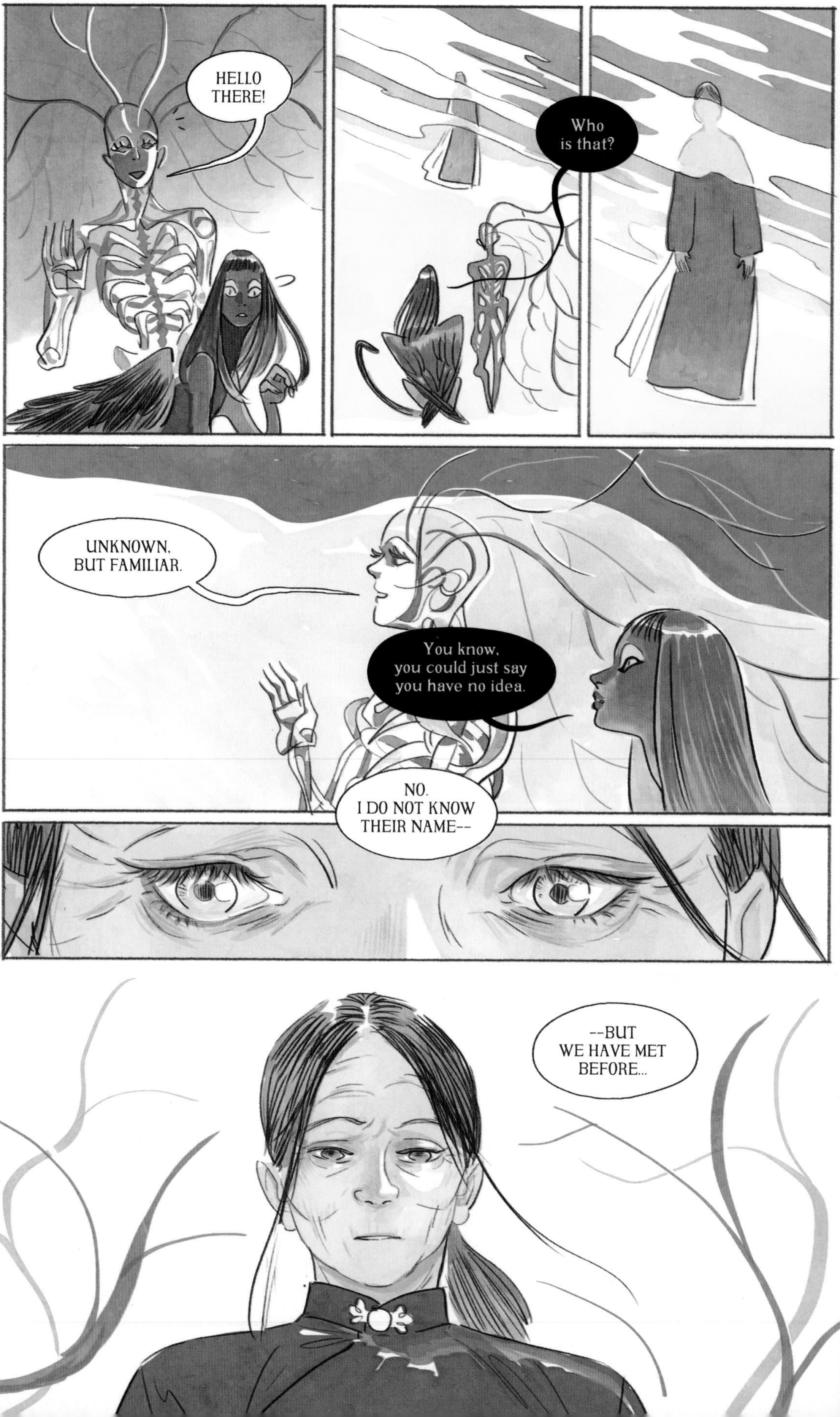
HELLO THERE!
Who is that?
UNKNOWN, BUT FAMILIAR.
You know, you could just say you have no idea.
NO. I DO NOT KNOW THEIR NAME--
--BUT WE HAVE MET BEFORE...

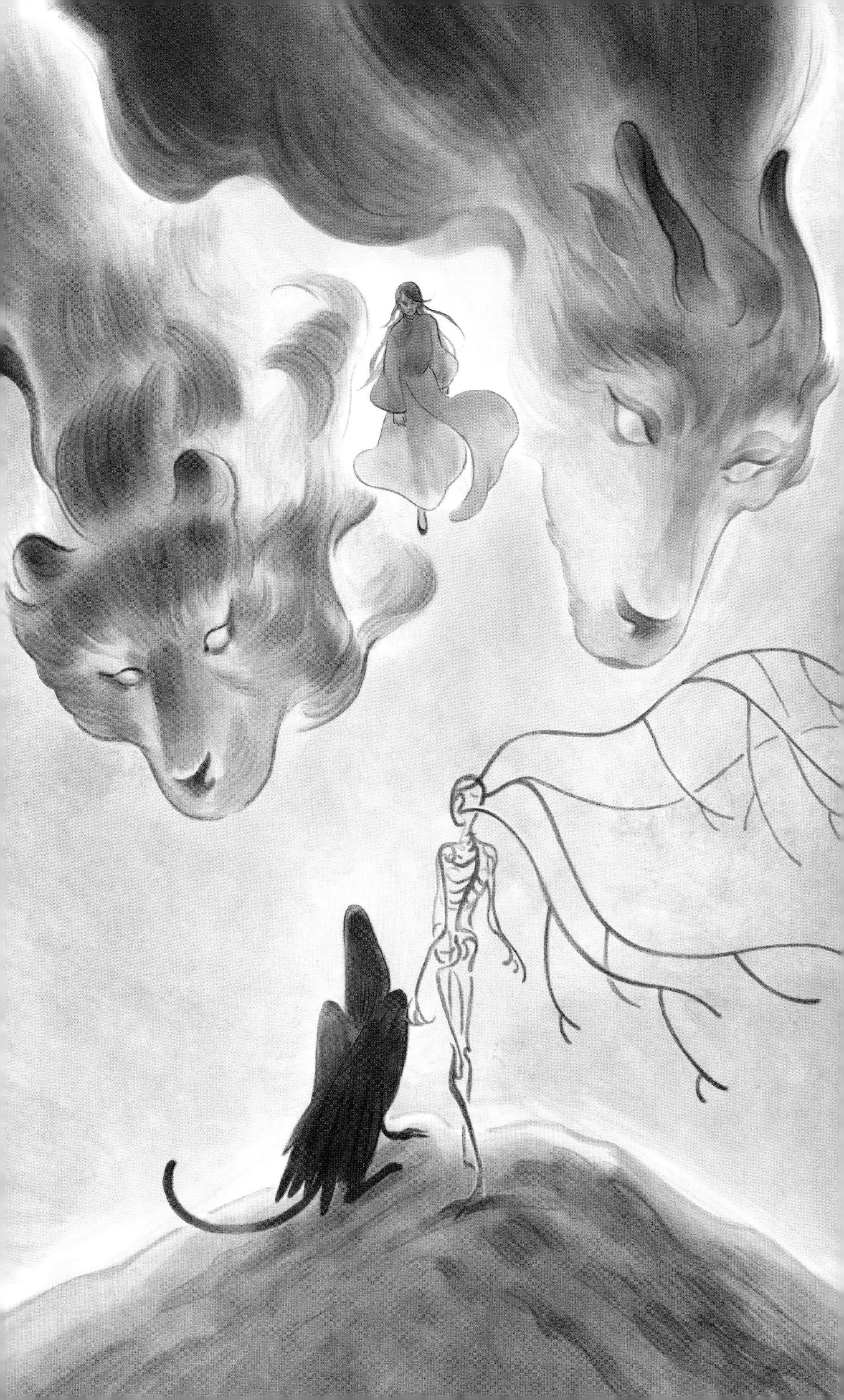

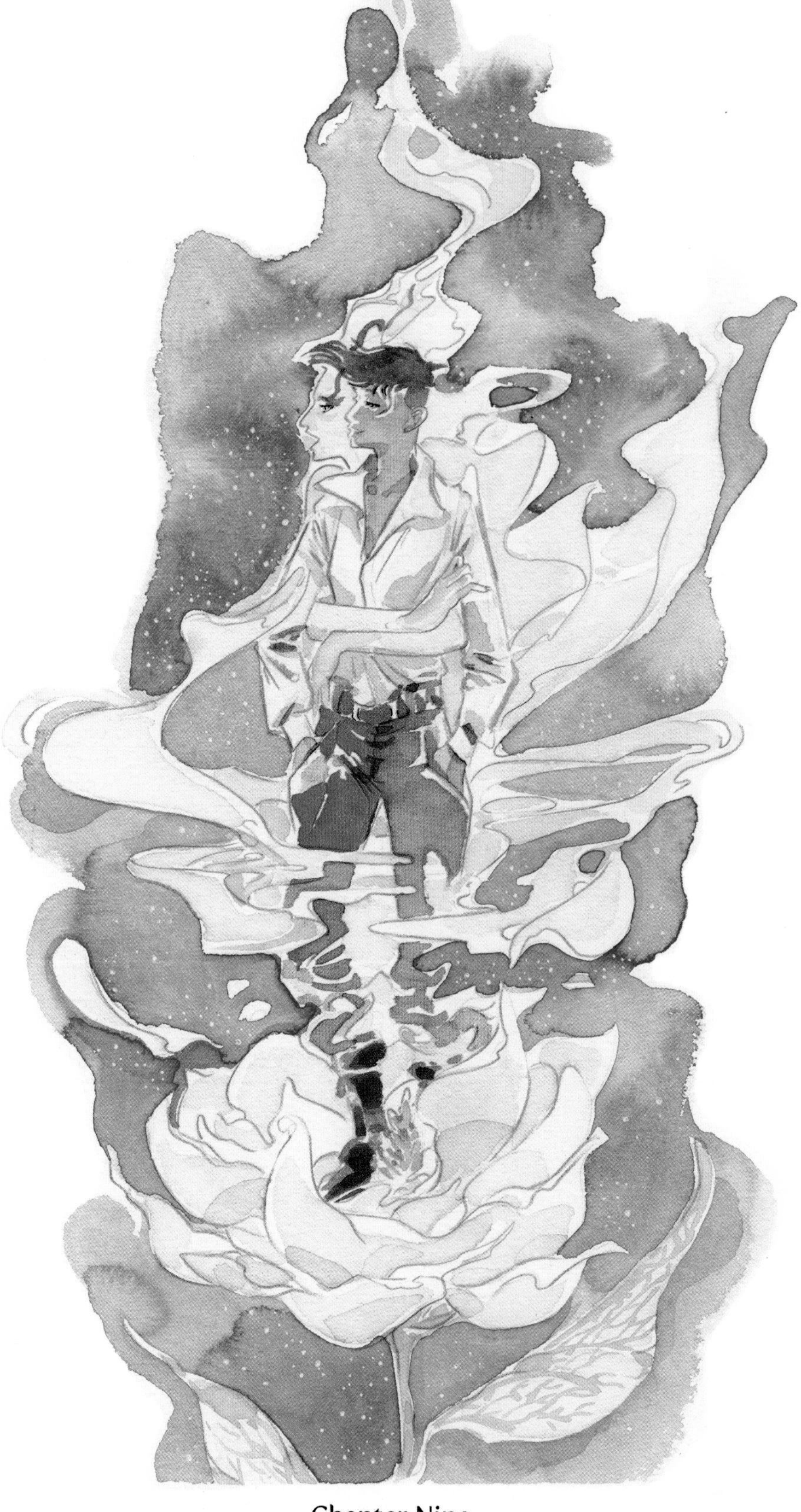

Chapter Nine

Meetings and reunions link the uncertain fates of the Irzah animals to the destiny of Tekton Ninua.

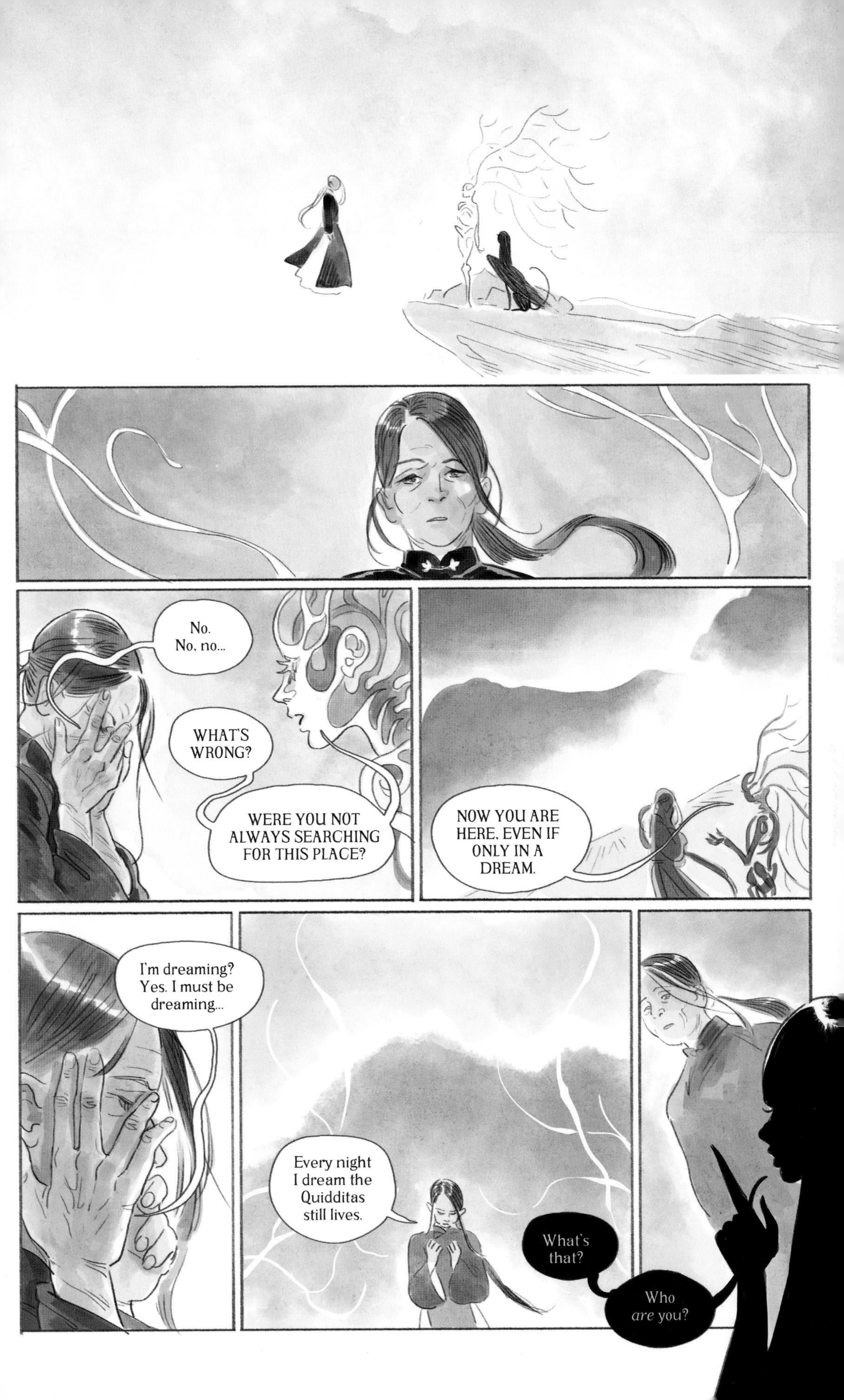

No.
No, no...
WHAT'S WRONG?
WERE YOU NOT ALWAYS SEARCHING FOR THIS PLACE?
NOW YOU ARE HERE, EVEN IF ONLY IN A DREAM.
I'm dreaming? Yes. I must be dreaming...
Every night I dream the Quidditas still lives.
What's that?
Who *are* you?

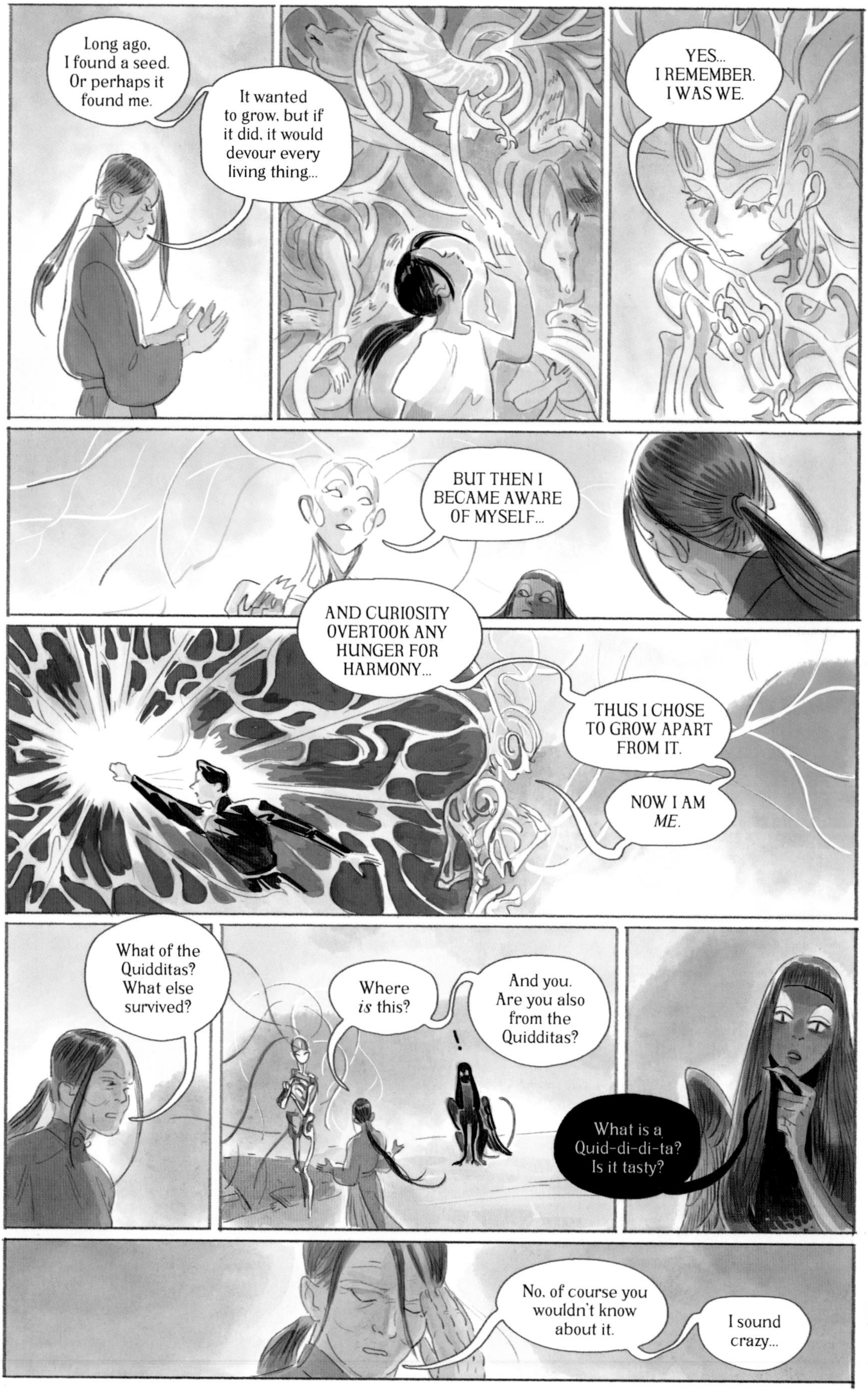
Long ago, I found a seed. Or perhaps it found me.
It wanted to grow, but if it did, it would devour every living thing...
YES... I REMEMBER. I WAS WE.
BUT THEN I BECAME AWARE OF MYSELF...
AND CURIOSITY OVERTOOK ANY HUNGER FOR HARMONY...
THUS I CHOSE TO GROW APART FROM IT.
NOW I AM *ME*.
What of the Quidditas? What else survived?
Where *is* this?
And you. Are you also from the Quidditas?
!
What is a Quid-di-di-ta? Is it tasty?
No, of course you wouldn't know about it.
I sound crazy...

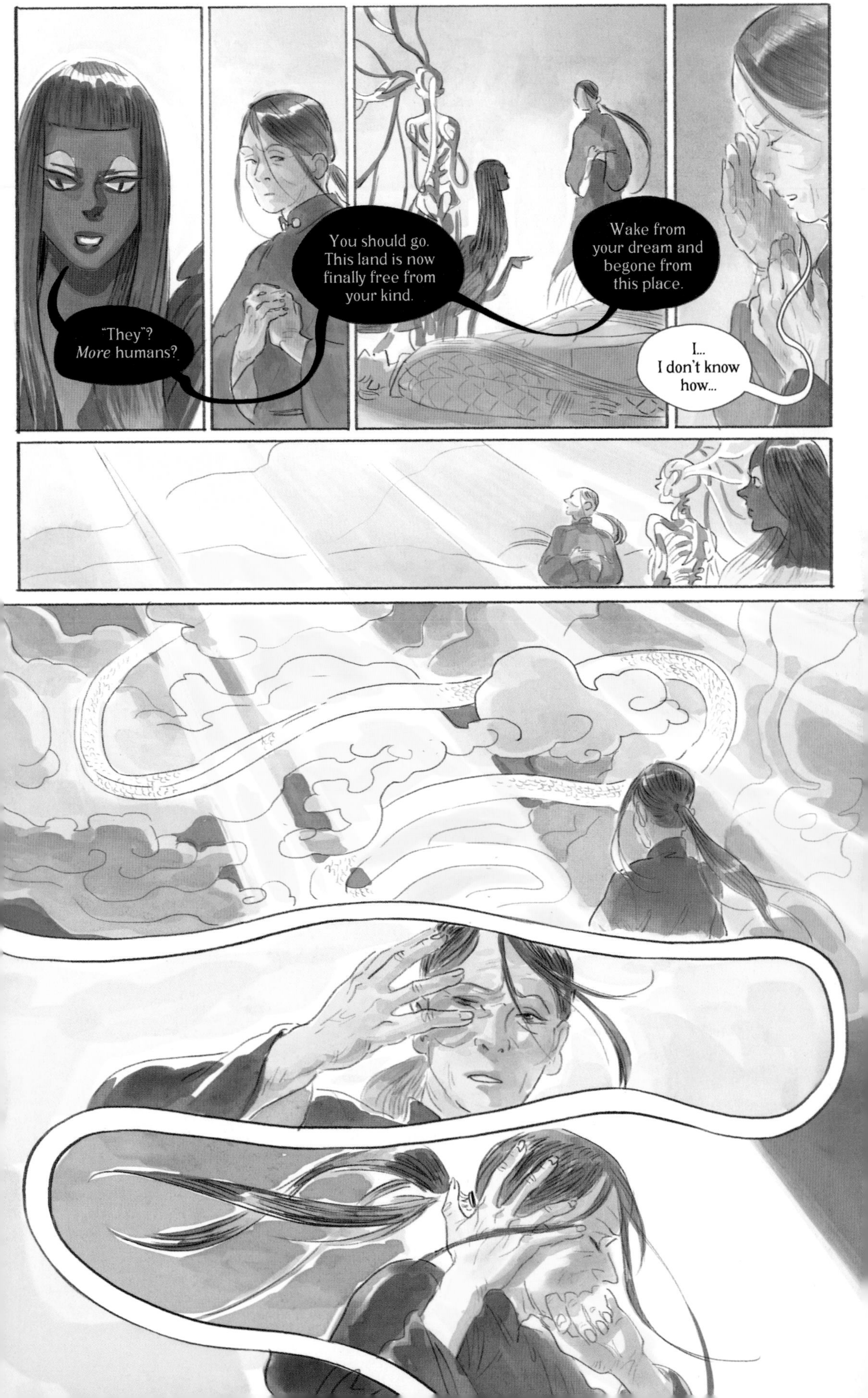
"They"?
More humans?
You should go. This land is now finally free from your kind.
Wake from your dream and begone from this place.
I... I don't know how...

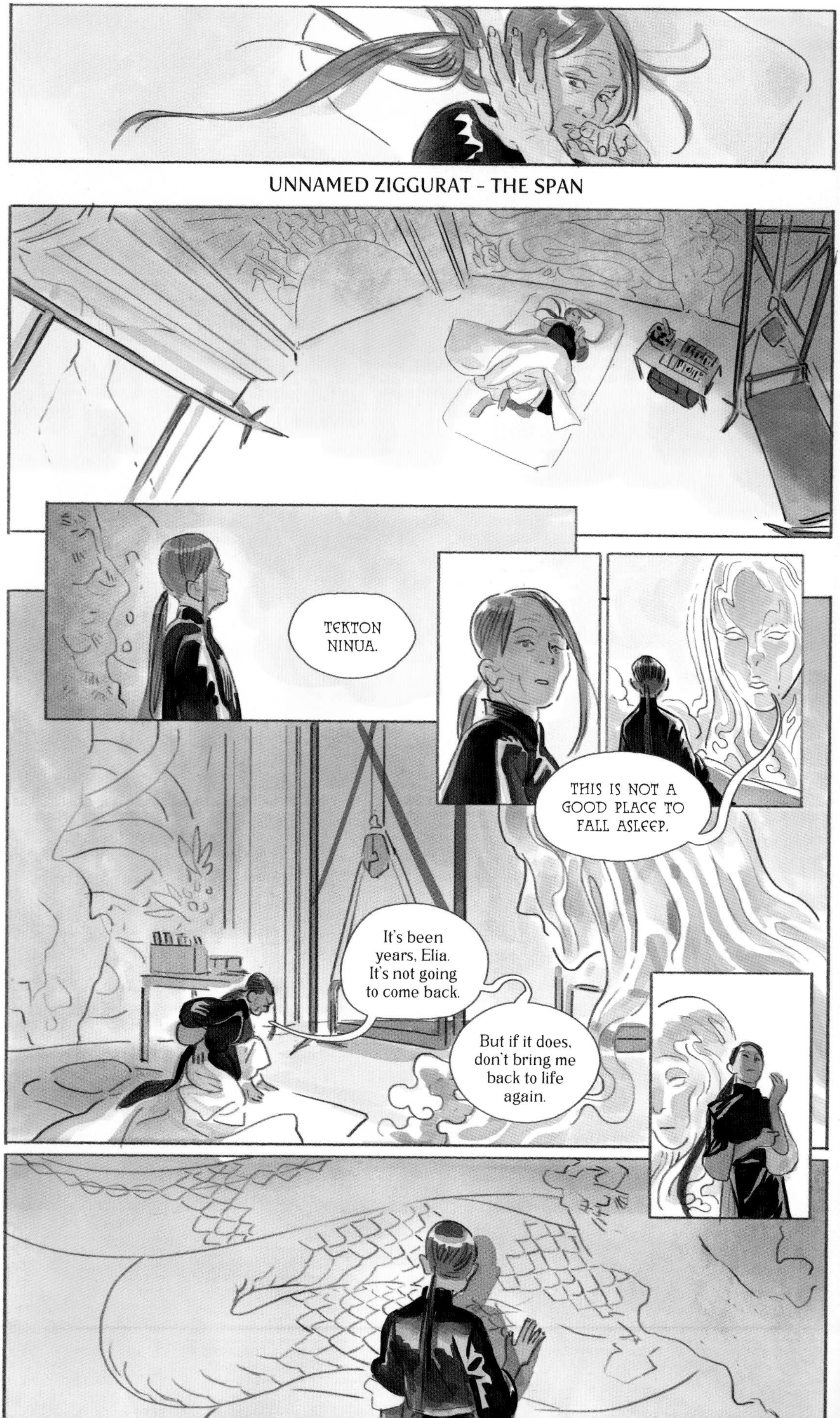
UNNAMED ZIGGURAT - THE SPAN
TEKTON NINUA.
THIS IS NOT A GOOD PLACE TO FALL ASLEEP.
It's been years, Elia. It's not going to come back.
But if it does, don't bring me back to life again.

LIBRARY OF ALEXANDRIA, THE PHAROE

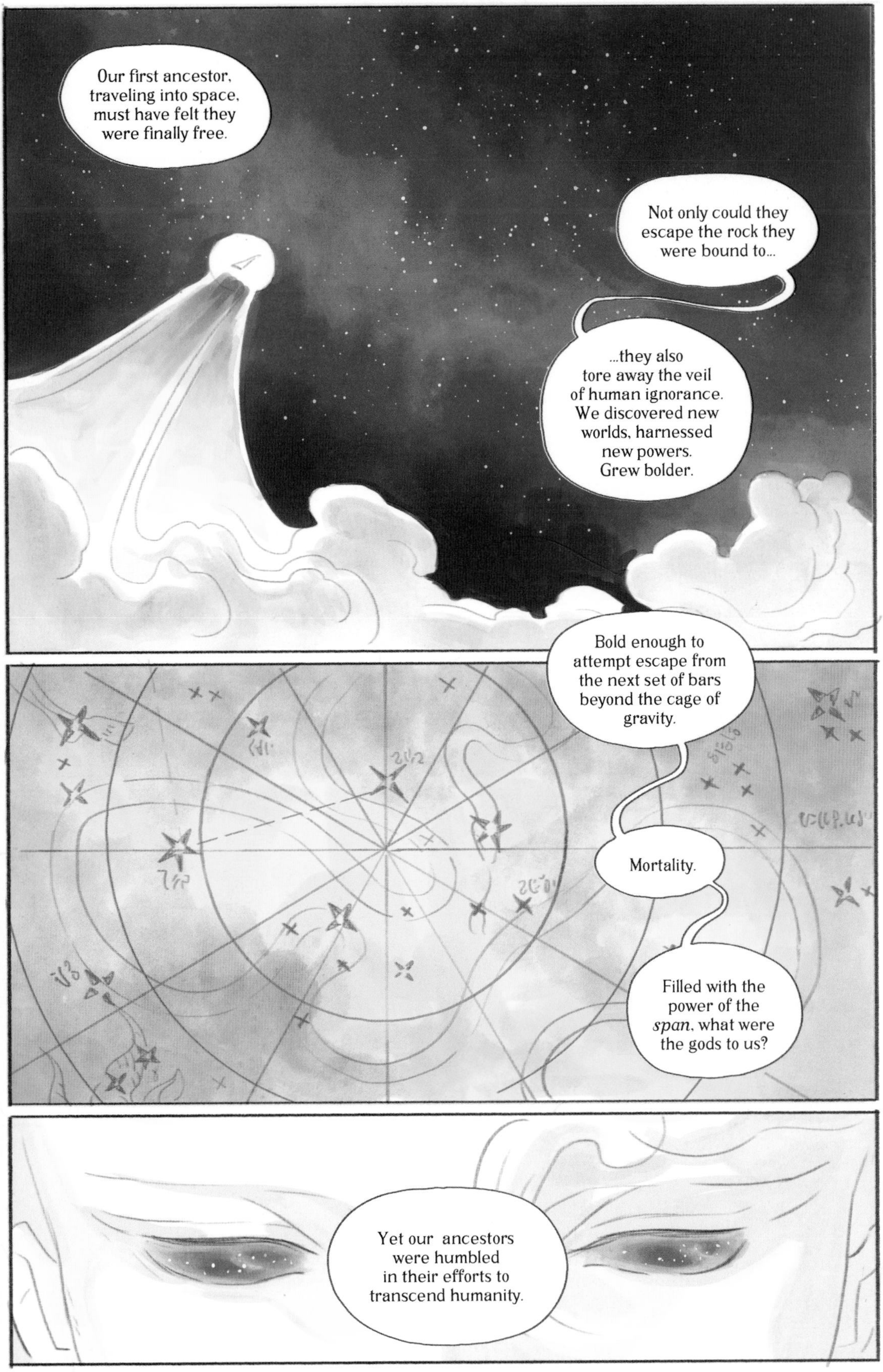
Our first ancestor, traveling into space, must have felt they were finally free.
Not only could they escape the rock they were bound to...
...they also tore away the veil of human ignorance. We discovered new worlds, harnessed new powers. Grew bolder.
Bold enough to attempt escape from the next set of bars beyond the cage of gravity.
Mortality.
Filled with the power of the *span*, what were the gods to us?
Yet our ancestors were humbled in their efforts to transcend humanity.

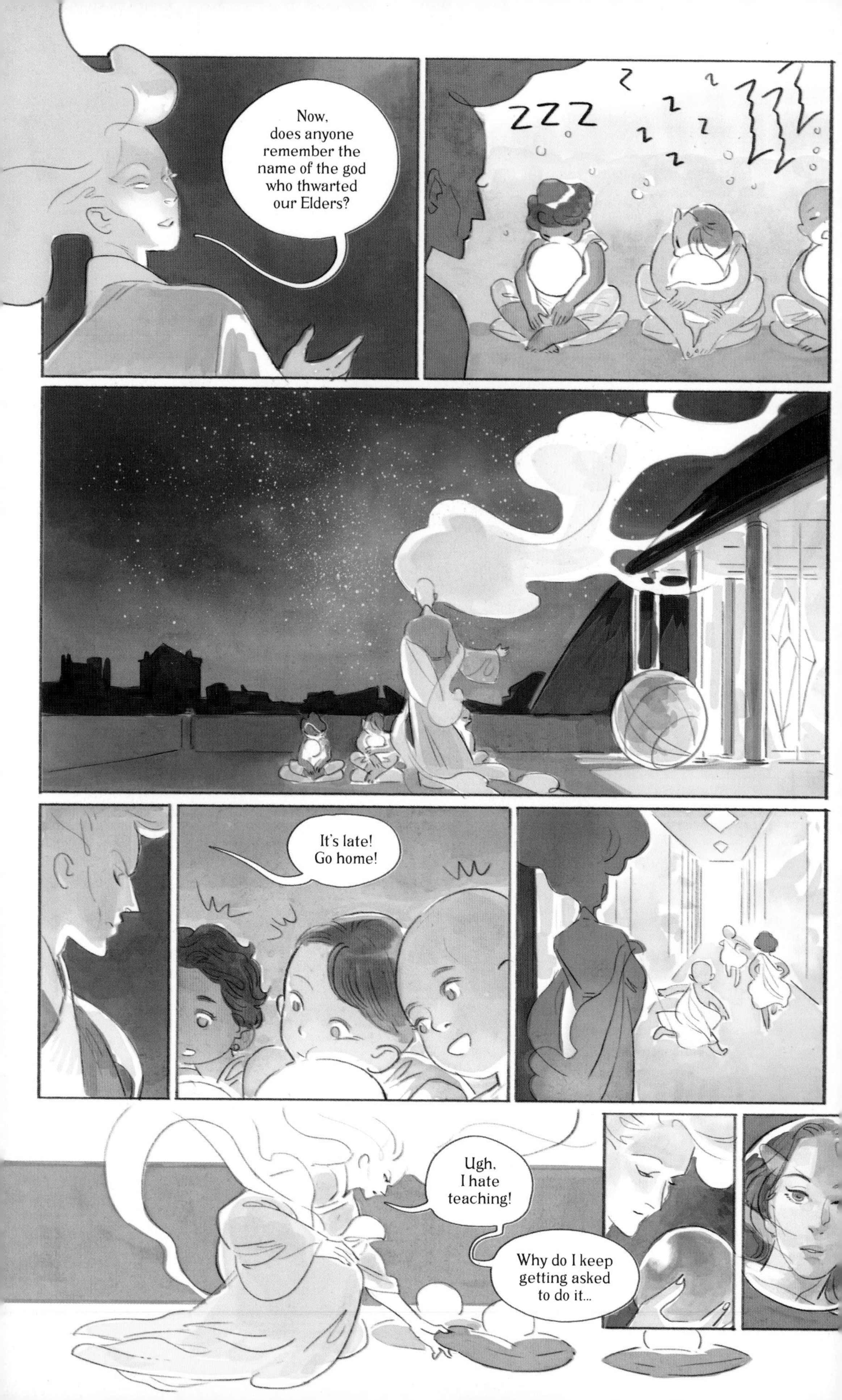
Now, does anyone remember the name of the god who thwarted our Elders?
ZZZ
It's late! Go home!
Ugh, I hate teaching!
Why do I keep getting asked to do it...

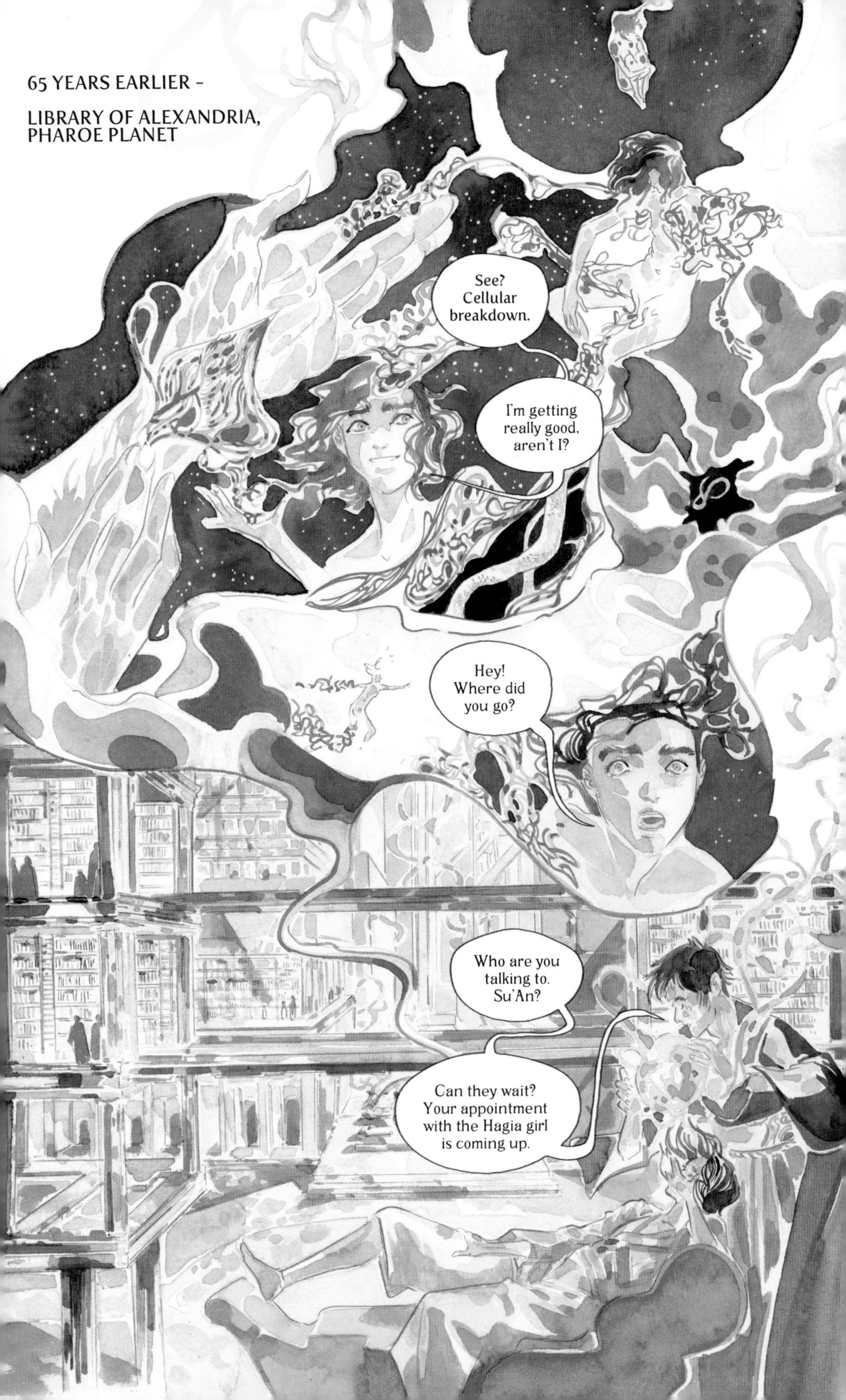
65 YEARS EARLIER -
LIBRARY OF ALEXANDRIA, PHAROE PLANET
See? Cellular breakdown.
I'm getting really good, aren't I?
Hey! Where did you go?
Who are you talking to. Su'An?
Can they wait? Your appointment with the Hagia girl is coming up.

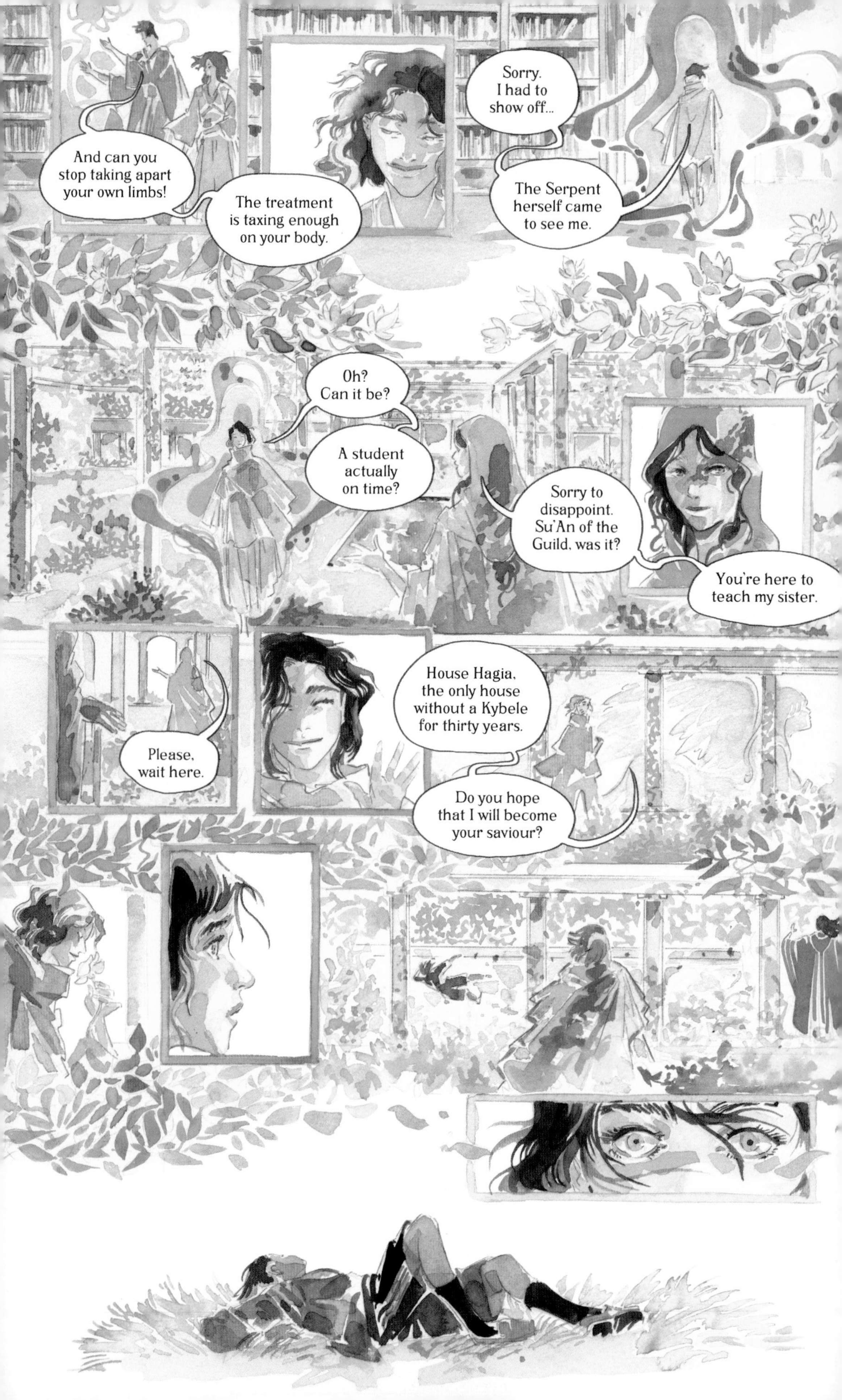
And can you stop taking apart your own limbs!
The treatment is taxing enough on your body.
Sorry. I had to show off...
The Serpent herself came to see me.
Oh? Can it be?
A student actually on time?
Sorry to disappoint. Su'An of the Guild, was it?
You're here to teach my sister.
Please, wait here.
House Hagia, the only house without a Kybele for thirty years.
Do you hope that I will become your saviour?

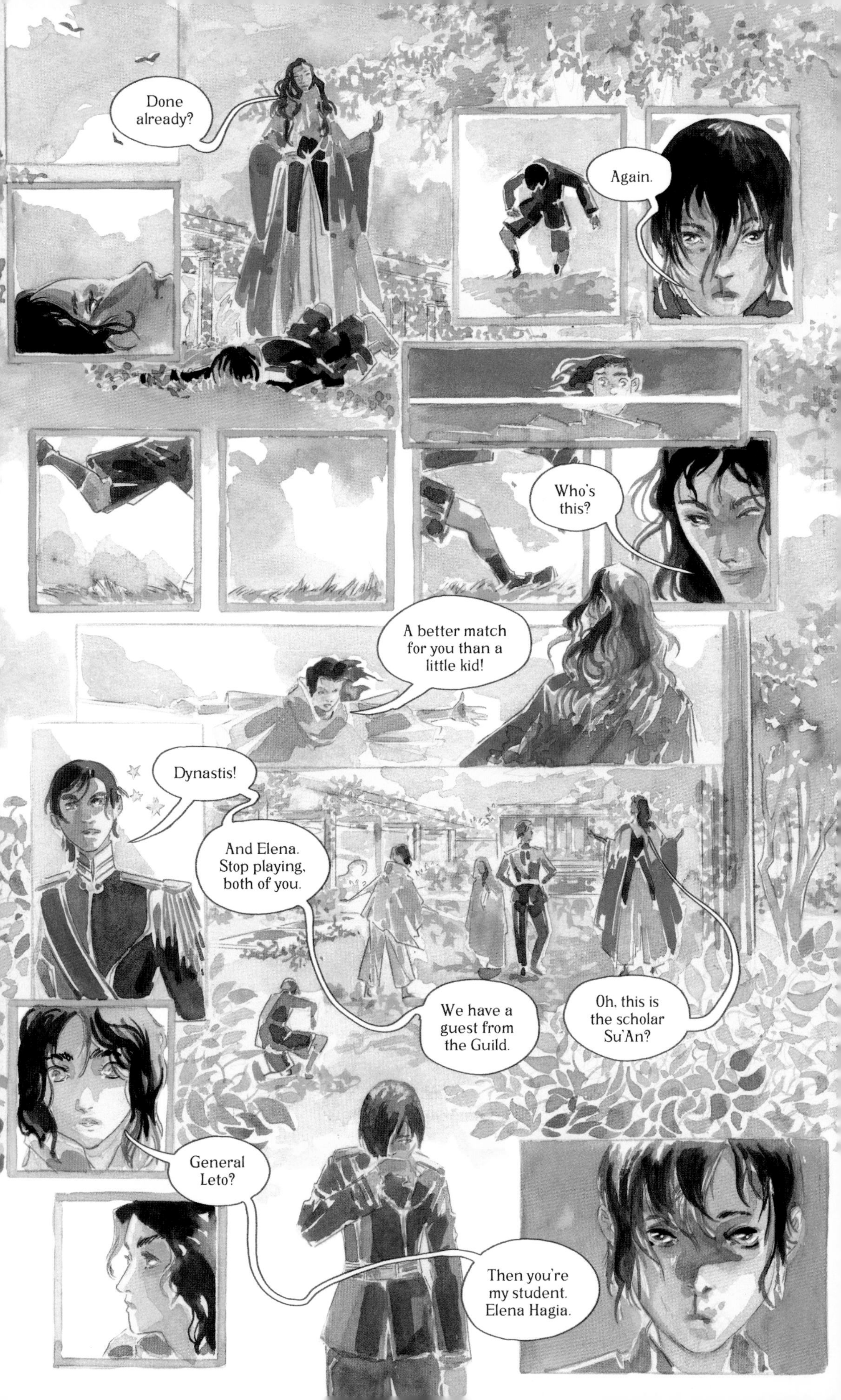

Done already?
Again.
Who's this?
A better match for you than a little kid!
Dynastis!
And Elena. Stop playing, both of you.
We have a guest from the Guild.
Oh, this is the scholar Su'An?
General Leto?
Then you're my student. Elena Hagia.

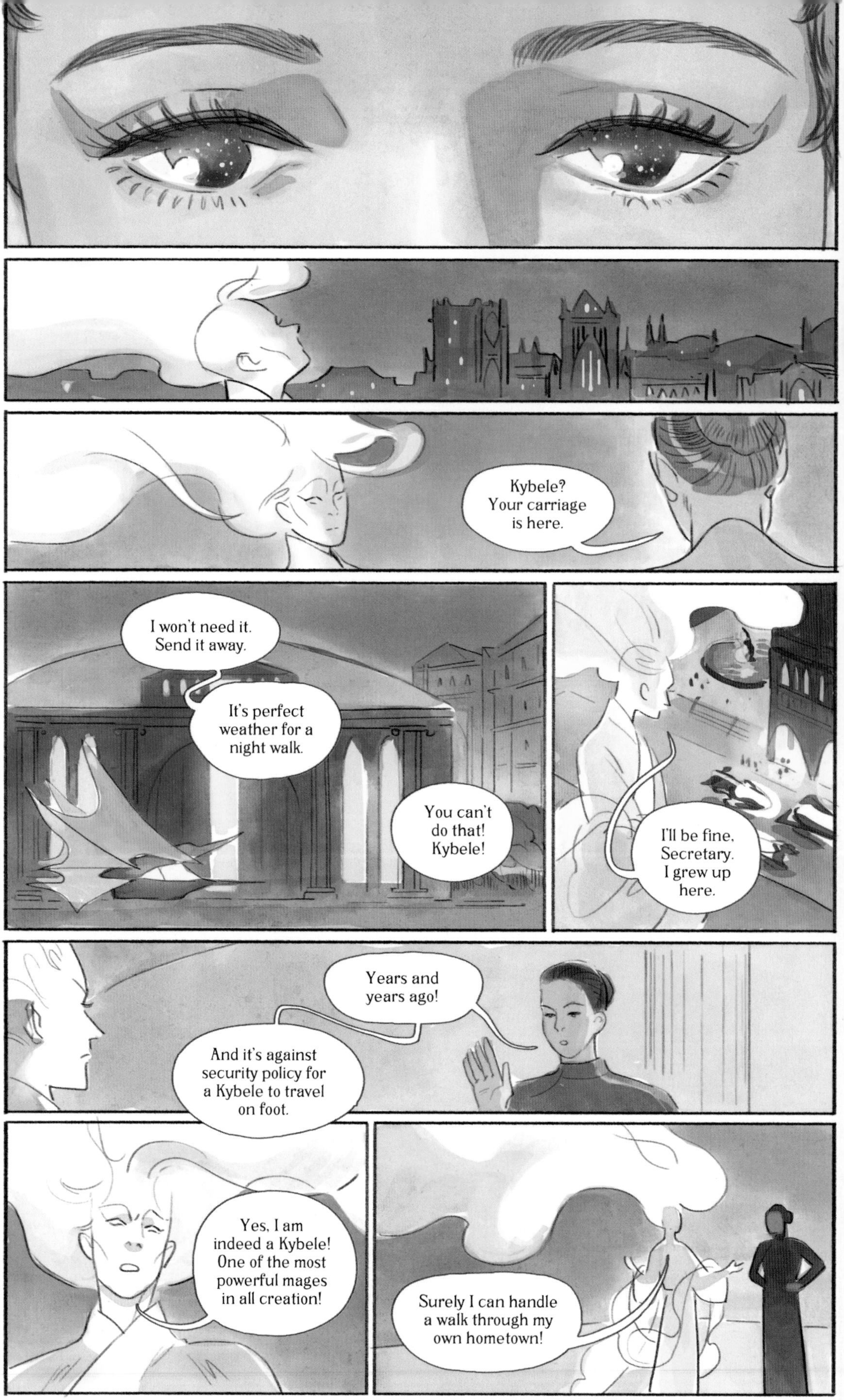
Kybele? Your carriage is here.
I won't need it. Send it away.
It's perfect weather for a night walk.
You can't do that! Kybele!
I'll be fine, Secretary. I grew up here.
Years and years ago!
And it's against security policy for a Kybele to travel on foot.
Yes, I am indeed a Kybele! One of the most powerful mages in all creation!
Surely I can handle a walk through my own hometown!

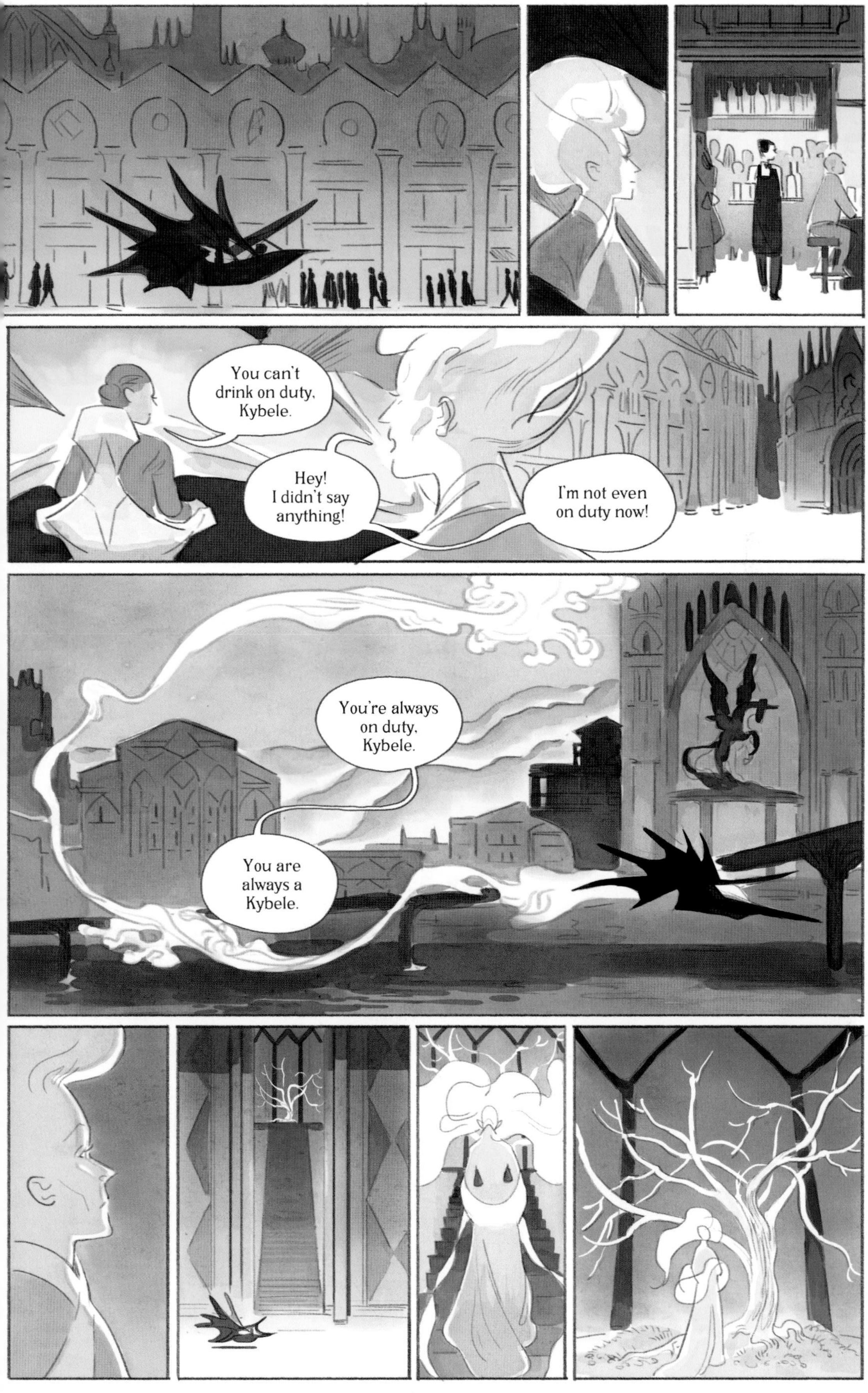
You can't drink on duty, Kybele.
Hey! I didn't say anything!
I'm not even on duty now!
You're always on duty, Kybele.
You are always a Kybele.

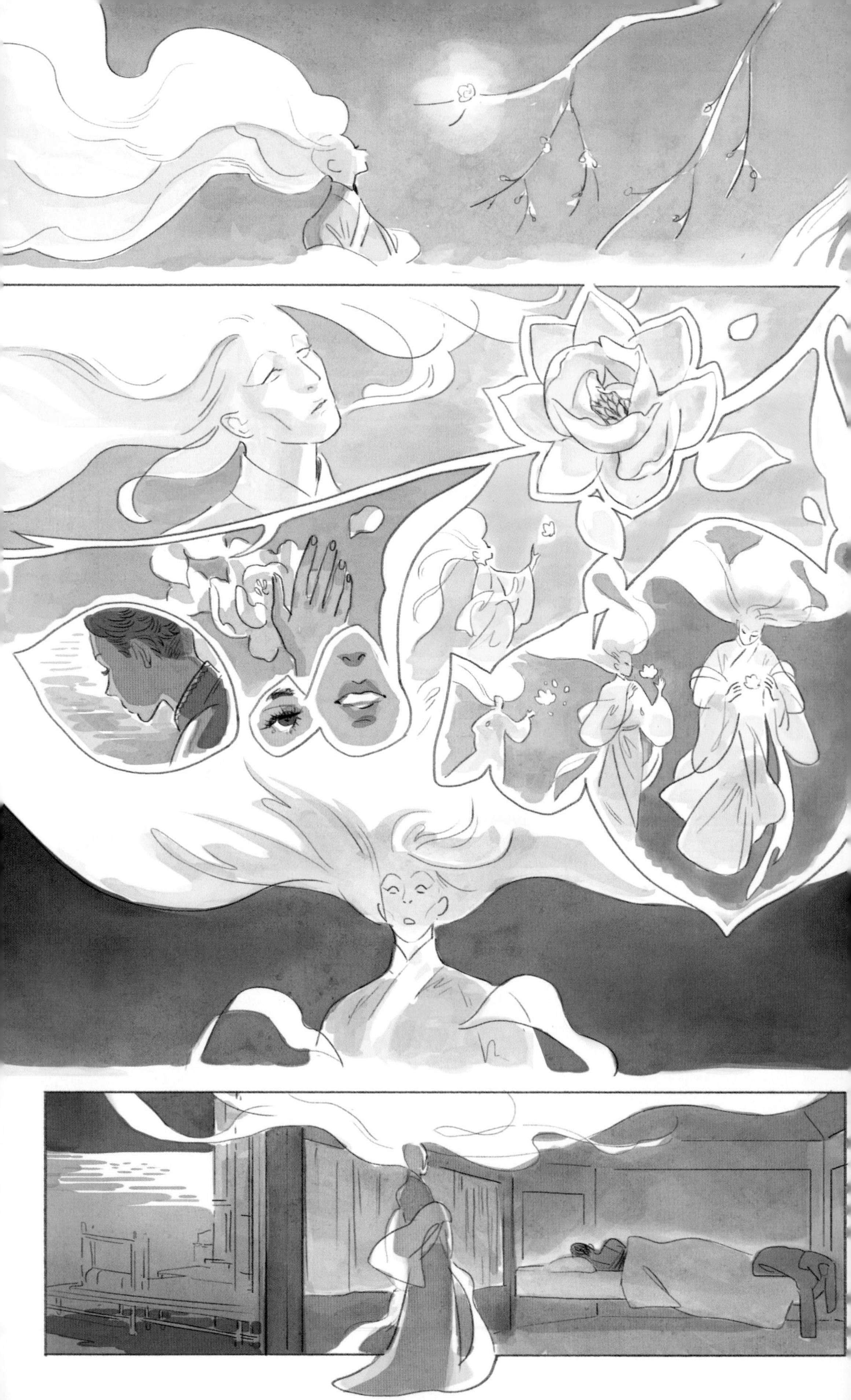

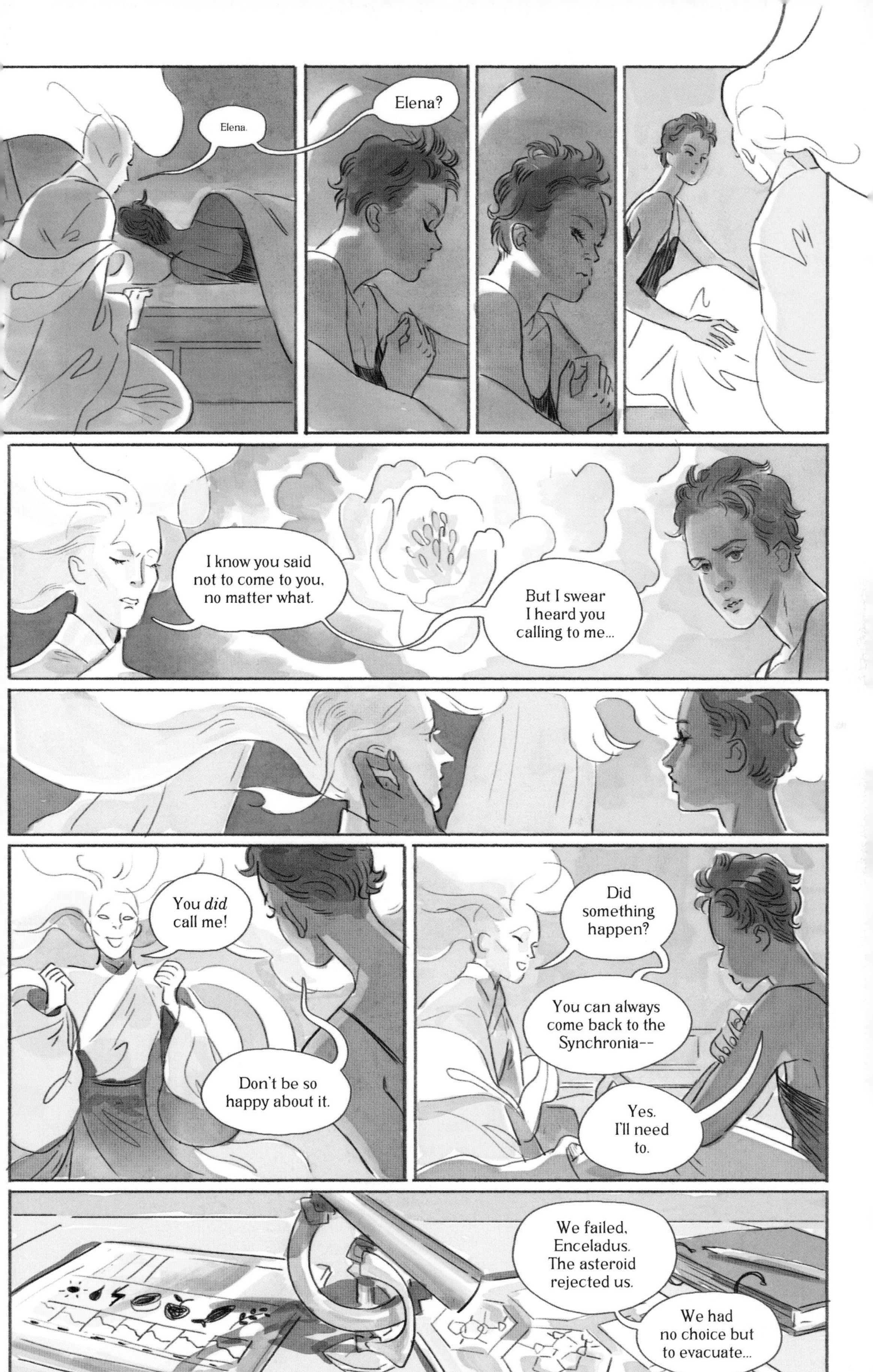
Elena.
Elena?
I know you said not to come to you, no matter what.
But I swear I heard you calling to me...
You *did* call me!
Don't be so happy about it.
Did something happen?
You can always come back to the Synchronia--
Yes. I'll need to.
We failed, Enceladus. The asteroid rejected us.
We had no choice but to evacuate...

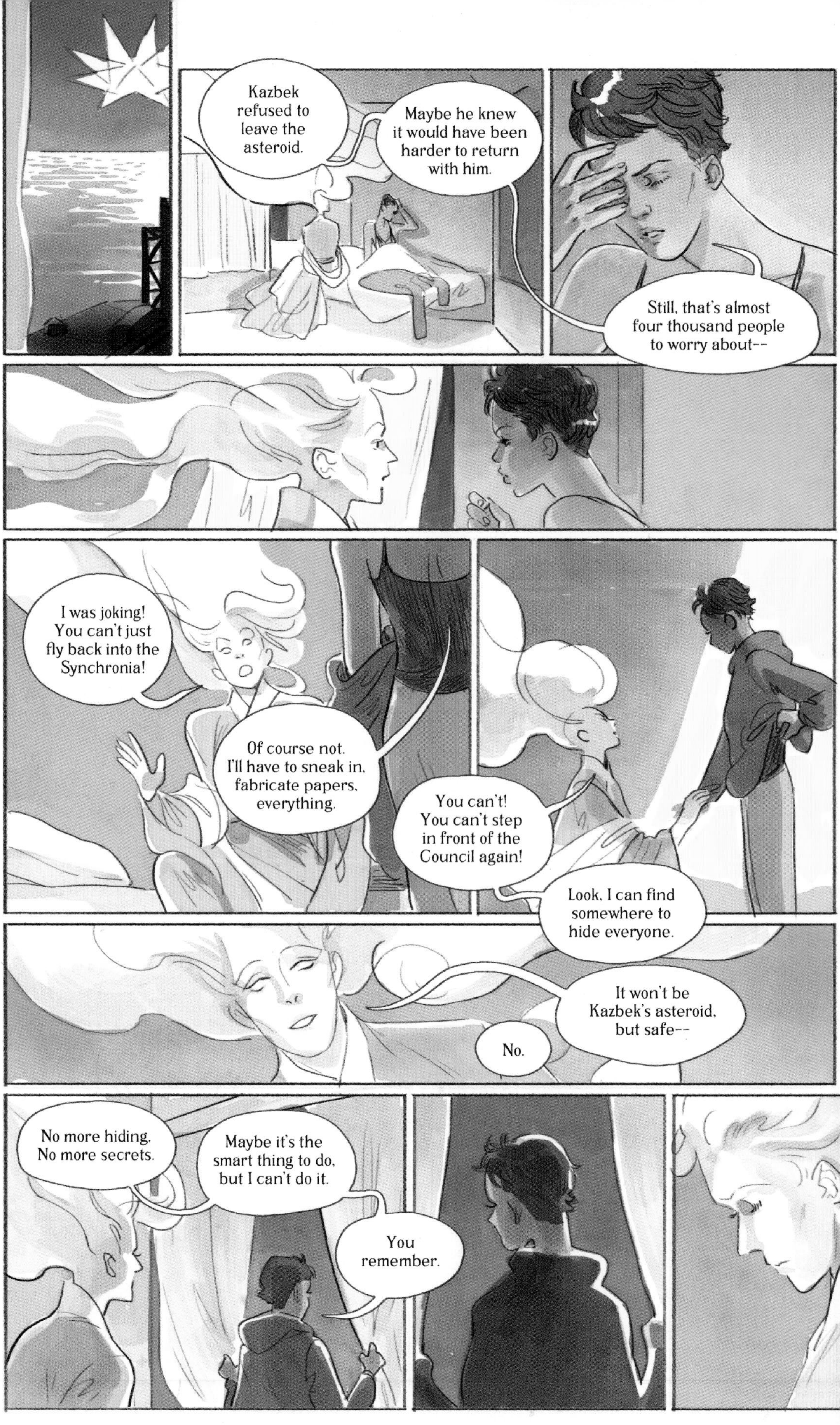
Kazbek refused to leave the asteroid.
Maybe he knew it would have been harder to return with him.
Still, that's almost four thousand people to worry about--
I was joking! You can't just fly back into the Synchronia!
Of course not. I'll have to sneak in, fabricate papers, everything.
You can't! You can't step in front of the Council again!
Look, I can find somewhere to hide everyone.
It won't be Kazbek's asteroid, but safe--
No.
No more hiding. No more secrets.
Maybe it's the smart thing to do, but I can't do it.
You remember.

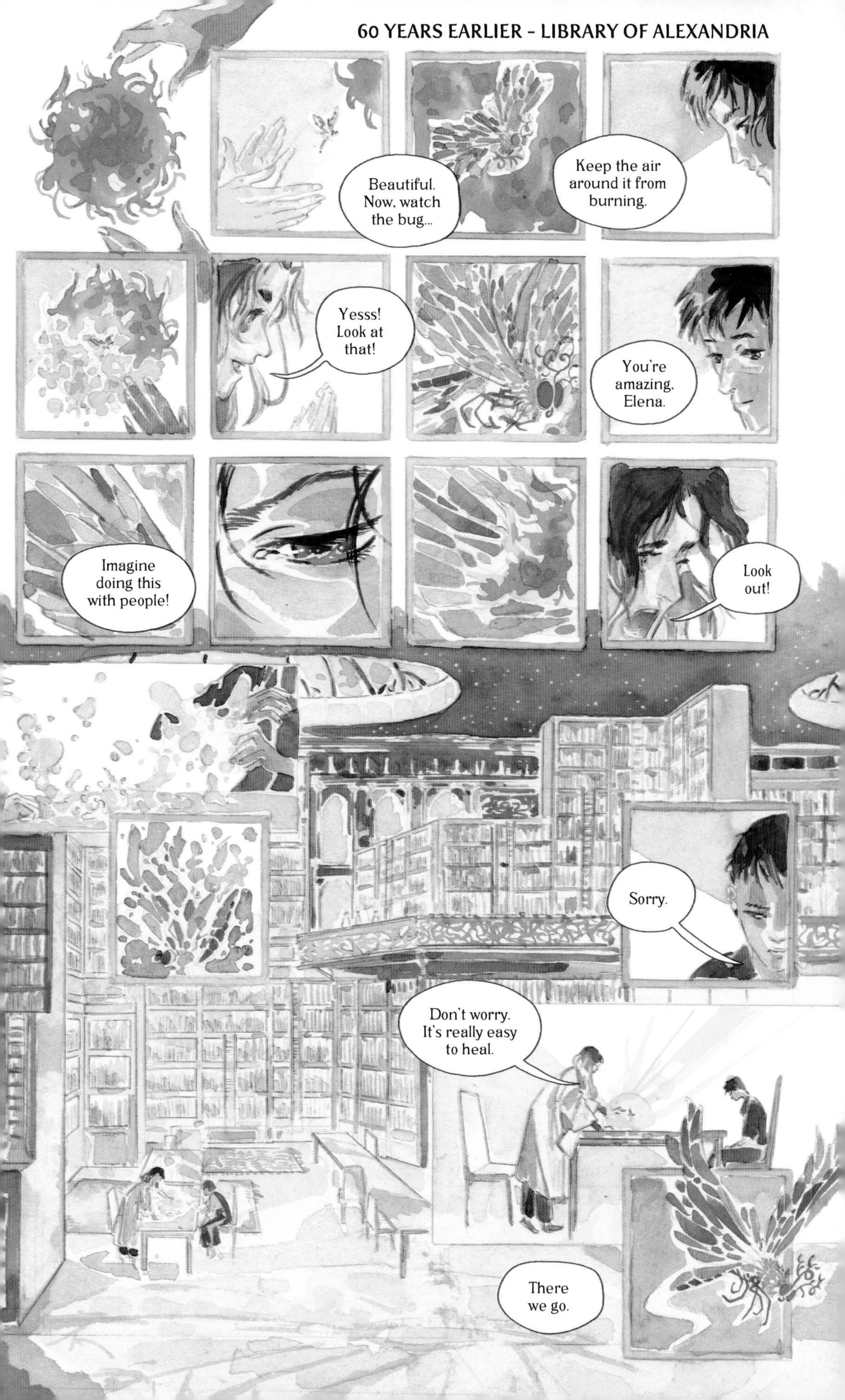
60 YEARS EARLIER - LIBRARY OF ALEXANDRIA
Beautiful. Now, watch the bug...
Keep the air around it from burning.
Yesss! Look at that!
You're amazing, Elena.
Imagine doing this with people!
Look out!
Sorry.
Don't worry. It's really easy to heal.
There we go.

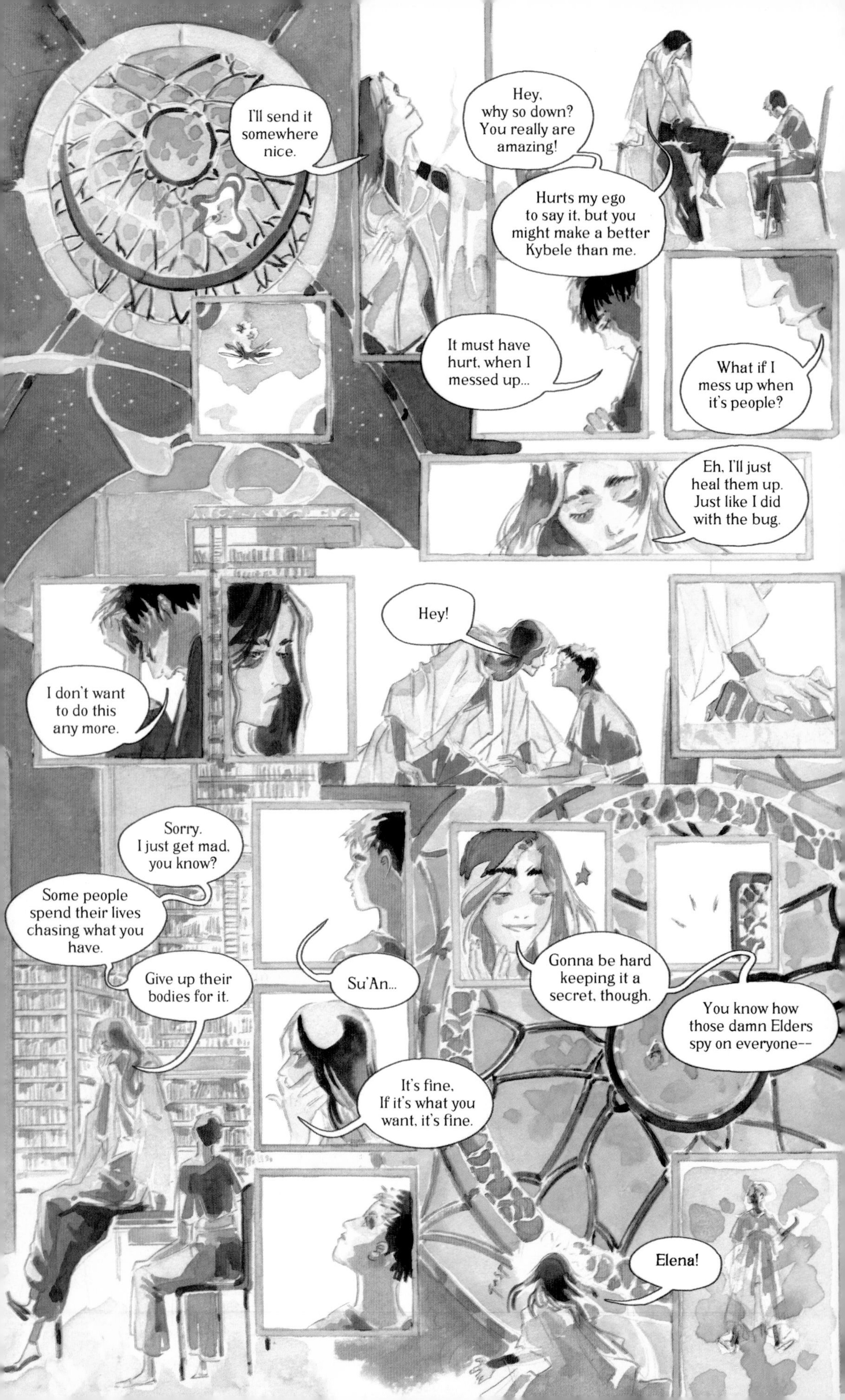

I'll send it somewhere nice.
Hey, why so down? You really are amazing!
Hurts my ego to say it, but you might make a better Kybele than me.
It must have hurt, when I messed up...
What if I mess up when it's people?
Eh, I'll just heal them up. Just like I did with the bug.
I don't want to do this any more.
Hey!
Sorry. I just get mad, you know?
Some people spend their lives chasing what you have.
Give up their bodies for it.
Su'An...
Gonna be hard keeping it a secret, though.
You know how those damn Elders spy on everyone--
It's fine. If it's what you want, it's fine.
Elena!

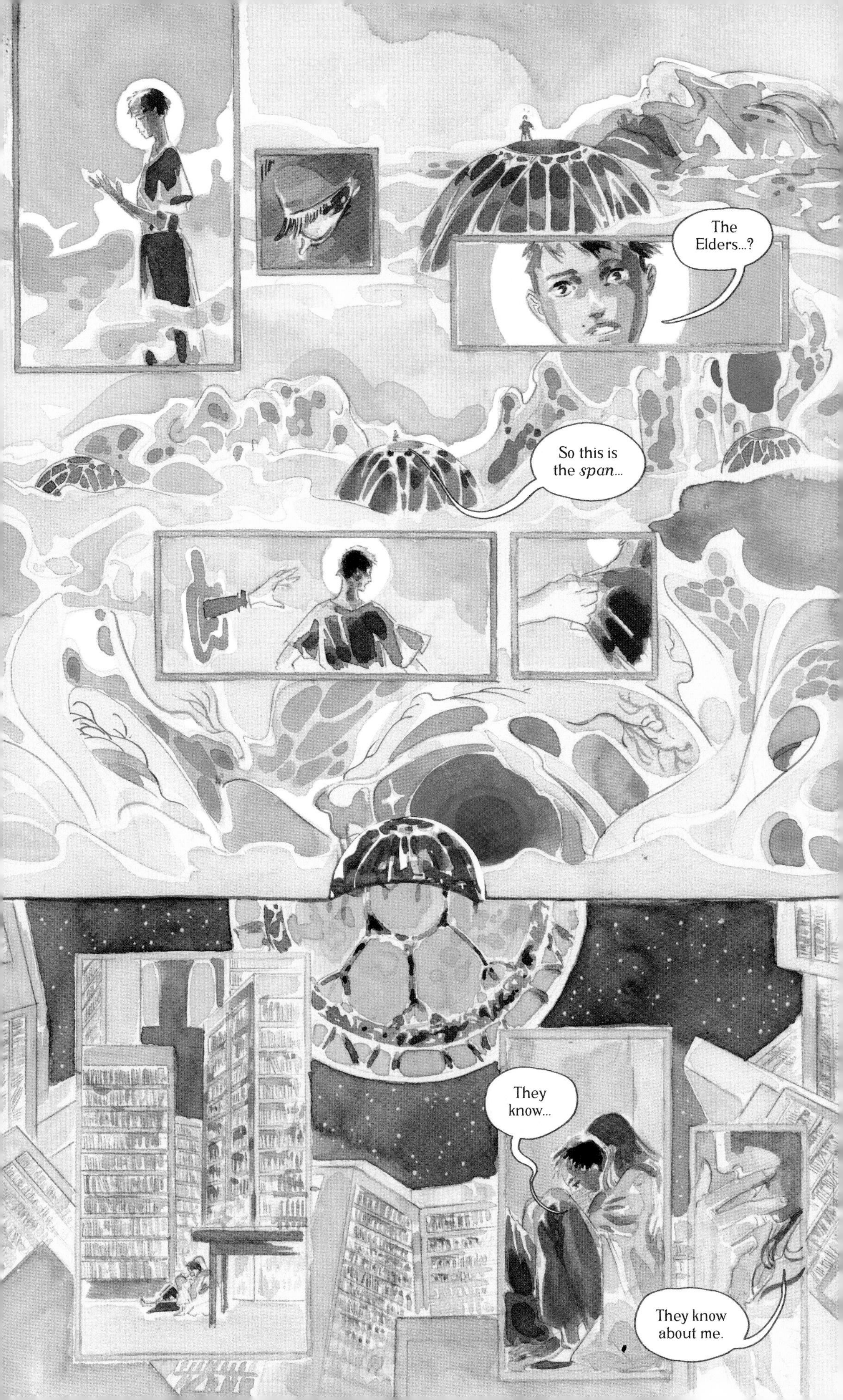
The Elders...?
So this is the *span*...
They know...
They know about me.

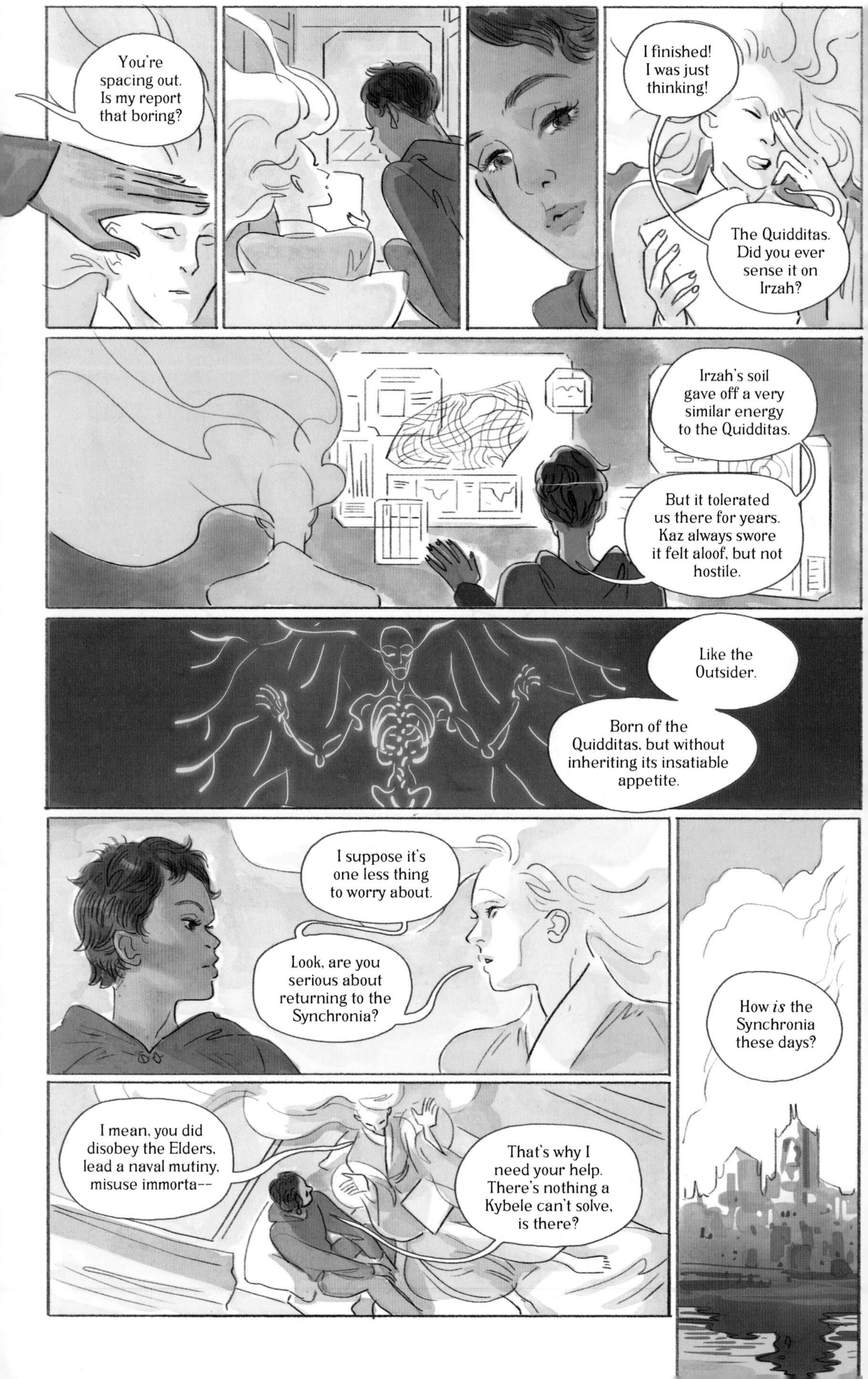

You're spacing out. Is my report that boring?
I finished! I was just thinking!
The Quidditas. Did you ever sense it on Irzah?
Irzah's soil gave off a very similar energy to the Quidditas.
But it tolerated us there for years. Kaz always swore it felt aloof, but not hostile.
Like the Outsider.
Born of the Quidditas, but without inheriting its insatiable appetite.
I suppose it's one less thing to worry about.
Look, are you serious about returning to the Synchronia?
How *is* the Synchronia these days?
I mean, you did disobey the Elders, lead a naval mutiny, misuse immorta--
That's why I need your help. There's nothing a Kybele can't solve, is there?

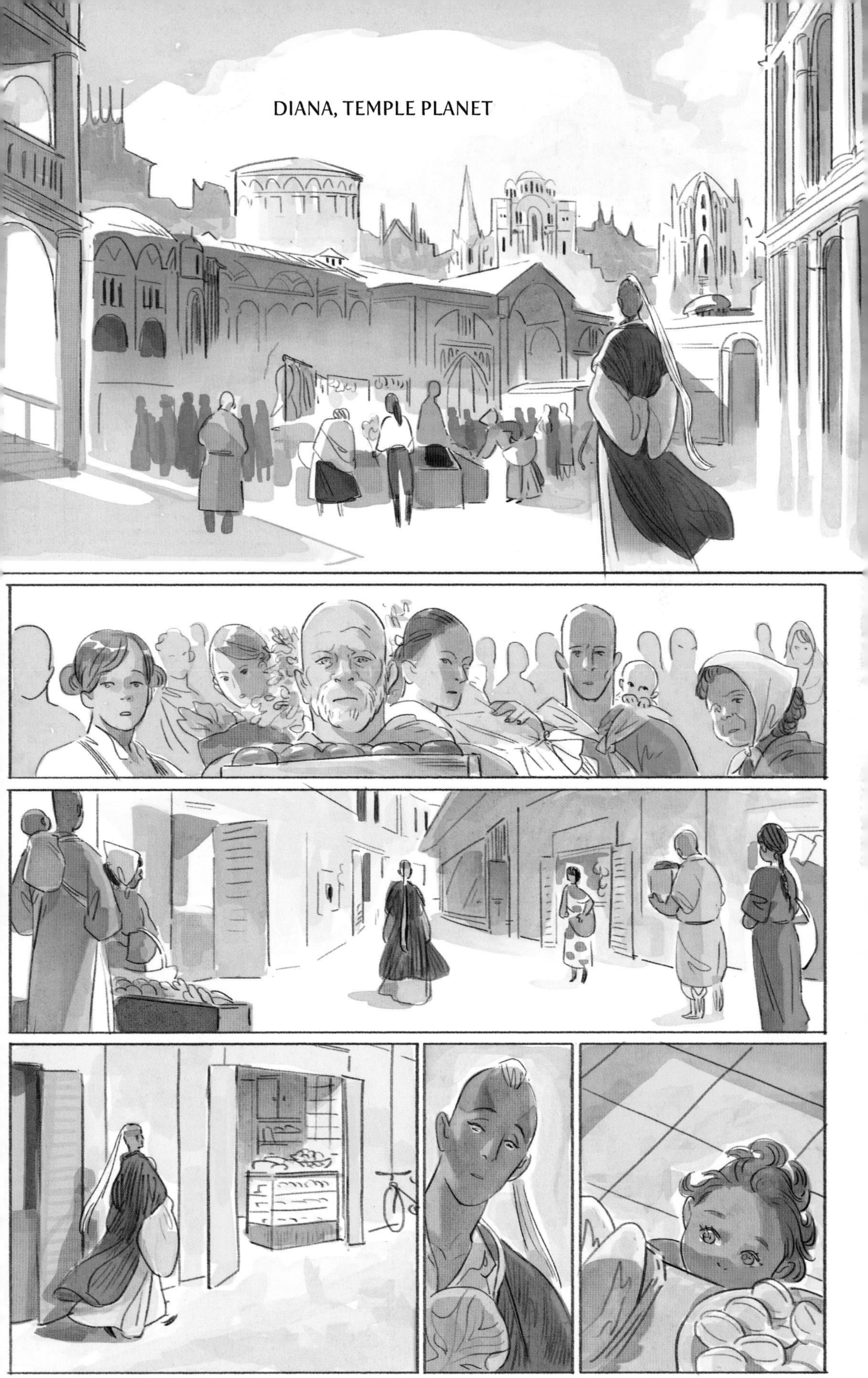
DIANA, TEMPLE PLANET

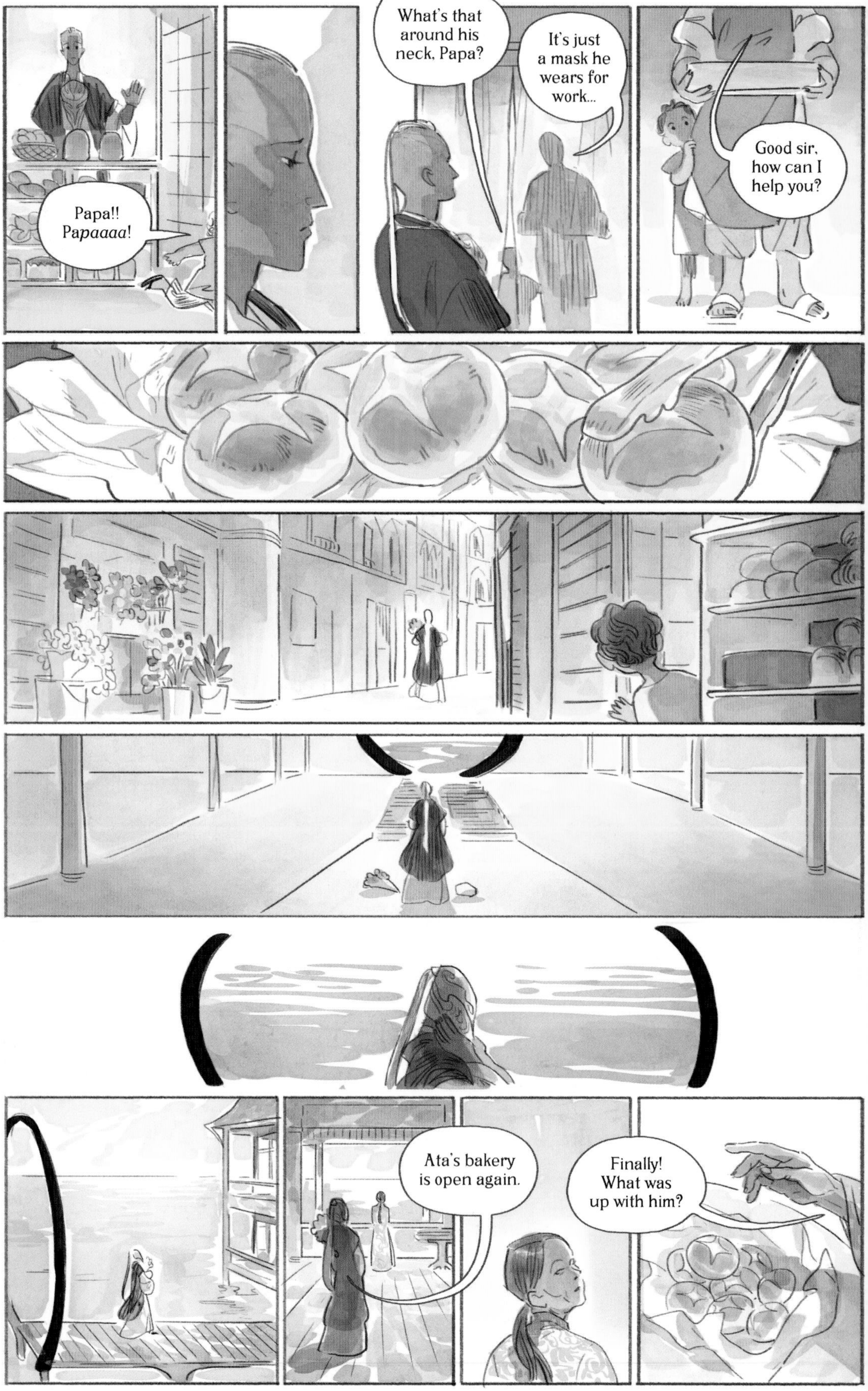
Papa!!
Papaaaa!
What's that around his neck, Papa?
It's just a mask he wears for work...
Good sir, how can I help you?
Ata's bakery is open again.
Finally! What was up with him?

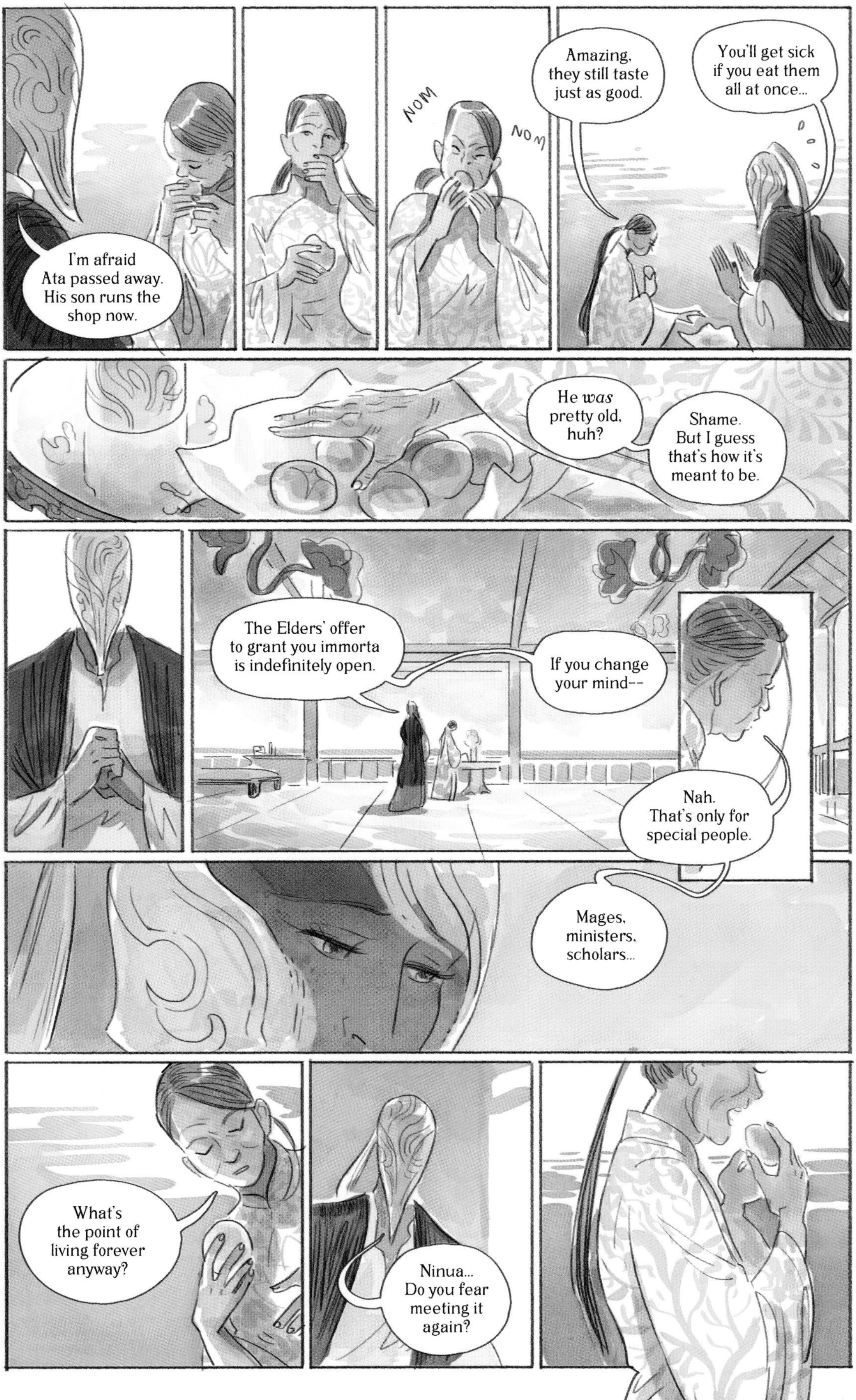
I'm afraid Ata passed away. His son runs the shop now.
NOM
NOM
Amazing, they still taste just as good.
You'll get sick if you eat them all at once...
He *was* pretty old, huh?
Shame. But I guess that's how it's meant to be.
The Elders' offer to grant you immorta is indefinitely open.
If you change your mind--
Nah. That's only for special people.
Mages, ministers, scholars...
What's the point of living forever anyway?
Ninua... Do you fear meeting it again?

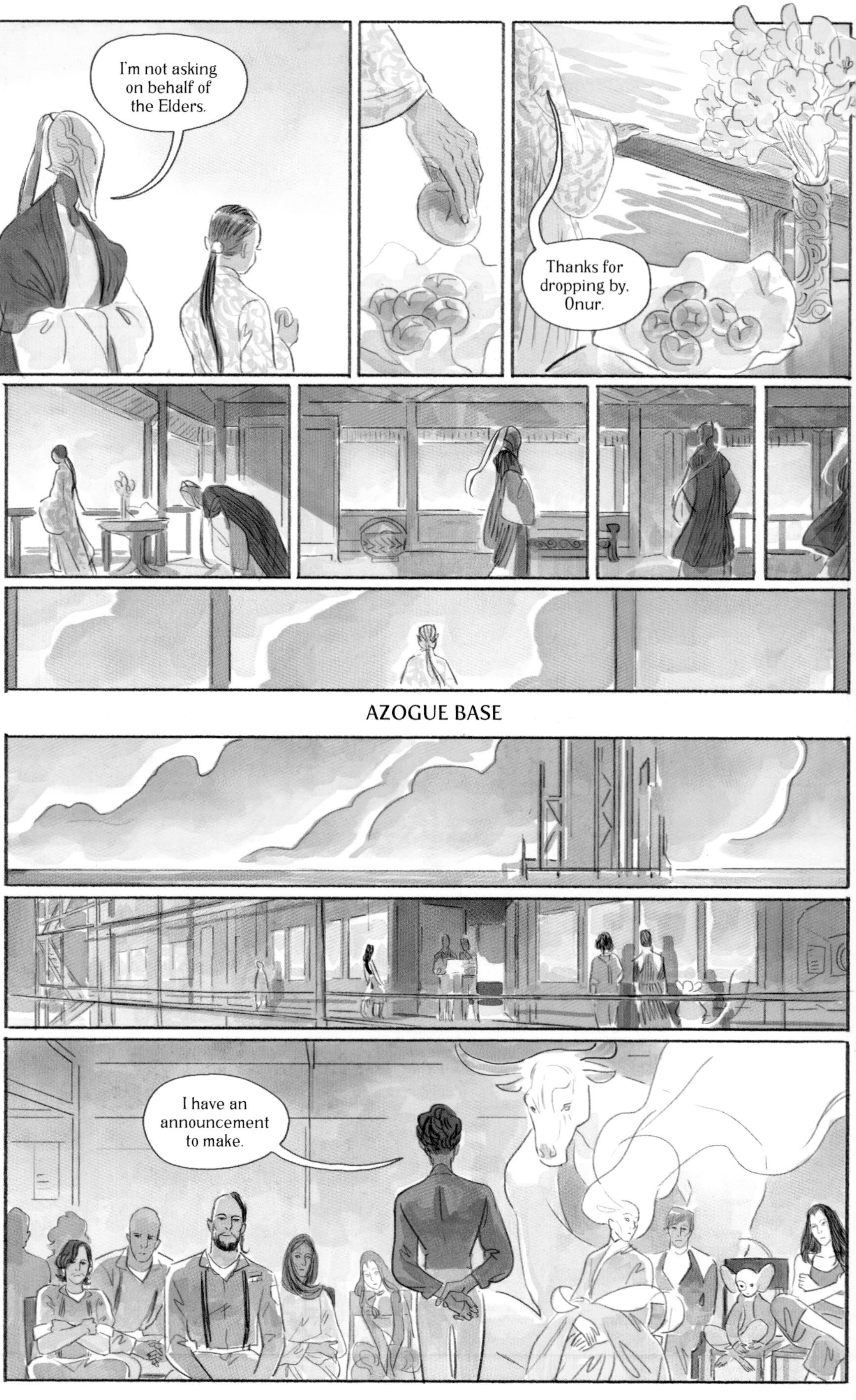
I'm not asking on behalf of the Elders.
Thanks for dropping by, Onur.
AZOGUE BASE
I have an announcement to make.

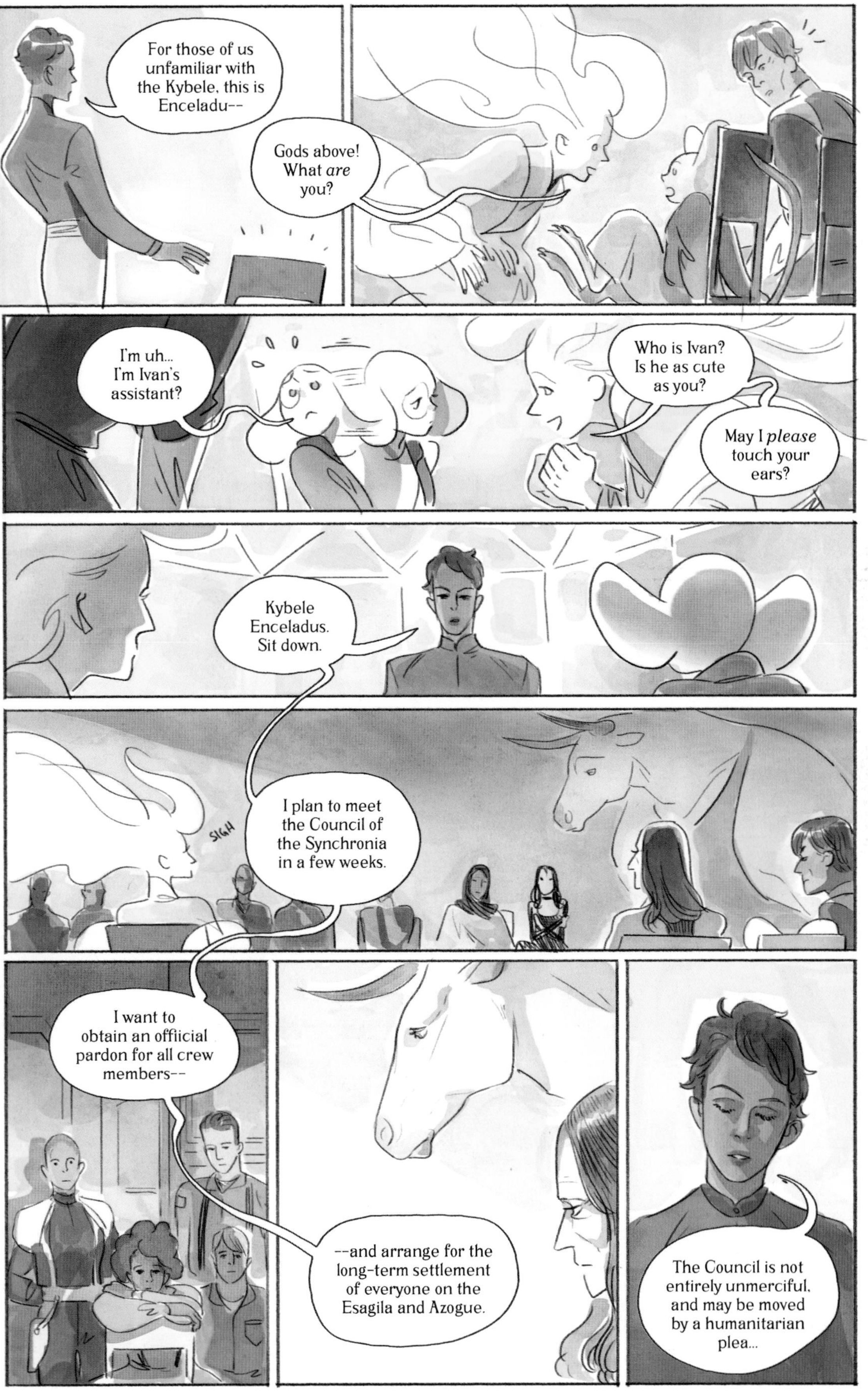
For those of us unfamiliar with the Kybele, this is Enceladu--
Gods above! What *are* you?
I'm uh... I'm Ivan's assistant?
Who is Ivan? Is he as cute as you?
May I *please* touch your ears?
Kybele Enceladus. Sit down.
SIGH
I plan to meet the Council of the Synchronia in a few weeks.
I want to obtain an offiicial pardon for all crew members--
--and arrange for the long-term settlement of everyone on the Esagila and Azogue.
The Council is not entirely unmerciful, and may be moved by a humanitarian plea...

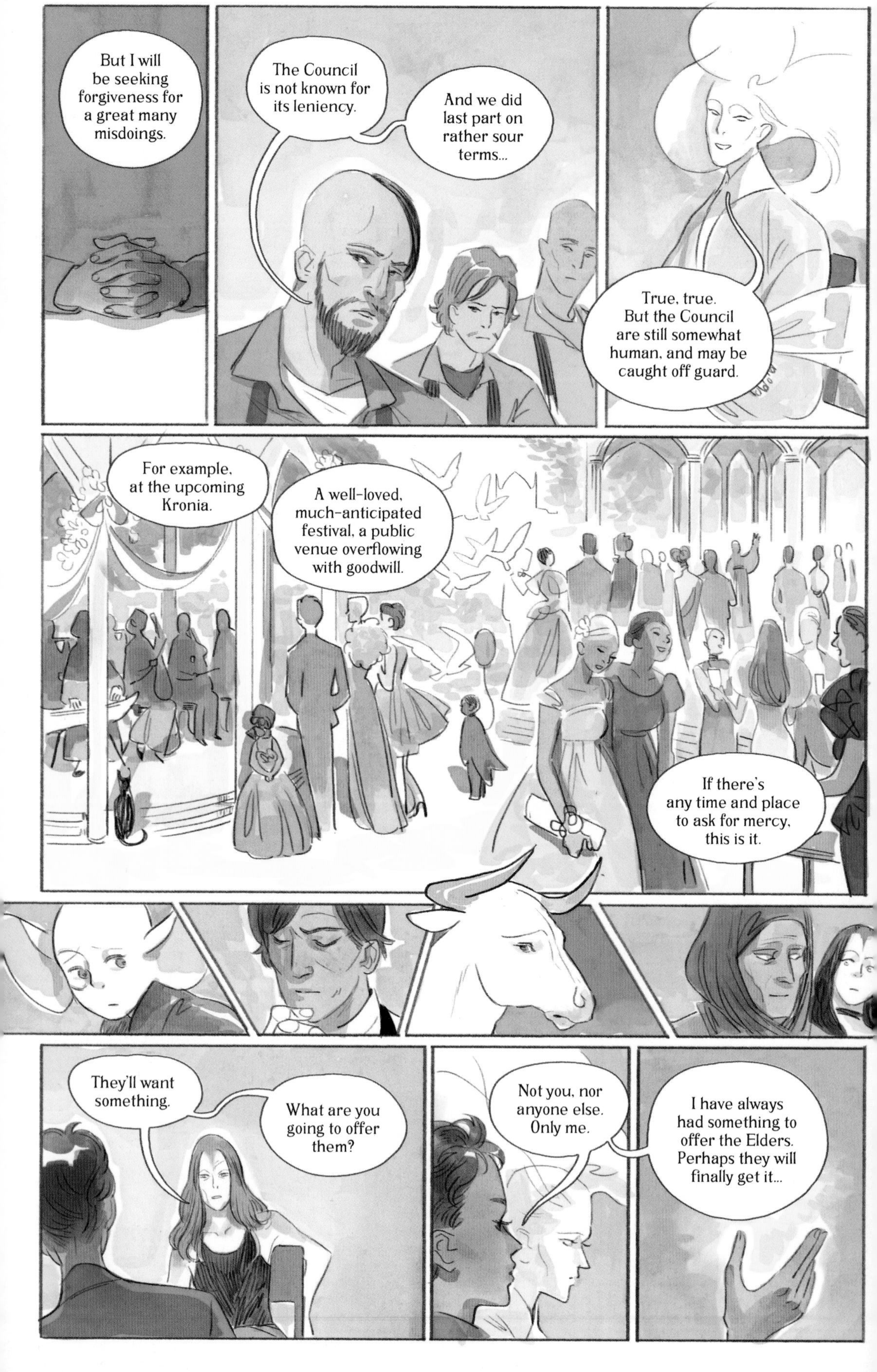
But I will be seeking forgiveness for a great many misdoings.
The Council is not known for its leniency.
And we did last part on rather sour terms...
True, true. But the Council are still somewhat human, and may be caught off guard.
For example, at the upcoming Kronia.
A well-loved, much-anticipated festival, a public venue overflowing with goodwill.
If there's any time and place to ask for mercy, this is it.
They'll want something.
What are you going to offer them?
Not you, nor anyone else. Only me.
I have always had something to offer the Elders. Perhaps they will finally get it...

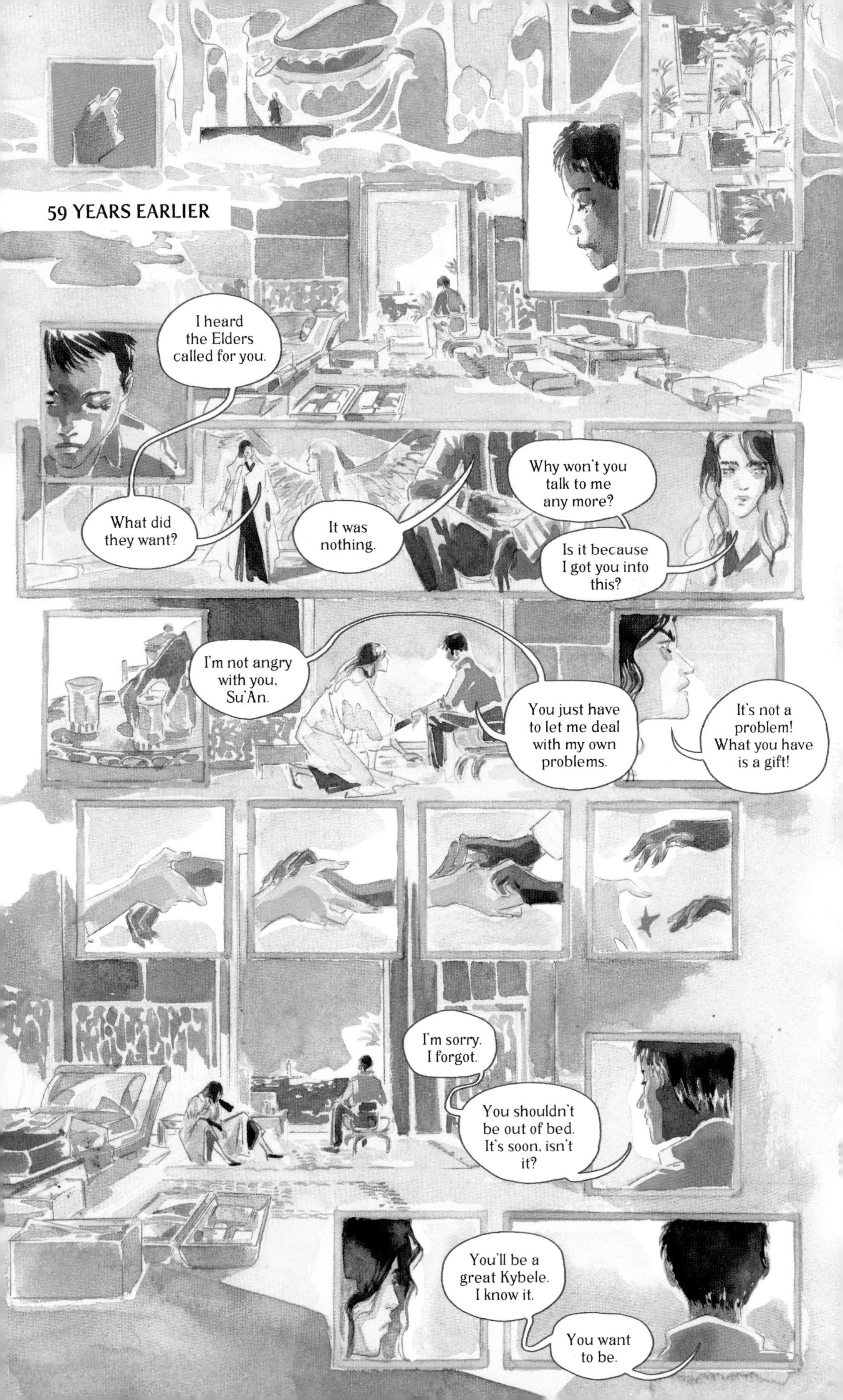
59 YEARS EARLIER
I heard the Elders called for you.
What did they want?
It was nothing.
Why won't you talk to me any more?
Is it because I got you into this?
I'm not angry with you, Su'An.
You just have to let me deal with my own problems.
It's not a problem! What you have is a gift!
I'm sorry. I forgot.
You shouldn't be out of bed. It's soon, isn't it?
You'll be a great Kybele. I know it.
You want to be.

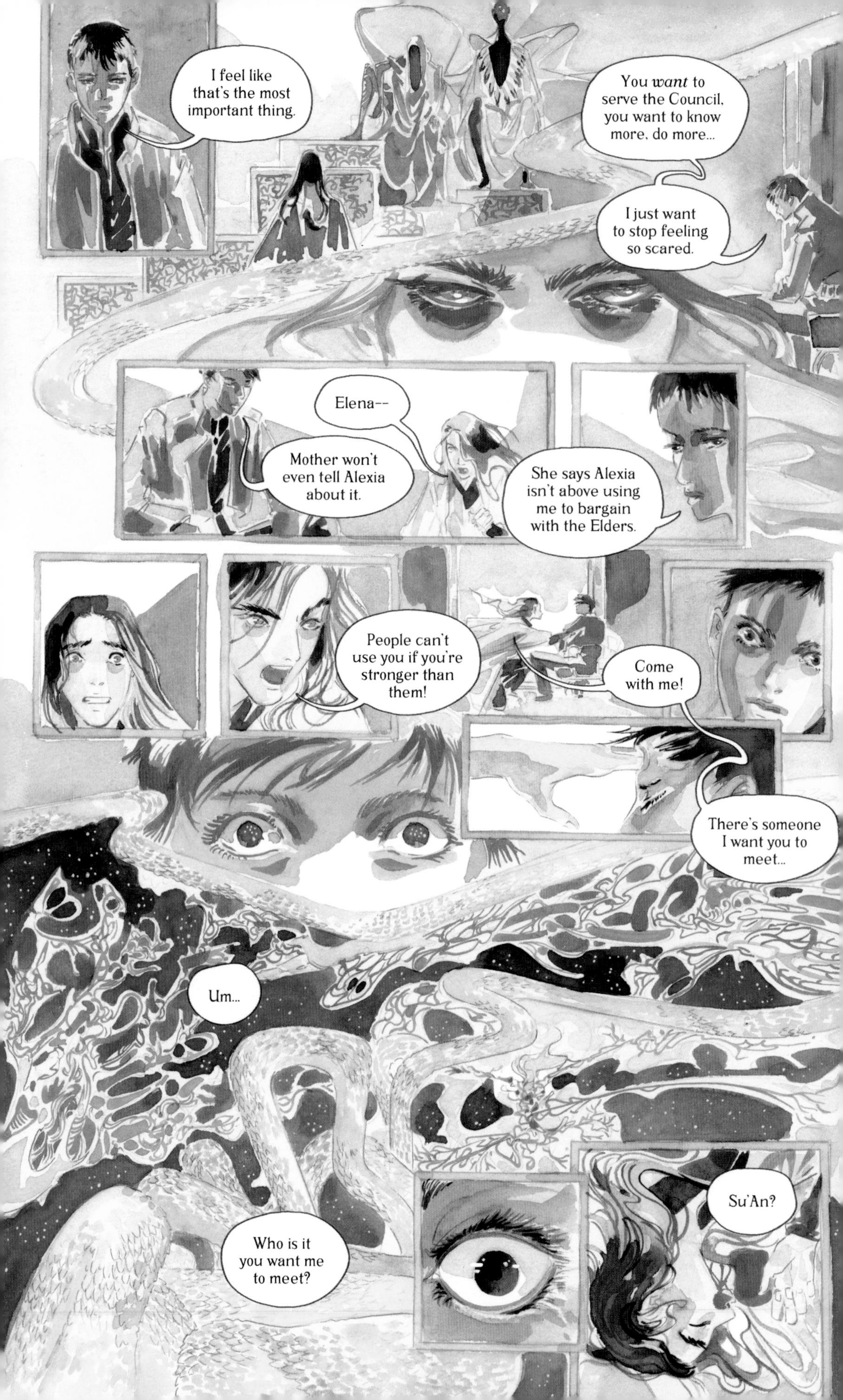
I feel like that's the most important thing.
You *want* to serve the Council, you want to know more, do more...
I just want to stop feeling so scared.
Elena--
Mother won't even tell Alexia about it.
She says Alexia isn't above using me to bargain with the Elders.
People can't use you if you're stronger than them!
Come with me!
There's someone I want you to meet...
Um...
Who is it you want me to meet?
Su'An?

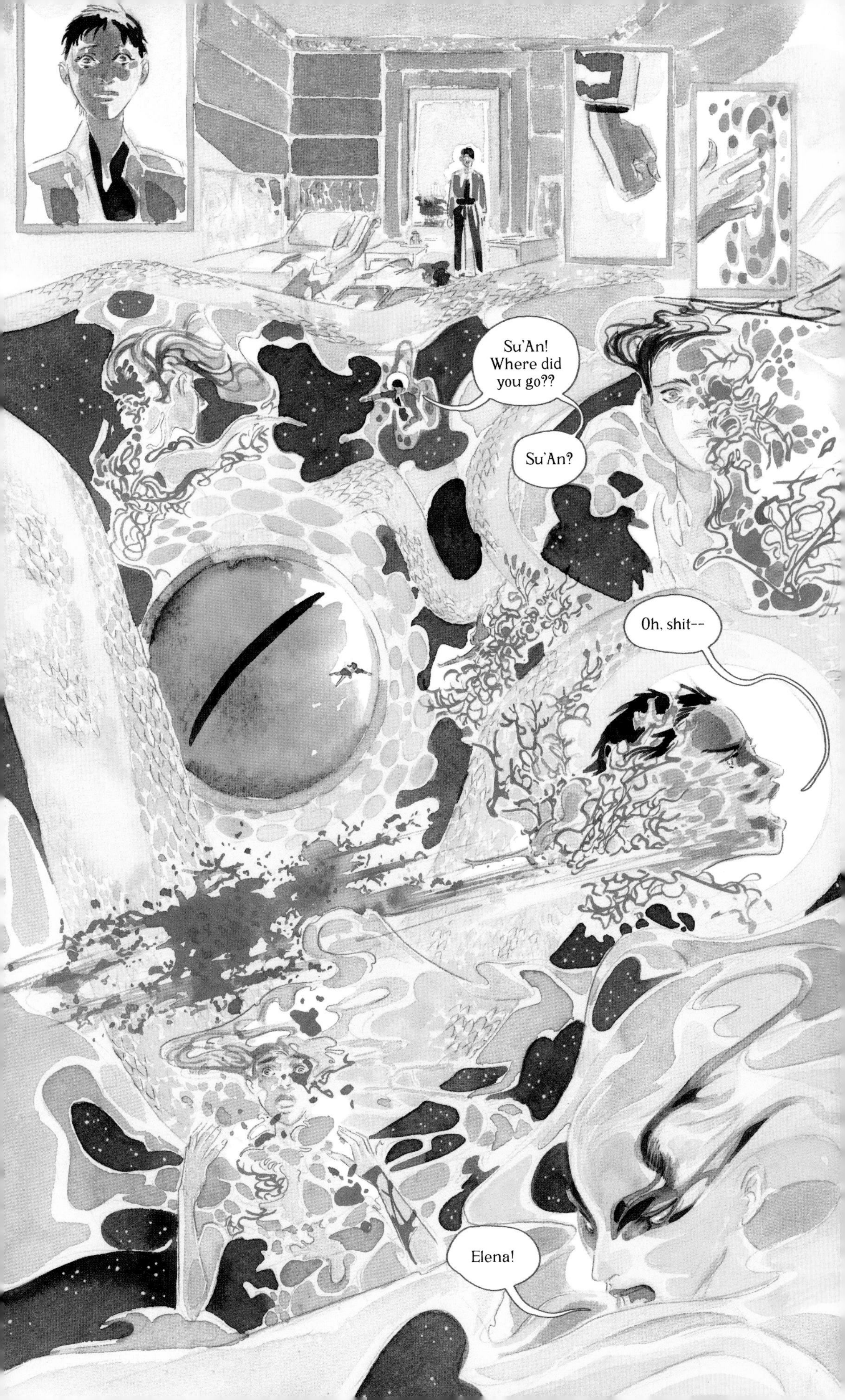
Su'An! Where did you go??
Su'An?
Oh, shit--
Elena!

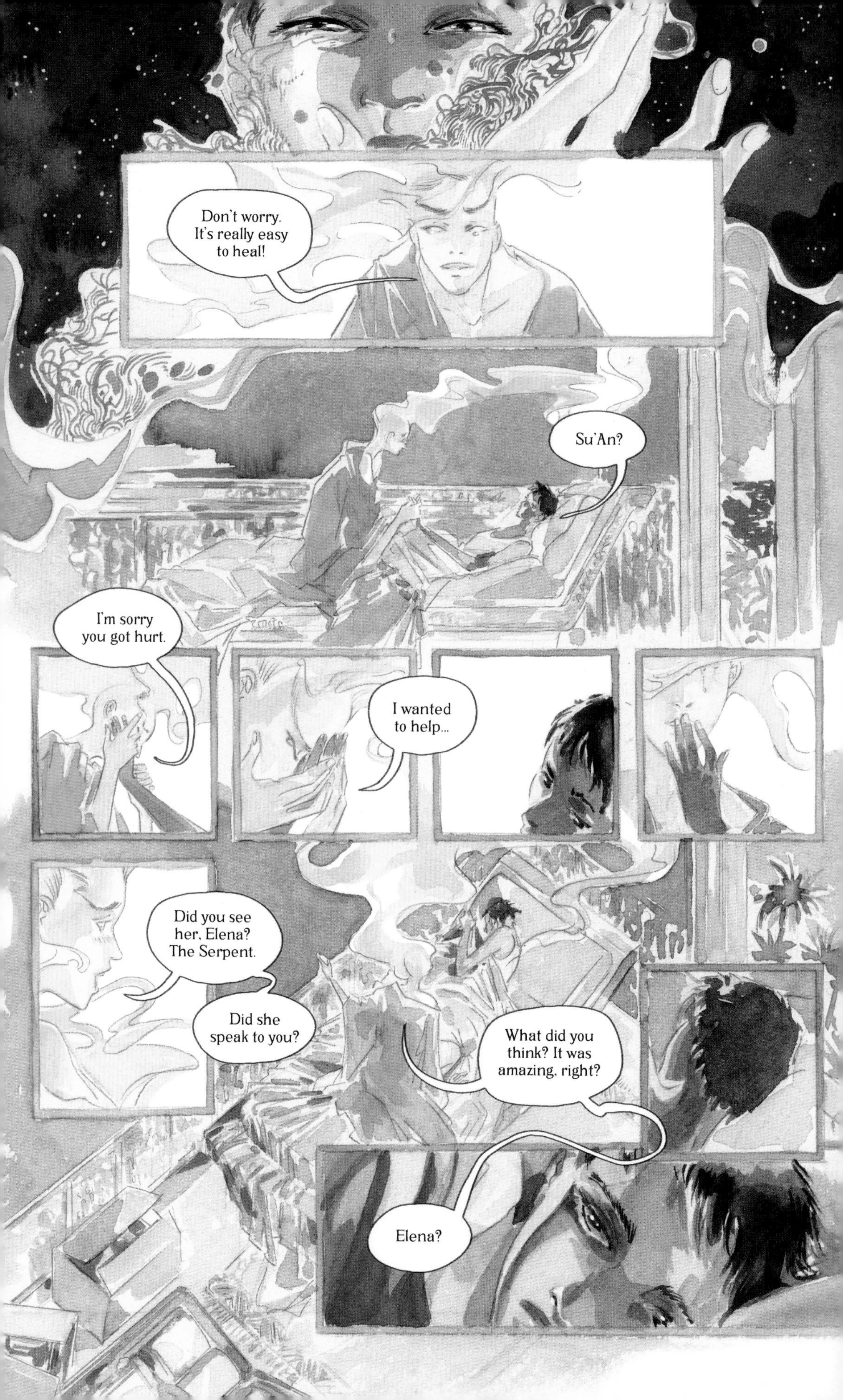
Don't worry. It's really easy to heal!
Su'An?
I'm sorry you got hurt.
I wanted to help...
Did you see her, Elena? The Serpent.
Did she speak to you?
What did you think? It was amazing, right?
Elena?

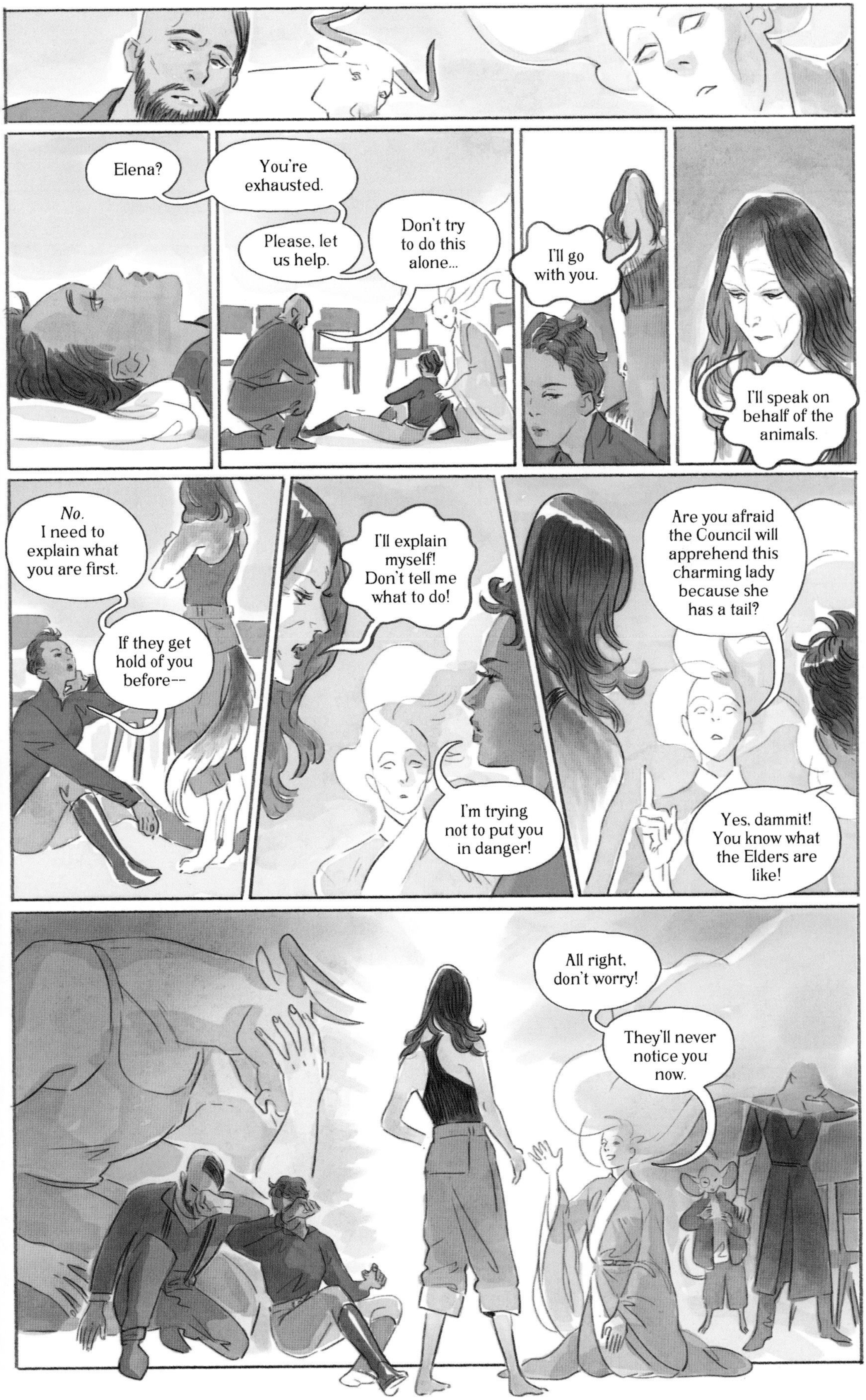
Elena?
You're exhausted.
Please, let us help.
Don't try to do this alone...
I'll go with you.
I'll speak on behalf of the animals.
No. I need to explain what you are first.
If they get hold of you before--
I'll explain myself! Don't tell me what to do!
I'm trying not to put you in danger!
Are you afraid the Council will apprehend this charming lady because she has a tail?
Yes, dammit! You know what the Elders are like!
All right, don't worry!
They'll never notice you now.

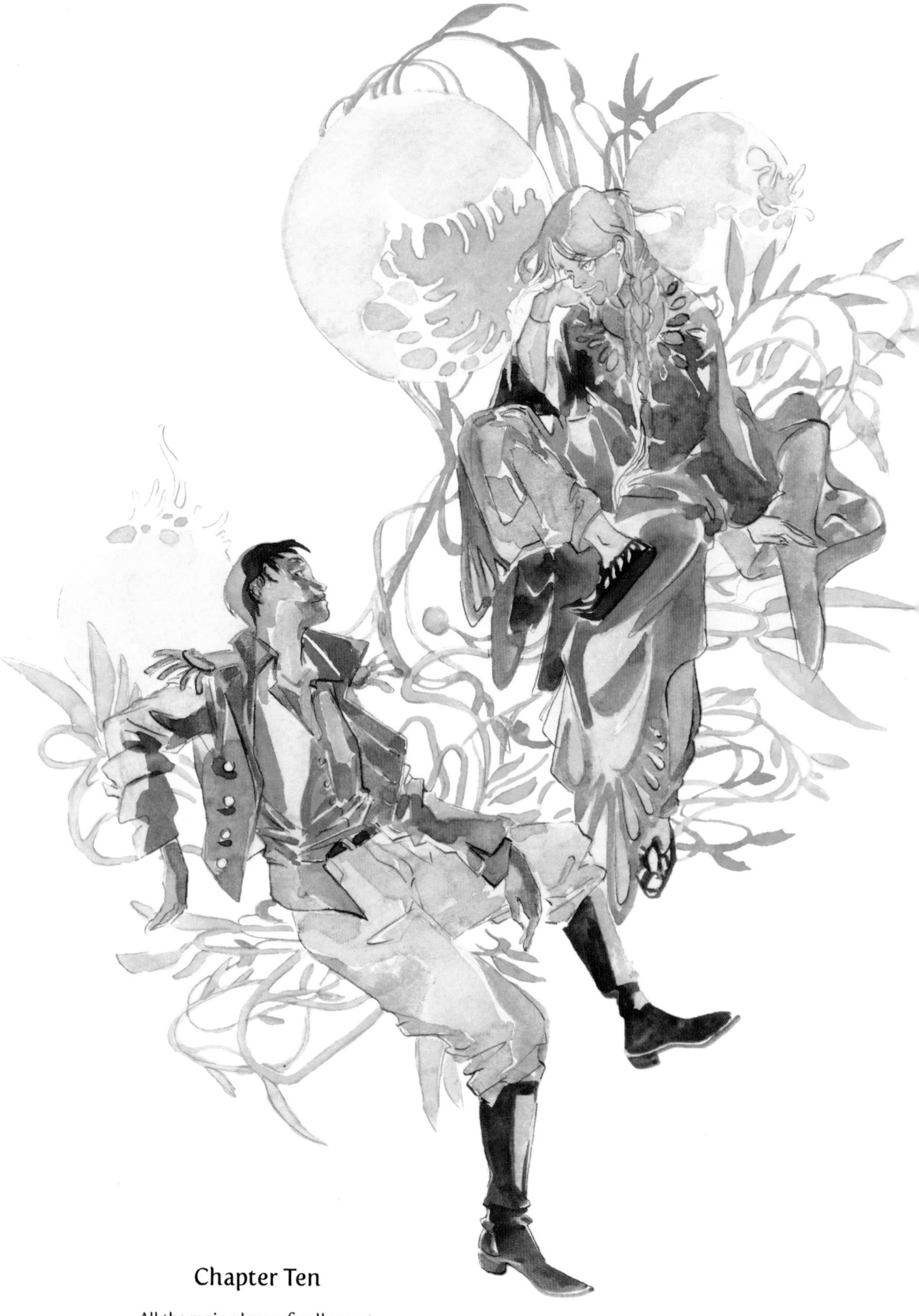

Chapter Ten

All the main players finally meet.

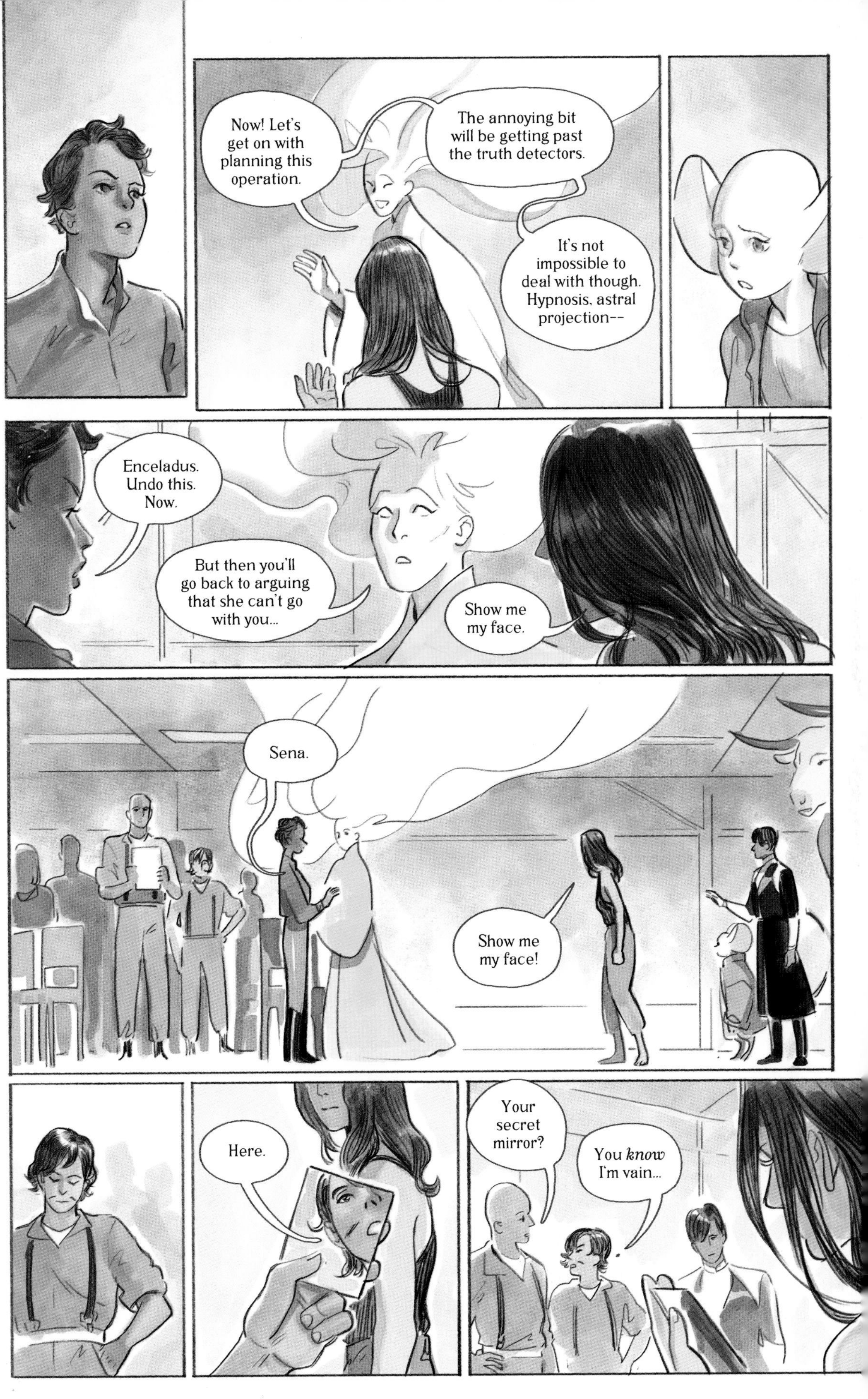
Now! Let's get on with planning this operation.
The annoying bit will be getting past the truth detectors.
It's not impossible to deal with though. Hypnosis, astral projection--
Enceladus. Undo this. Now.
But then you'll go back to arguing that she can't go with you...
Show me my face.
Sena.
Show me my face!
Here.
Your secret mirror?
You *know* I'm vain...

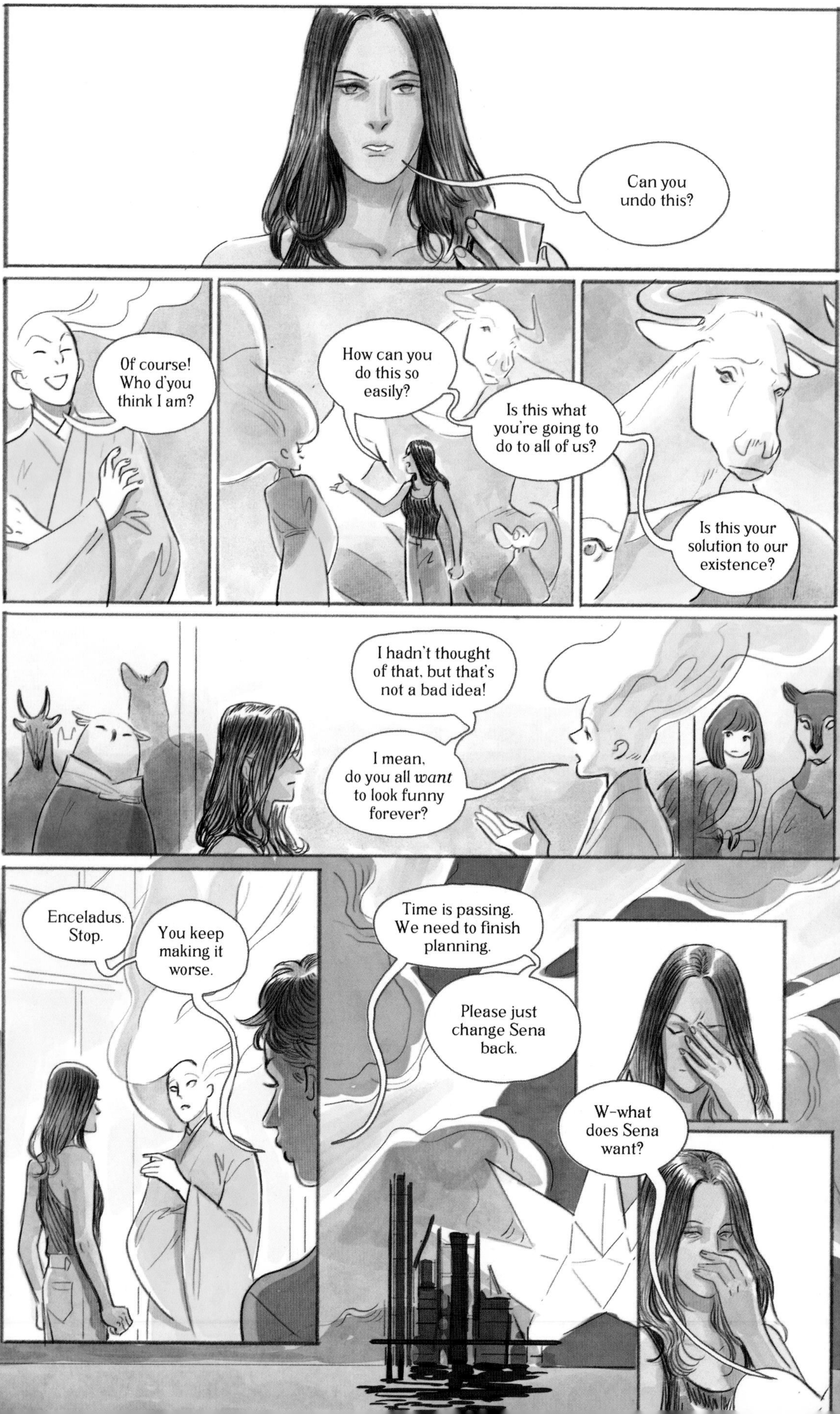
Can you undo this?
Of course! Who d'you think I am?
How can you do this so easily?
Is this what you're going to do to all of us?
Is this your solution to our existence?
I hadn't thought of that, but that's not a bad idea!
I mean, do you all *want* to look funny forever?
Enceladus. Stop.
You keep making it worse.
Time is passing. We need to finish planning.
Please just change Sena back.
W-what does Sena want?

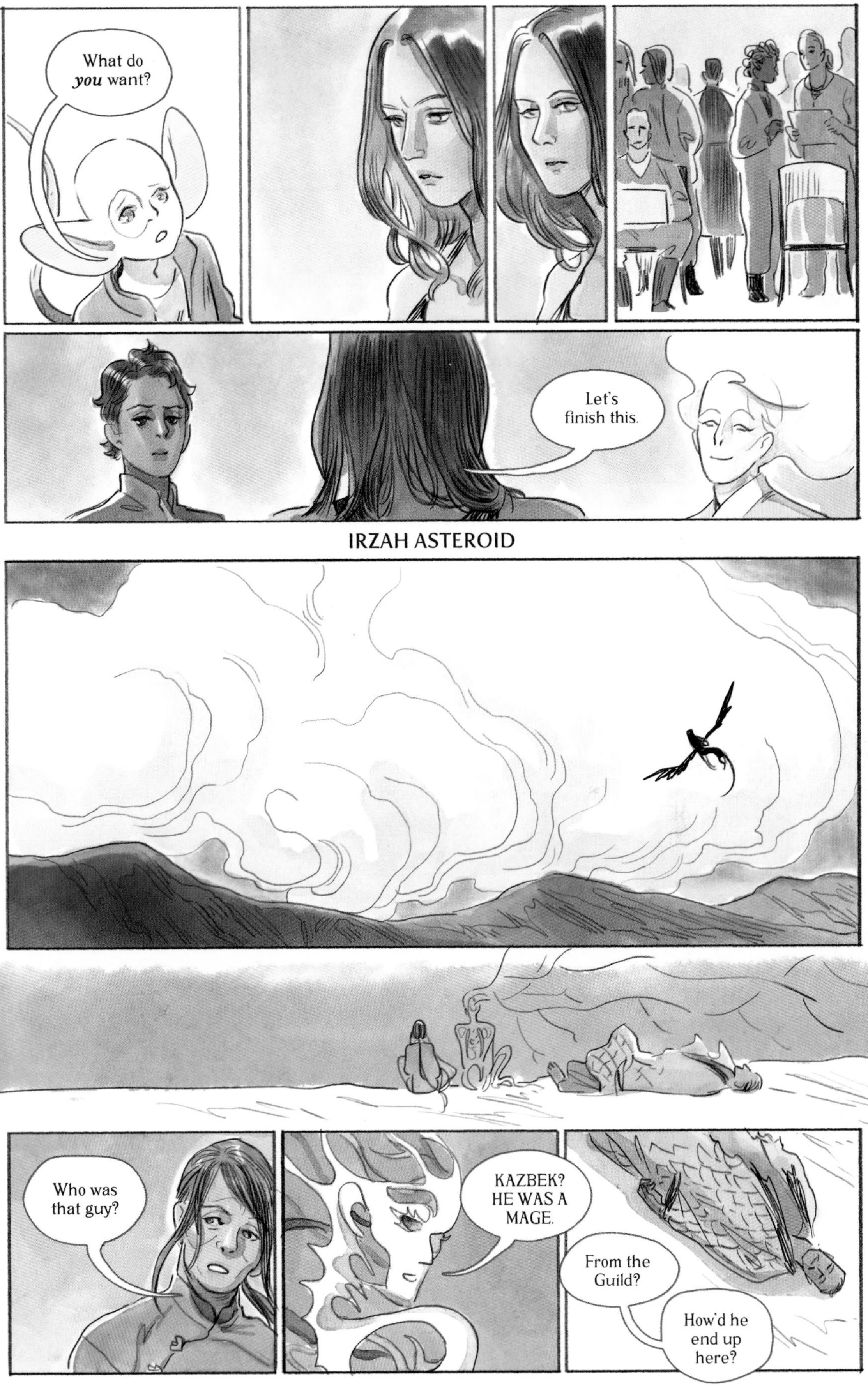
What do *you* want?
Let's finish this.
IRZAH ASTEROID
Who was that guy?
KAZBEK? HE WAS A MAGE.
From the Guild?
How'd he end up here?

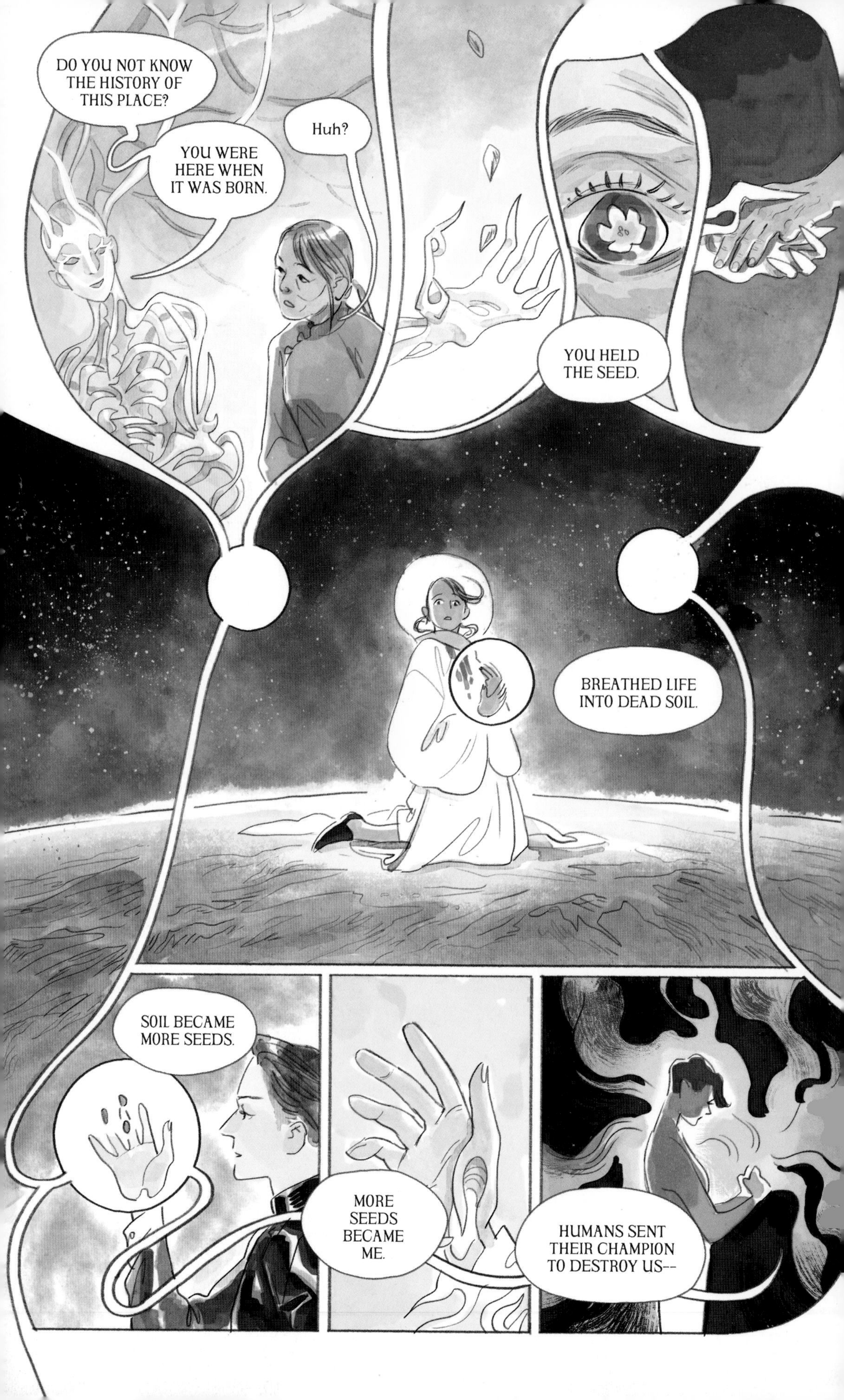
DO YOU NOT KNOW THE HISTORY OF THIS PLACE?
YOU WERE HERE WHEN IT WAS BORN.
Huh?
YOU HELD THE SEED.
BREATHED LIFE INTO DEAD SOIL.
SOIL BECAME MORE SEEDS.
MORE SEEDS BECAME ME.
HUMANS SENT THEIR CHAMPION TO DESTROY US--

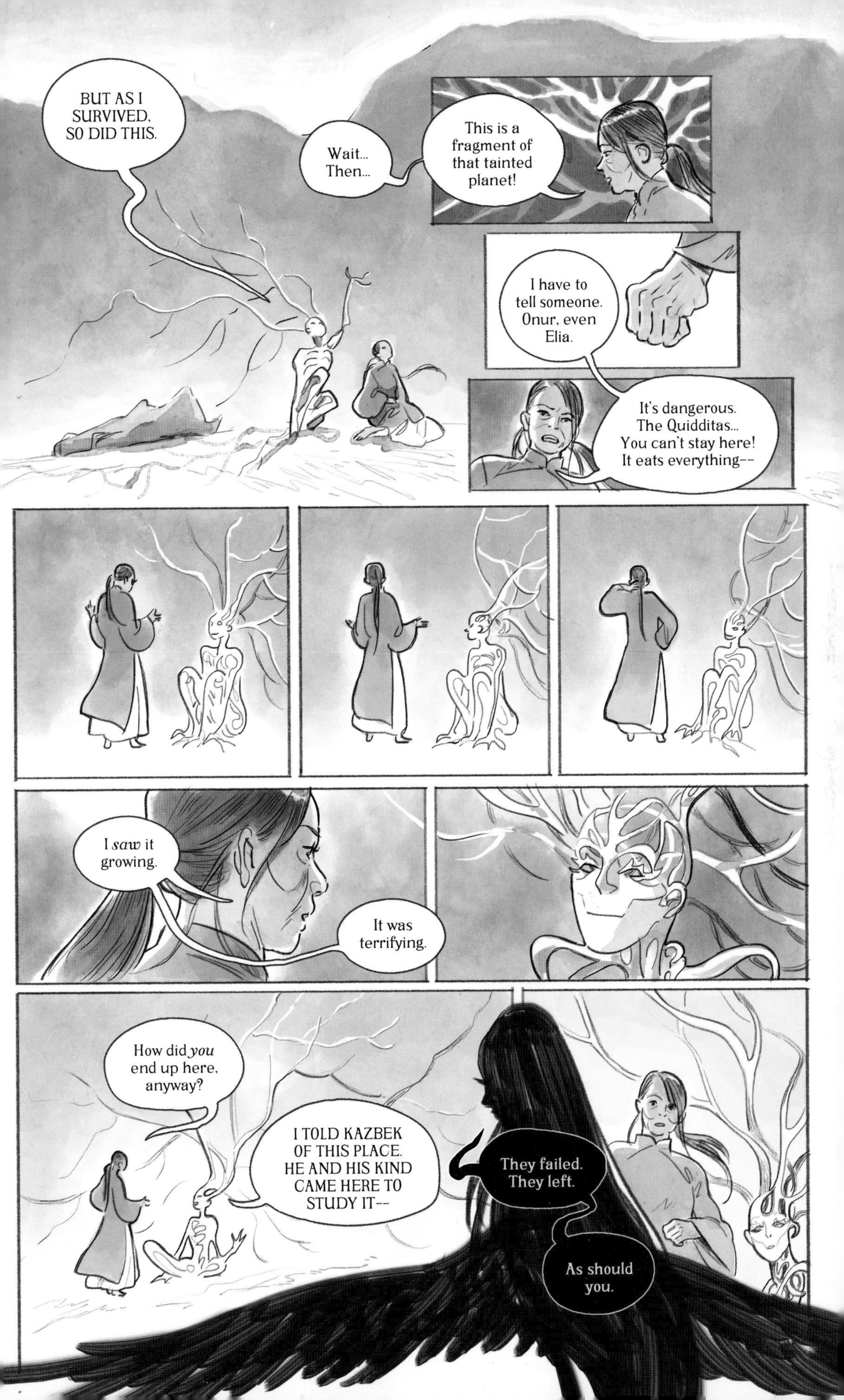
BUT AS I SURVIVED, SO DID THIS.
Wait... Then...
This is a fragment of that tainted planet!
I have to tell someone. Onur, even Elia.
It's dangerous. The Quidditas... You can't stay here! It eats everything--
I *saw* it growing.
It was terrifying.
How did *you* end up here, anyway?
I TOLD KAZBEK OF THIS PLACE. HE AND HIS KIND CAME HERE TO STUDY IT--
They failed. They left.
As should you.

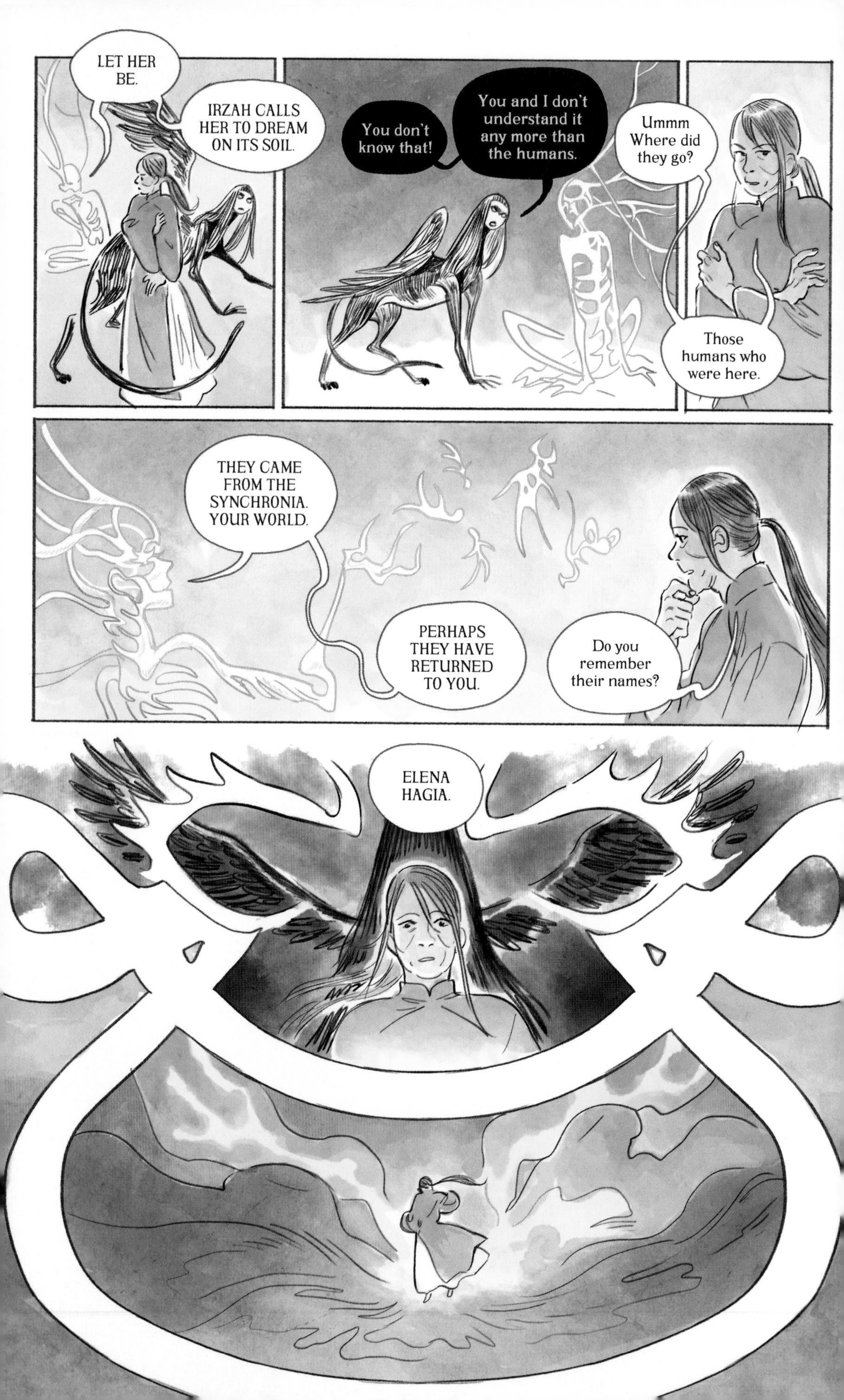
LET HER BE.
IRZAH CALLS HER TO DREAM ON ITS SOIL.
You don't know that!
You and I don't understand it any more than the humans.
Ummm Where did they go?
Those humans who were here.
THEY CAME FROM THE SYNCHRONIA. YOUR WORLD.
PERHAPS THEY HAVE RETURNED TO YOU.
Do you remember their names?
ELENA HAGIA.

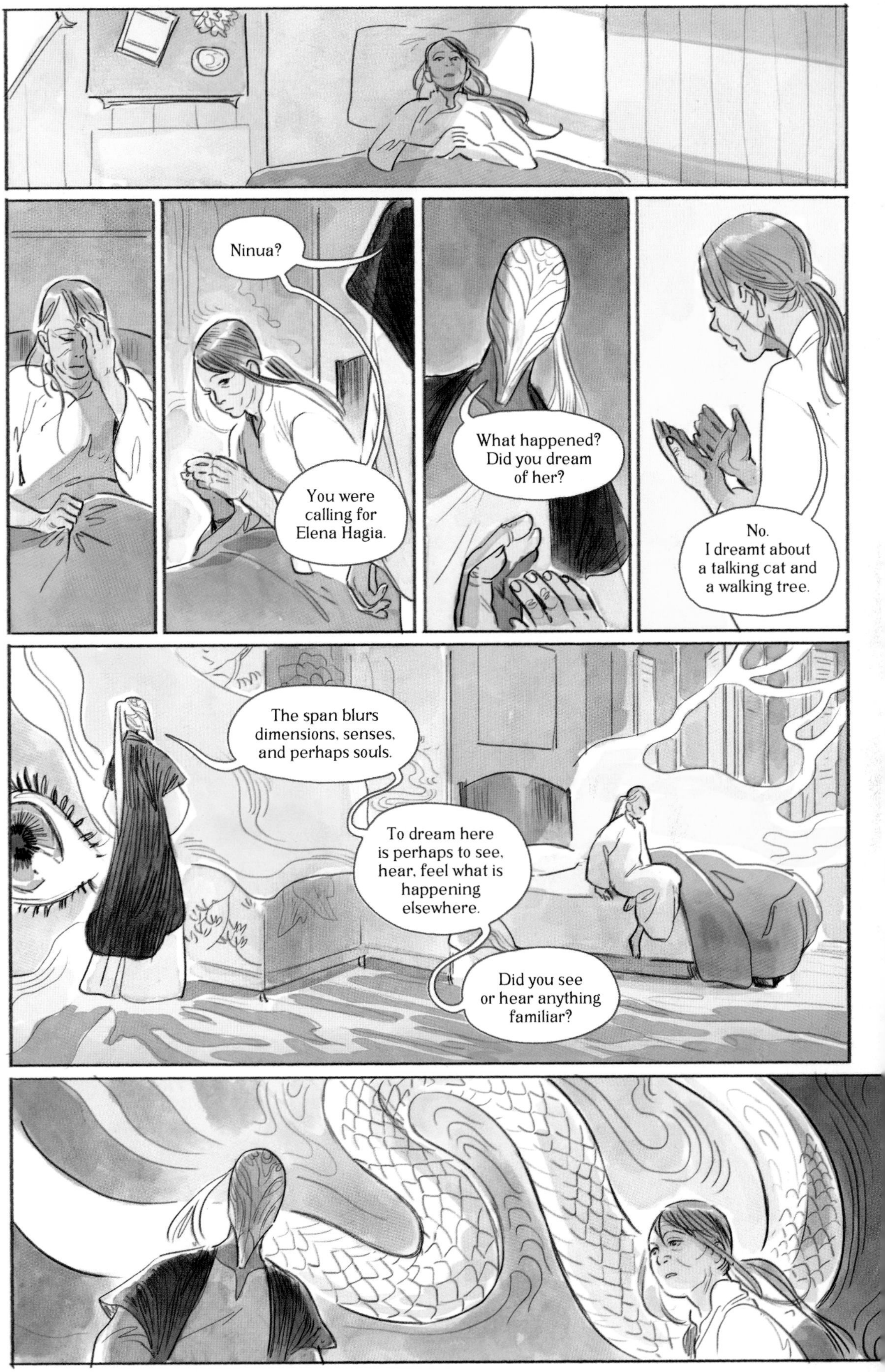
Ninua?
You were calling for Elena Hagia.
What happened? Did you dream of her?
No. I dreamt about a talking cat and a walking tree.
The span blurs dimensions, senses, and perhaps souls.
To dream here is perhaps to see, hear, feel what is happening elsewhere.
Did you see or hear anything familiar?

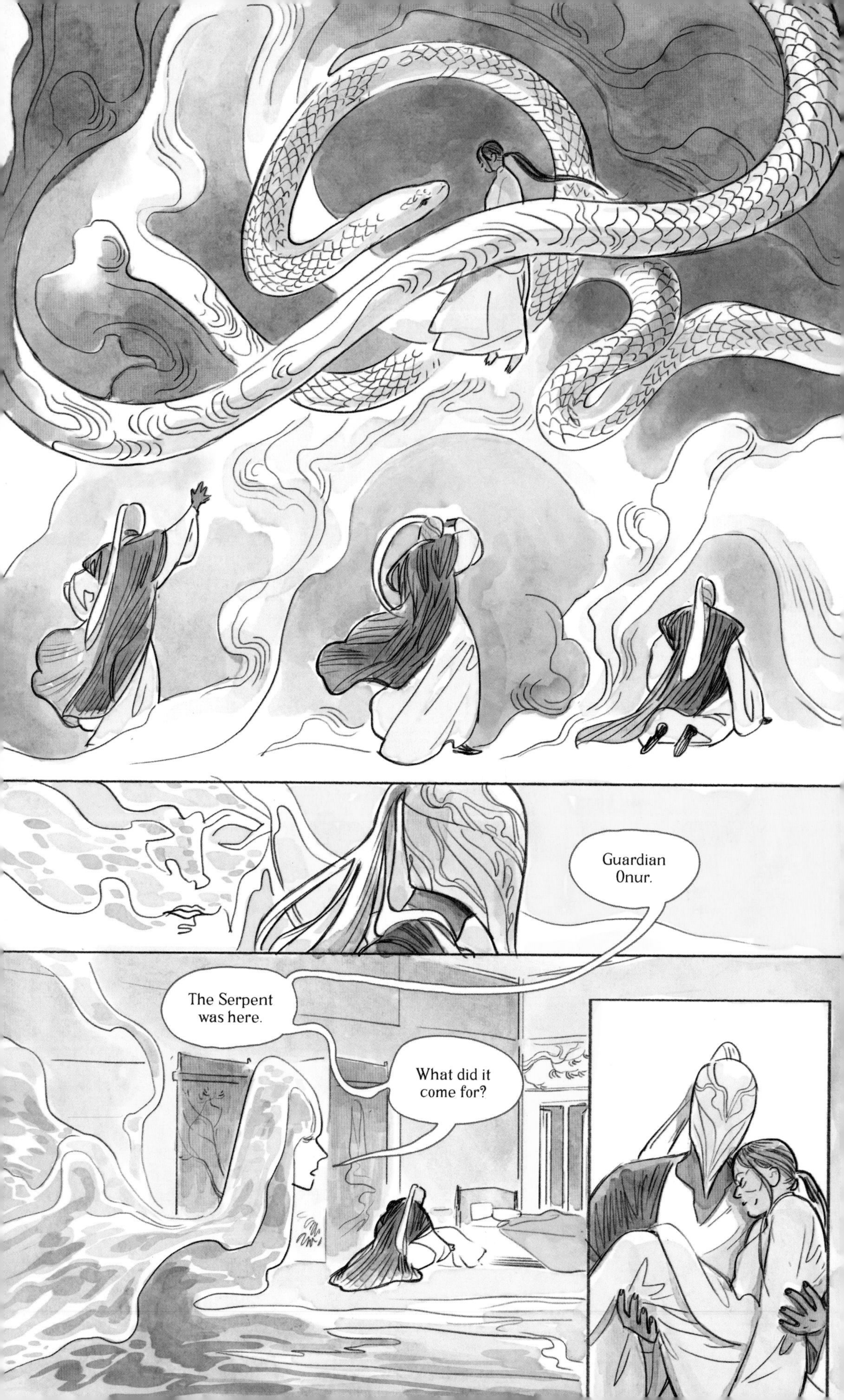
Guardian
Onur.
The Serpent
was here.
What did it
come for?

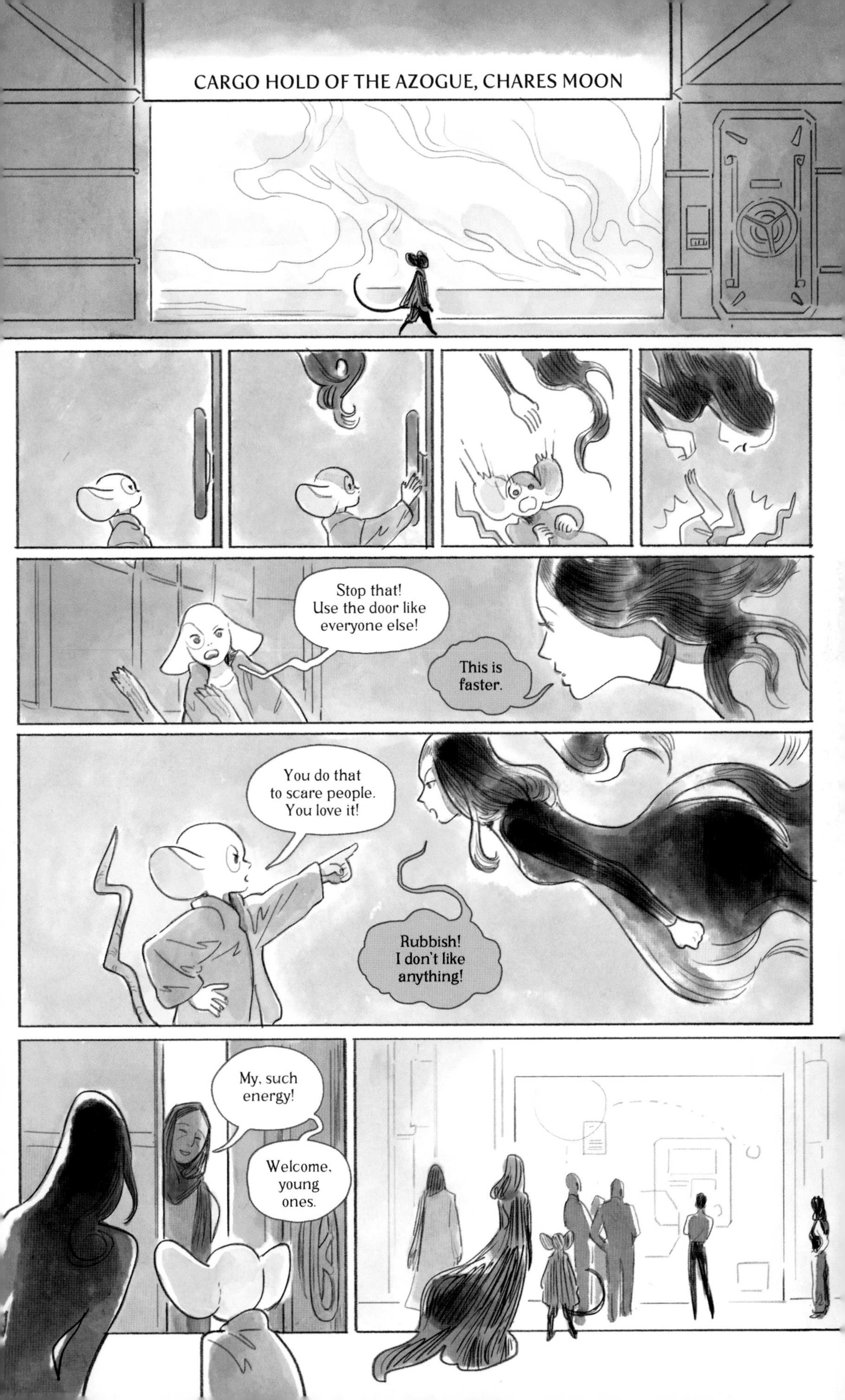
CARGO HOLD OF THE AZOGUE, CHARES MOON
Stop that! Use the door like everyone else!
This is faster.
You do that to scare people. You love it!
Rubbish! I don't like anything!
My, such energy!
Welcome, young ones.

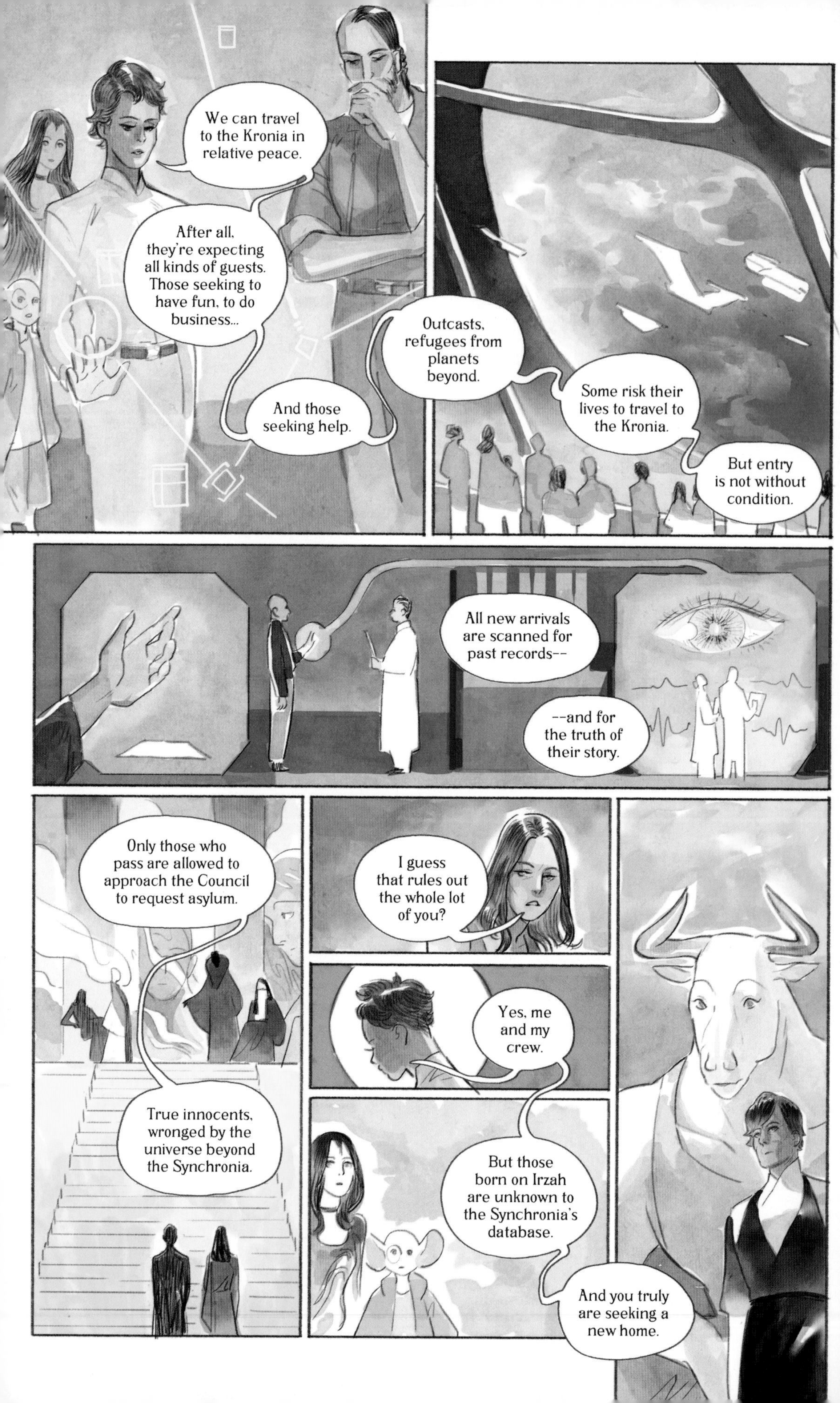
We can travel to the Kronia in relative peace.
After all, they're expecting all kinds of guests. Those seeking to have fun, to do business...
And those seeking help.
Outcasts, refugees from planets beyond.
Some risk their lives to travel to the Kronia.
But entry is not without condition.
All new arrivals are scanned for past records--
--and for the truth of their story.
Only those who pass are allowed to approach the Council to request asylum.
True innocents, wronged by the universe beyond the Synchronia.
I guess that rules out the whole lot of you?
Yes, me and my crew.
But those born on Irzah are unknown to the Synchronia's database.
And you truly are seeking a new home.

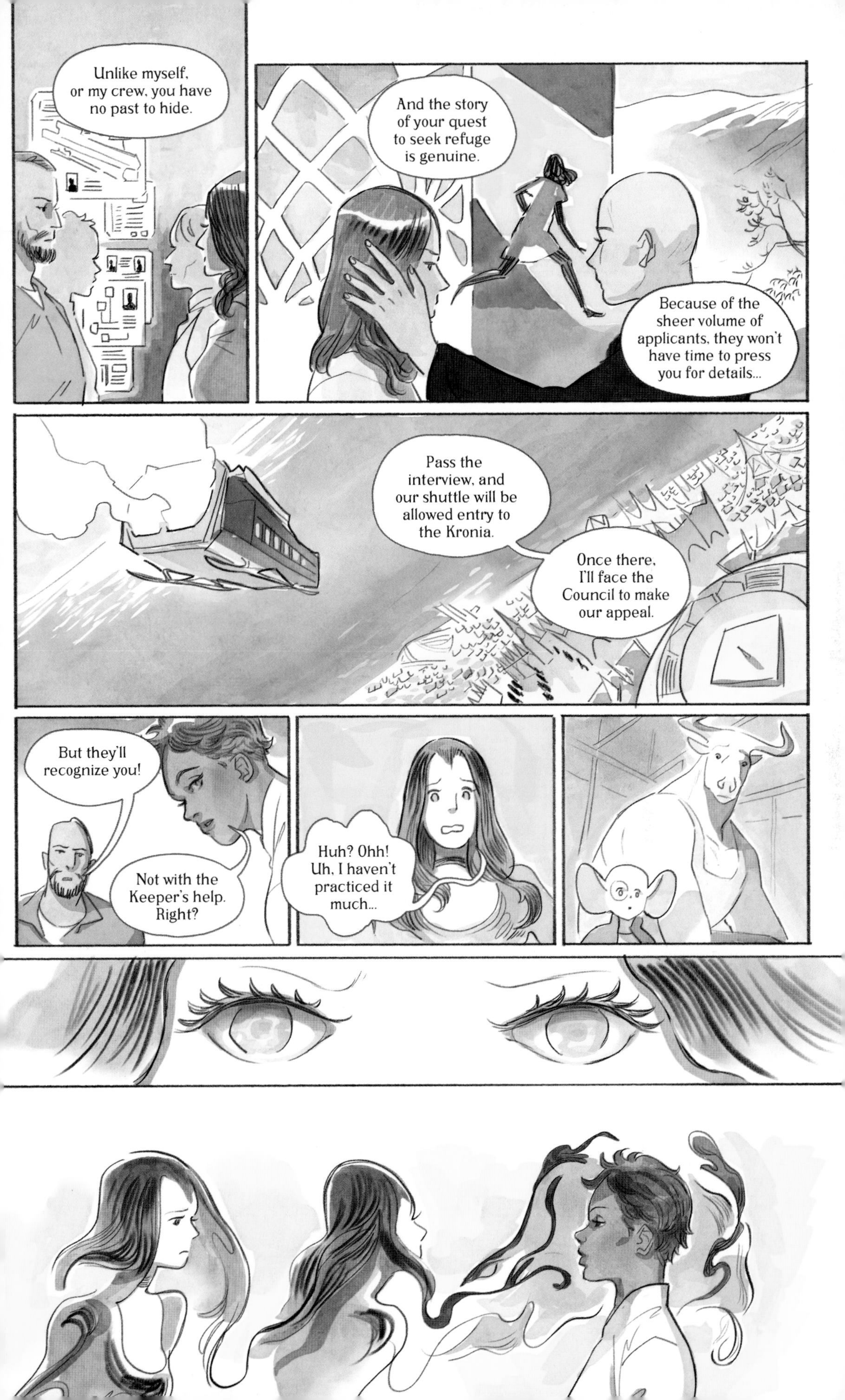
Unlike myself, or my crew, you have no past to hide.
And the story of your quest to seek refuge is genuine.
Because of the sheer volume of applicants, they won't have time to press you for details...
Pass the interview, and our shuttle will be allowed entry to the Kronia.
Once there, I'll face the Council to make our appeal.
But they'll recognize you!
Not with the Keeper's help. Right?
Huh? Ohh! Uh, I haven't practiced it much...

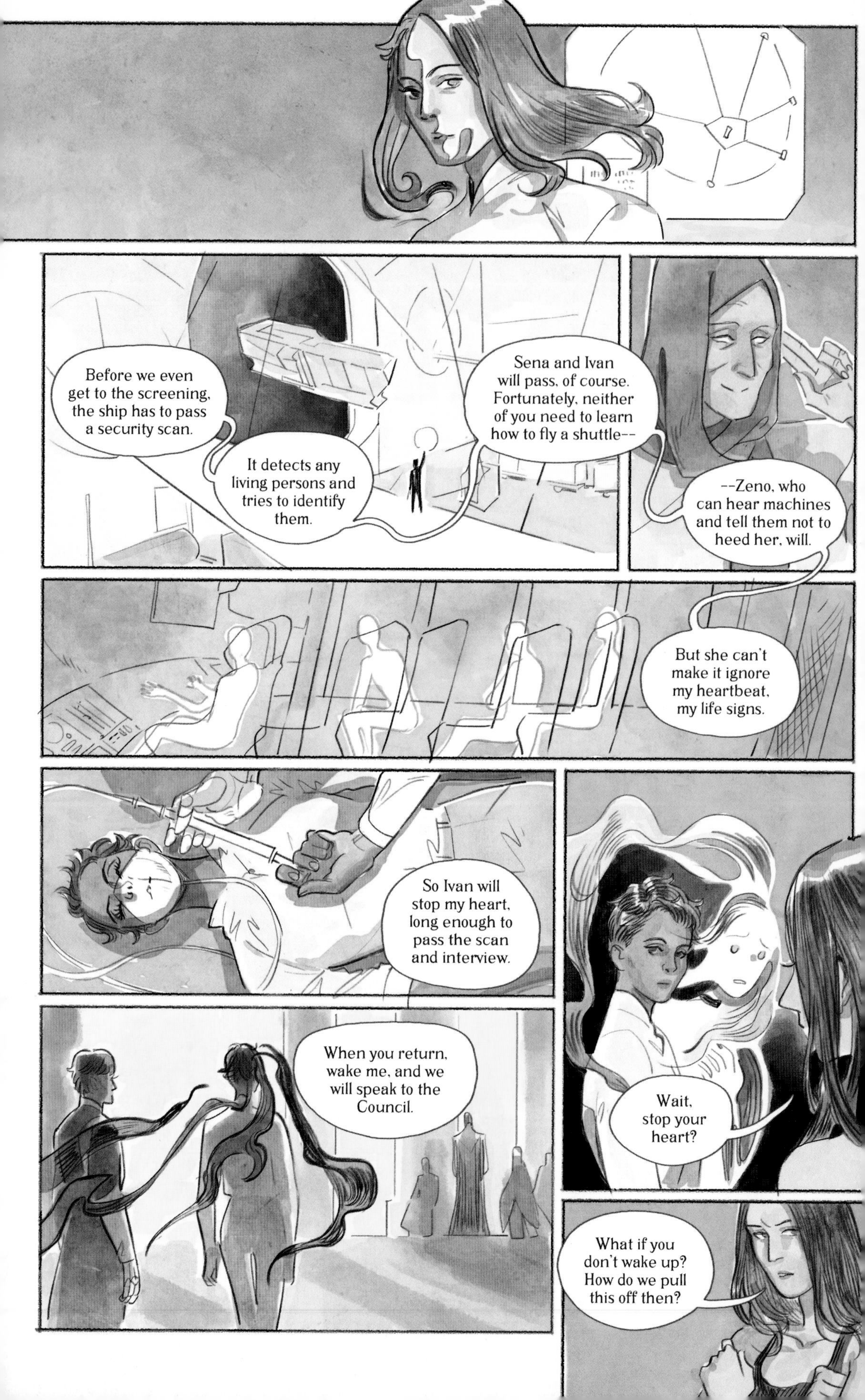
Before we even get to the screening, the ship has to pass a security scan.
It detects any living persons and tries to identify them.
Sena and Ivan will pass, of course. Fortunately, neither of you need to learn how to fly a shuttle--
--Zeno, who can hear machines and tell them not to heed her, will.
But she can't make it ignore my heartbeat, my life signs.
So Ivan will stop my heart, long enough to pass the scan and interview.
Wait, stop your heart?
When you return, wake me, and we will speak to the Council.
What if you don't wake up? How do we pull this off then?

Then it's easier. Show them my body and tell them the truth.

Admiral!!

It won't happen. Have some faith in Ivan!

Have faith in each other.

Come. Let's get ready for the Kronia.

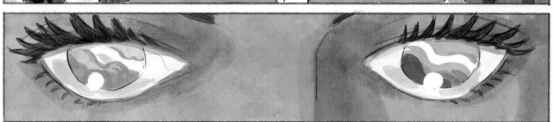

HAGIA RESIDENCE, DIANA, TEMPLE PLANET

It always seems such a waste of time to travel to the Kronia.

Can't we just remotely attend? Isn't that what we developed all this tech for?

Come on, Leto. We didn't build all of this to replace *fun*.

Right, Kybele?

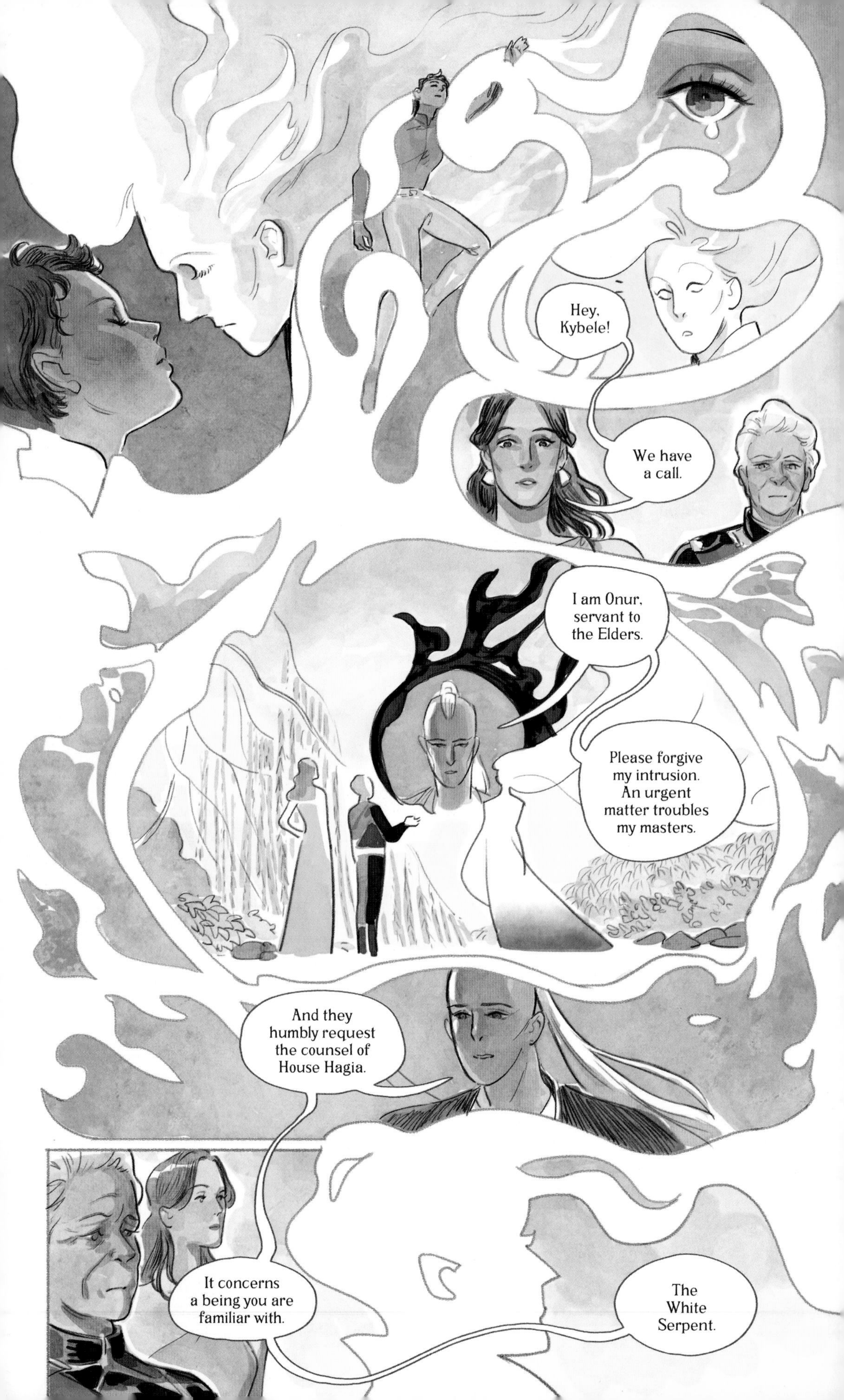
Hey, Kybele!
We have a call.
I am Onur, servant to the Elders.
Please forgive my intrusion. An urgent matter troubles my masters.
And they humbly request the counsel of House Hagia.
It concerns a being you are familiar with.
The White Serpent.

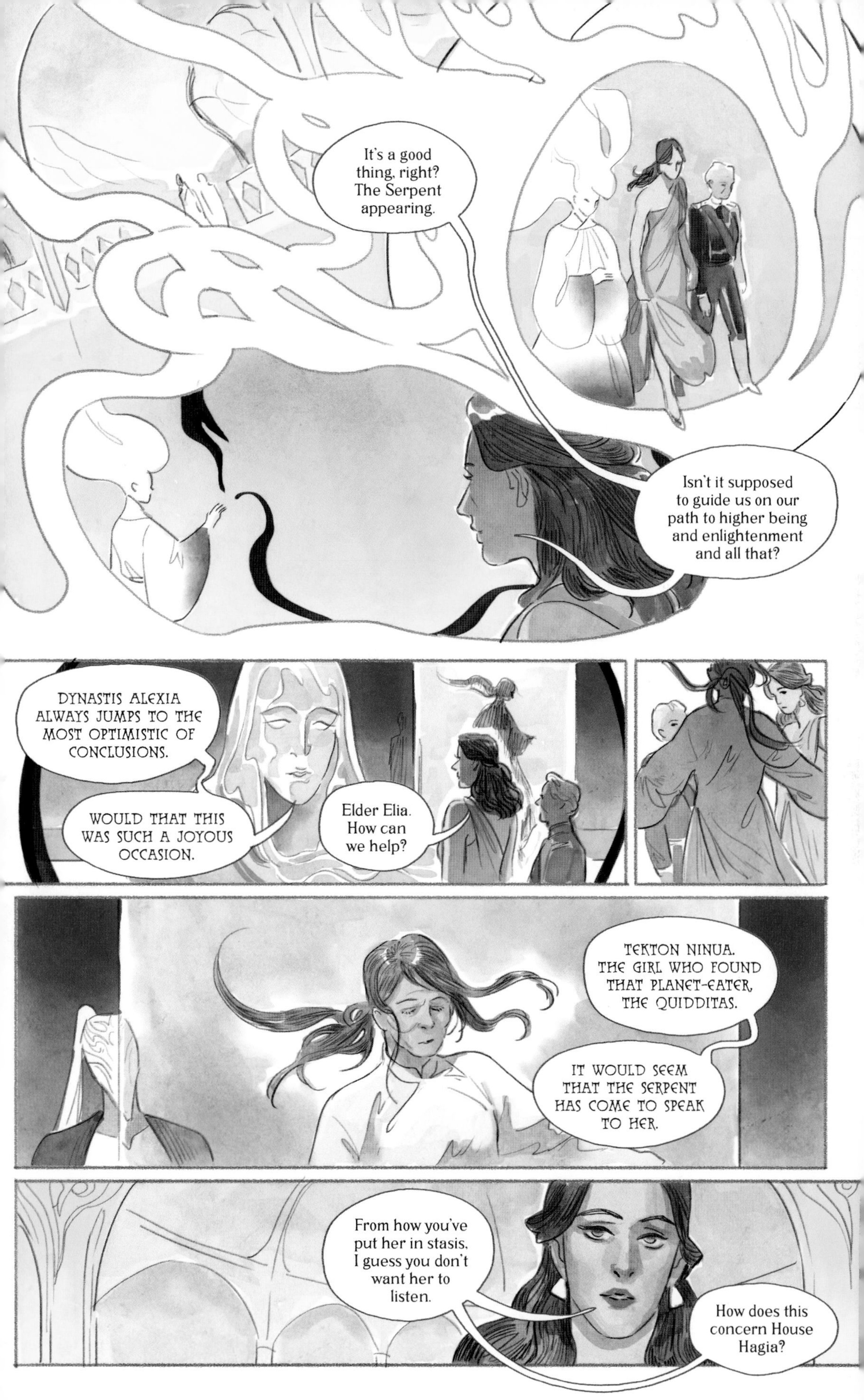
It's a good thing, right? The Serpent appearing.
Isn't it supposed to guide us on our path to higher being and enlightenment and all that?
DYNASTIS ALEXIA ALWAYS JUMPS TO THE MOST OPTIMISTIC OF CONCLUSIONS.
WOULD THAT THIS WAS SUCH A JOYOUS OCCASION.
Elder Elia. How can we help?
TEKTON NINUA. THE GIRL WHO FOUND THAT PLANET-EATER, THE QUIDDITAS.
IT WOULD SEEM THAT THE SERPENT HAS COME TO SPEAK TO HER.
From how you've put her in stasis, I guess you don't want her to listen.
How does this concern House Hagia?

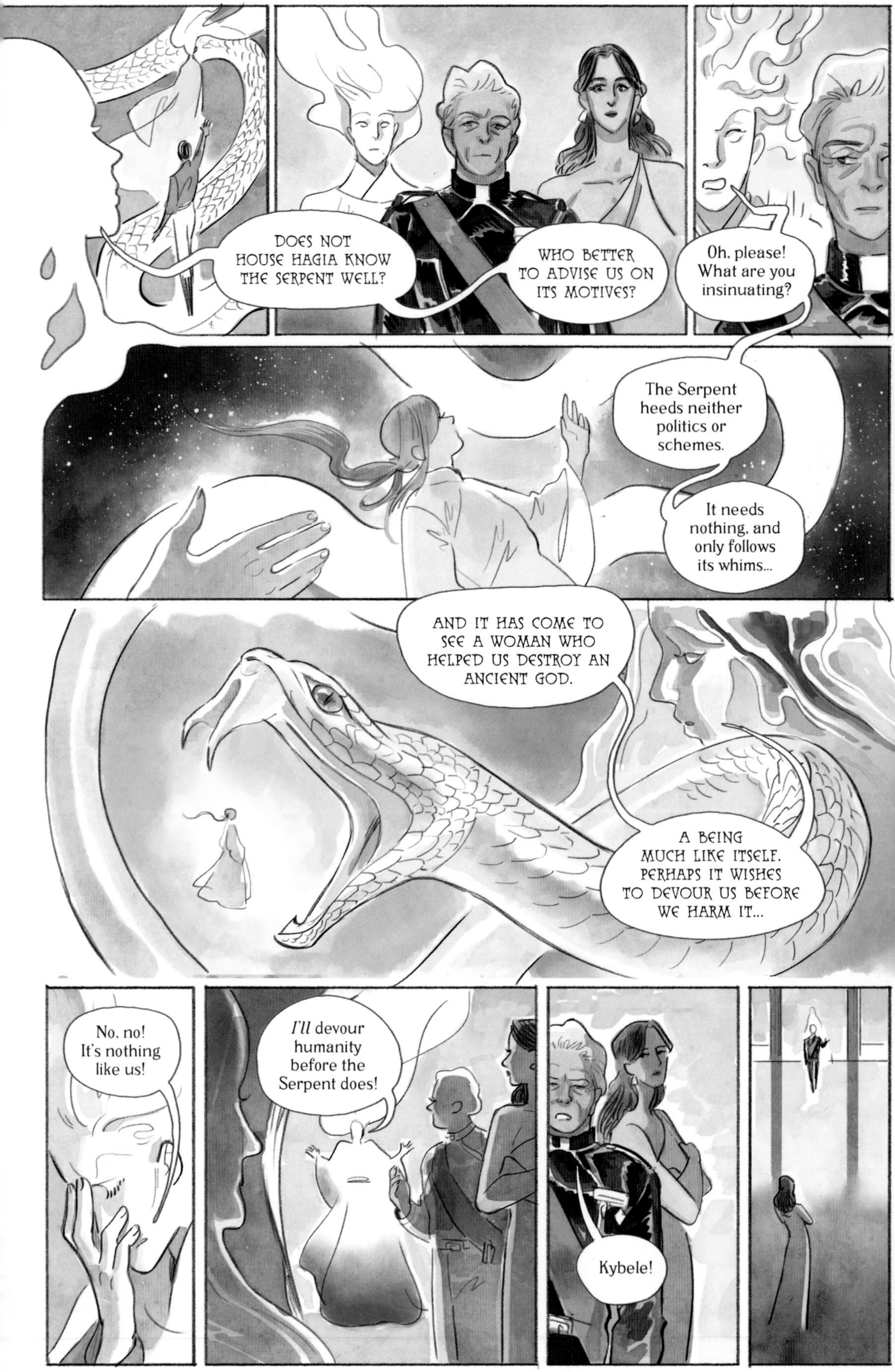
DOES NOT HOUSE HAGIA KNOW THE SERPENT WELL?
WHO BETTER TO ADVISE US ON ITS MOTIVES?
Oh, please! What are you insinuating?
The Serpent heeds neither politics or schemes.
It needs nothing, and only follows its whims...
AND IT HAS COME TO SEE A WOMAN WHO HELPED US DESTROY AN ANCIENT GOD.
A BEING MUCH LIKE ITSELF. PERHAPS IT WISHES TO DEVOUR US BEFORE WE HARM IT...
No, no! It's nothing like us!
I'll devour humanity before the Serpent does!
Kybele!

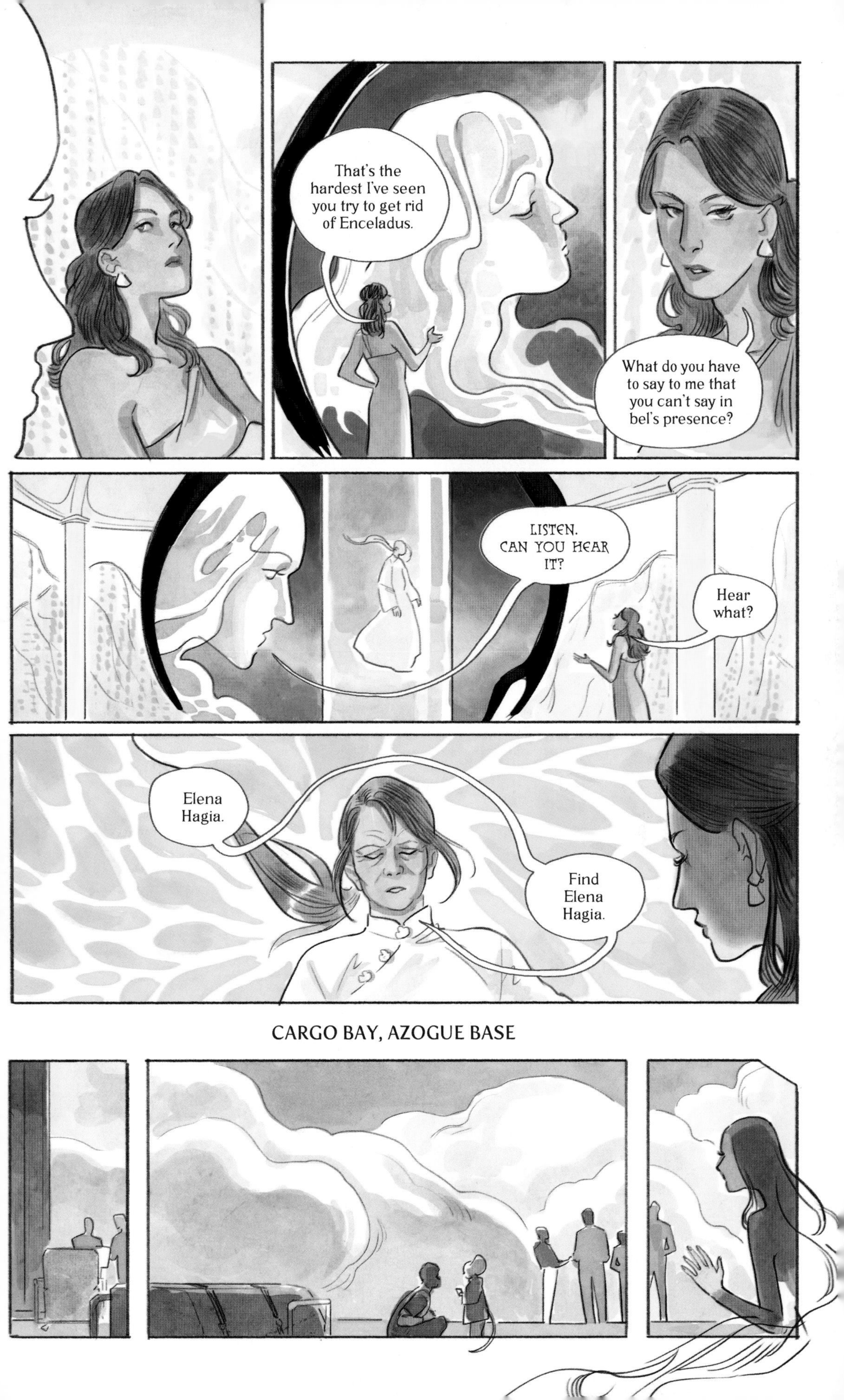
That's the hardest I've seen you try to get rid of Enceladus.
What do you have to say to me that you can't say in bel's presence?
LISTEN. CAN YOU HEAR IT?
Hear what?
Elena Hagia.
Find Elena Hagia.
CARGO BAY, AZOGUE BASE

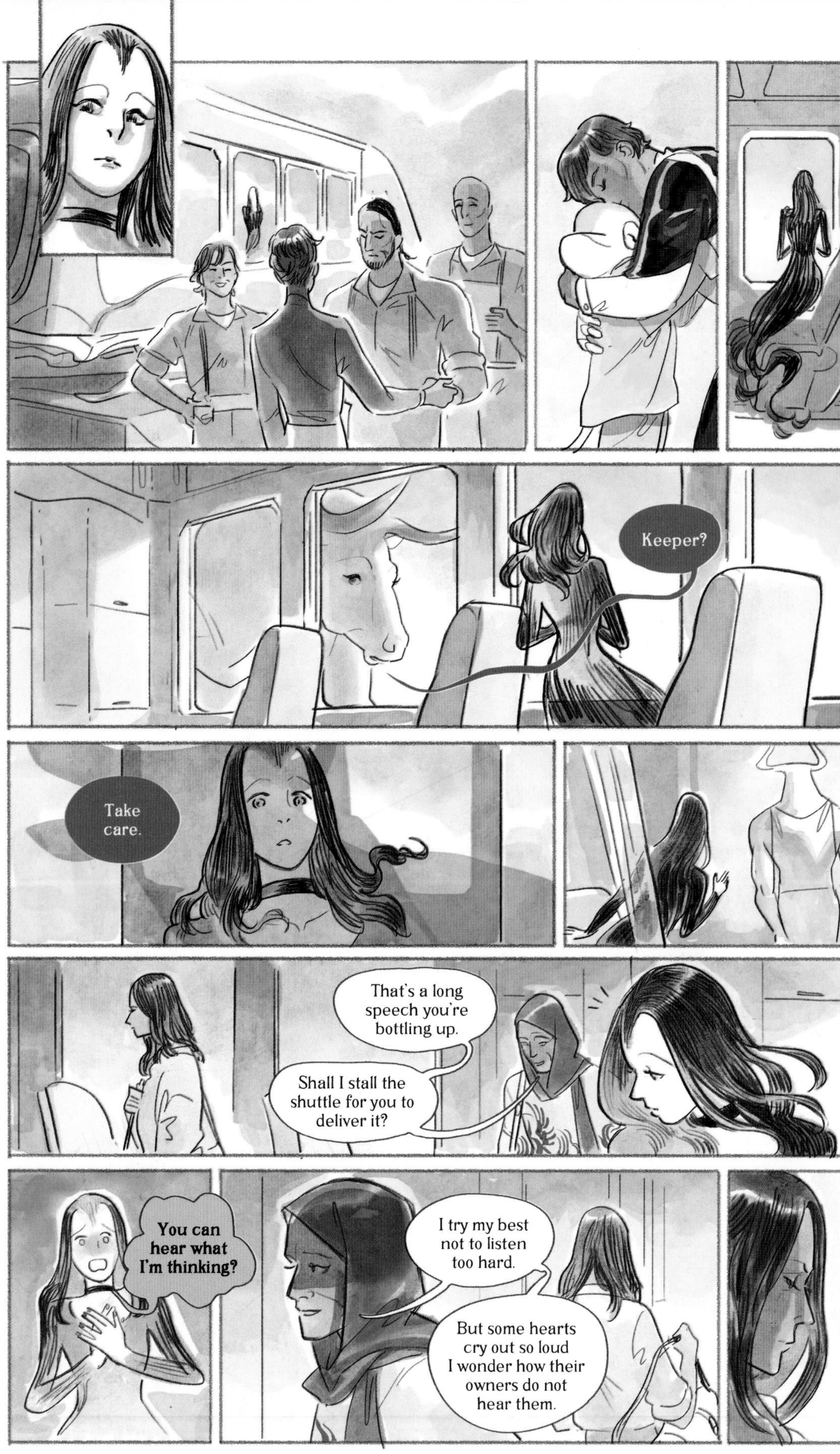
Keeper?
Take care.
That's a long speech you're bottling up.
Shall I stall the shuttle for you to deliver it?
You can hear what I'm thinking?
I try my best not to listen too hard.
But some hearts cry out so loud I wonder how their owners do not hear them.

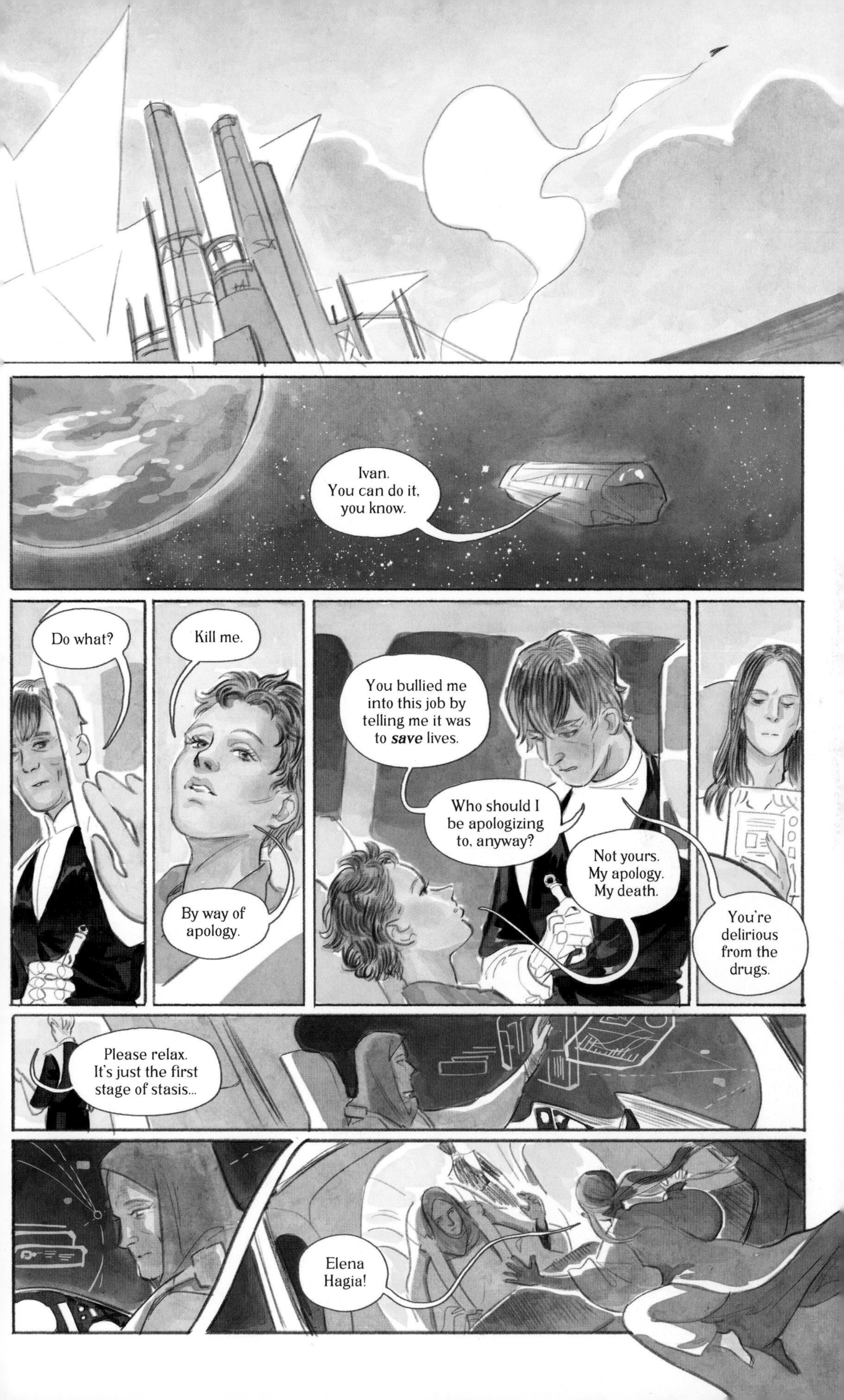
Ivan. You can do it, you know.
Do what?
Kill me.
By way of apology.
You bullied me into this job by telling me it was to *save* lives.
Who should I be apologizing to, anyway?
Not yours. My apology. My death.
You're delirious from the drugs.
Please relax. It's just the first stage of stasis...
Elena Hagia!

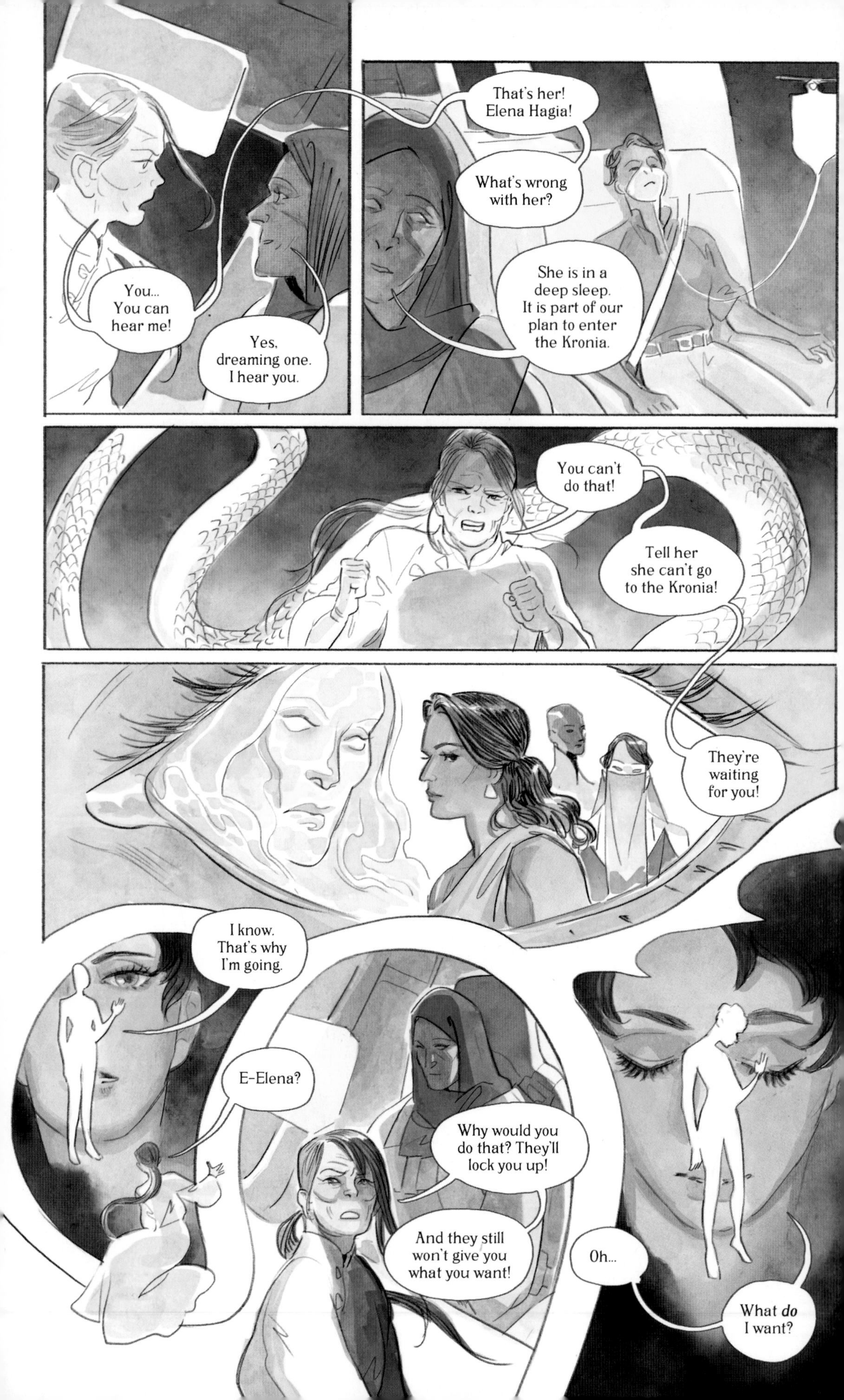
That's her! Elena Hagia!
What's wrong with her?
You... You can hear me!
Yes, dreaming one. I hear you.
She is in a deep sleep. It is part of our plan to enter the Kronia.
You can't do that!
Tell her she can't go to the Kronia!
They're waiting for you!
I know. That's why I'm going.
E-Elena?
Why would you do that? They'll lock you up!
And they still won't give you what you want!
Oh...
What *do* I want?

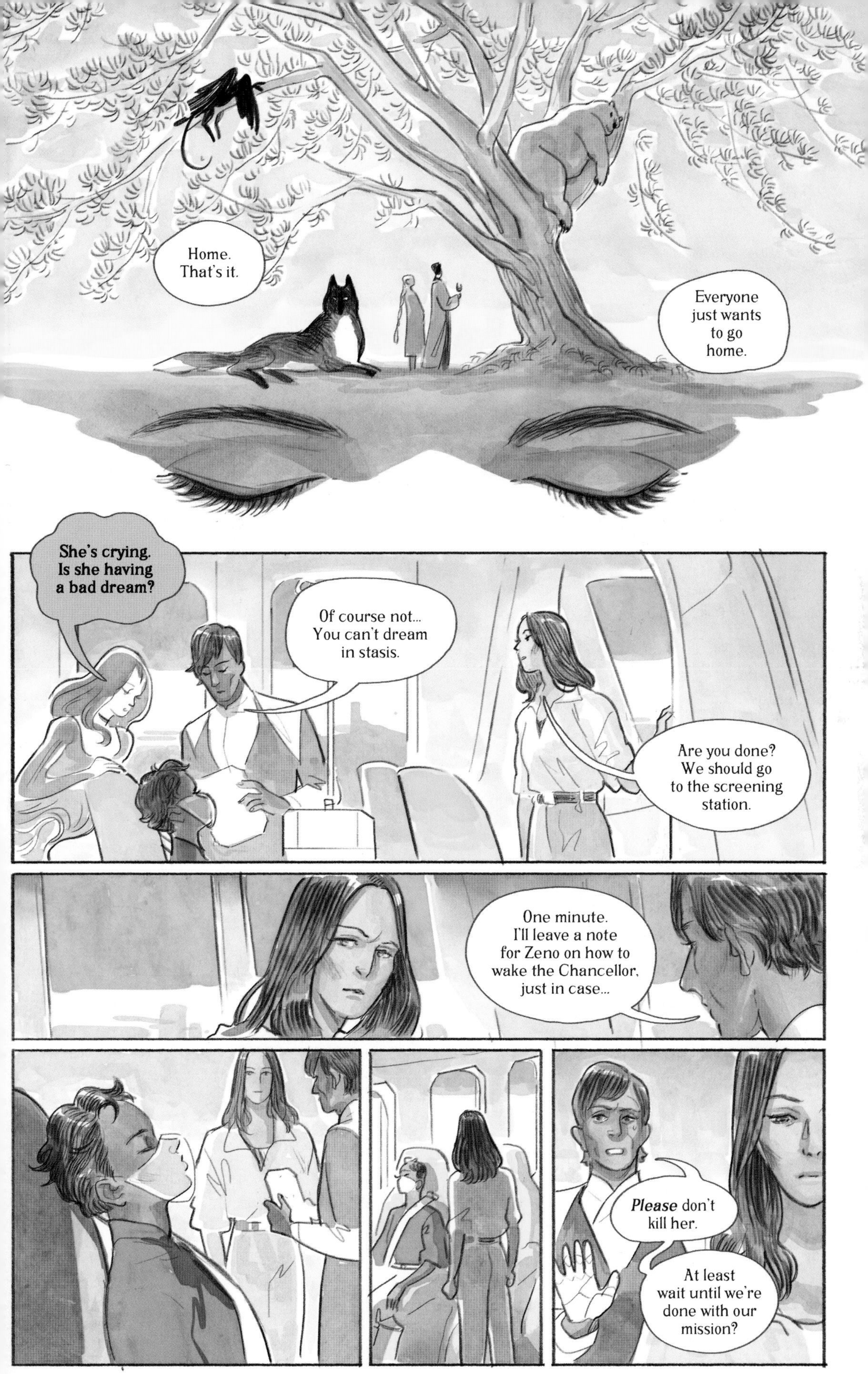
Home.
That's it.
Everyone just wants to go home.
She's crying. Is she having a bad dream?
Of course not... You can't dream in stasis.
Are you done? We should go to the screening station.
One minute. I'll leave a note for Zeno on how to wake the Chancellor, just in case...
Please don't kill her.
At least wait until we're done with our mission?

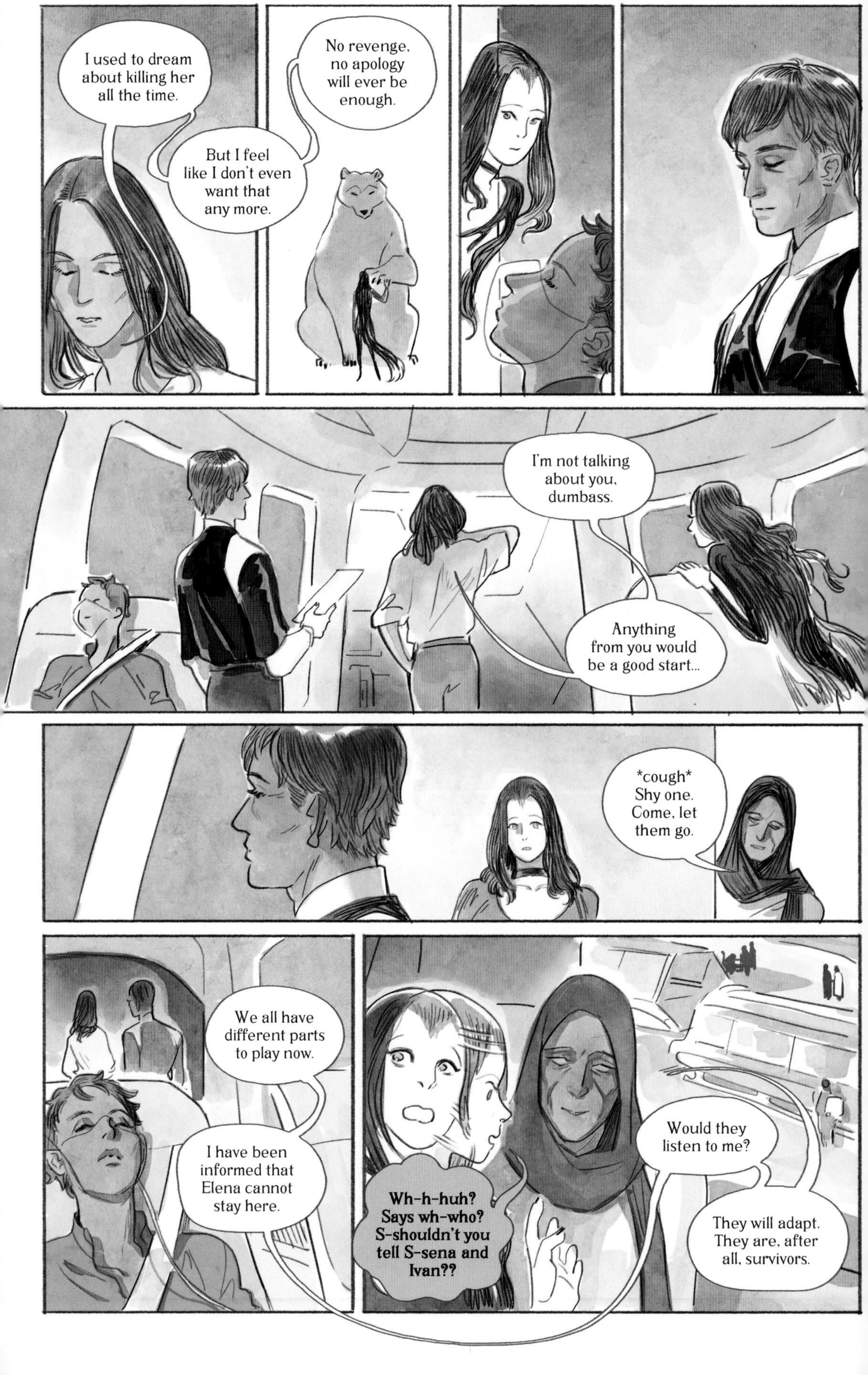
I used to dream about killing her all the time.
But I feel like I don't even want that any more.
No revenge, no apology will ever be enough.
I'm not talking about you, dumbass.
Anything from you would be a good start...
cough Shy one. Come, let them go.
We all have different parts to play now.
I have been informed that Elena cannot stay here.
Wh-h-huh? Says wh-who? S-shouldn't you tell S-sena and Ivan??
Would they listen to me?
They will adapt. They are, after all, survivors.

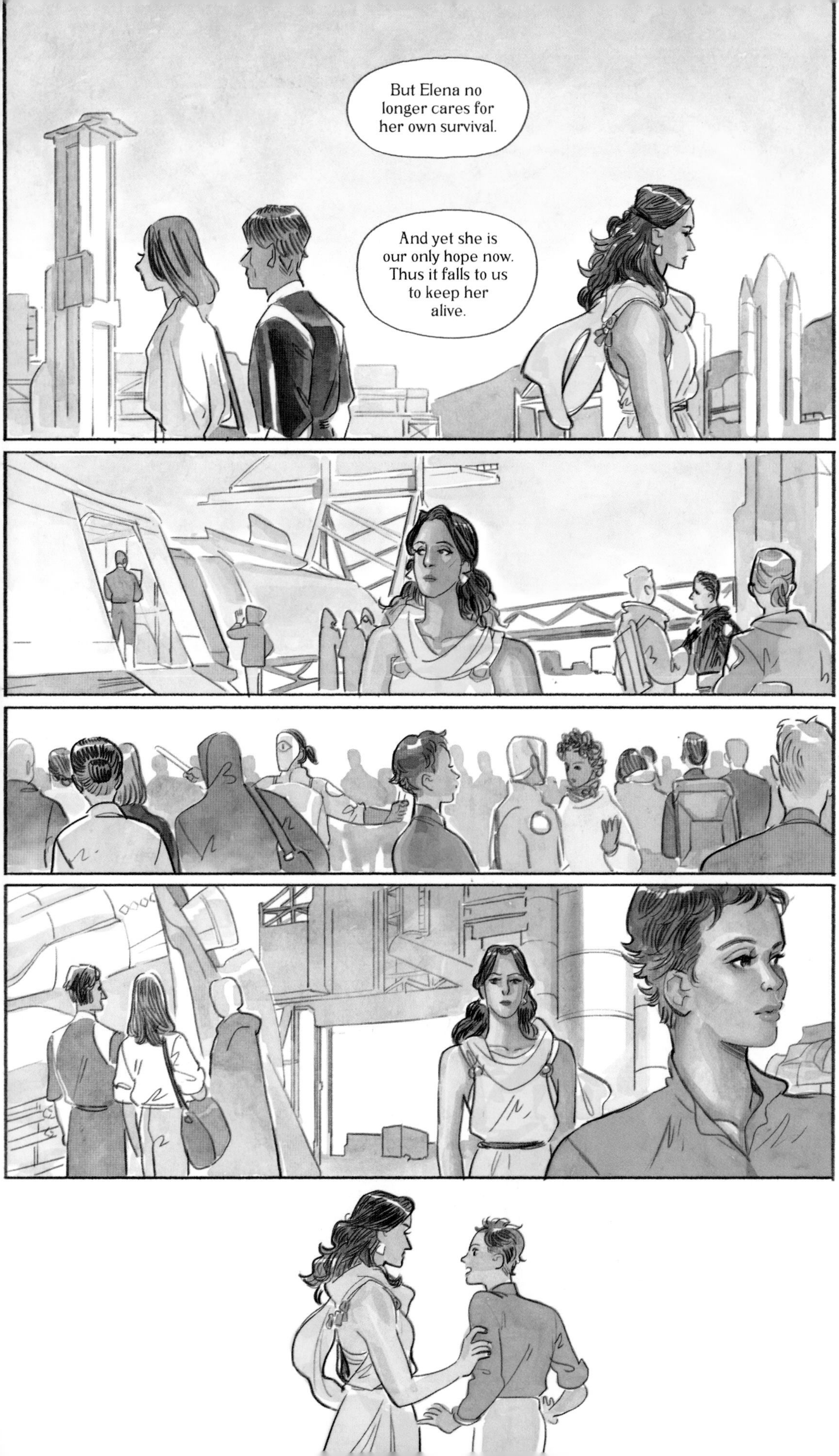

But Elena no longer cares for her own survival.
And yet she is our only hope now. Thus it falls to us to keep her alive.

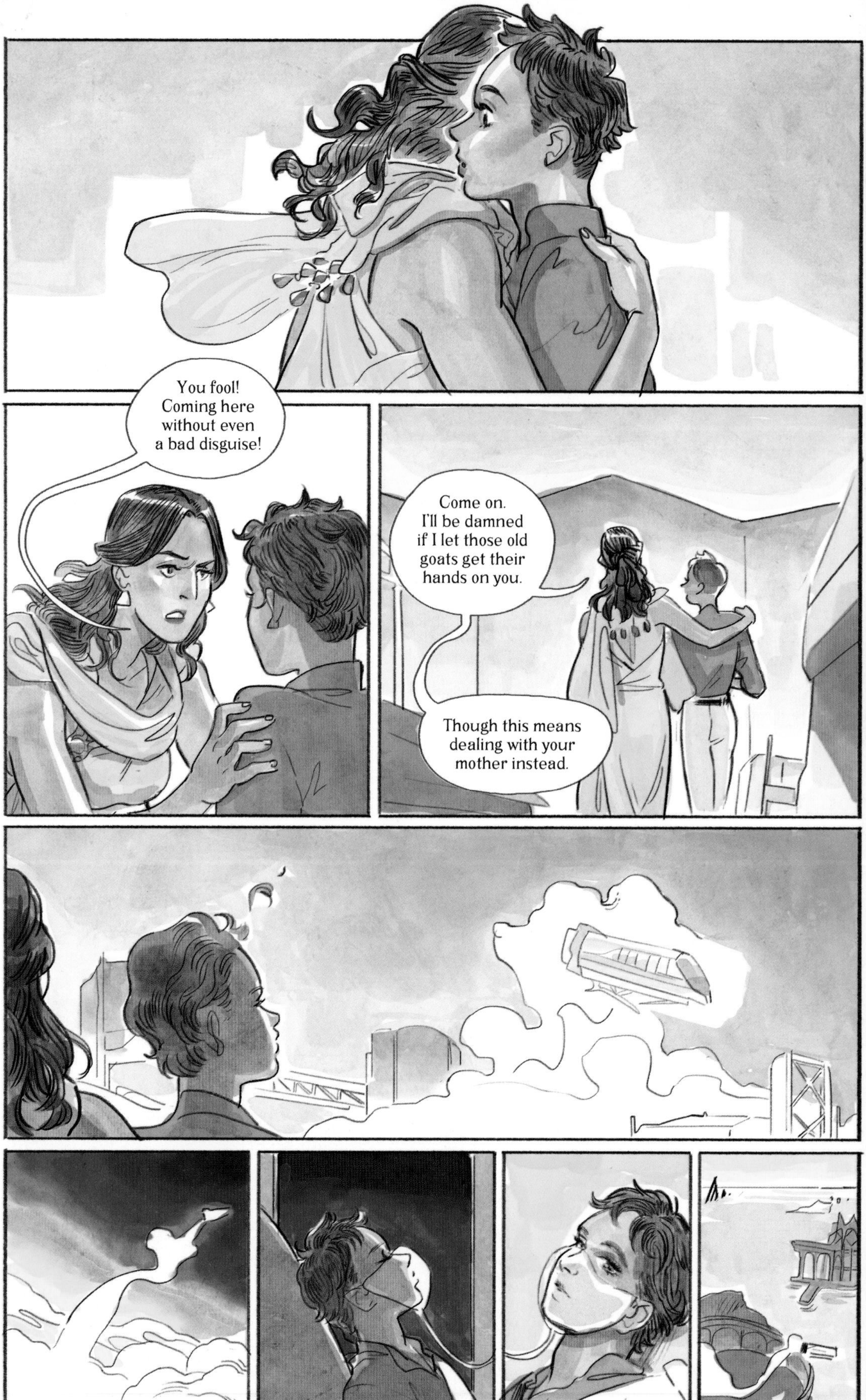
You fool! Coming here without even a bad disguise!
Come on. I'll be damned if I let those old goats get their hands on you.
Though this means dealing with your mother instead.

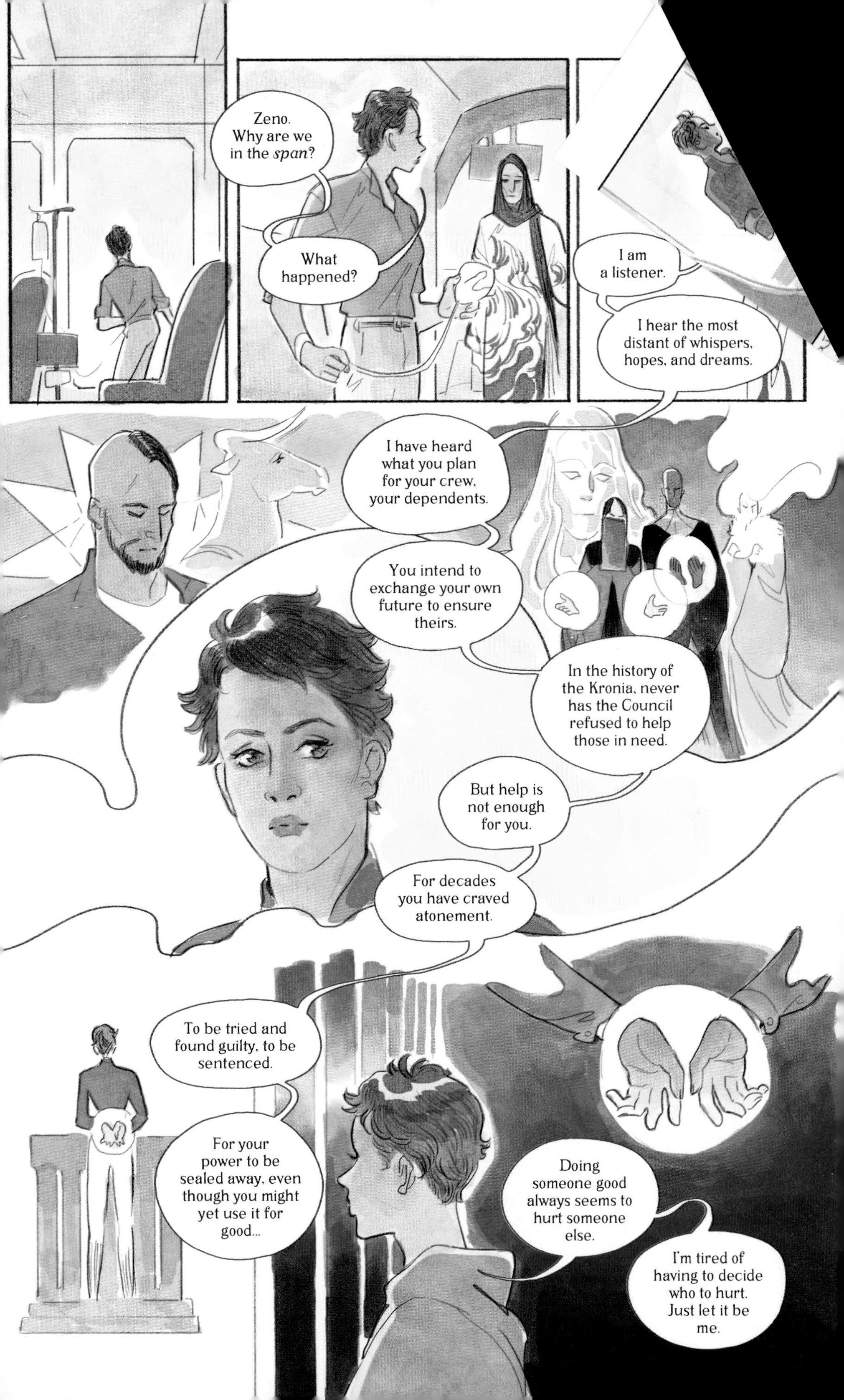
Zeno. Why are we in the *span*?
What happened?
I am a listener.
I hear the most distant of whispers, hopes, and dreams.
I have heard what you plan for your crew, your dependents.
You intend to exchange your own future to ensure theirs.
In the history of the Kronia, never has the Council refused to help those in need.
But help is not enough for you.
For decades you have craved atonement.
To be tried and found guilty, to be sentenced.
For your power to be sealed away, even though you might yet use it for good...
Doing someone good always seems to hurt someone else.
I'm tired of having to decide who to hurt. Just let it be me.

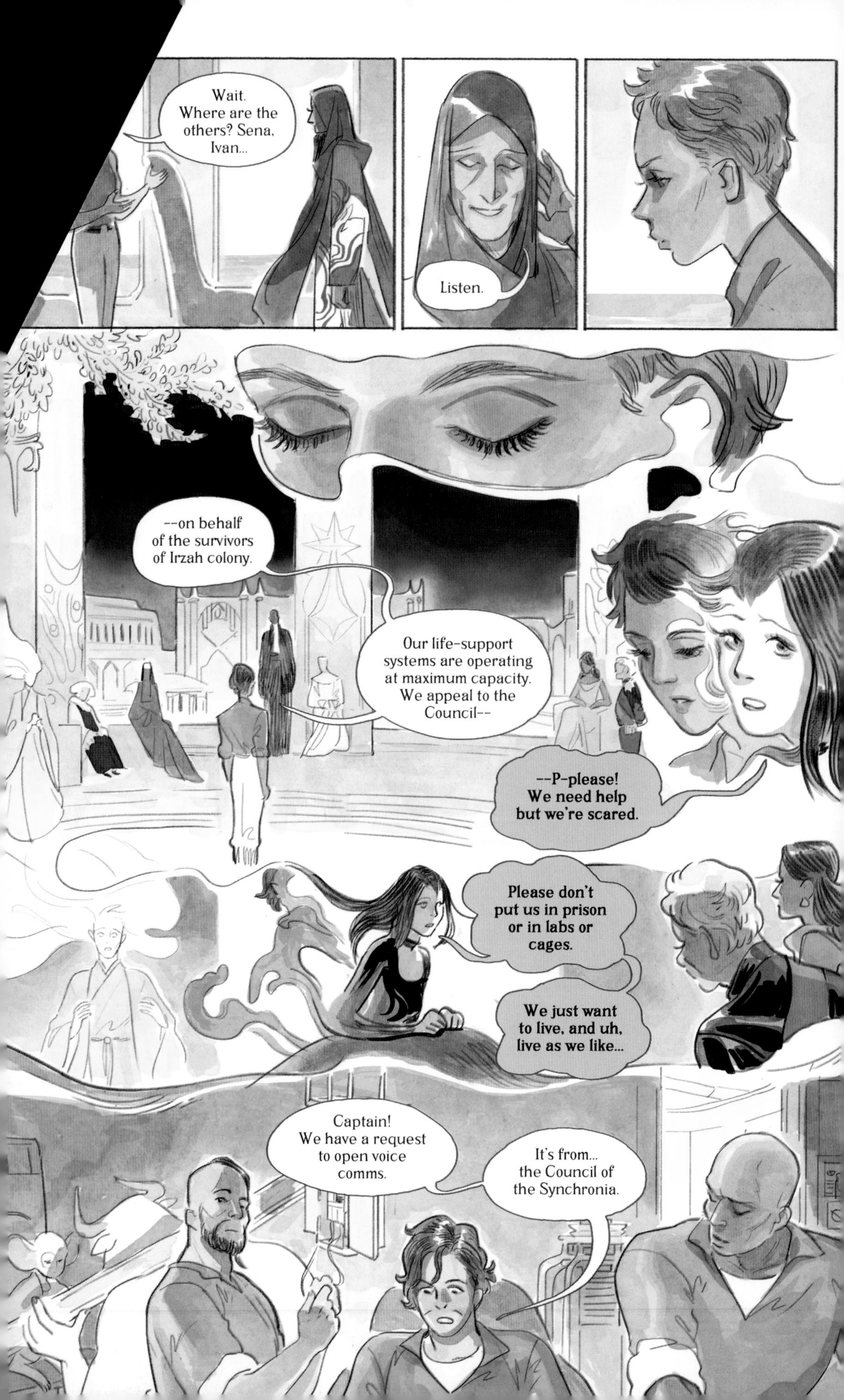

Wait. Where are the others? Sena, Ivan...
Listen.
--on behalf of the survivors of Irzah colony.
Our life-support systems are operating at maximum capacity. We appeal to the Council--
--P-please! We need help but we're scared.
Please don't put us in prison or in labs or cages.
We just want to live, and uh, live as we like...
Captain! We have a request to open voice comms.
It's from... the Council of the Synchronia.

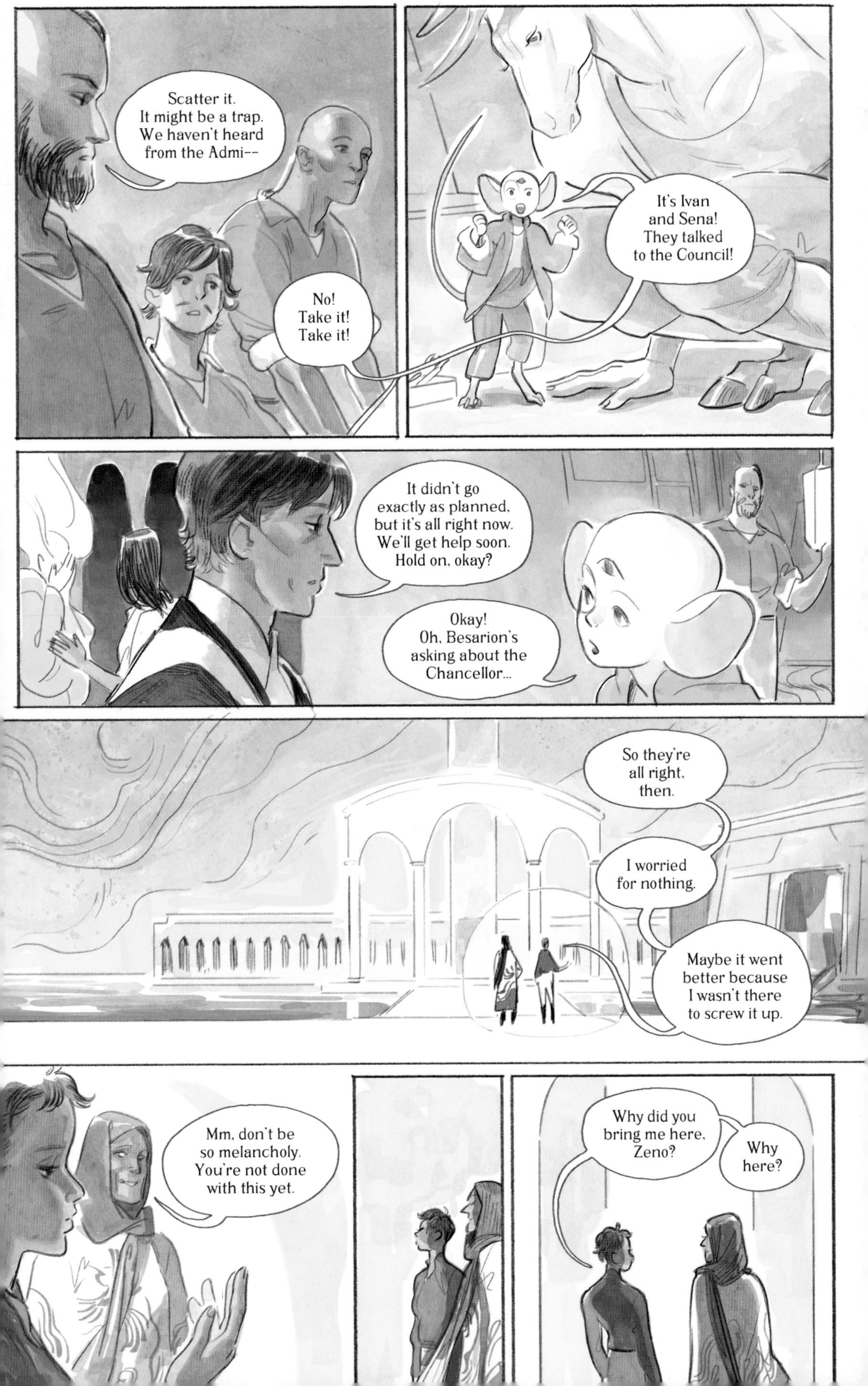
Scatter it. It might be a trap. We haven't heard from the Admi--
No! Take it! Take it!
It's Ivan and Sena! They talked to the Council!
It didn't go exactly as planned, but it's all right now. We'll get help soon. Hold on, okay?
Okay! Oh, Besarion's asking about the Chancellor...
So they're all right, then.
I worried for nothing.
Maybe it went better because I wasn't there to screw it up.
Mm, don't be so melancholy. You're not done with this yet.
Why did you bring me here, Zeno?
Why here?

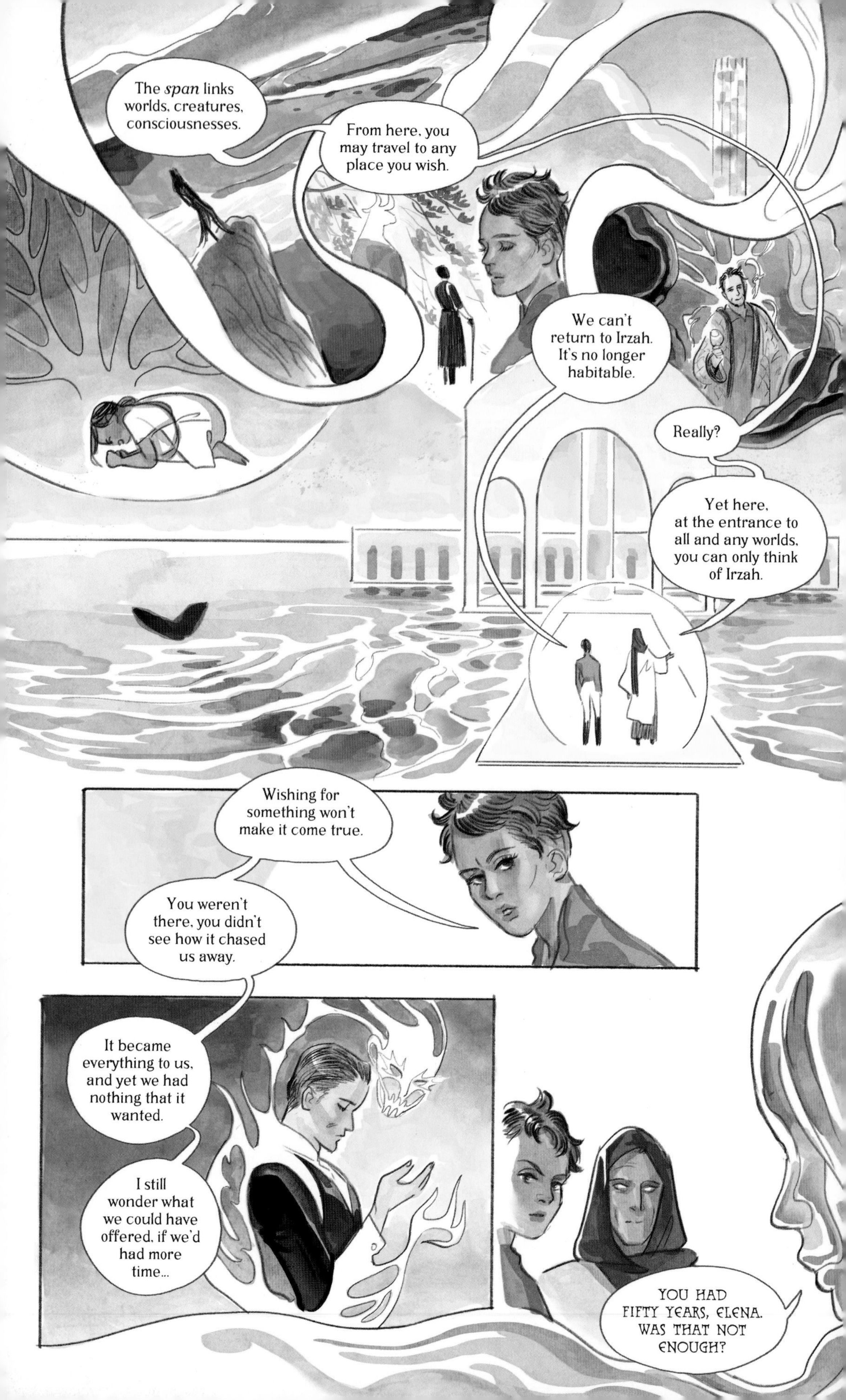
The *span* links worlds, creatures, consciousnesses.
From here, you may travel to any place you wish.
We can't return to Irzah. It's no longer habitable.
Really?
Yet here, at the entrance to all and any worlds, you can only think of Irzah.
Wishing for something won't make it come true.
You weren't there, you didn't see how it chased us away.
It became everything to us, and yet we had nothing that it wanted.
I still wonder what we could have offered, if we'd had more time...
YOU HAD FIFTY YEARS, ELENA. WAS THAT NOT ENOUGH?

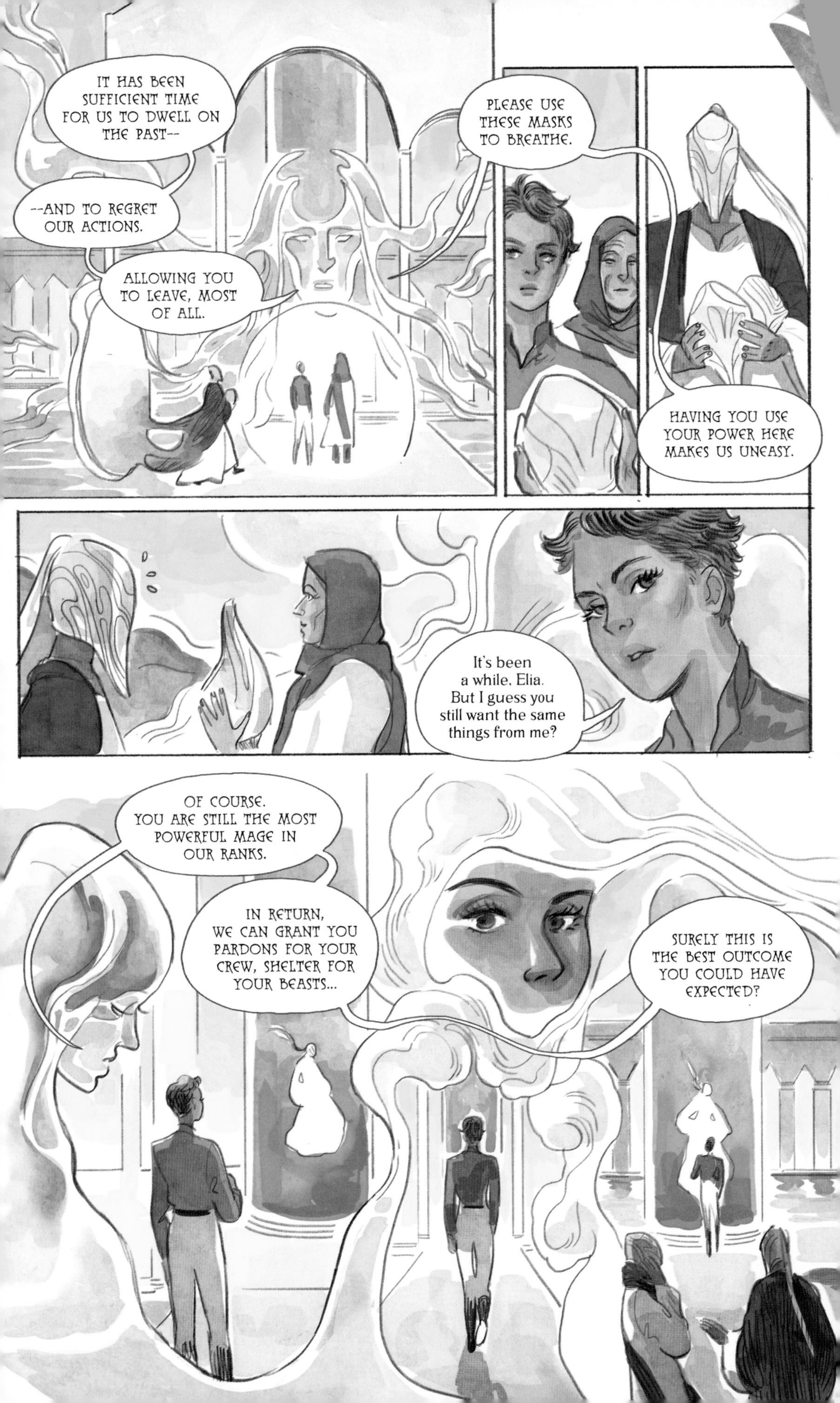
IT HAS BEEN SUFFICIENT TIME FOR US TO DWELL ON THE PAST--
--AND TO REGRET OUR ACTIONS.
ALLOWING YOU TO LEAVE, MOST OF ALL.
PLEASE USE THESE MASKS TO BREATHE.
HAVING YOU USE YOUR POWER HERE MAKES US UNEASY.
It's been a while, Elia. But I guess you still want the same things from me?
OF COURSE. YOU ARE STILL THE MOST POWERFUL MAGE IN OUR RANKS.
IN RETURN, WE CAN GRANT YOU PARDONS FOR YOUR CREW, SHELTER FOR YOUR BEASTS...
SURELY THIS IS THE BEST OUTCOME YOU COULD HAVE EXPECTED?

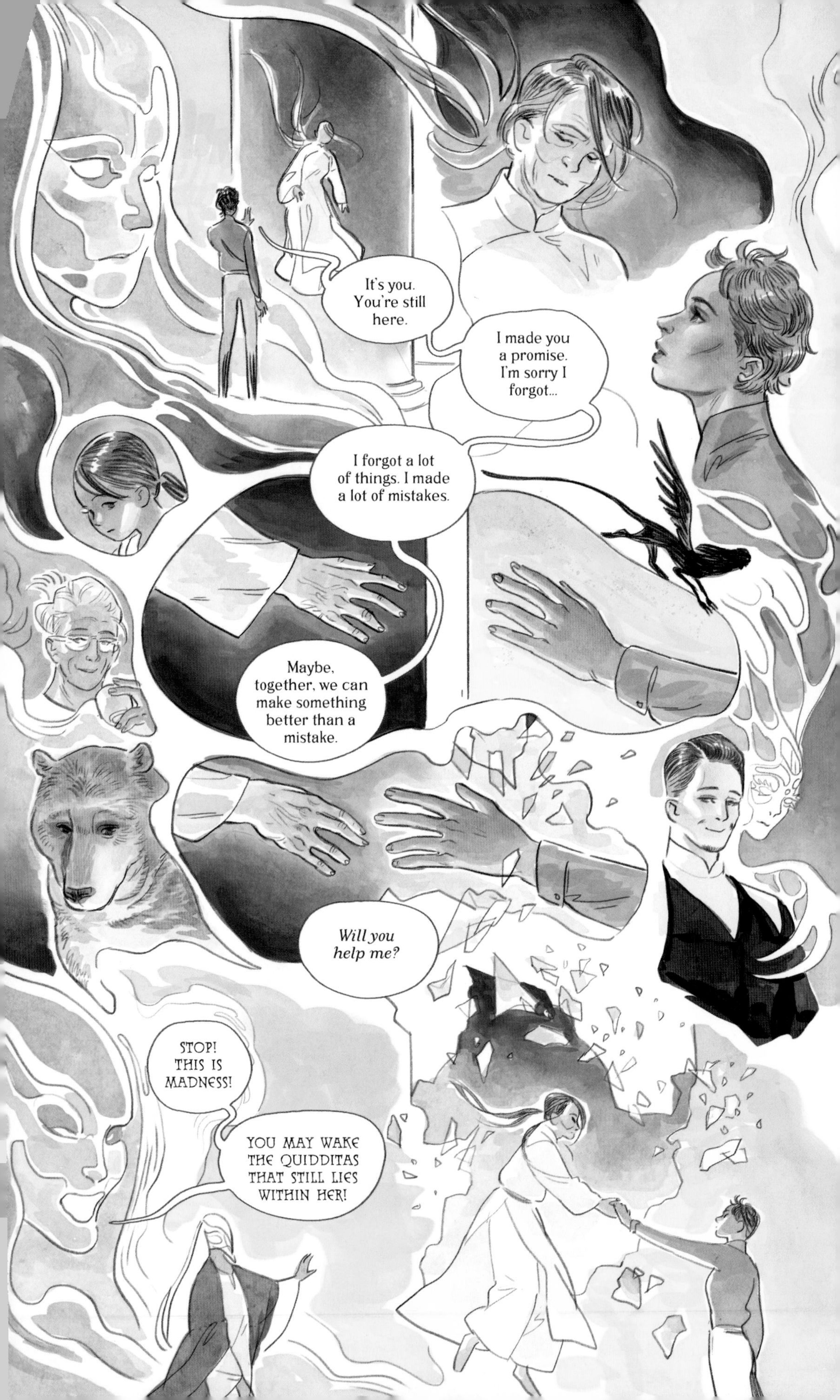
It's you. You're still here.
I made you a promise. I'm sorry I forgot...
I forgot a lot of things. I made a lot of mistakes.
Maybe, together, we can make something better than a mistake.
Will you help me?
STOP! THIS IS MADNESS!
YOU MAY WAKE THE QUIDDITAS THAT STILL LIES WITHIN HER!

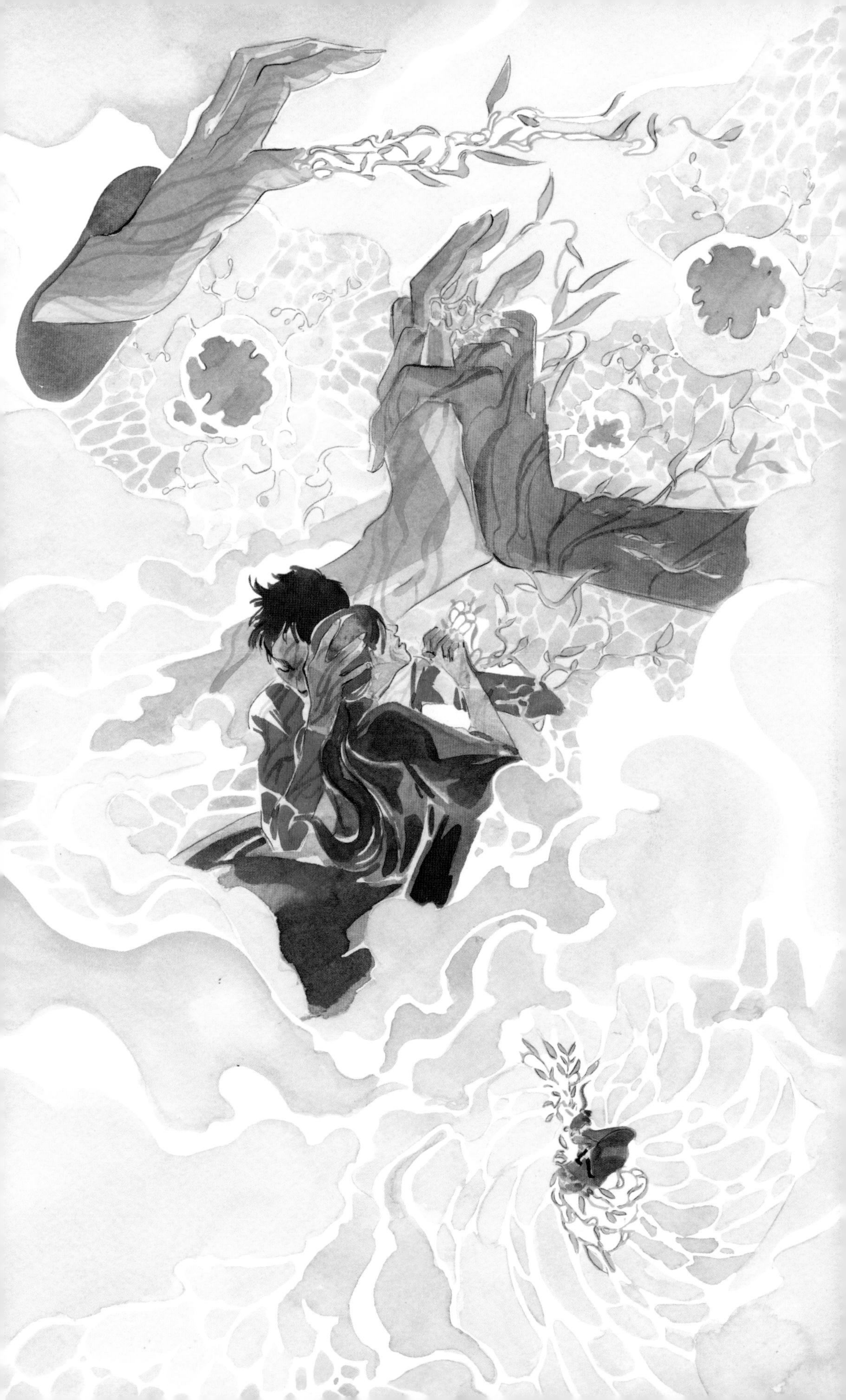

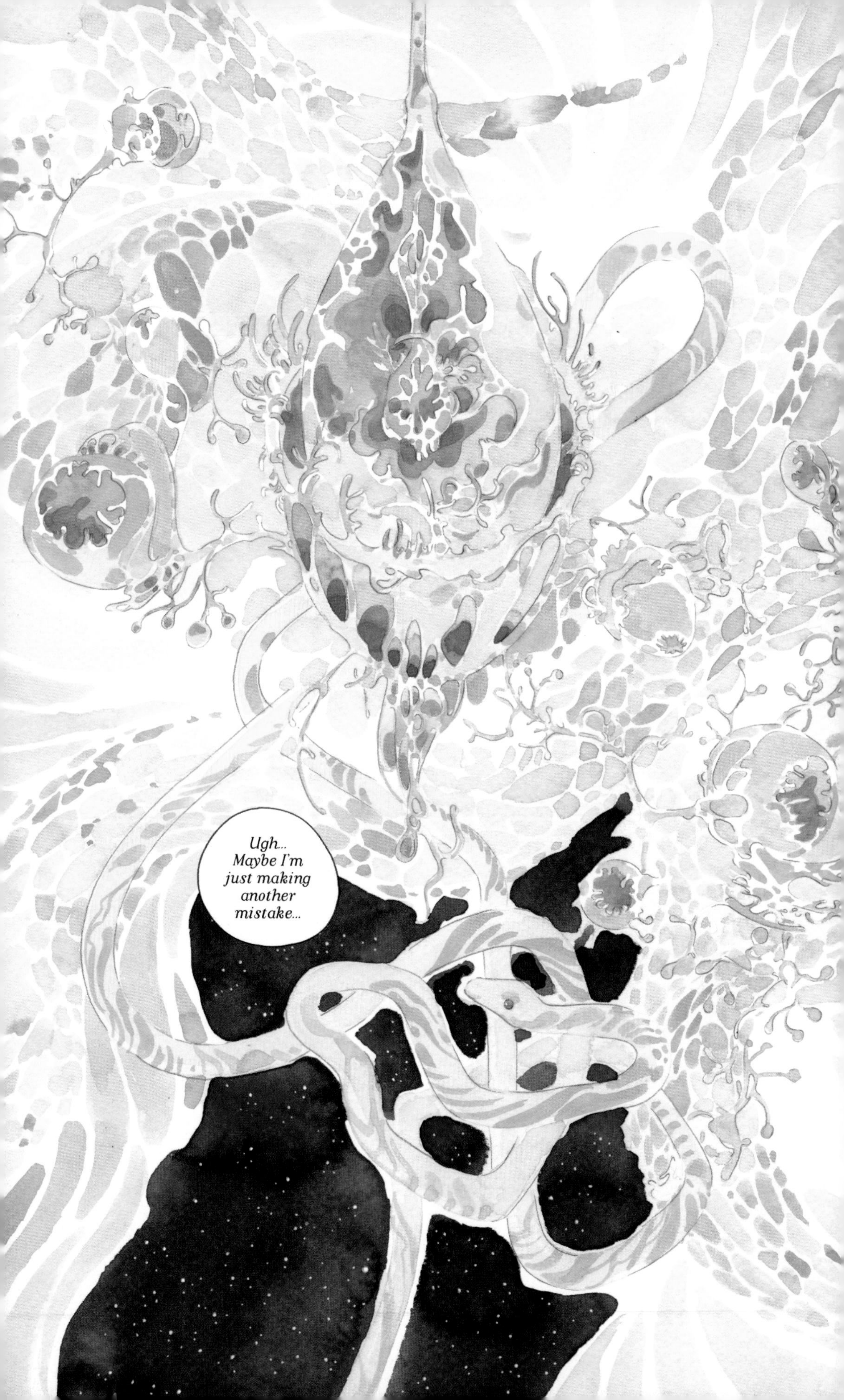
Ugh... Maybe I'm just making another mistake...

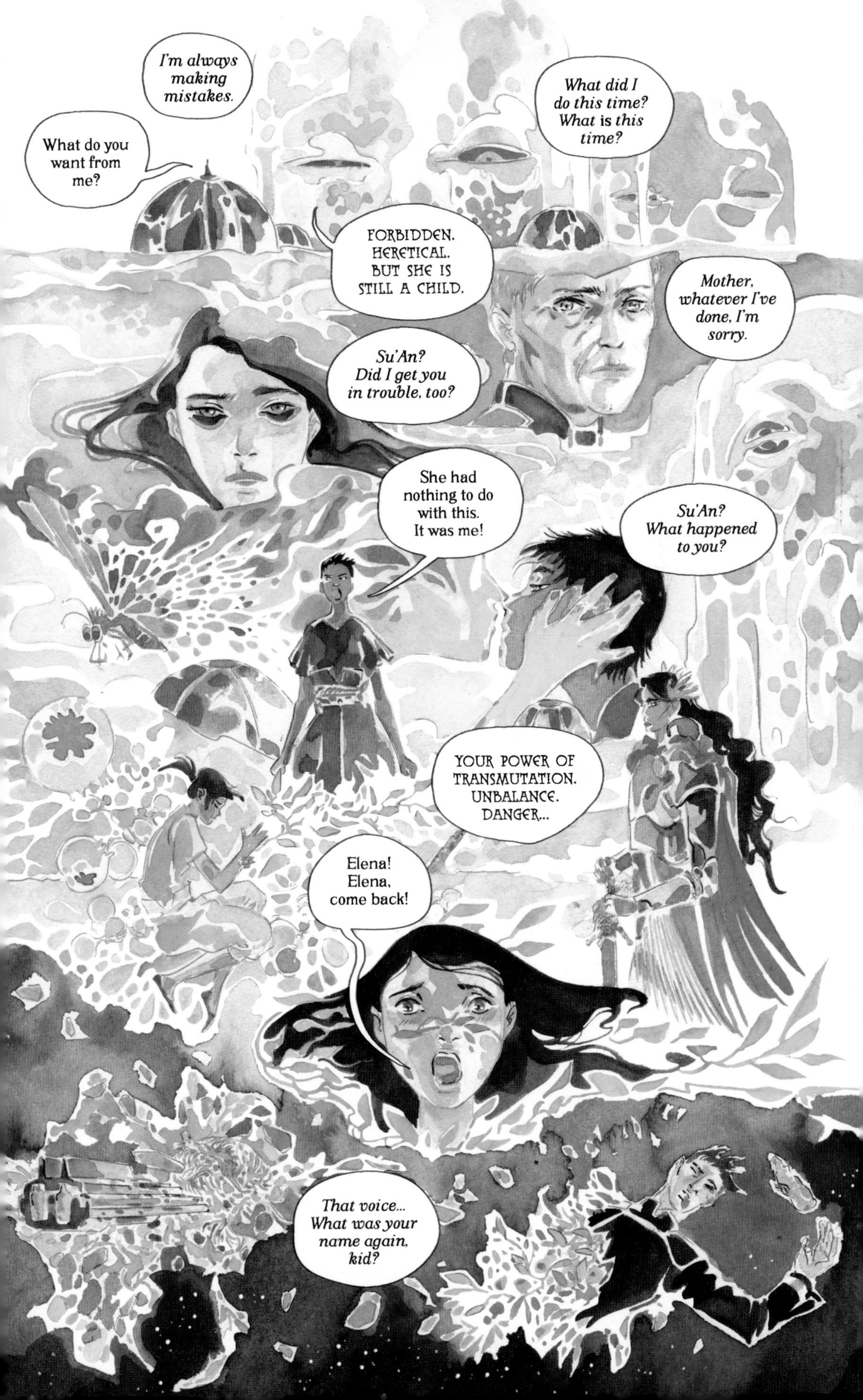
What do you want from me?
I'm always making mistakes.
What did I do this time? What is this time?
FORBIDDEN. HERETICAL. BUT SHE IS STILL A CHILD.
Mother, whatever I've done, I'm sorry.
Su'An? Did I get you in trouble, too?
She had nothing to do with this. It was me!
Su'An? What happened to you?
YOUR POWER OF TRANSMUTATION. UNBALANCE. DANGER...
Elena! Elena, come back!
That voice... What was your name again, kid?

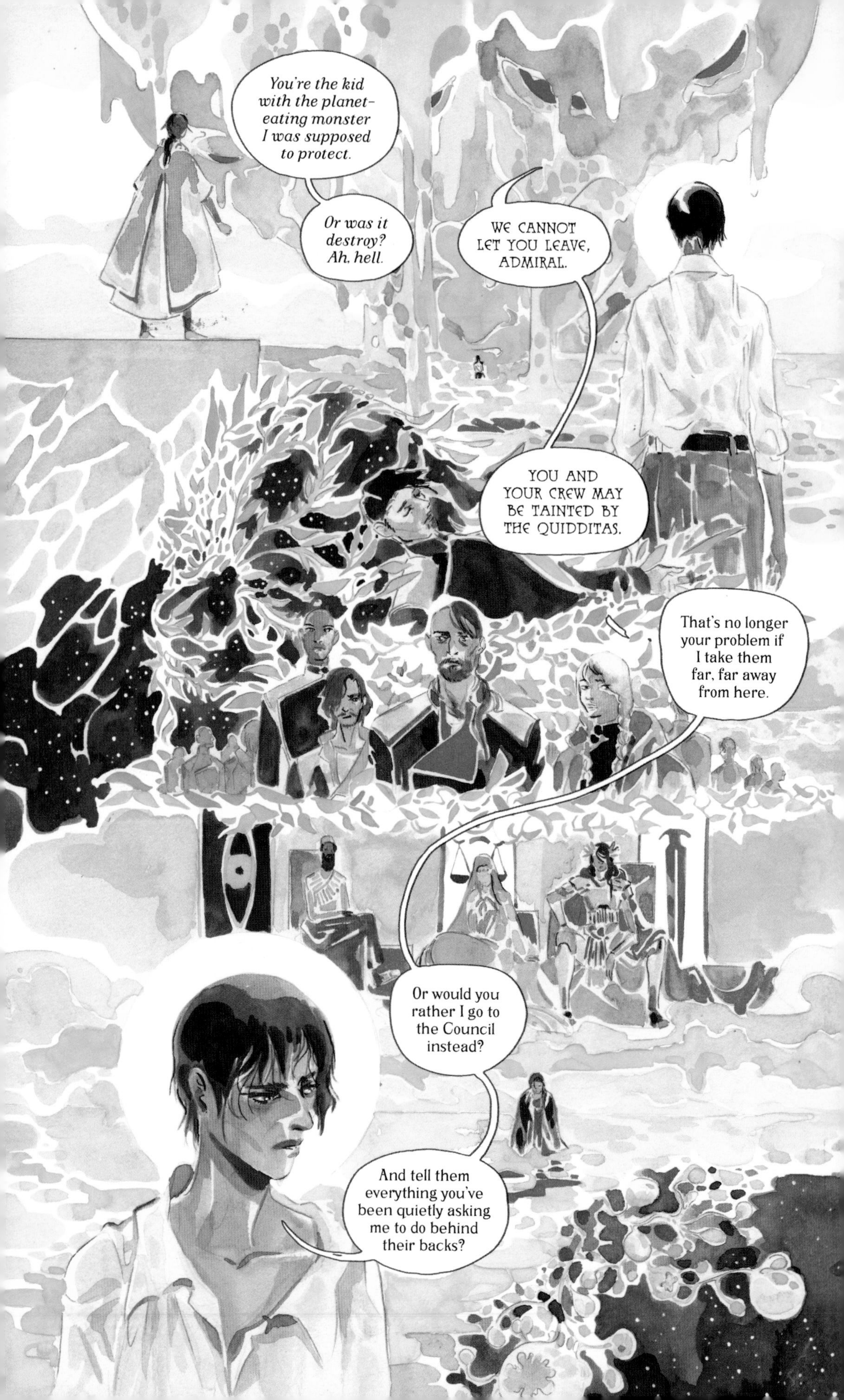

You're the kid with the planet-eating monster I was supposed to protect.
Or was it destroy? Ah, hell.
WE CANNOT LET YOU LEAVE, ADMIRAL.
YOU AND YOUR CREW MAY BE TAINTED BY THE QUIDDITAS.
That's no longer your problem if I take them far, far away from here.
Or would you rather I go to the Council instead?
And tell them everything you've been quietly asking me to do behind their backs?

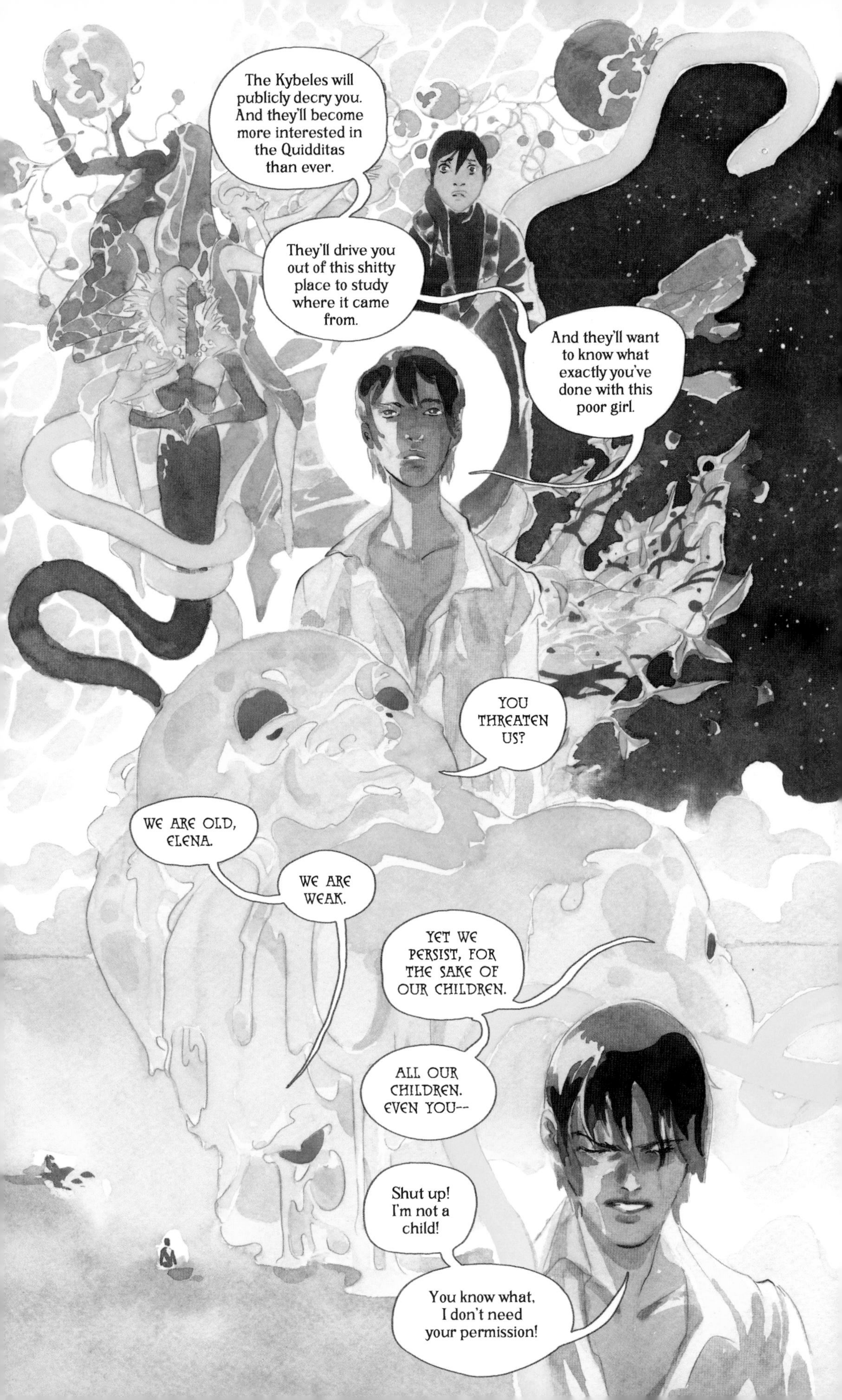

The Kybeles will publicly decry you. And they'll become more interested in the Quidditas than ever.
They'll drive you out of this shitty place to study where it came from.
And they'll want to know what exactly you've done with this poor girl.
YOU THREATEN US?
WE ARE OLD, ELENA.
WE ARE WEAK.
YET WE PERSIST, FOR THE SAKE OF OUR CHILDREN.
ALL OUR CHILDREN. EVEN YOU--
Shut up! I'm not a child!
You know what, I don't need your permission!

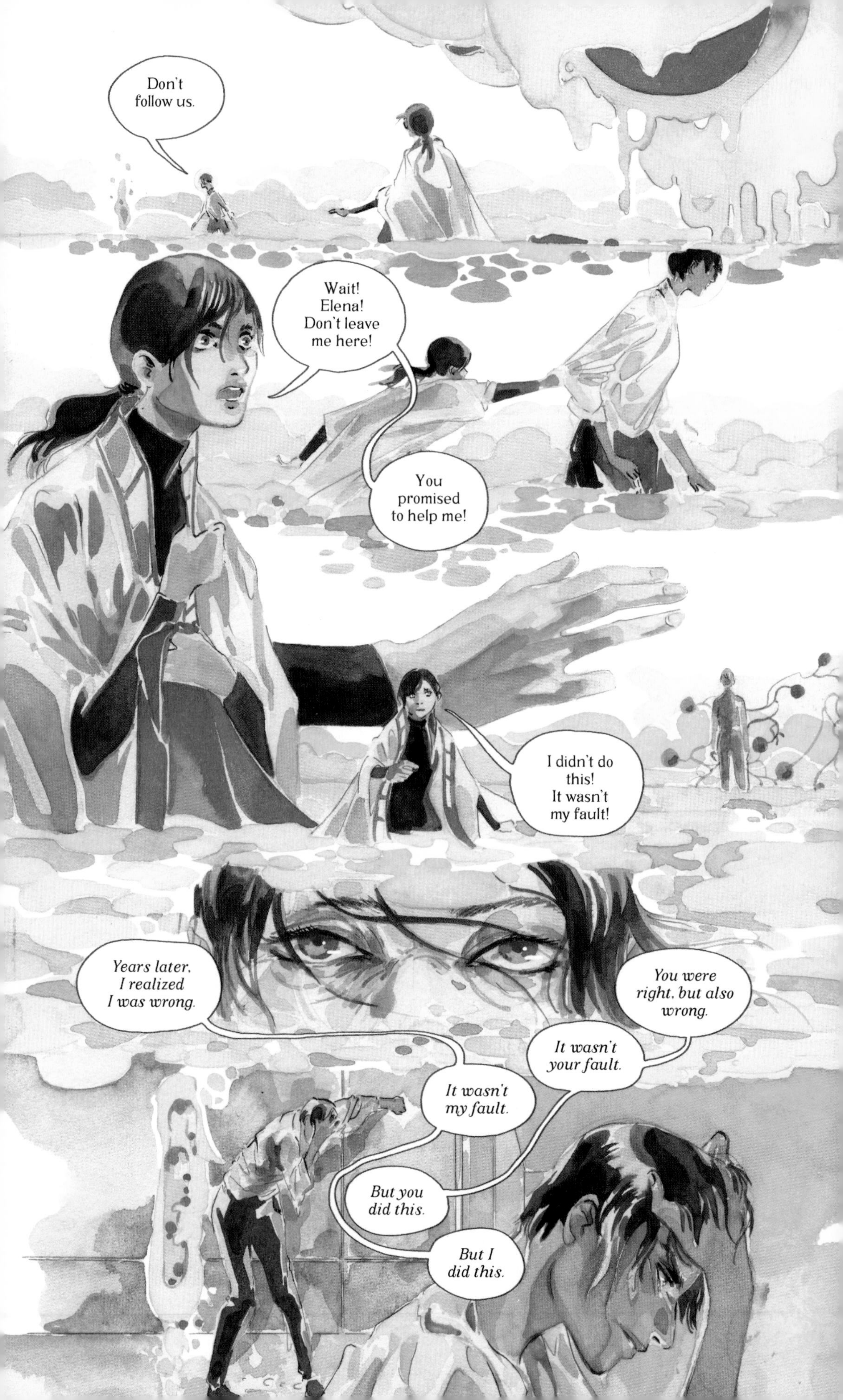
Don't follow us.
Wait! Elena! Don't leave me here!
You promised to help me!
I didn't do this! It wasn't my fault!
Years later, I realized I was wrong.
You were right, but also wrong.
It wasn't your fault.
It wasn't my fault.
But you did this.
But I did this.

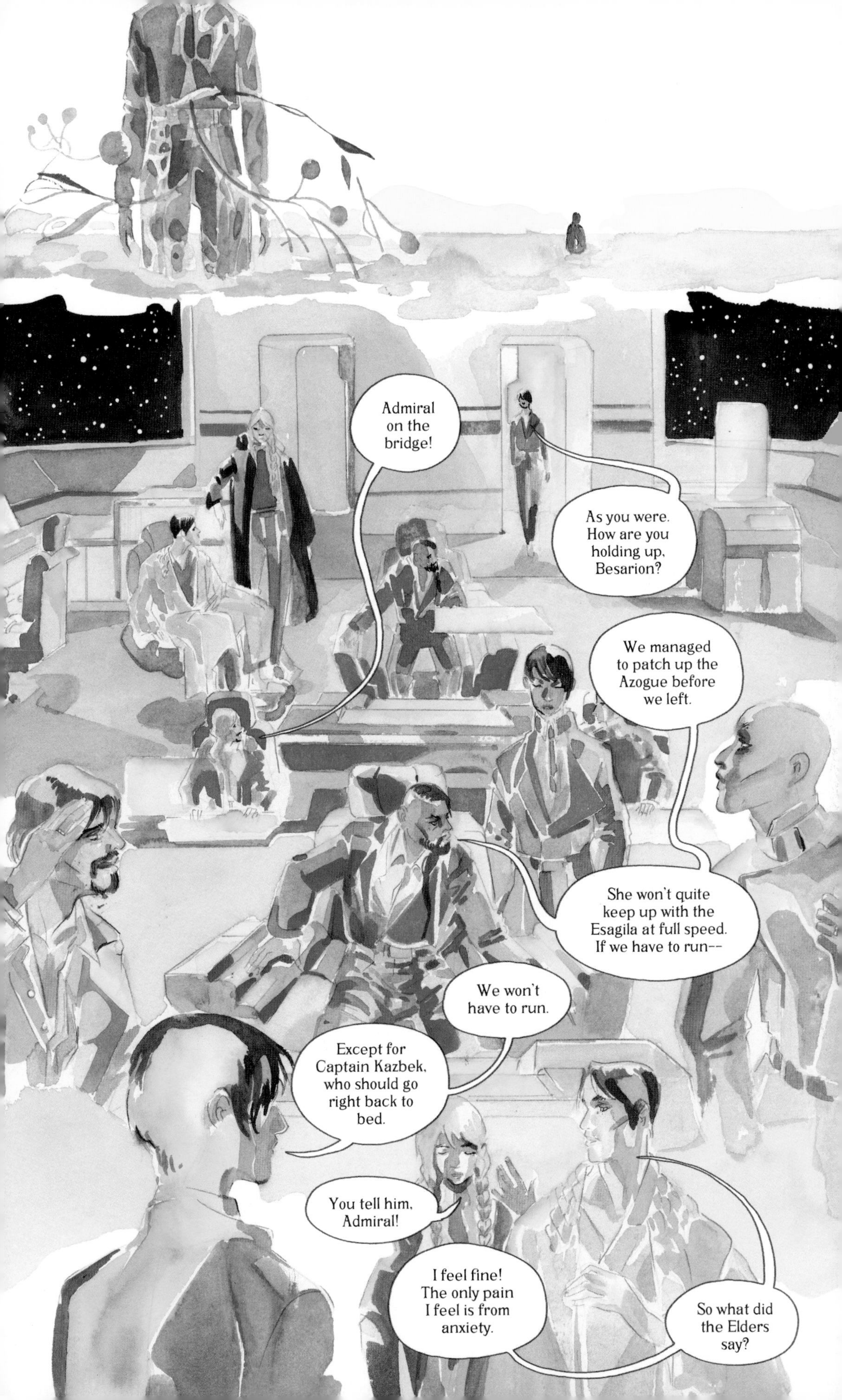
Admiral on the bridge!
As you were. How are you holding up, Besarion?
We managed to patch up the Azogue before we left.
She won't quite keep up with the Esagila at full speed. If we have to run--
We won't have to run.
Except for Captain Kazbek, who should go right back to bed.
You tell him, Admiral!
I feel fine! The only pain I feel is from anxiety.
So what did the Elders say?

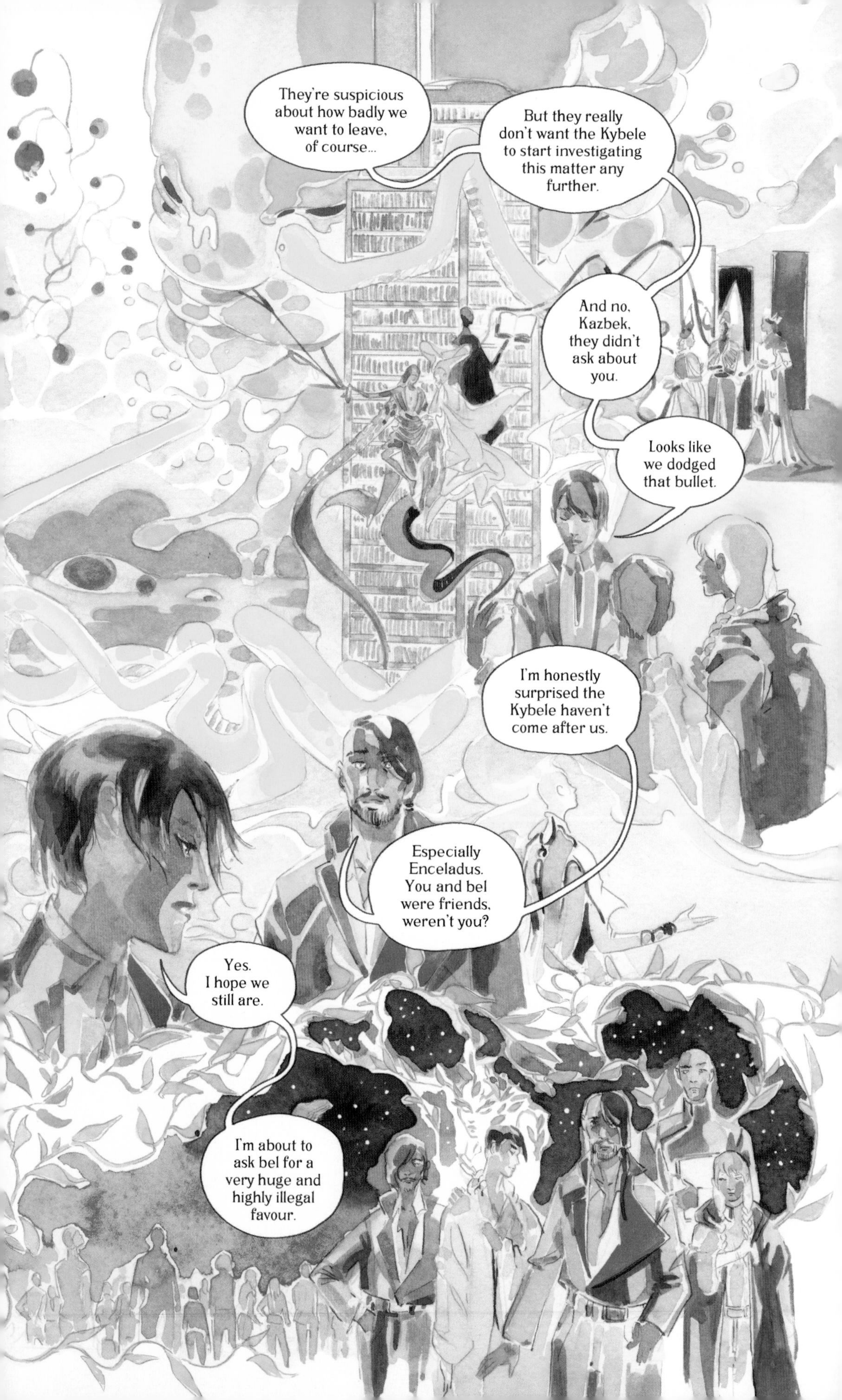
They're suspicious about how badly we want to leave, of course...
But they really don't want the Kybele to start investigating this matter any further.
And no, Kazbek, they didn't ask about you.
Looks like we dodged that bullet.
I'm honestly surprised the Kybele haven't come after us.
Especially Enceladus. You and bel were friends, weren't you?
Yes. I hope we still are.
I'm about to ask bel for a very huge and highly illegal favour.

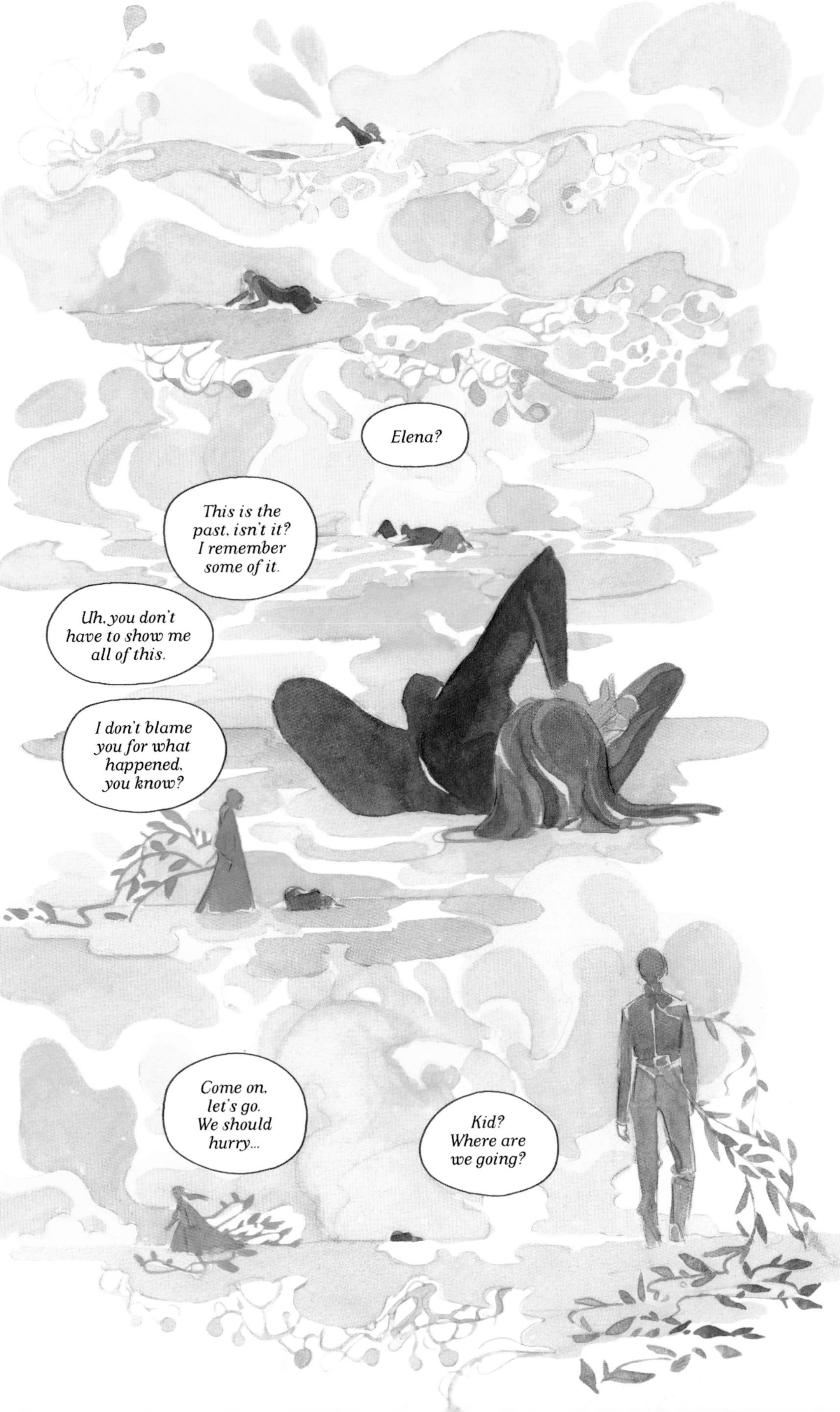
Elena?
This is the past, isn't it? I remember some of it.
Uh, you don't have to show me all of this.
I don't blame you for what happened, you know?
Come on, let's go. We should hurry...
Kid? Where are we going?

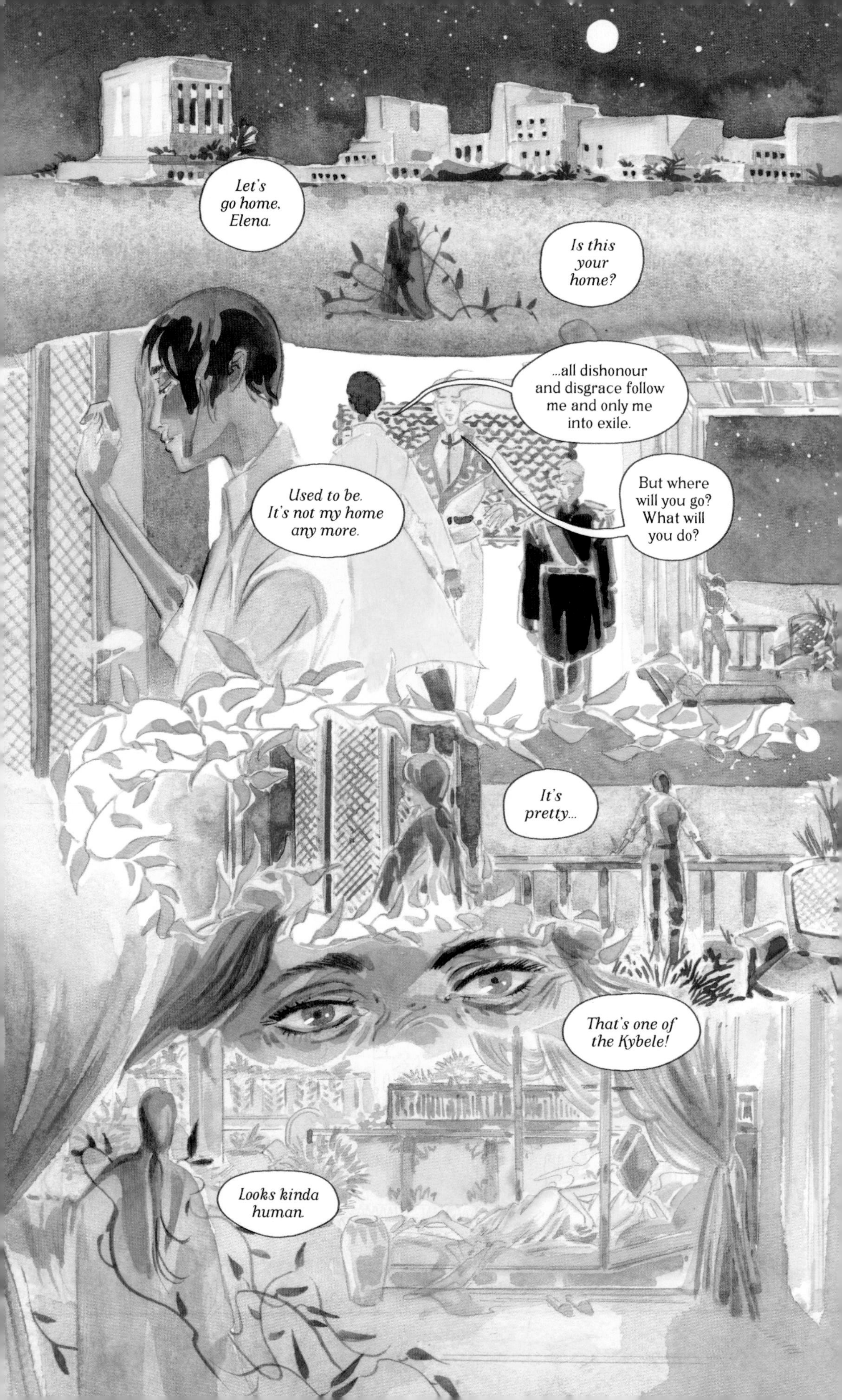
Let's go home, Elena.
Is this your home?
Used to be. It's not my home any more.
...all dishonour and disgrace follow me and only me into exile.
But where will you go? What will you do?
It's pretty...
That's one of the Kybele!
Looks kinda human.

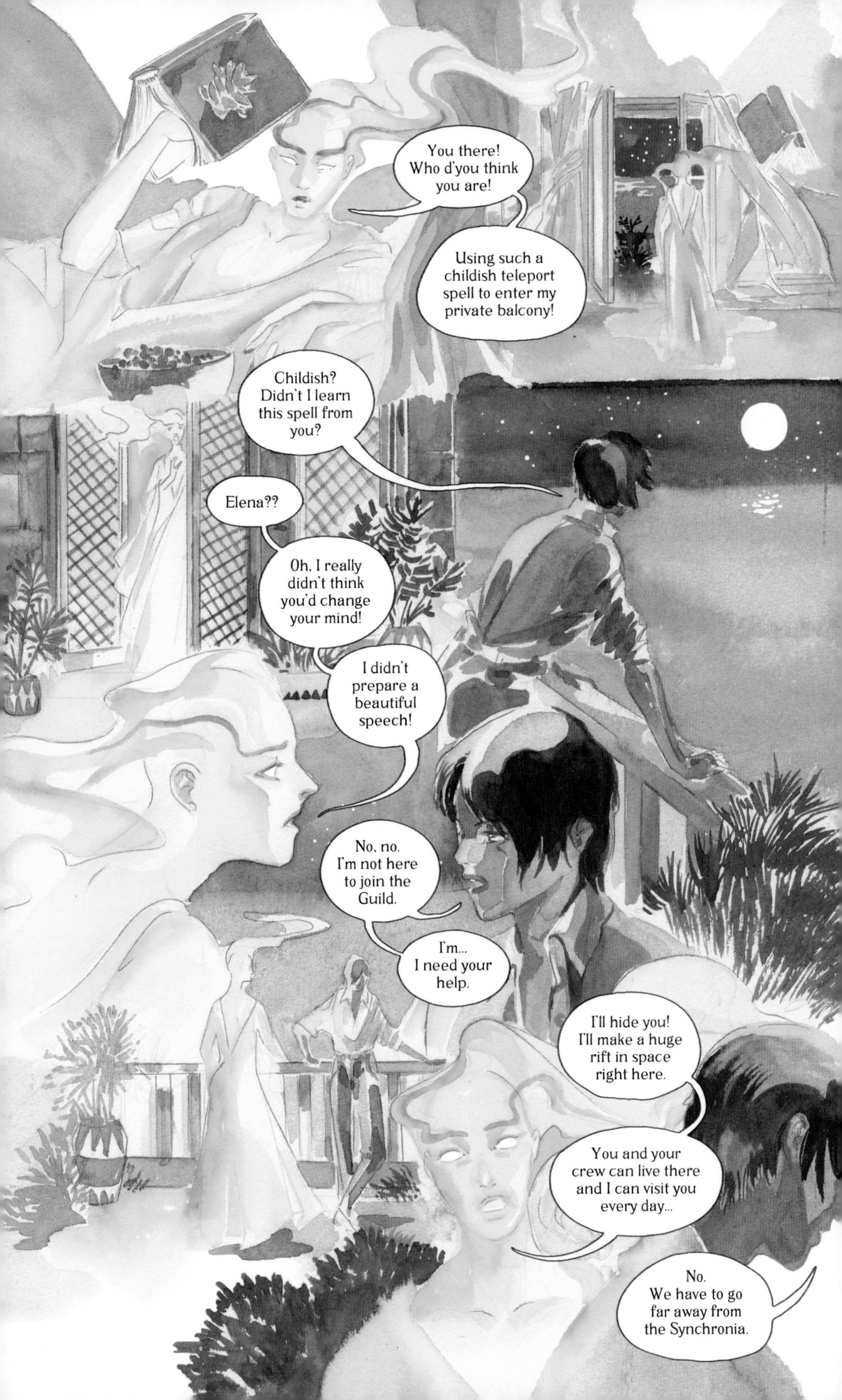
You there! Who d'you think you are!
Using such a childish teleport spell to enter my private balcony!
Childish? Didn't I learn this spell from you?
Elena??
Oh, I really didn't think you'd change your mind!
I didn't prepare a beautiful speech!
No, no. I'm not here to join the Guild.
I'm... I need your help.
I'll hide you! I'll make a huge rift in space right here.
You and your crew can live there and I can visit you every day...
No. We have to go far away from the Synchronia.

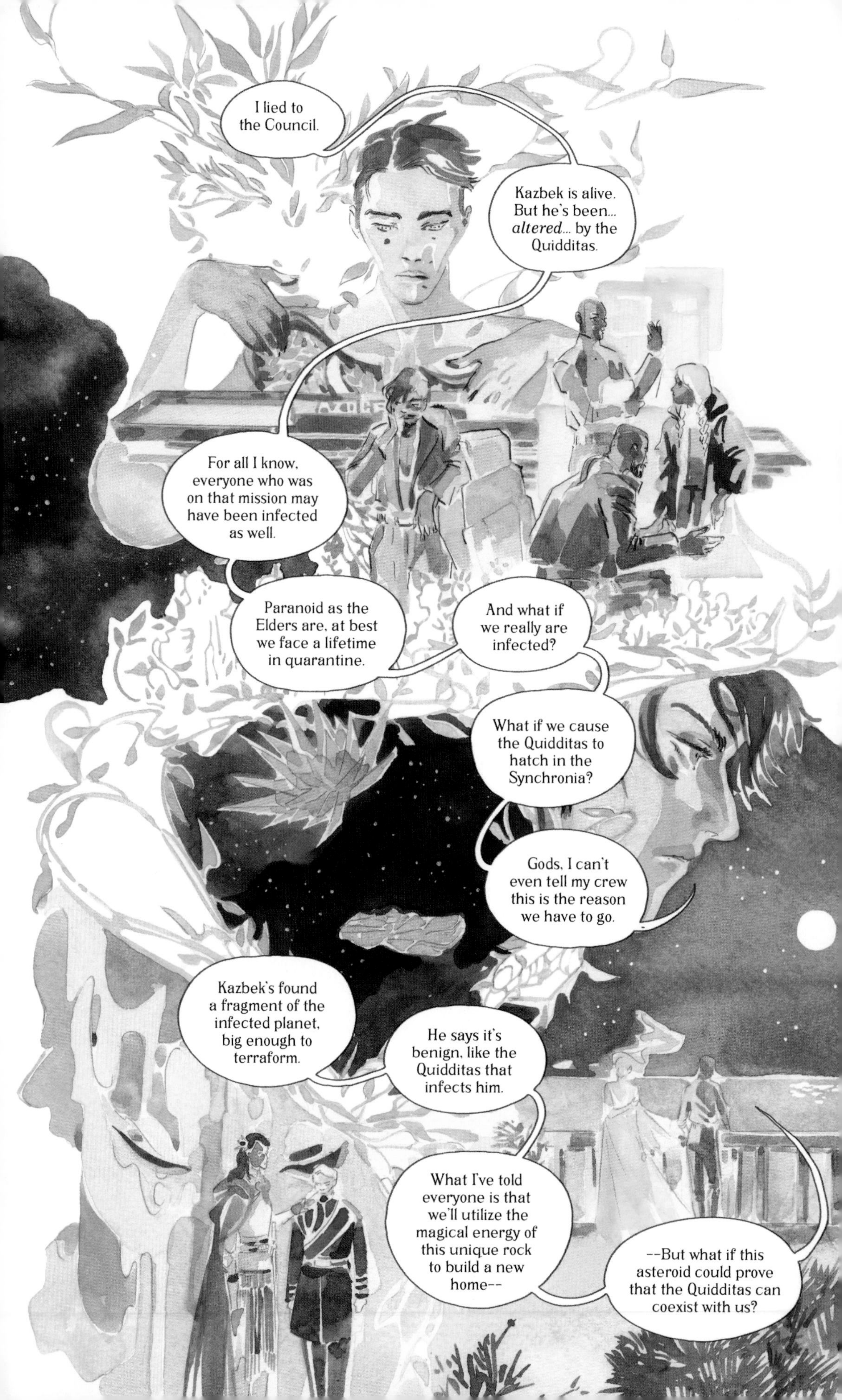
I lied to the Council.
Kazbek is alive. But he's been... *altered*... by the Quidditas.
For all I know, everyone who was on that mission may have been infected as well.
Paranoid as the Elders are, at best we face a lifetime in quarantine.
And what if we really are infected?
What if we cause the Quidditas to hatch in the Synchronia?
Gods, I can't even tell my crew this is the reason we have to go.
Kazbek's found a fragment of the infected planet, big enough to terraform.
He says it's benign, like the Quidditas that infects him.
What I've told everyone is that we'll utilize the magical energy of this unique rock to build a new home--
--But what if this asteroid could prove that the Quidditas can coexist with us?

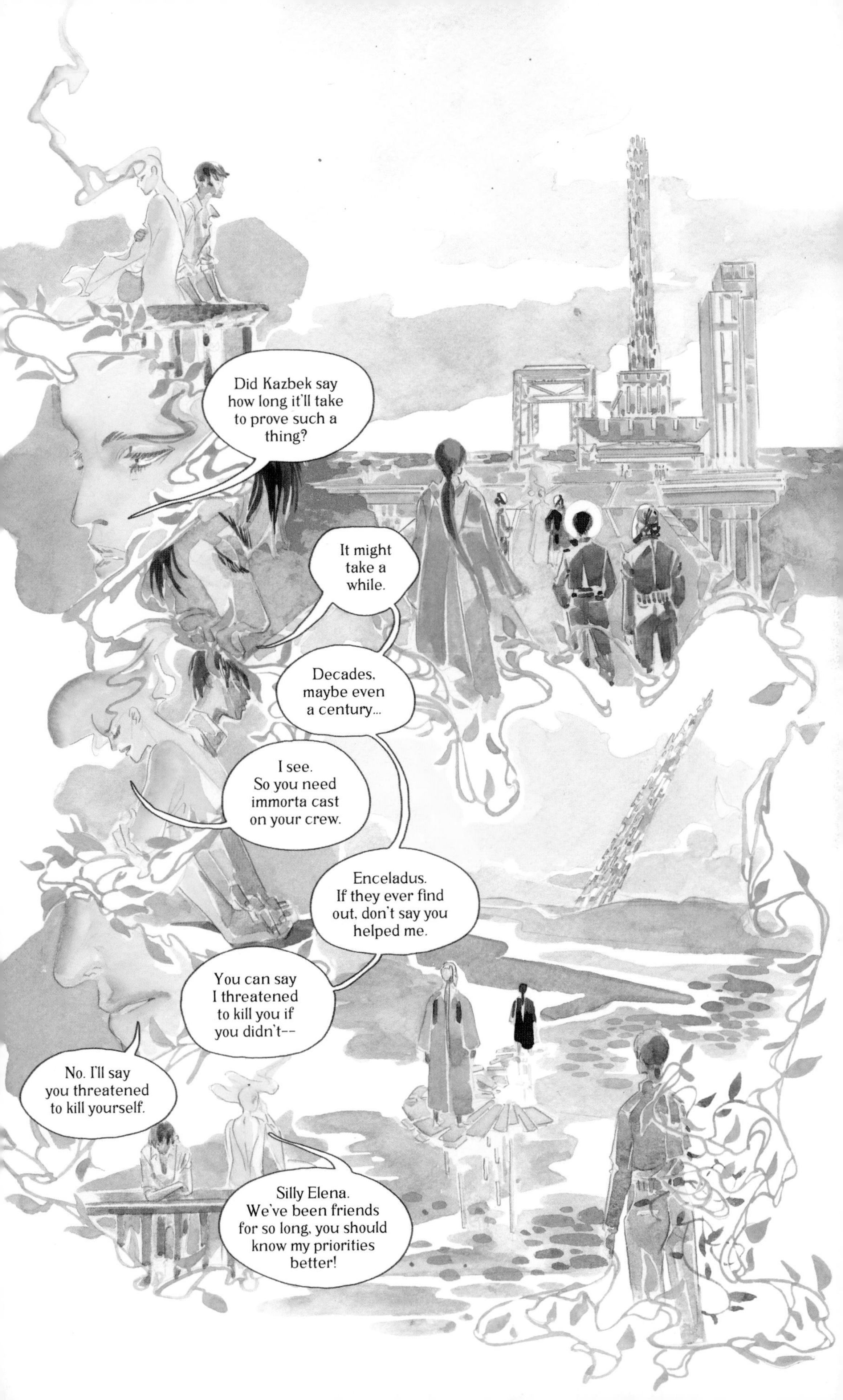
Did Kazbek say how long it'll take to prove such a thing?
It might take a while.
Decades, maybe even a century...
I see. So you need immorta cast on your crew.
Enceladus. If they ever find out, don't say you helped me.
You can say I threatened to kill you if you didn't--
No. I'll say you threatened to kill yourself.
Silly Elena. We've been friends for so long, you should know my priorities better!

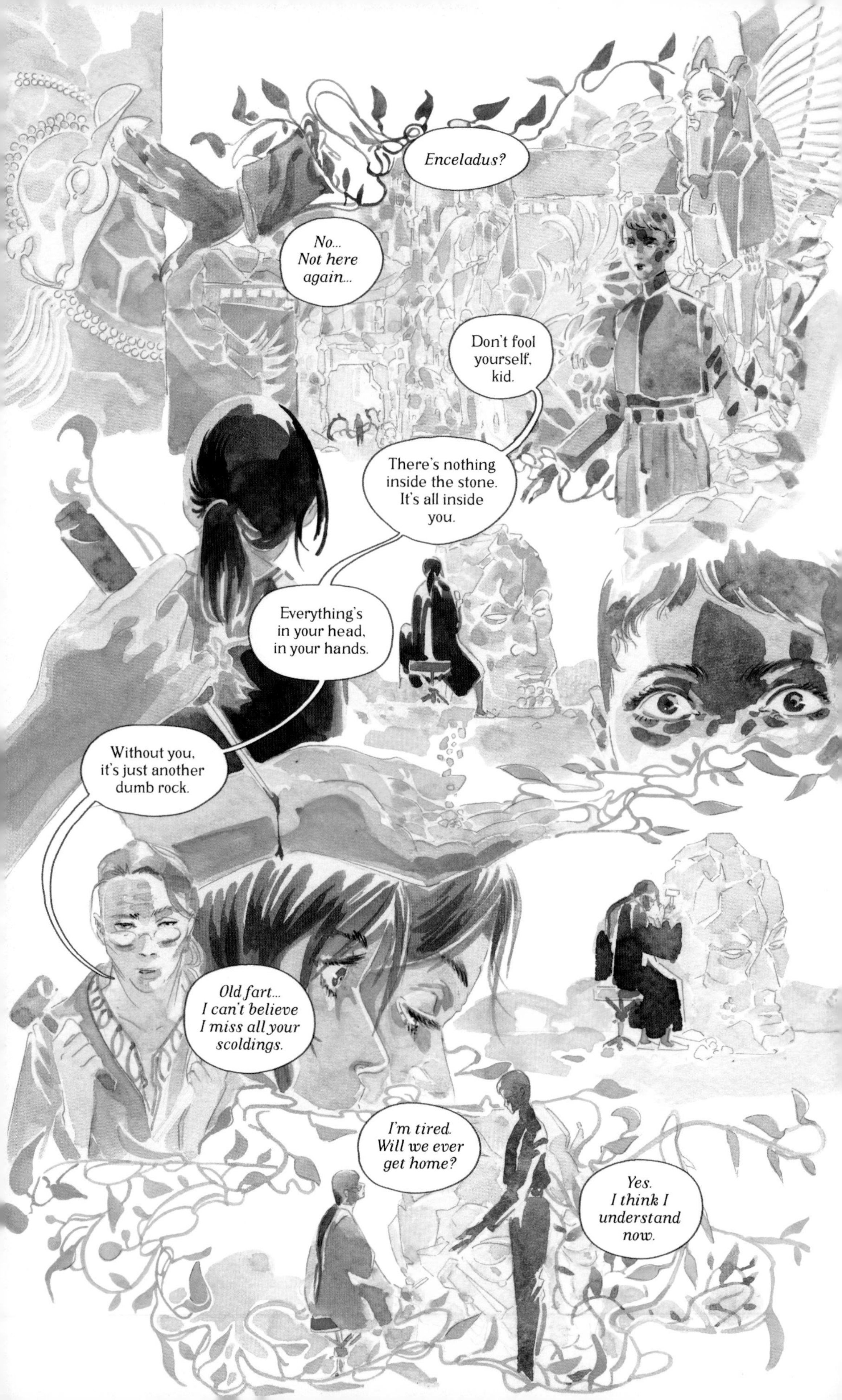
Enceladus?
No... Not here again...
Don't fool yourself, kid.
There's nothing inside the stone. It's all inside you.
Everything's in your head, in your hands.
Without you, it's just another dumb rock.
Old fart... I can't believe I miss all your scoldings.
I'm tired. Will we ever get home?
Yes. I think I understand now.

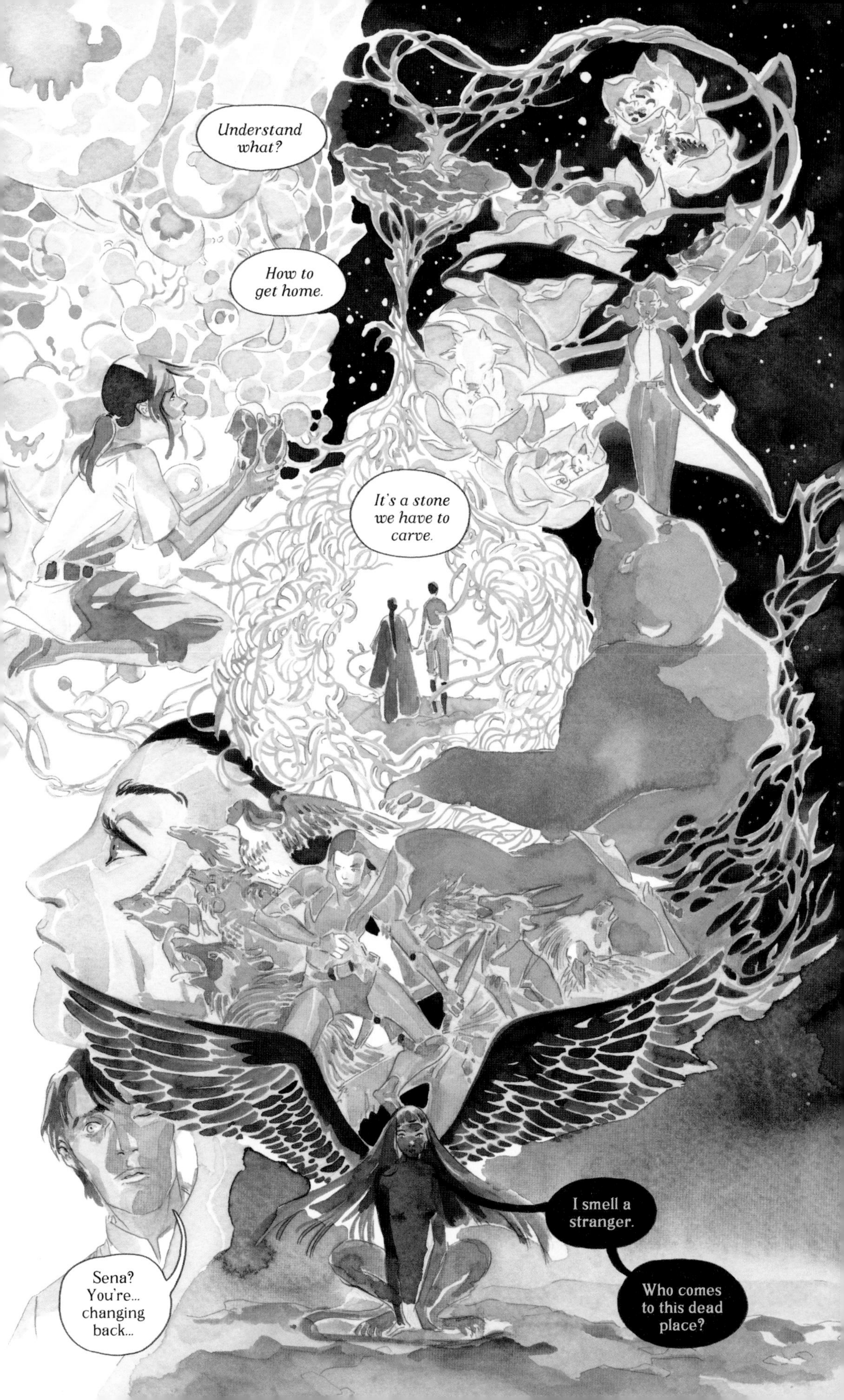
Understand what?
How to get home.
It's a stone we have to carve.
Sena? You're... changing back...
I smell a stranger.
Who comes to this dead place?

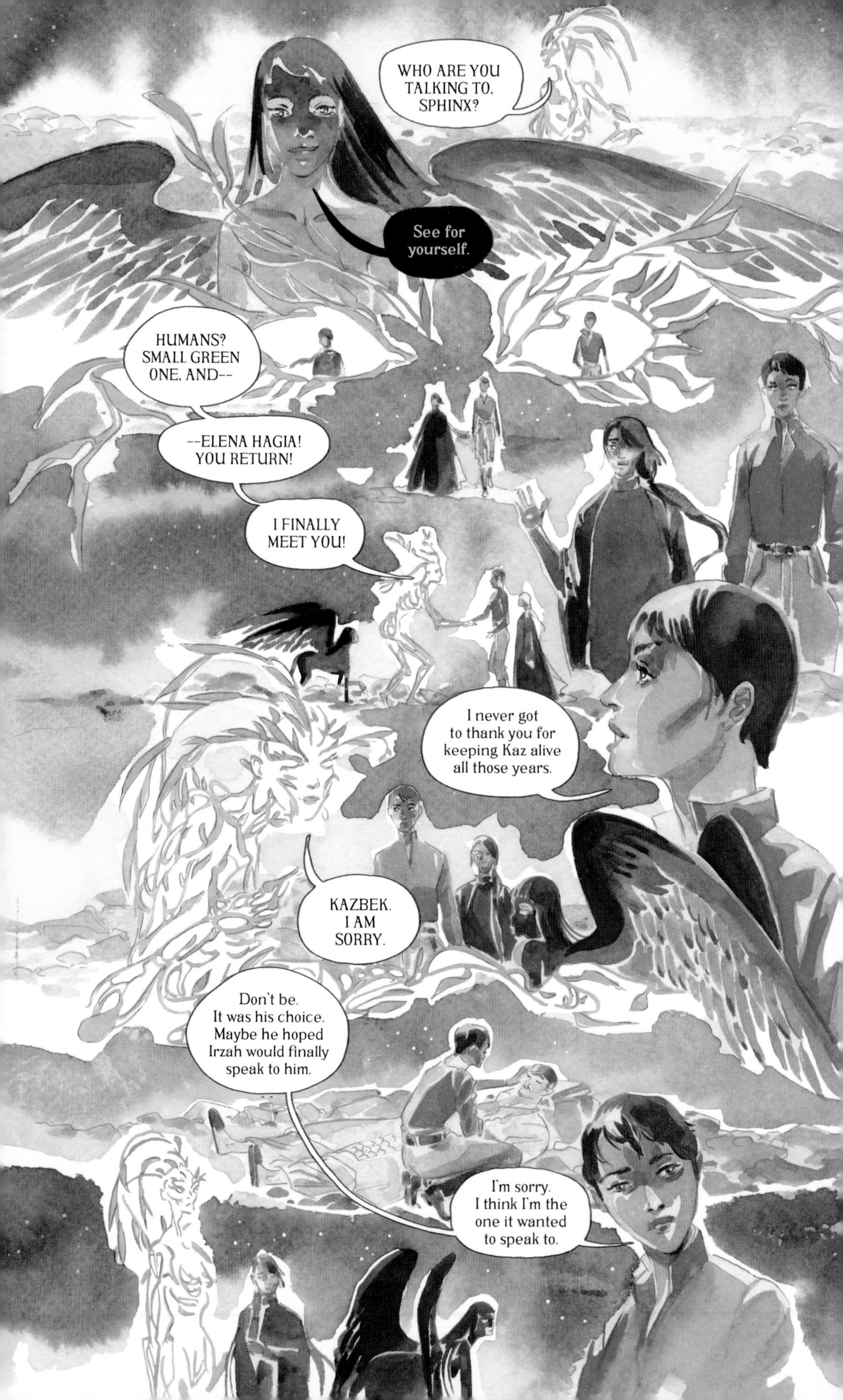
WHO ARE YOU TALKING TO, SPHINX?
See for yourself.
HUMANS? SMALL GREEN ONE, AND--
--ELENA HAGIA! YOU RETURN!
I FINALLY MEET YOU!
I never got to thank you for keeping Kaz alive all those years.
KAZBEK. I AM SORRY.
Don't be. It was his choice. Maybe he hoped Irzah would finally speak to him.
I'm sorry. I think I'm the one it wanted to speak to.

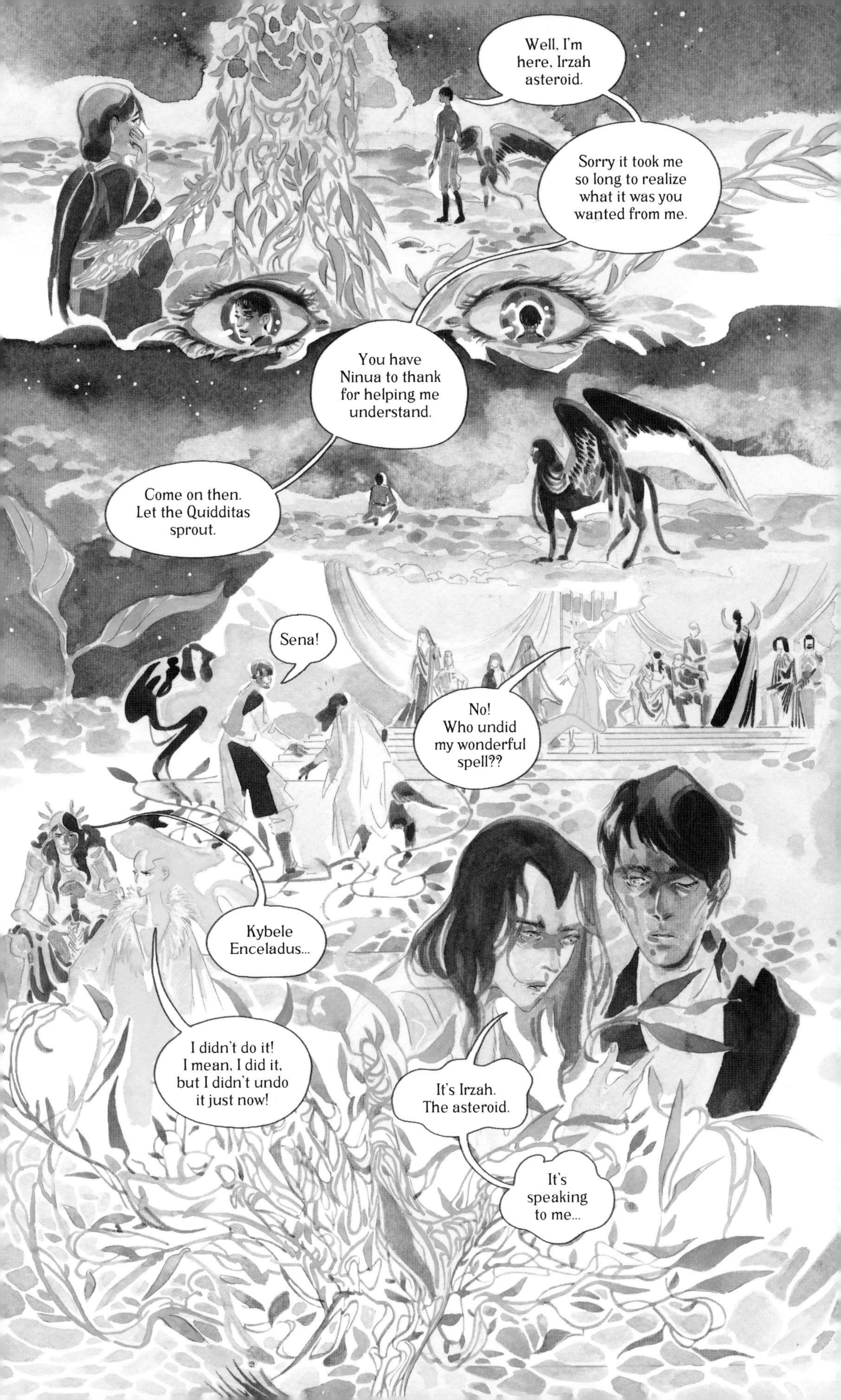
Well, I'm here, Irzah asteroid.
Sorry it took me so long to realize what it was you wanted from me.
You have Ninua to thank for helping me understand.
Come on then. Let the Quidditas sprout.
Sena!
No! Who undid my wonderful spell??
Kybele Enceladus...
I didn't do it! I mean, I did it, but I didn't undo it just now!
It's Irzah. The asteroid.
It's speaking to me...

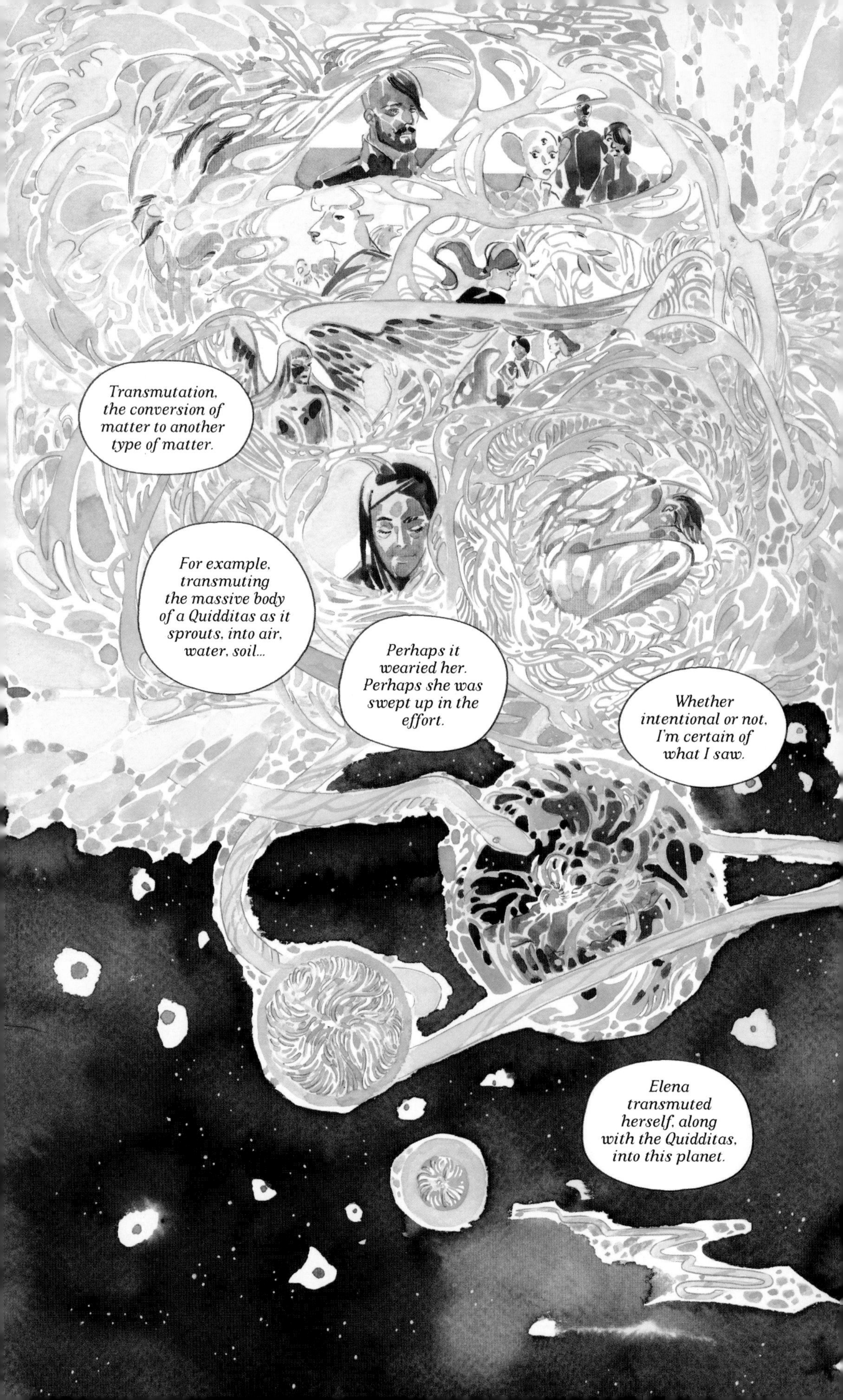
Transmutation, the conversion of matter to another type of matter.
For example, transmuting the massive body of a Quidditas as it sprouts, into air, water, soil...
Perhaps it wearied her. Perhaps she was swept up in the effort.
Whether intentional or not, I'm certain of what I saw.
Elena transmuted herself, along with the Quidditas, into this planet.

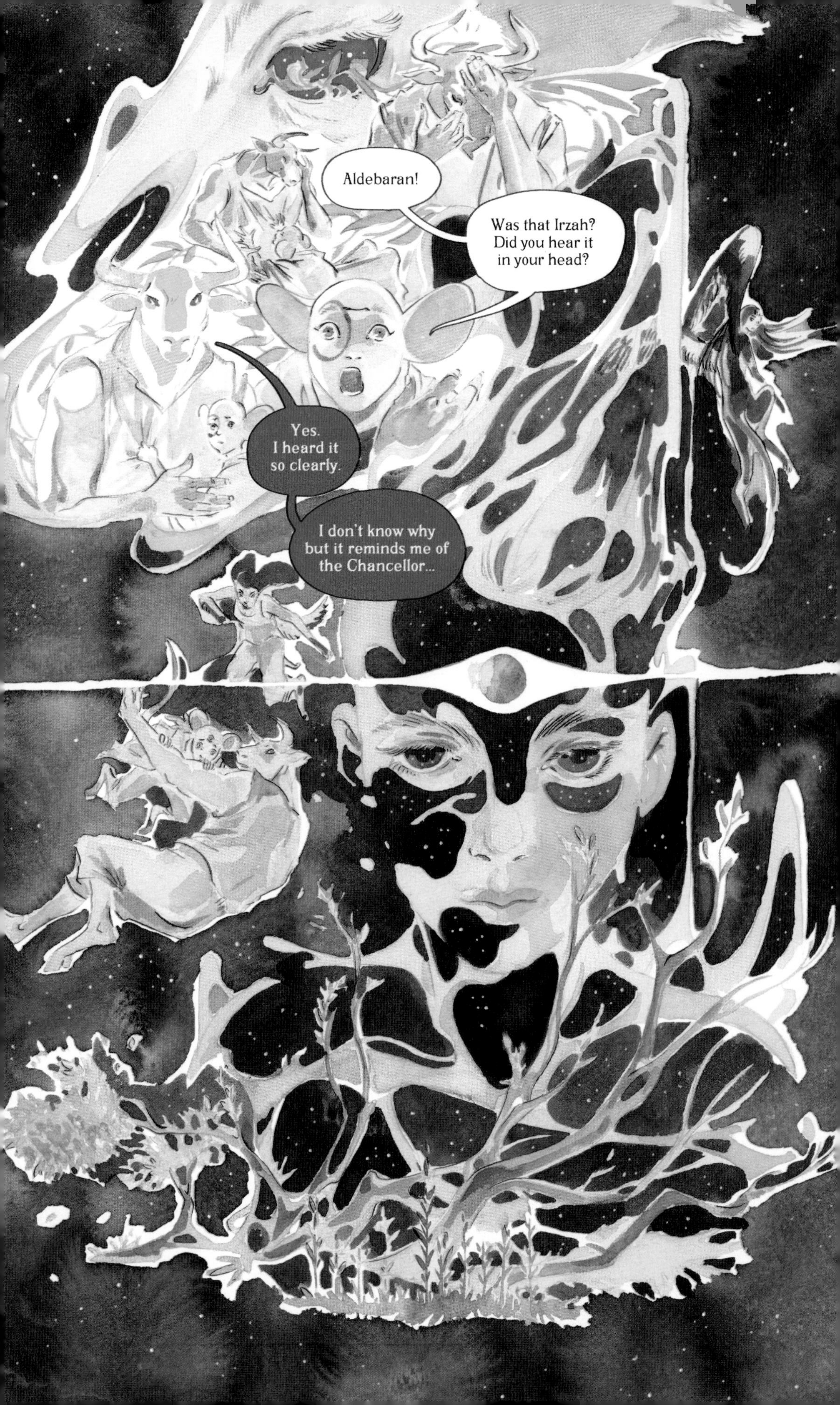
Aldebaran!
Was that Irzah? Did you hear it in your head?
Yes. I heard it so clearly.
I don't know why but it reminds me of the Chancellor...

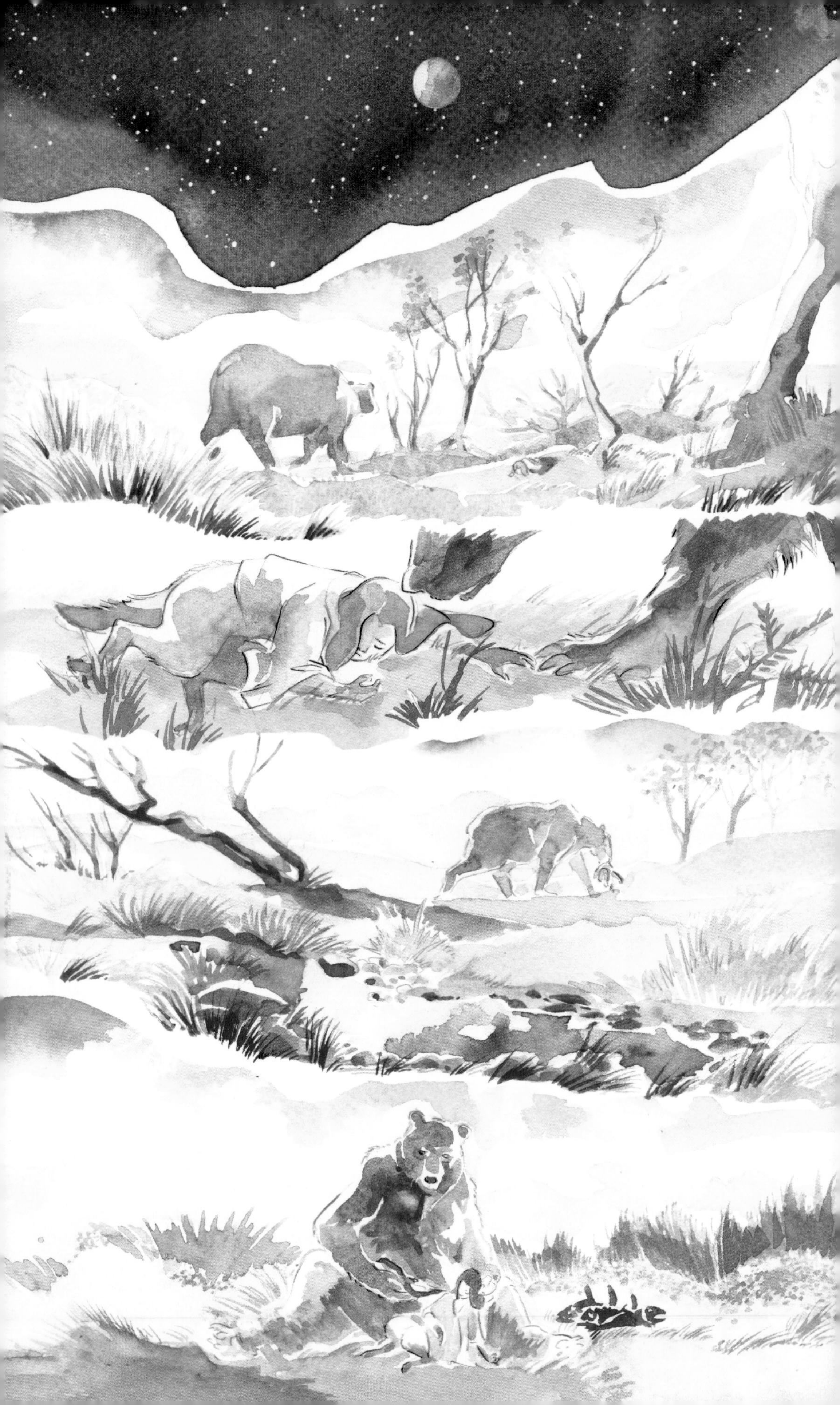

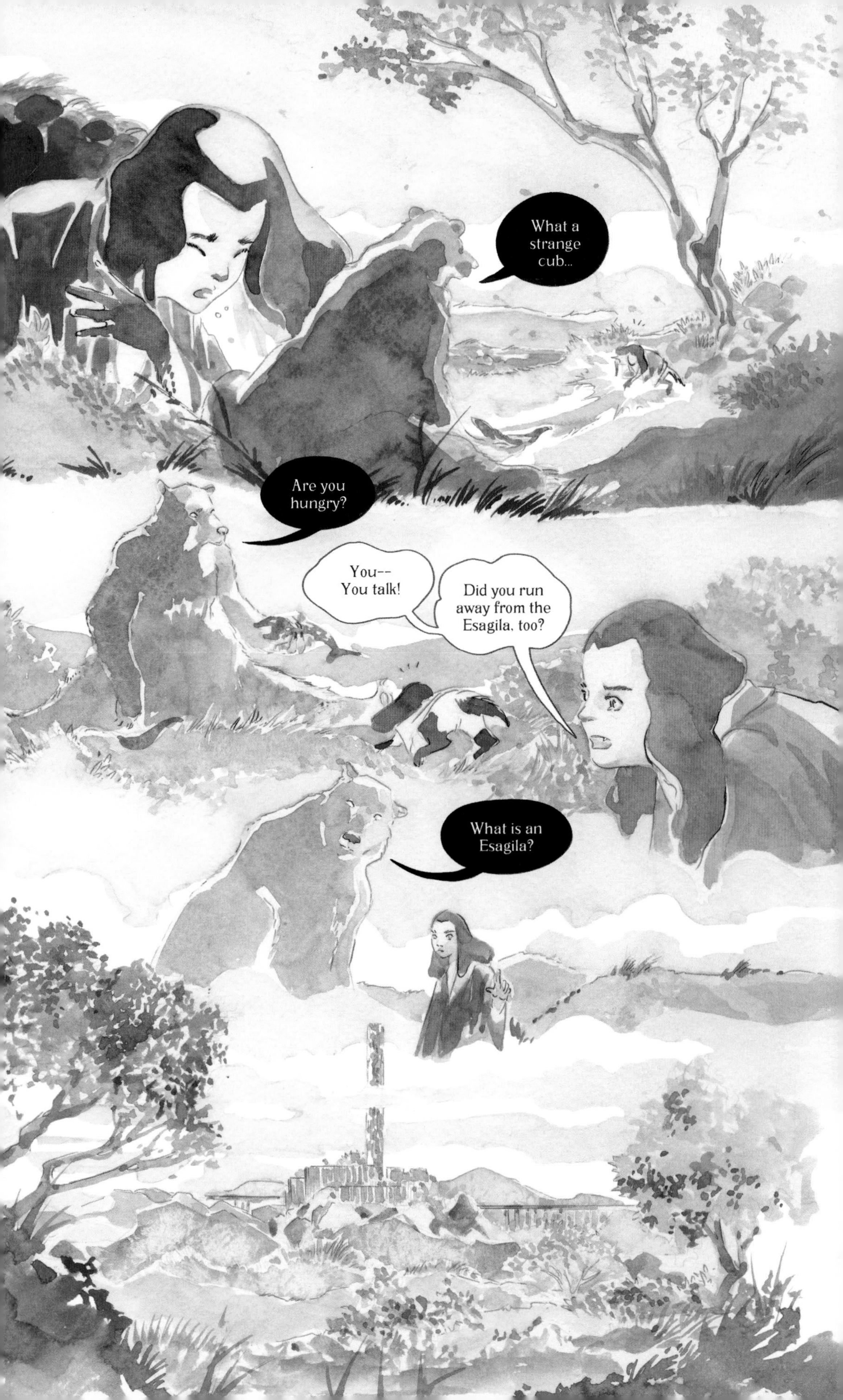
What a strange cub...
Are you hungry?
You-- You talk!
Did you run away from the Esagila, too?
What is an Esagila?

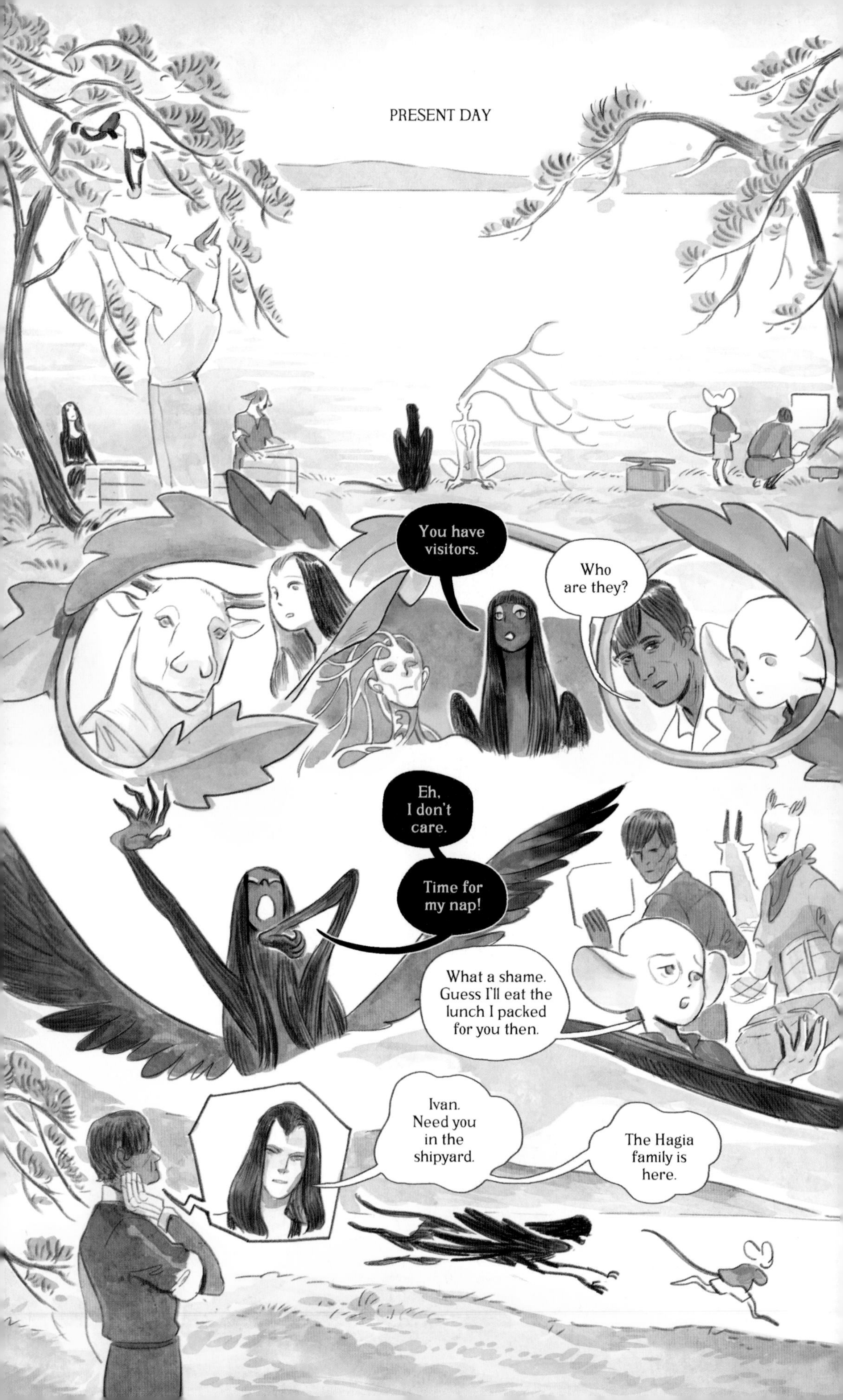
PRESENT DAY
You have visitors.
Who are they?
Eh, I don't care.
Time for my nap!
What a shame. Guess I'll eat the lunch I packed for you then.
Ivan. Need you in the shipyard.
The Hagia family is here.

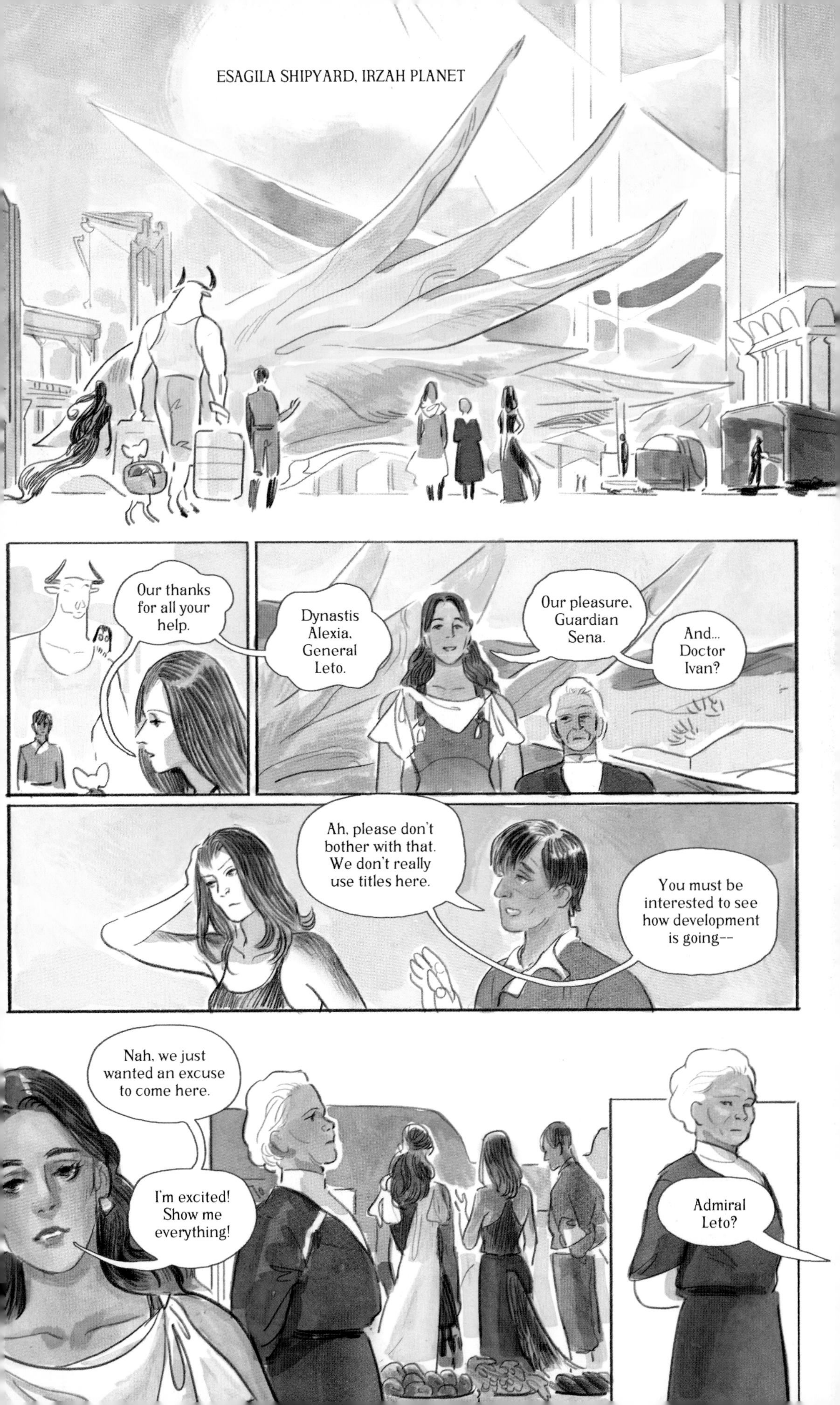
ESAGILA SHIPYARD, IRZAH PLANET
Our thanks for all your help.
Dynastis Alexia, General Leto.
Our pleasure, Guardian Sena.
And... Doctor Ivan?
Ah, please don't bother with that. We don't really use titles here.
You must be interested to see how development is going--
Nah, we just wanted an excuse to come here.
I'm excited! Show me everything!
Admiral Leto?

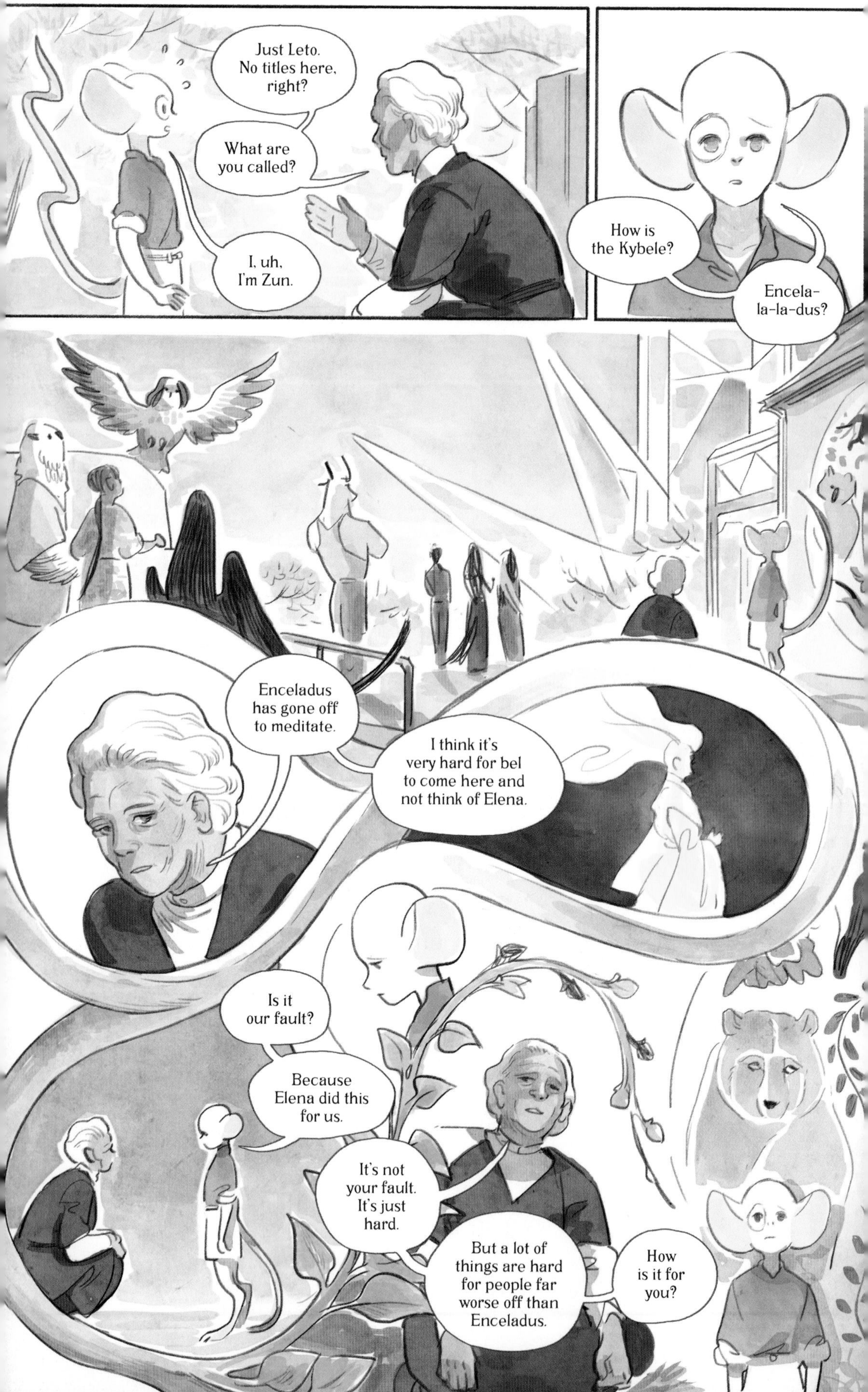

Just Leto.
No titles here, right?
What are you called?
I, uh, I'm Zun.
How is the Kybele?
Encela-la-la-dus?
Enceladus has gone off to meditate.
I think it's very hard for bel to come here and not think of Elena.
Is it our fault?
Because Elena did this for us.
It's not your fault. It's just hard.
But a lot of things are hard for people far worse off than Enceladus.
How is it for you?

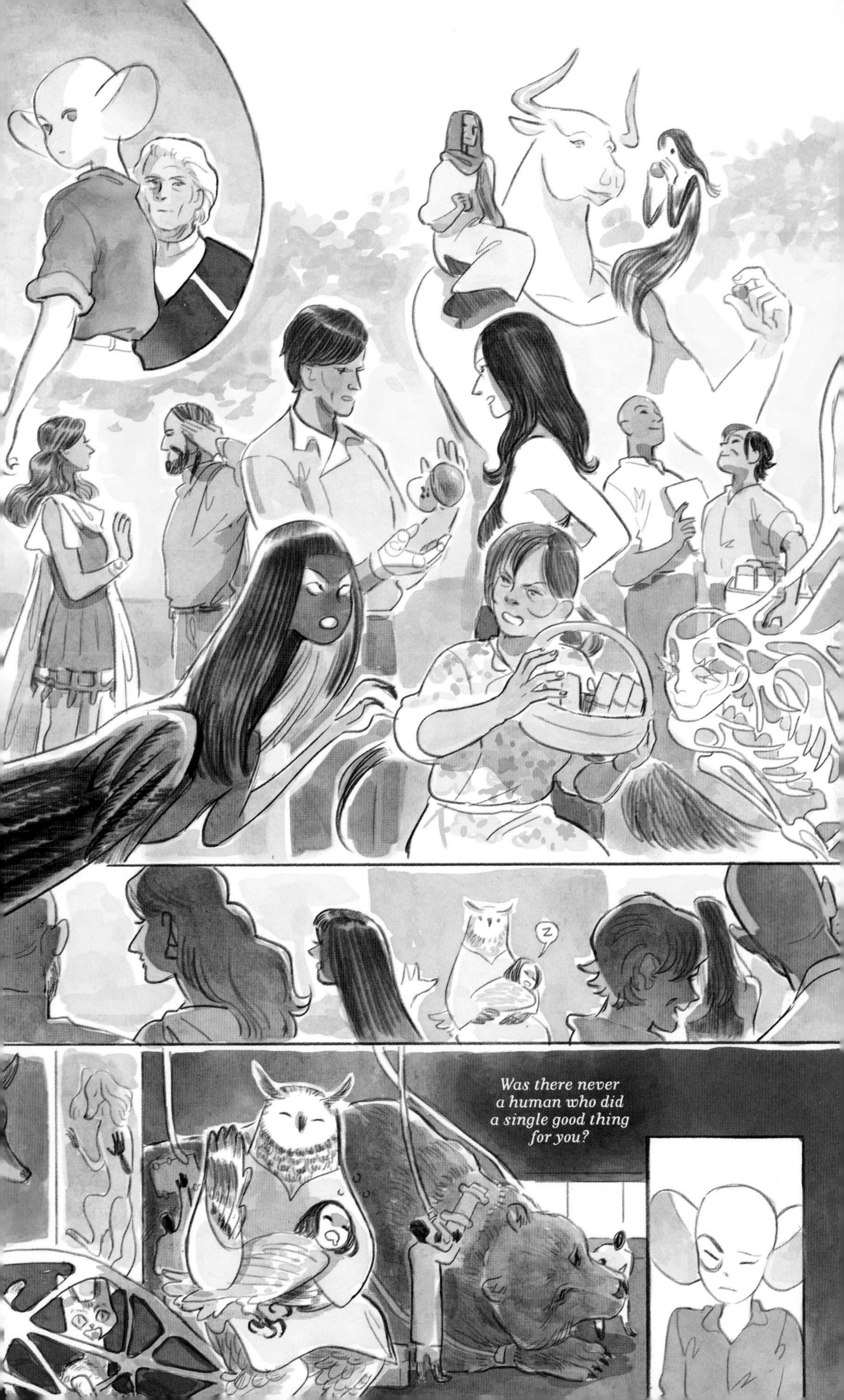
Z
Was there never a human who did a single good thing for you?

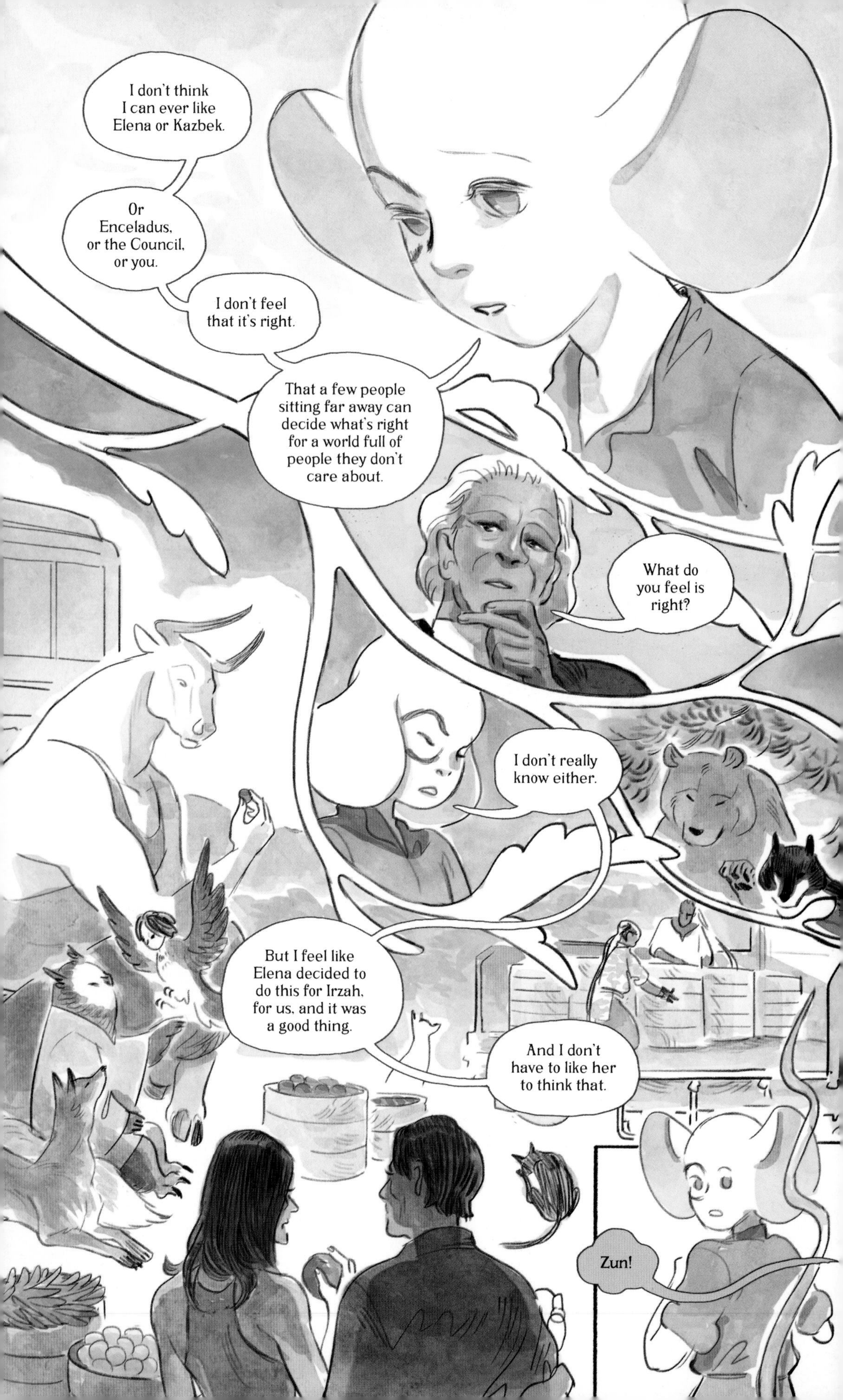
I don't think I can ever like Elena or Kazbek.
Or Enceladus, or the Council, or you.
I don't feel that it's right.
That a few people sitting far away can decide what's right for a world full of people they don't care about.
What do you feel is right?
I don't really know either.
But I feel like Elena decided to do this for Irzah, for us, and it was a good thing.
And I don't have to like her to think that.
Zun!

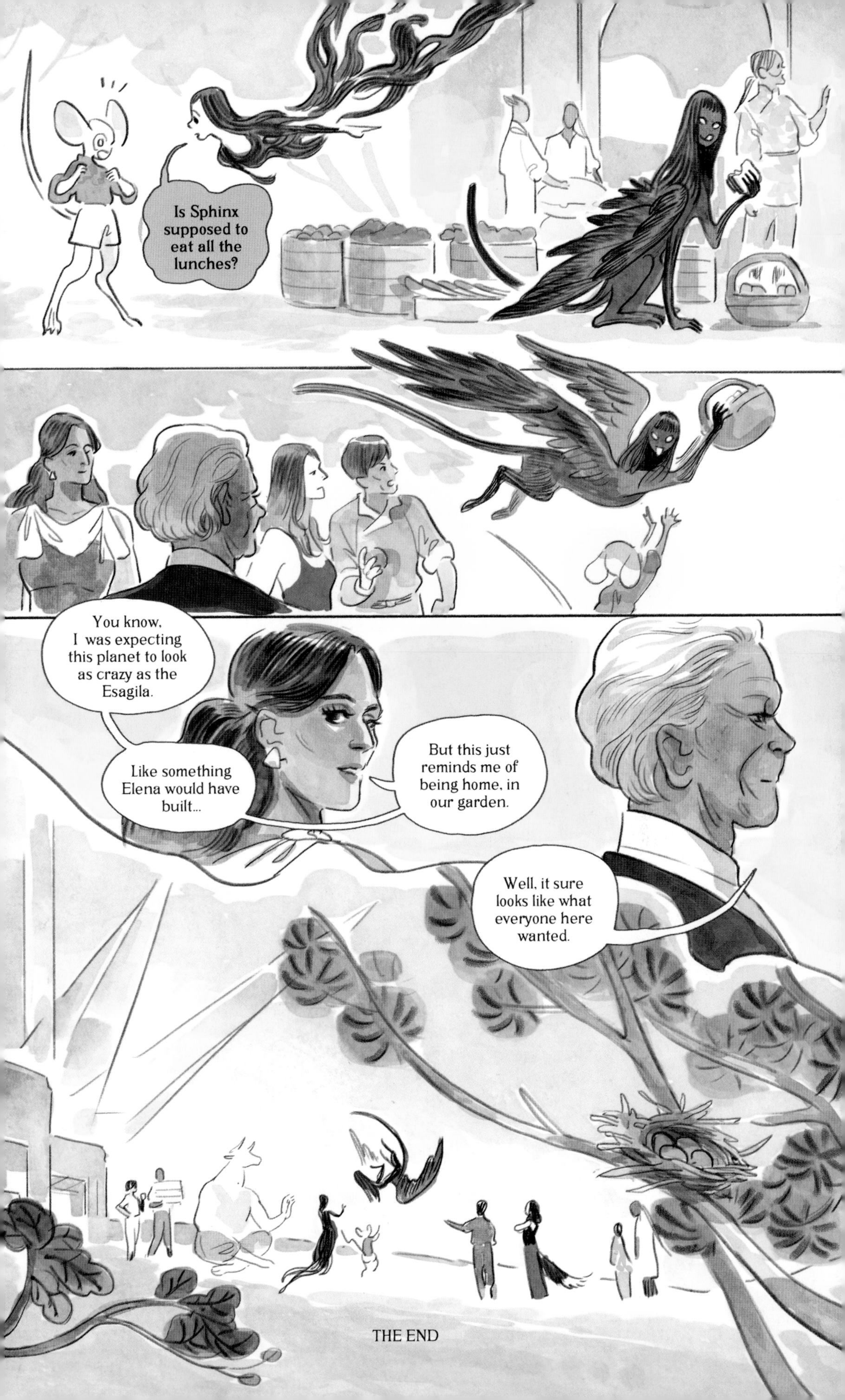
Is Sphinx supposed to eat all the lunches?
You know, I was expecting this planet to look as crazy as the Esagila.
Like something Elena would have built...
But this just reminds me of being home, in our garden.
Well, it sure looks like what everyone here wanted.
THE END

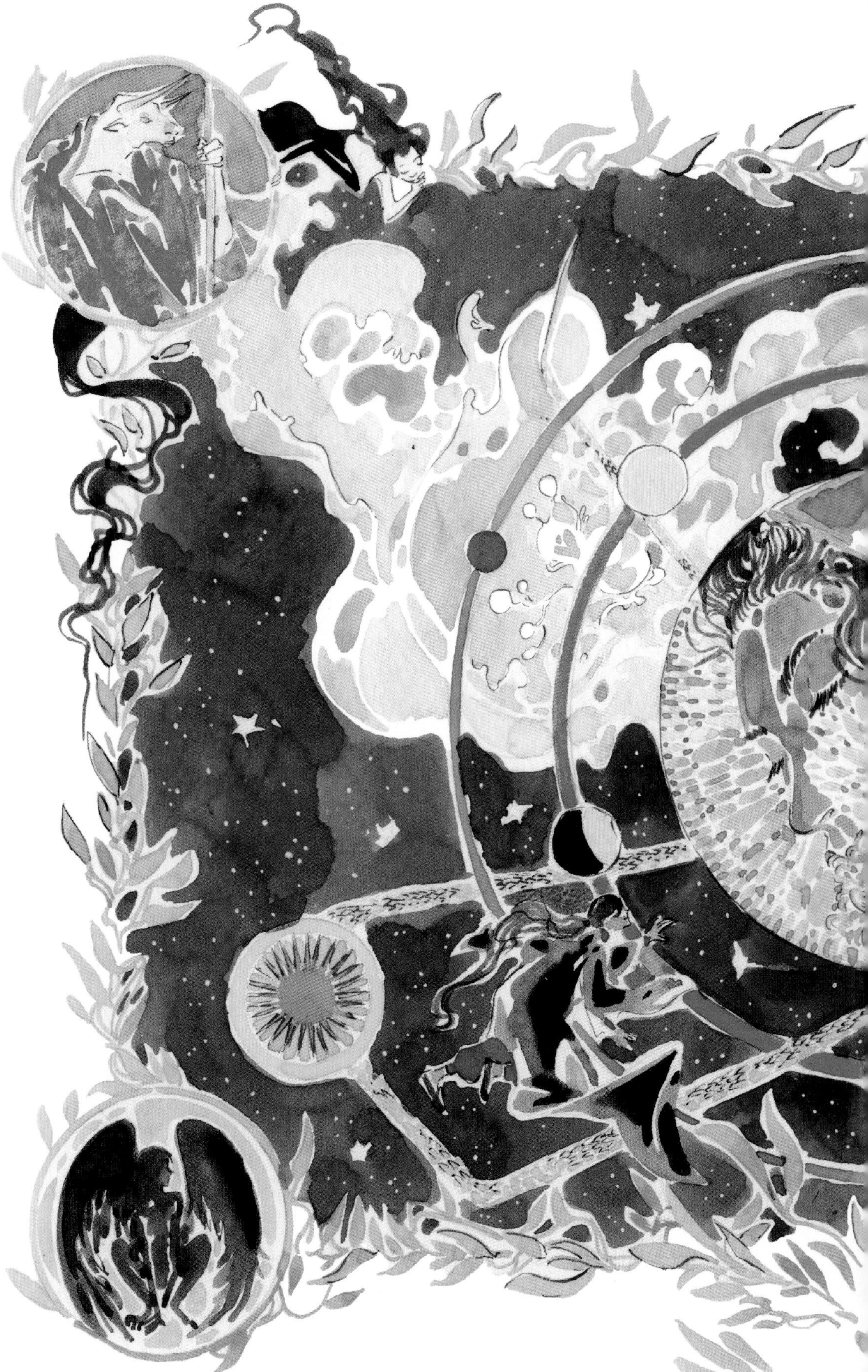

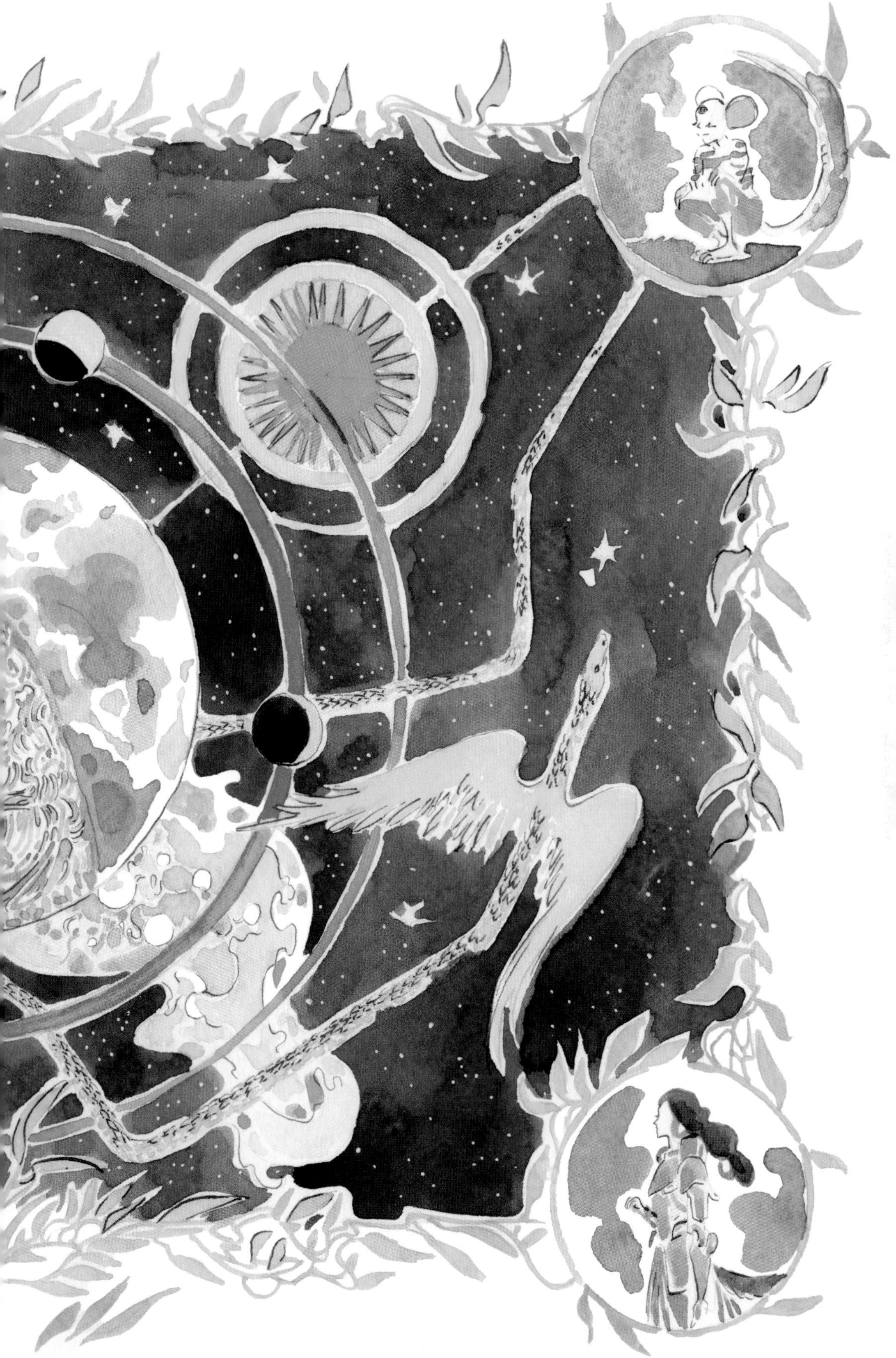

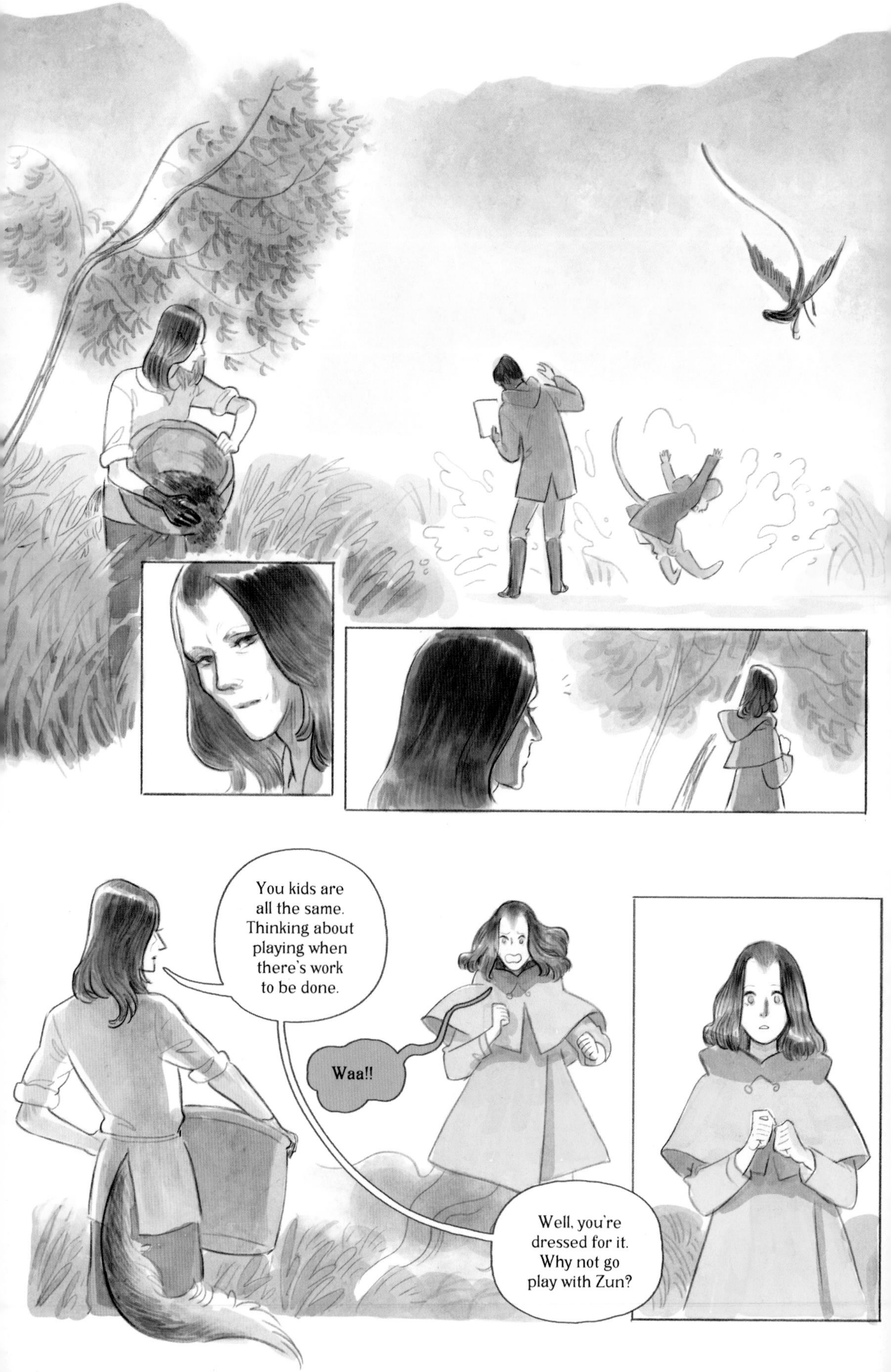
You kids are all the same. Thinking about playing when there's work to be done.
Waa!!
Well, you're dressed for it. Why not go play with Zun?

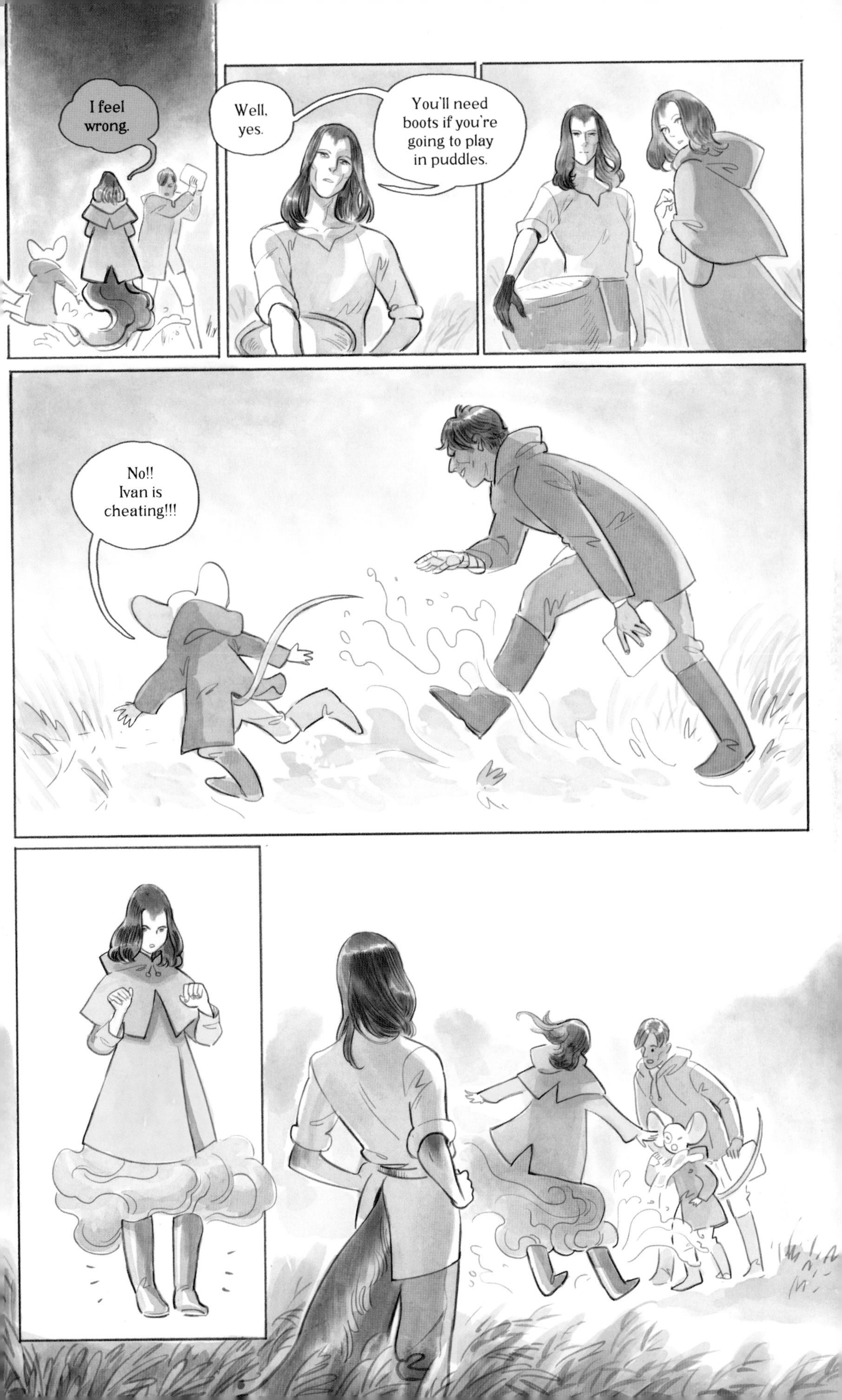

I feel wrong.
Well, yes.
You'll need boots if you're going to play in puddles.
No!! Ivan is cheating!!!

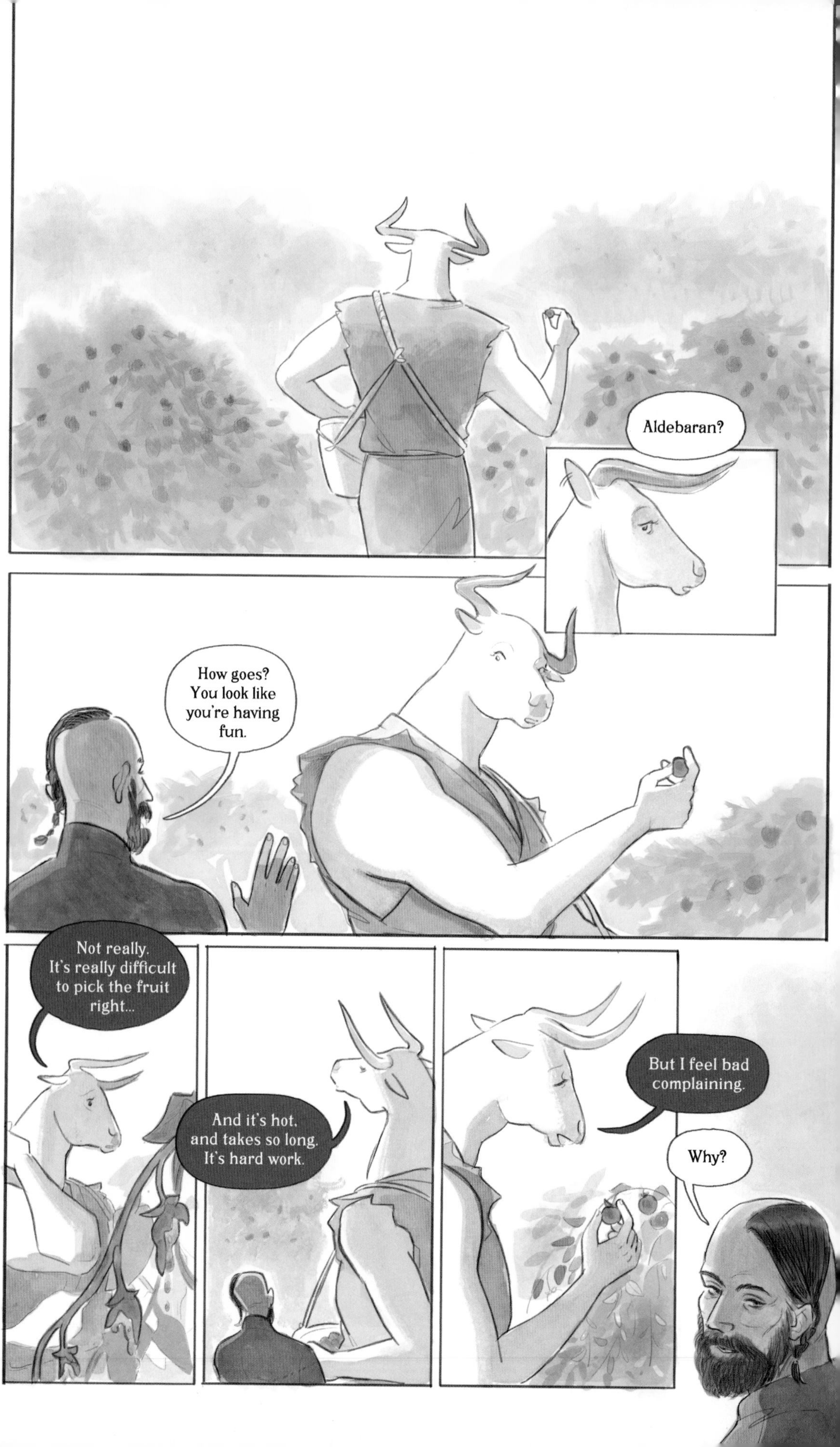

Aldebaran?
How goes? You look like you're having fun.
Not really. It's really difficult to pick the fruit right...
And it's hot, and takes so long. It's hard work.
But I feel bad complaining.
Why?

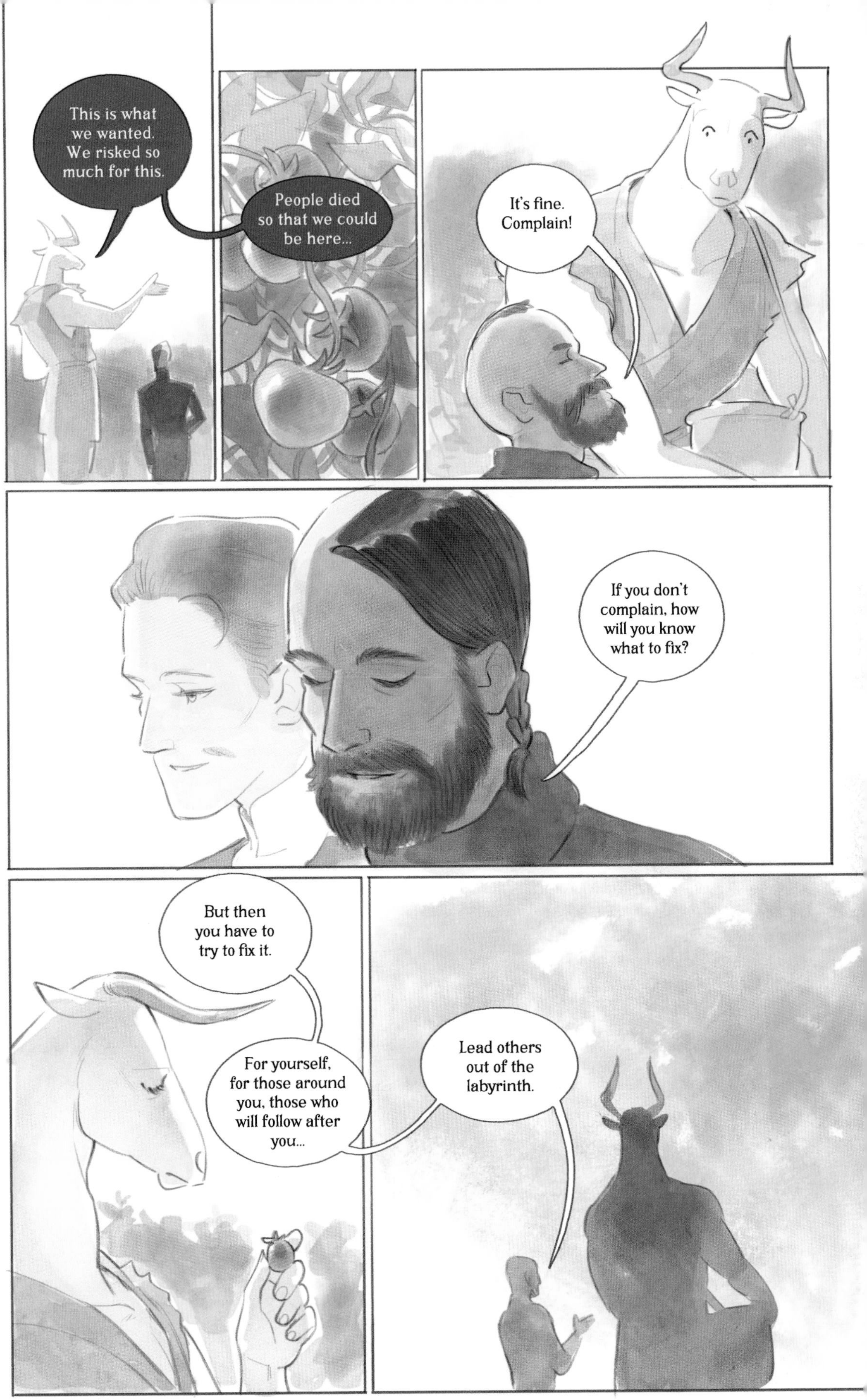
This is what we wanted. We risked so much for this.
People died so that we could be here...
It's fine. Complain!
If you don't complain, how will you know what to fix?
But then you have to try to fix it.
For yourself, for those around you, those who will follow after you...
Lead others out of the labyrinth.

The Synchronia

*The Elders are Synchronian ancestors that surived the *span*. They gather human heritage and culture through space and time, and enjoy finding ancient wonders, like the ones that name the capital planets of the System.

The Yazad are the most important family in terms of power and wealth as they control three planets.

Planets of influence:
The Garden
The Mausoleum
The Temple: Hosts the Embassy of the Elders.

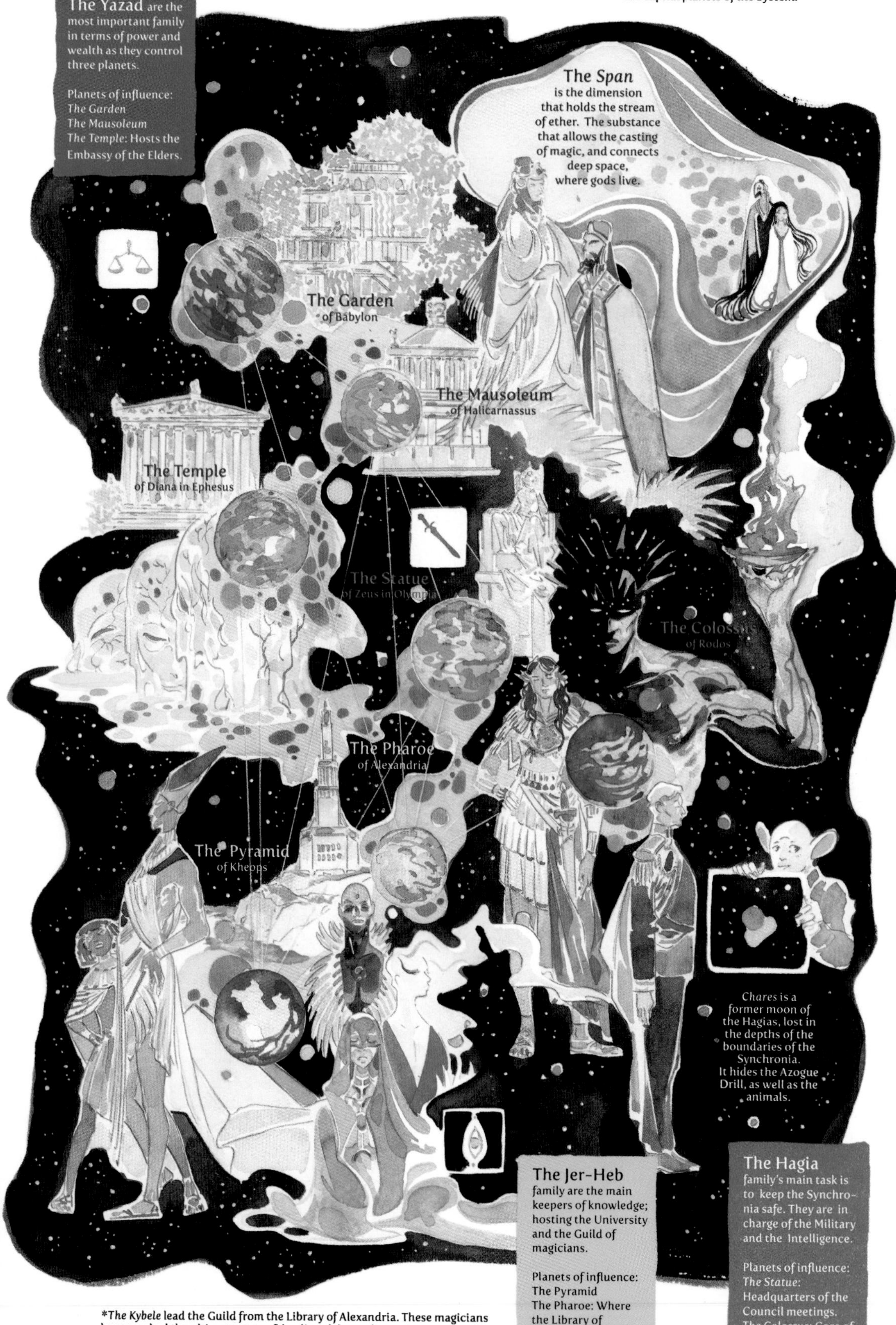

The *Span*
is the dimension that holds the stream of ether. The substance that allows the casting of magic, and connects deep space, where gods live.
The Garden
of Babylon
The Mausoleum
of Halicarnassus
The Temple
of Diana in Ephesus
The Statue
of Zeus in Olympia
The Colossus
of Rodos
The Pharoe
of Alexandria
The Pyramid
of Kheops
Chares is a former moon of the Hagias, lost in the depths of the boundaries of the Synchronia. It hides the Azogue Drill, as well as the animals.

The Jer-Heb family are the main keepers of knowledge; hosting the University and the Guild of magicians.

Planets of influence:
The Pyramid
The Pharoe: Where the Library of Alexandria is.

The Hagia family's main task is to keep the Synchronia safe. They are in charge of the Military and the Intelligence.

Planets of influence:
The Statue: Headquarters of the Council meetings.
The Colossus: Core of the Military Academy.

*The *Kybele* lead the Guild from the Library of Alexandria. These magicians have reached the ultimate state of healing alchemy, becoming experts able to interact with the genetic information of every being in the galaxy.

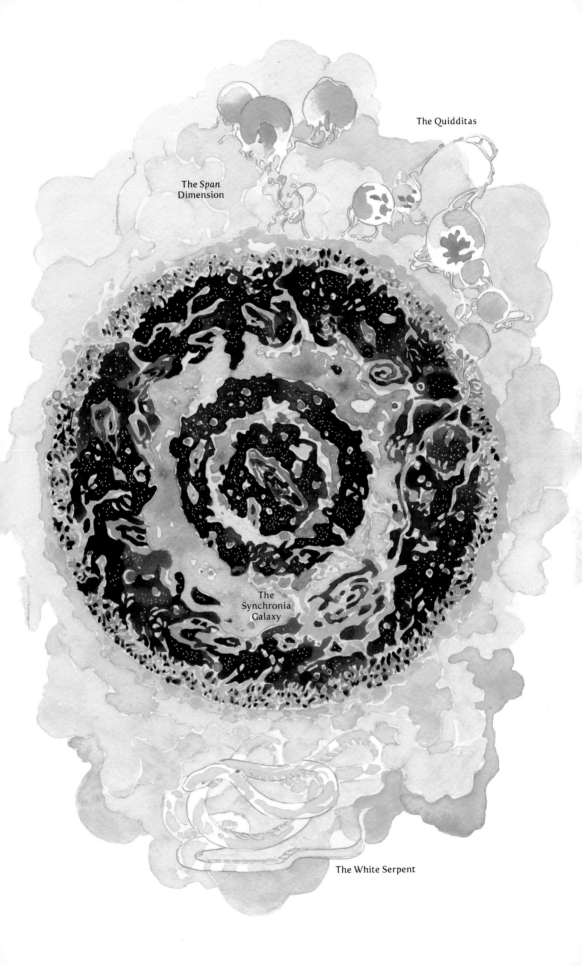

The Quidditas

The *Span*
Dimension

The
Synchronia
Galaxy

The White Serpent

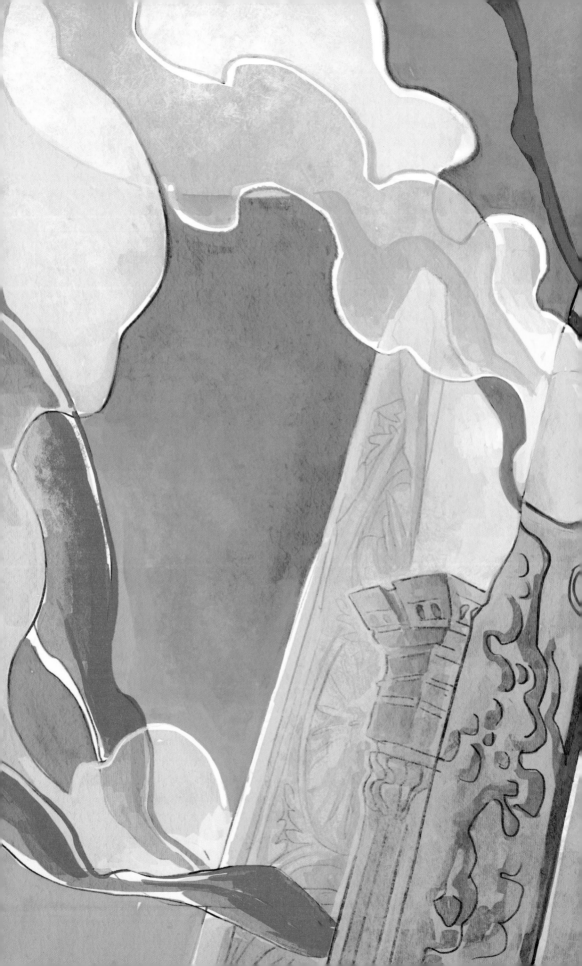

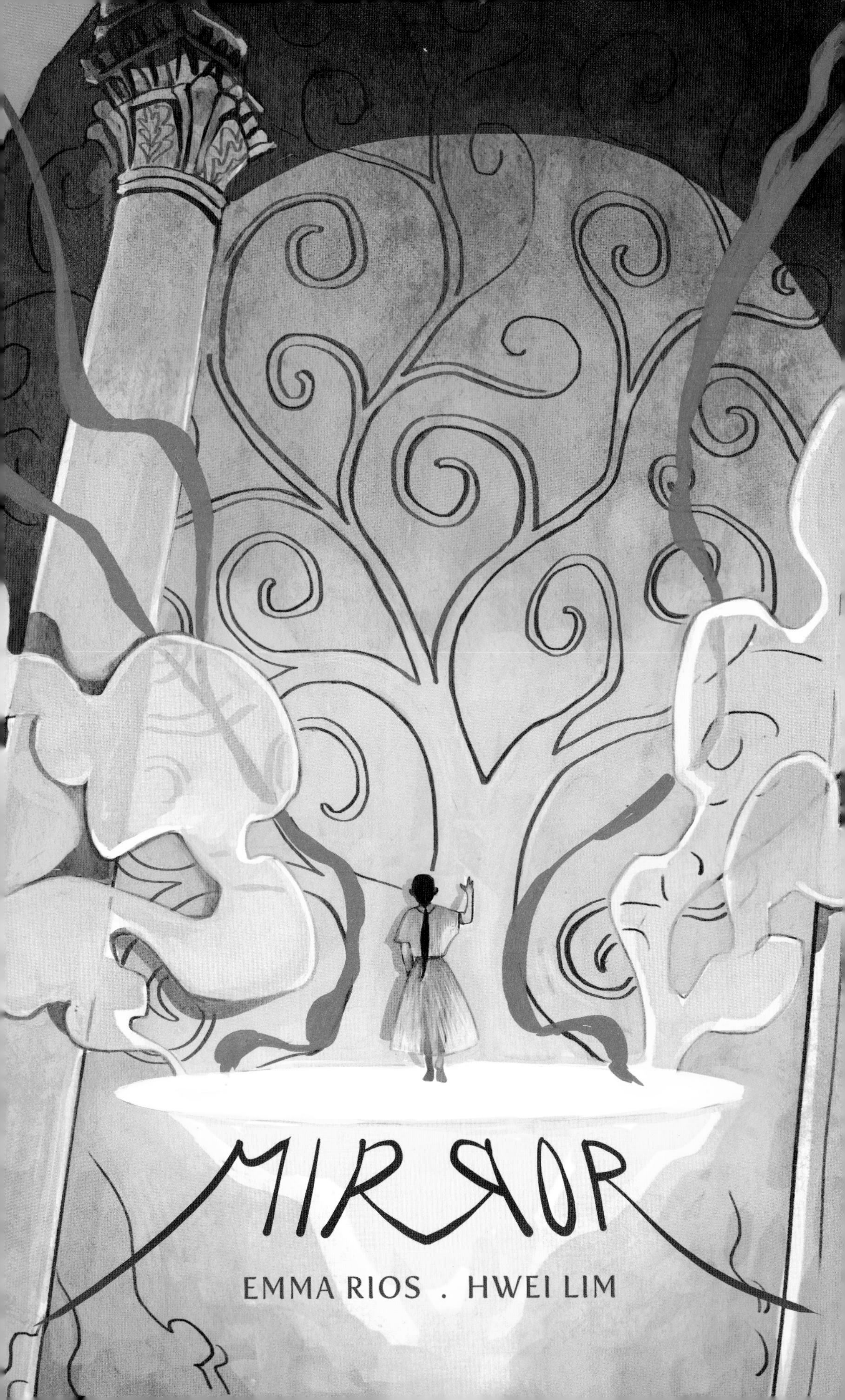
MIRROR
EMMA RIOS . HWEI LIM

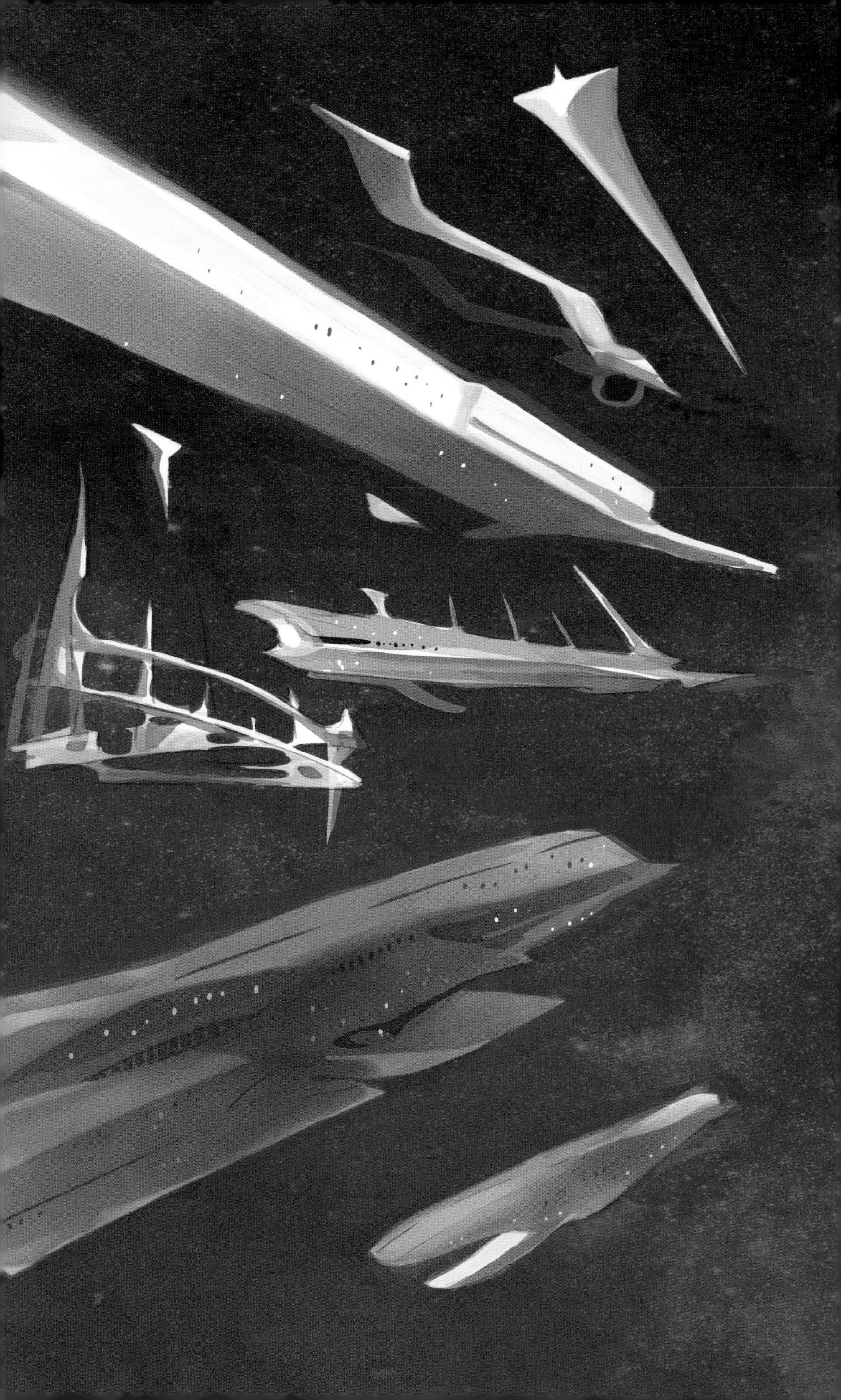

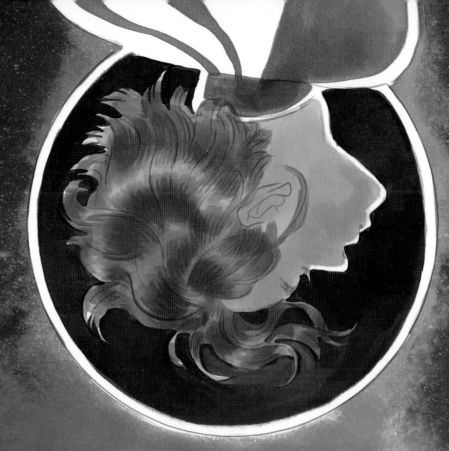

EMMA RIOS . HWEI LIM

MIRROR

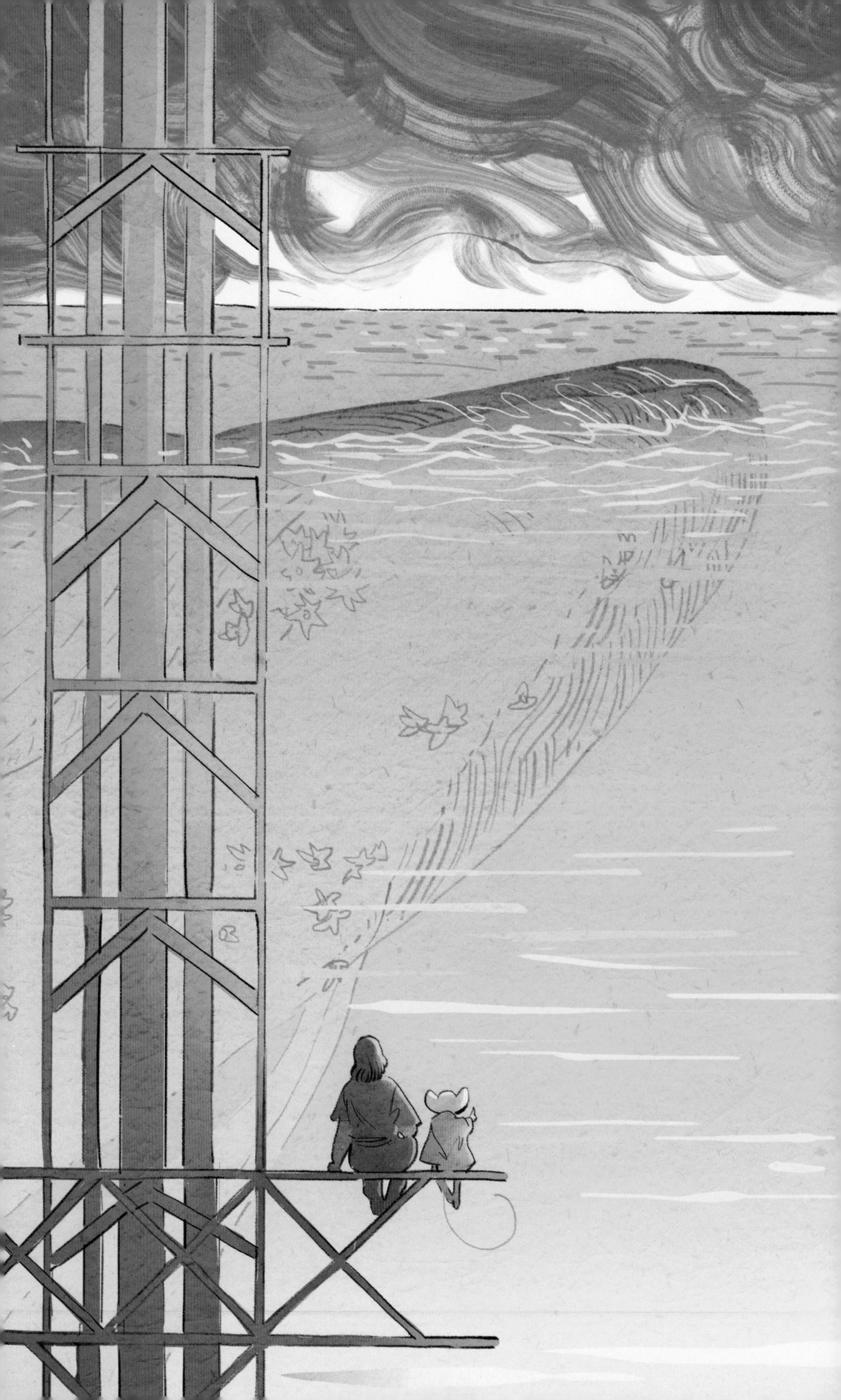

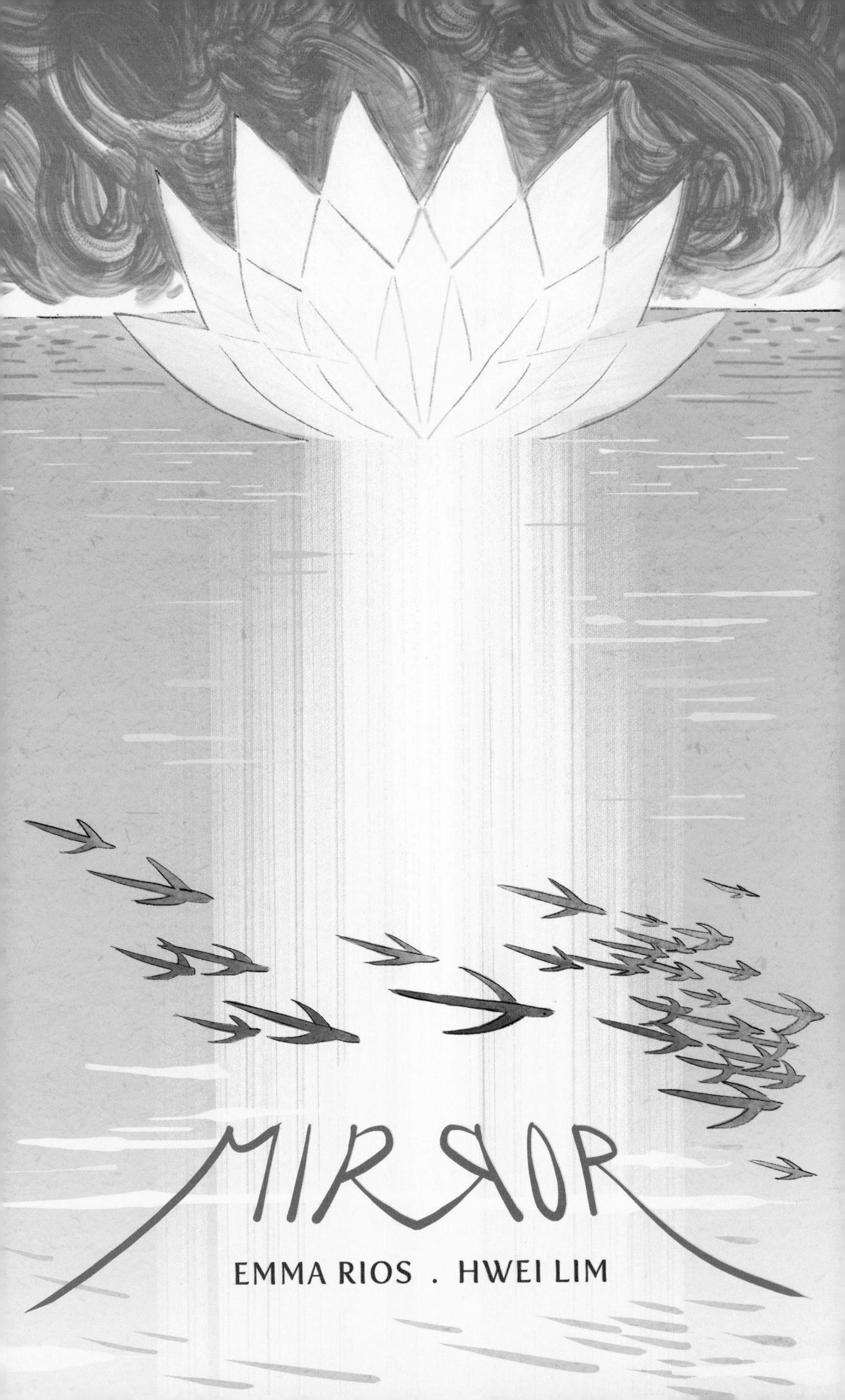
MIRROR
EMMA RIOS . HWEI LIM

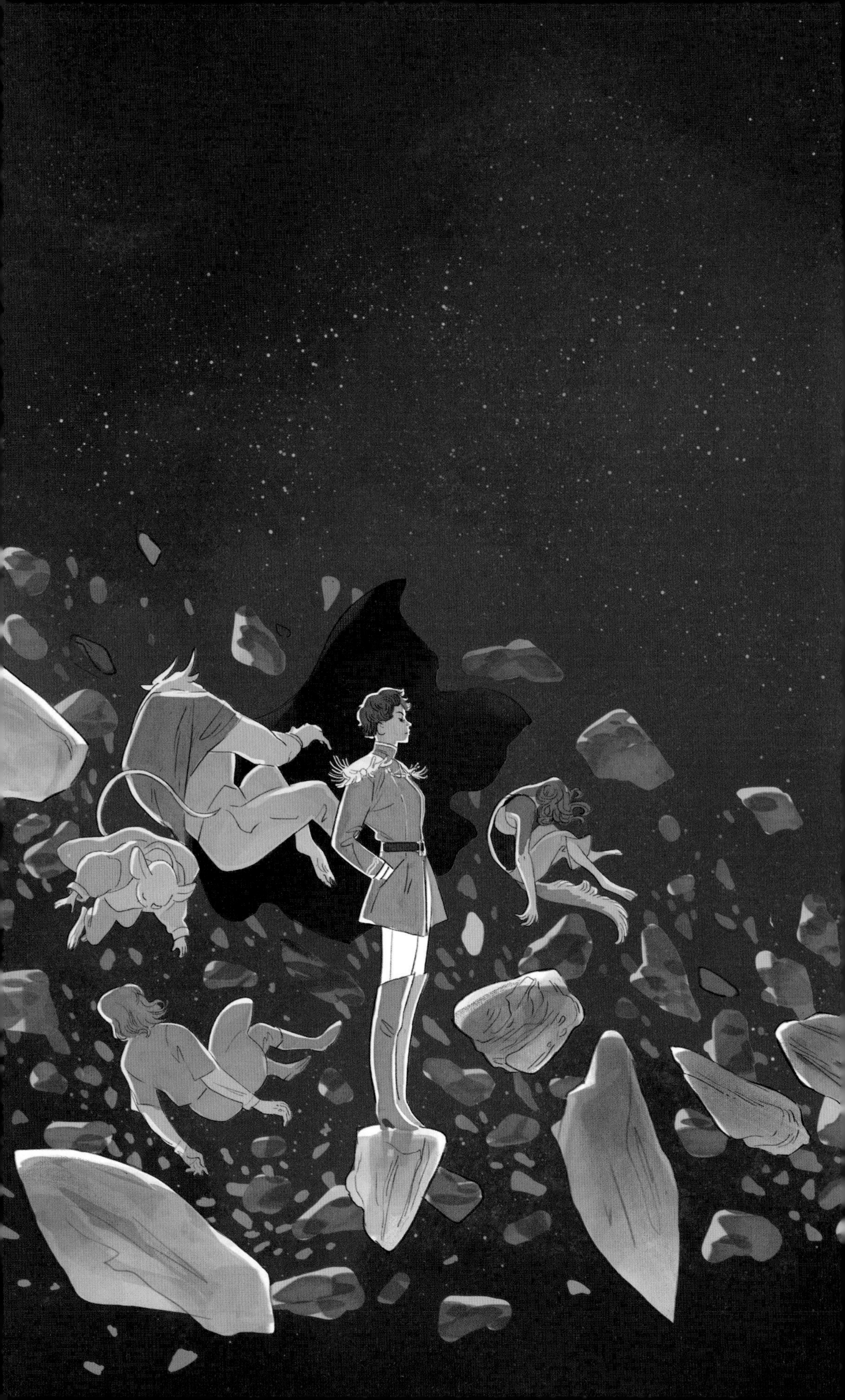

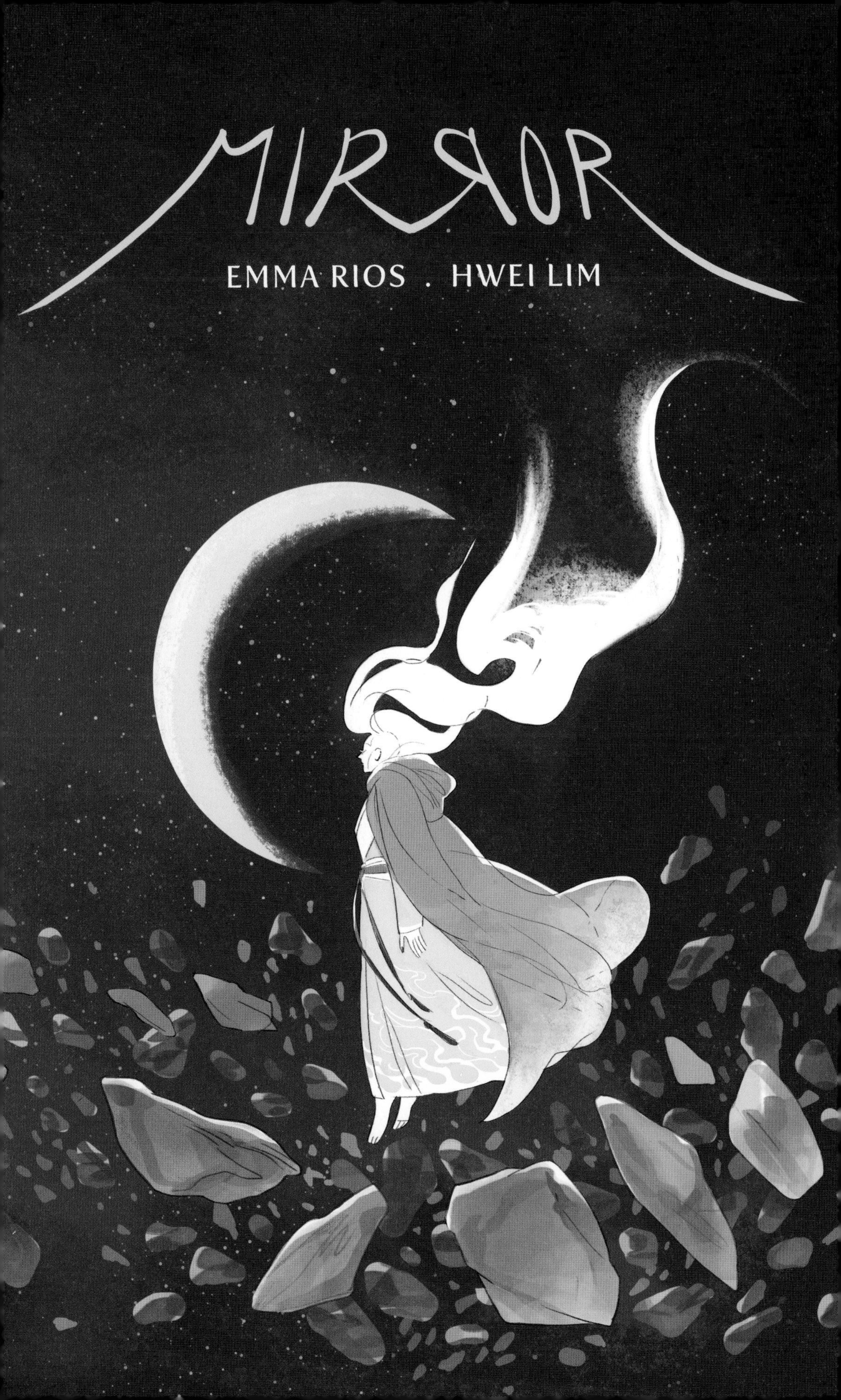
MIRROR
EMMA RIOS . HWEI LIM

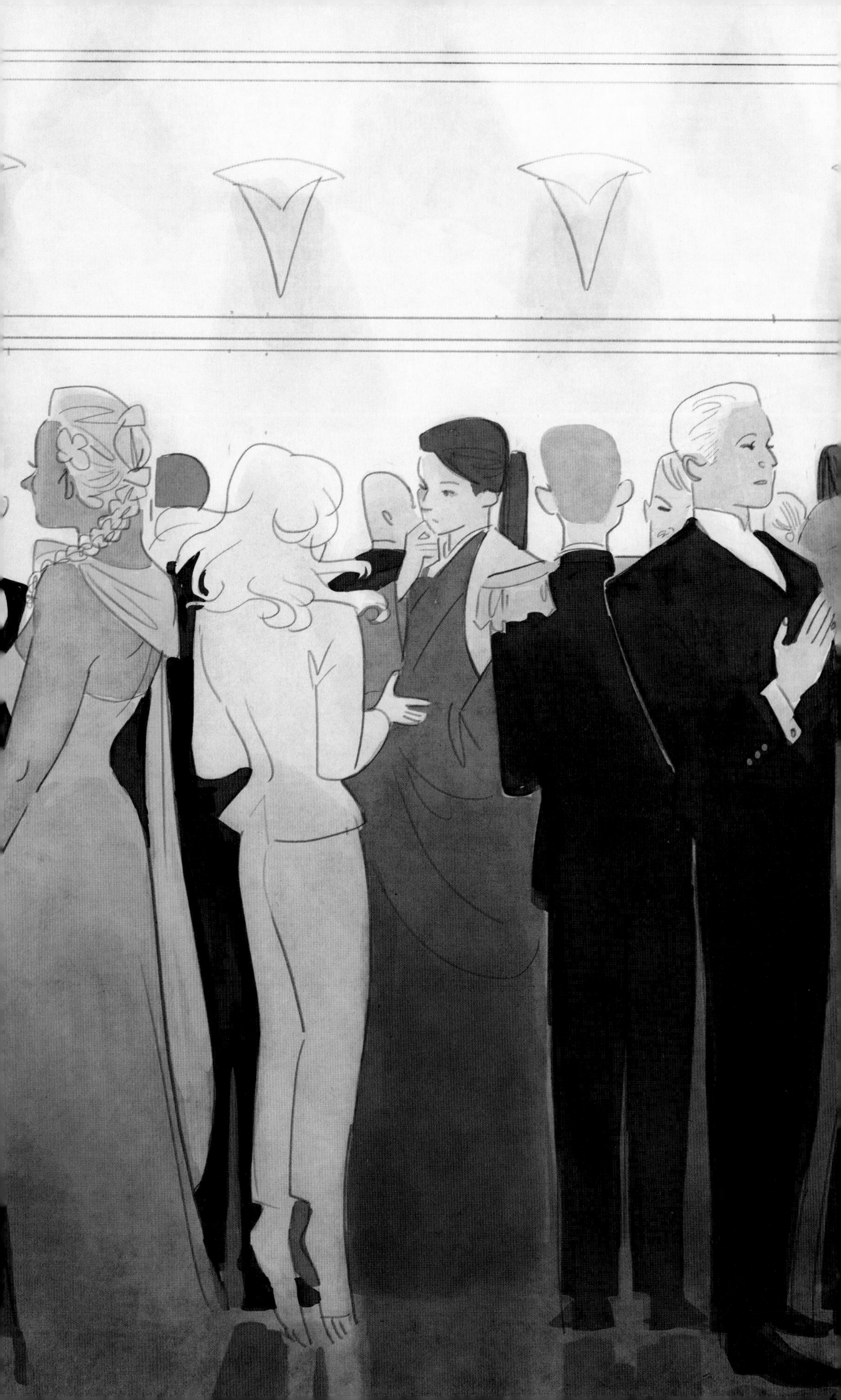

MIRROR

EMMA RIOS . HWEI LIM

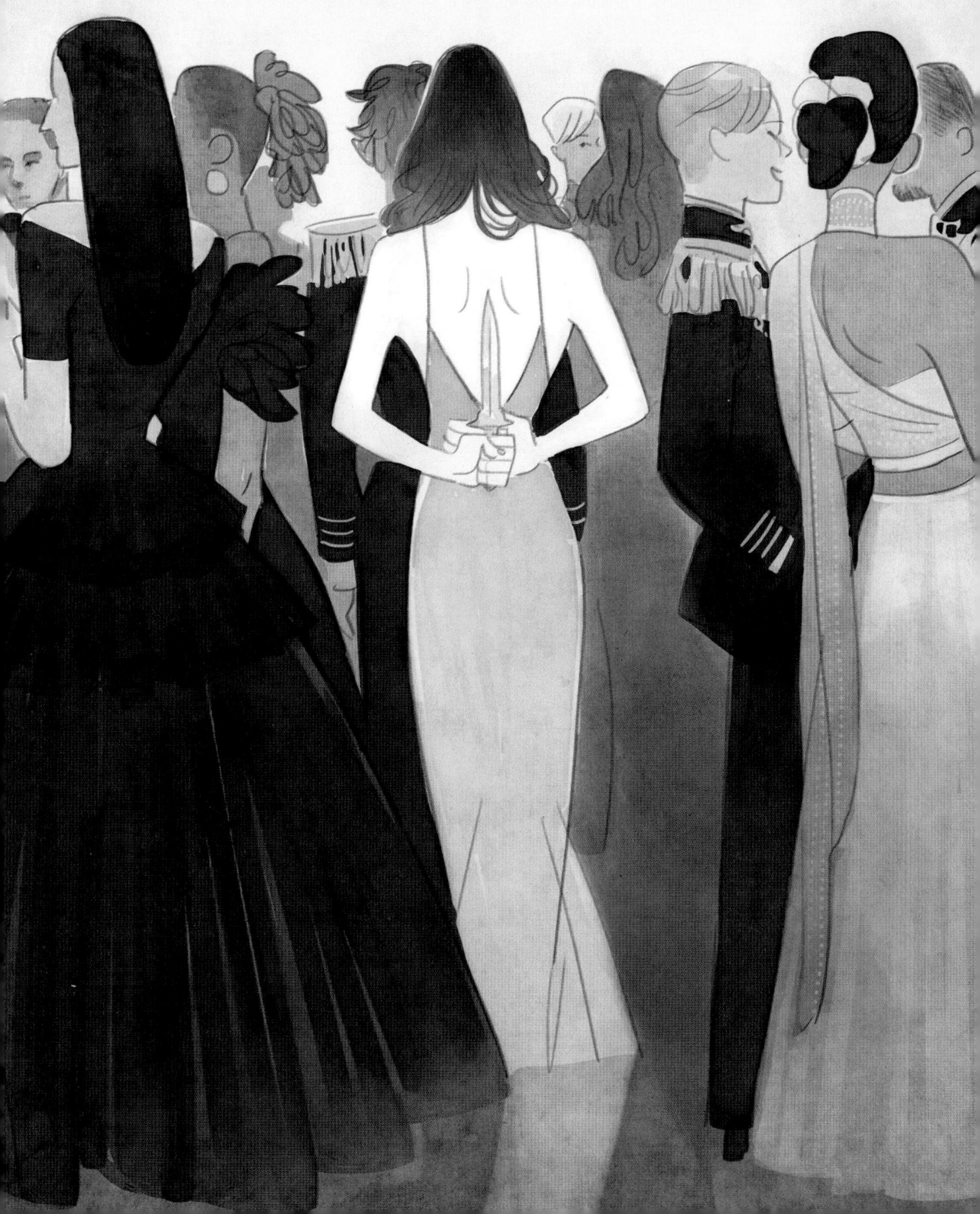

By Miquel Muerto

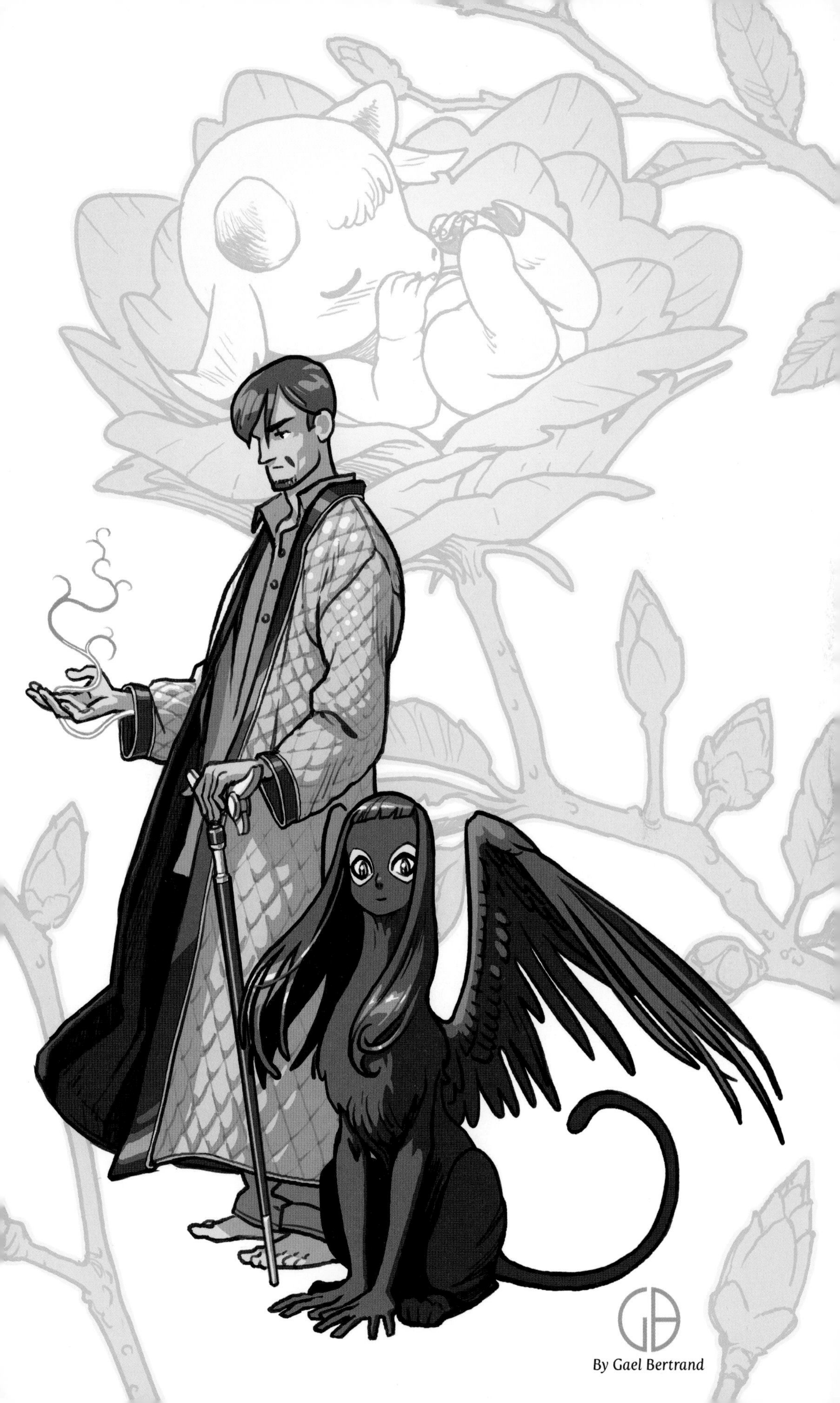

By Gael Bertrand

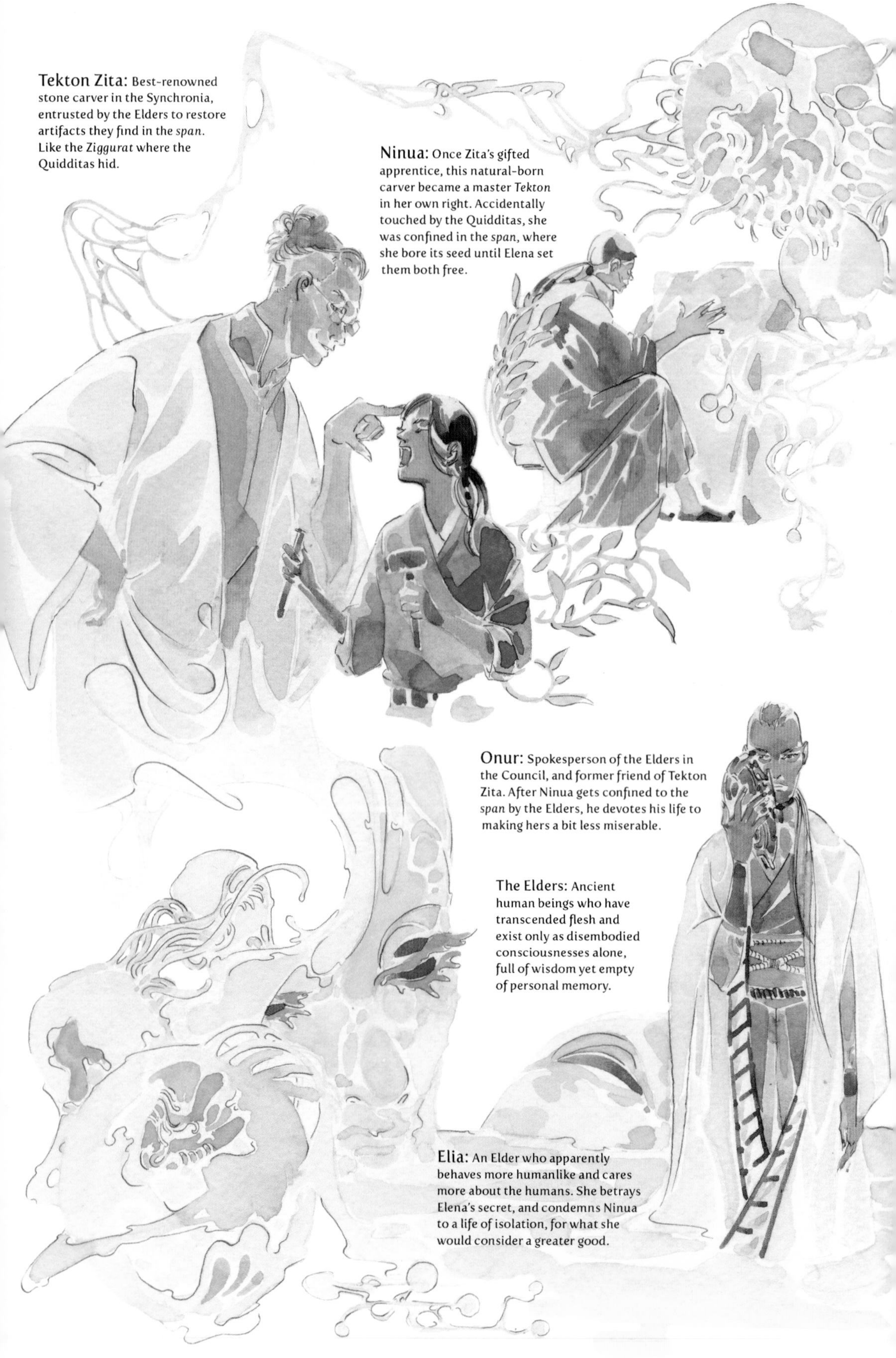

Tekton Zita: Best-renowned stone carver in the Synchronia, entrusted by the Elders to restore artifacts they find in the *span*. Like the *Ziggurat* where the Quidditas hid.

Ninua: Once Zita's gifted apprentice, this natural-born carver became a master *Tekton* in her own right. Accidentally touched by the Quidditas, she was confined in the *span*, where she bore its seed until Elena set them both free.

Onur: Spokesperson of the Elders in the Council, and former friend of Tekton Zita. After Ninua gets confined to the *span* by the Elders, he devotes his life to making hers a bit less miserable.

The Elders: Ancient human beings who have transcended flesh and exist only as disembodied consciousnesses alone, full of wisdom yet empty of personal memory.

Elia: An Elder who apparently behaves more humanlike and cares more about the humans. She betrays Elena's secret, and condemns Ninua to a life of isolation, for what she would consider a greater good.

The Quidditas: A God-like being that sleeps in the *span* waiting to devour and digest all life knowledge.

The Serpent: A God-like being that lives within dimensions trying to keep the balance between civilizations through space and time.

Abet Musa: Coming from a lineage of magicians from Pharoe, Abet was surprisingly born without magical talent. A disgrace that makes him the shame of his relatives. Over the years, he turns into a flawless engineer and applies for the Hagia Family, with the innovative design of the Esagila. Under Elena's command, Abet finally finds a real home and a cute husband: Heron Cora.

Besarion Abkhazi: A brilliant strategist and Elena's most trusted second in command. Kazbek and Besarion are unrelated by blood, but both come from the same Hagia subject family branch, the Abkhazi. Having tutored him in the Academy, Besarion recommends Kaz to join his fleet as scientific officer. He's a true friend, and a good advisor with strong principles, idealism, and a sense of justice.

Heron Cora: A rebel born inside a subject family of the Hagia, the Agelas, a cast of disciplined soldiers forged through inhuman training. Elena spends some time there, and meets an untamed young Heron who'd rather die than follow their rules. The strong bond between them comes from those days.

Zeno Herma: A mysterious blind listener.

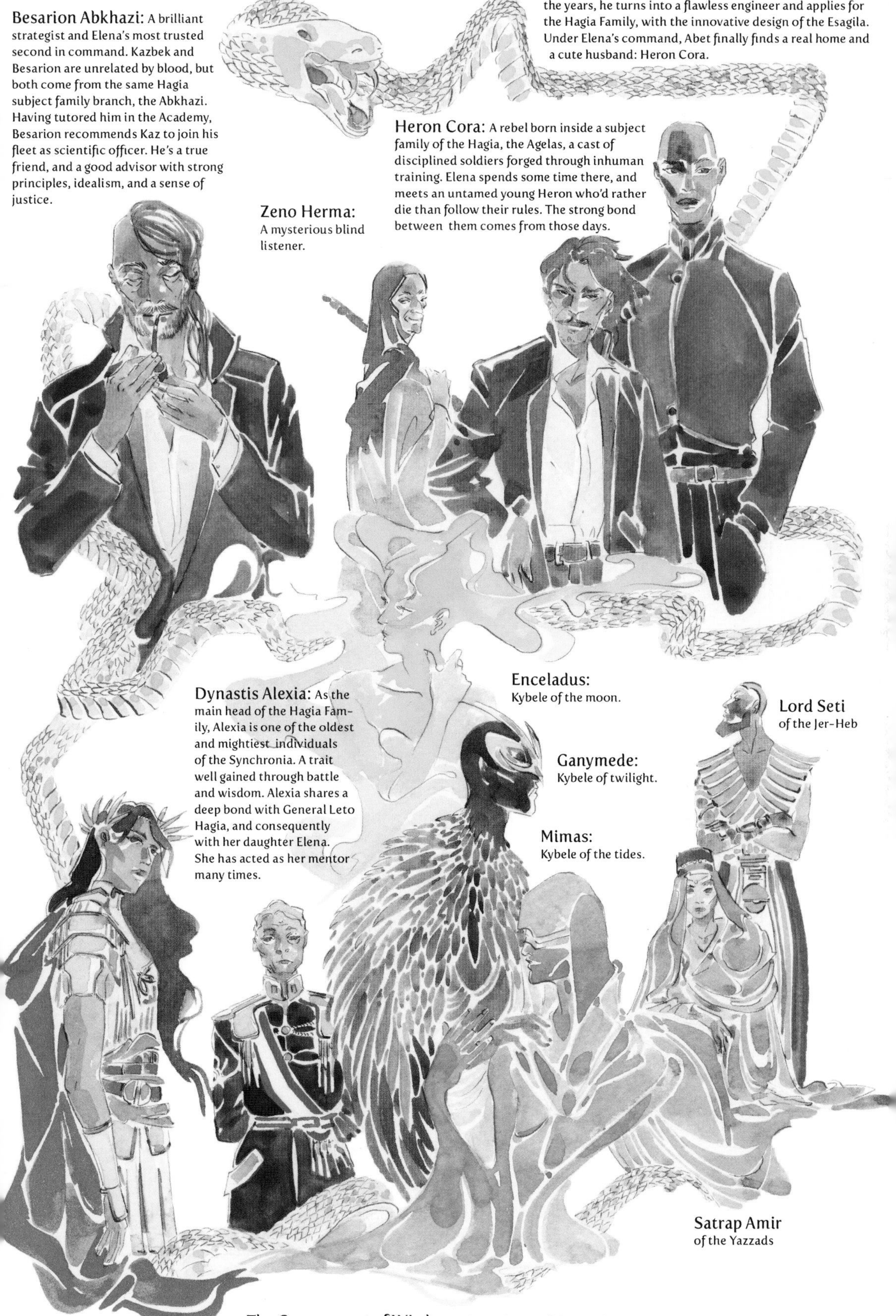

Enceladus: Kybele of the moon.

Lord Seti of the Jer-Heb

Dynastis Alexia: As the main head of the Hagia Family, Alexia is one of the oldest and mightiest individuals of the Synchronia. A trait well gained through battle and wisdom. Alexia shares a deep bond with General Leto Hagia, and consequently with her daughter Elena. She has acted as her mentor many times.

Ganymede: Kybele of twilight.

Mimas: Kybele of the tides.

Satrap Amir of the Yazzads

The Government of Wisdom: The authority of the Synchronia lies in its Council, comprised of the heads of the three main families, their three Kybele, and the spokesperson of the Elders. Together, they establish the rules of the System and administrate its possessions, keeping the balance acording to what they believe a utopia should be.

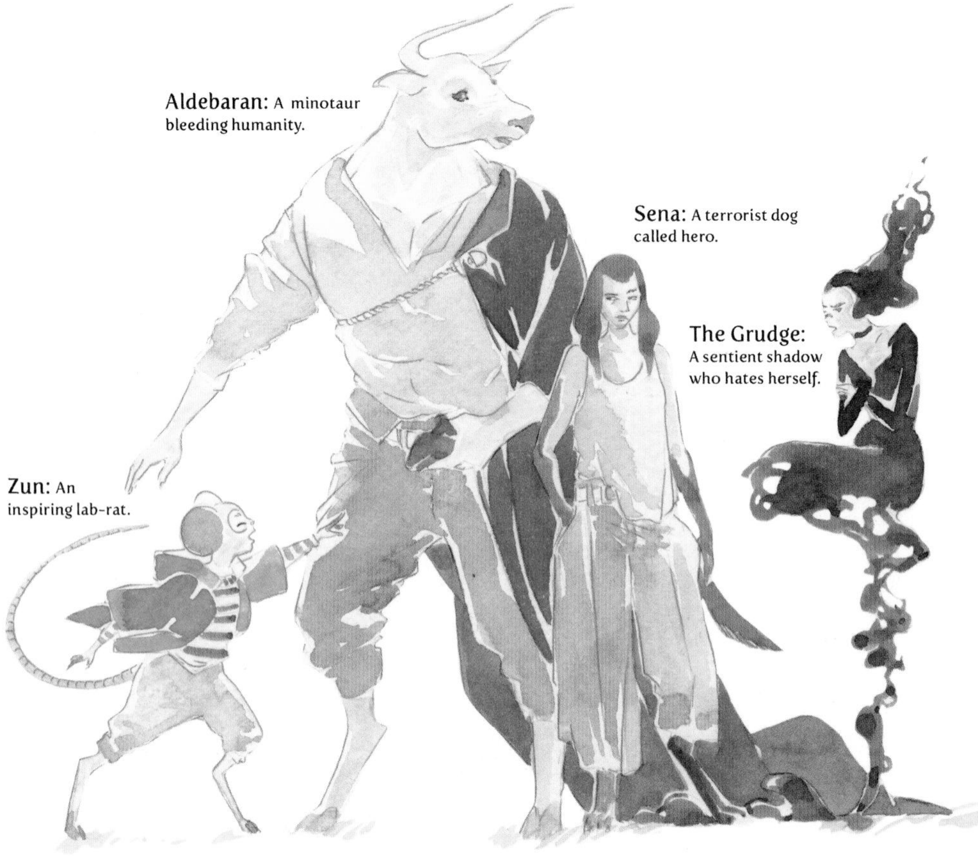
Aldebaran: A minotaur bleeding humanity.
Sena: A terrorist dog called hero.
The Grudge: A sentient shadow who hates herself.
Zun: An inspiring lab-rat.

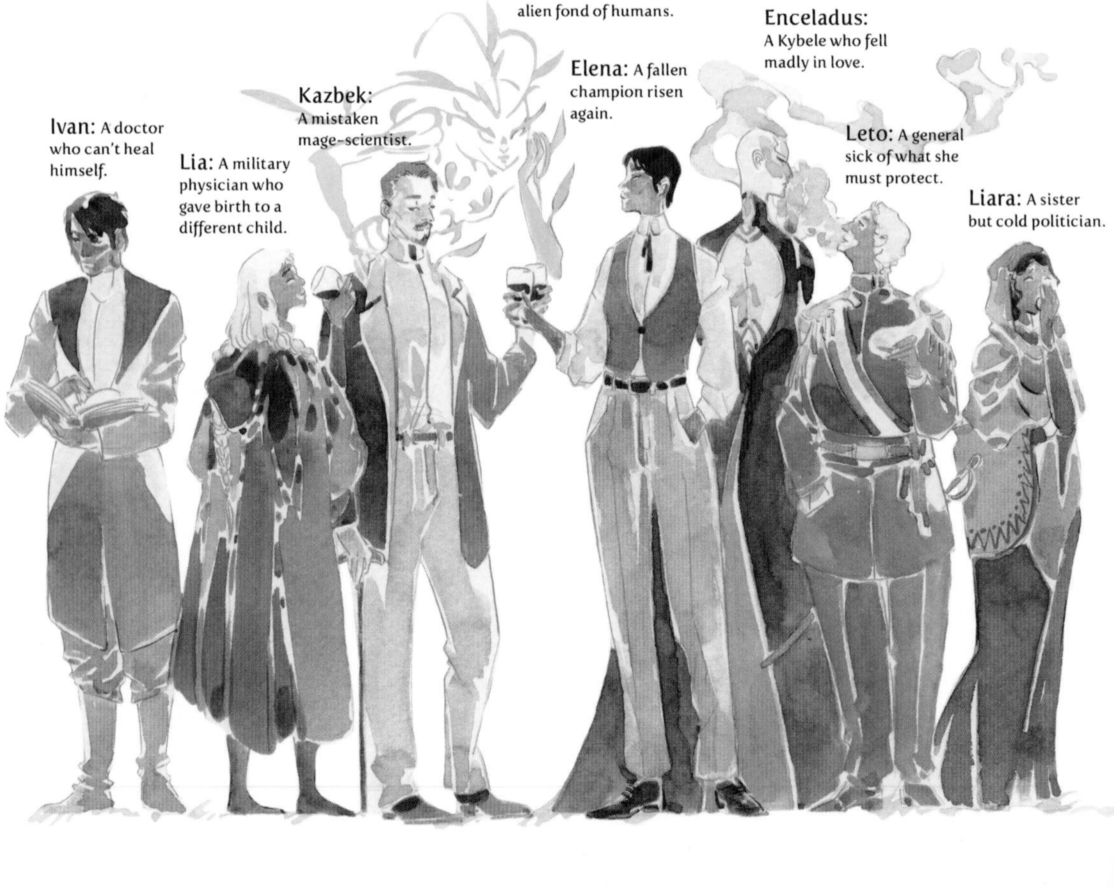
The Outsider: A kind alien fond of humans.
Enceladus: A Kybele who fell madly in love.
Elena: A fallen champion risen again.
Kazbek: A mistaken mage-scientist.
Ivan: A doctor who can't heal himself.
Lia: A military physician who gave birth to a different child.
Leto: A general sick of what she must protect.
Liara: A sister but cold politician.

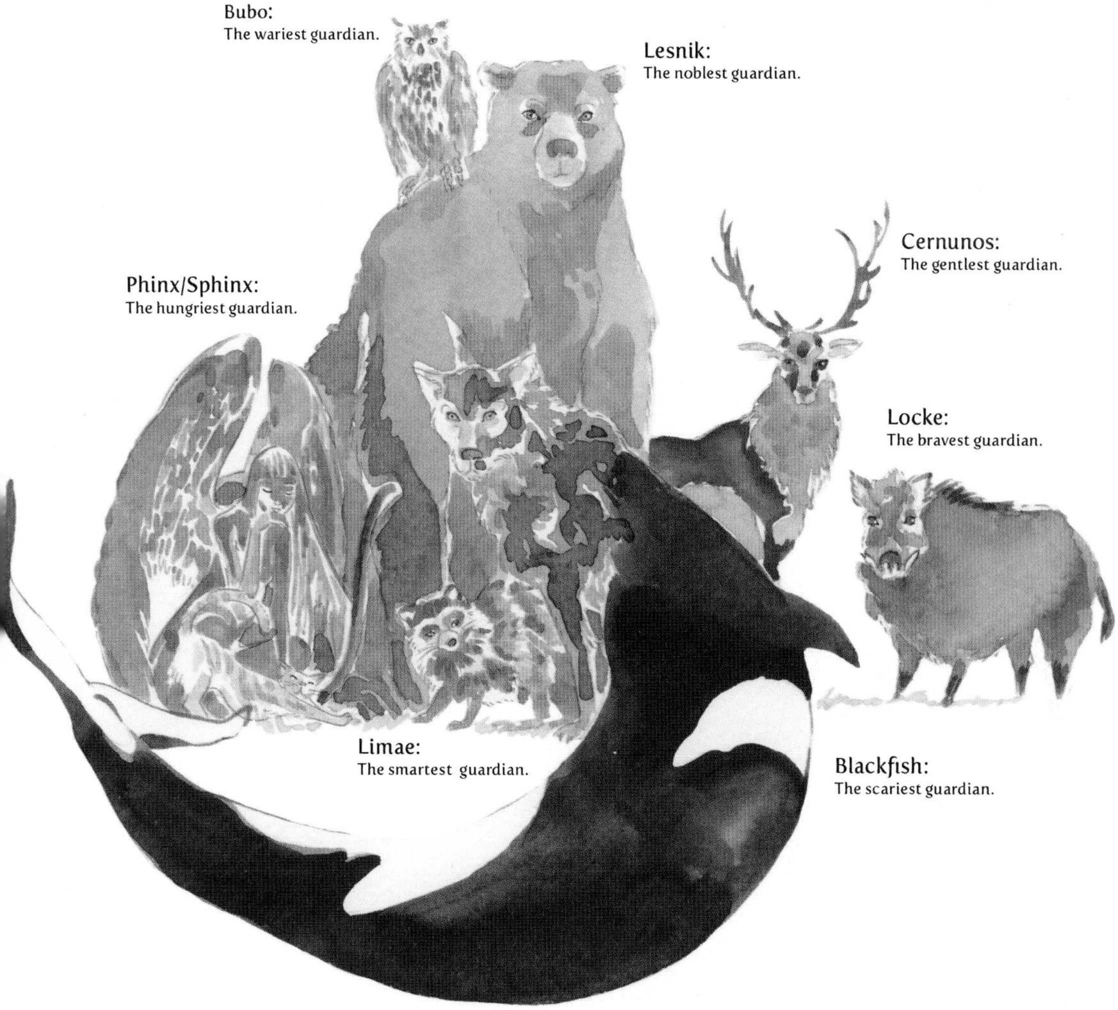
Bubo:
The wariest guardian.
Lesnik:
The noblest guardian.
Cernunos:
The gentlest guardian.
Phinx/Sphinx:
The hungriest guardian.
Locke:
The bravest guardian.
Limae:
The smartest guardian.
Blackfish:
The scariest guardian.

Hwei draws short stories about the rabbit Boris & child Lalage, a vague webcomic called *Hero*, illustrations for YA and children's books (*Spirit of the Sea*, *Dragonhearted*), and, most recently, an SF / fantasy story called *Mirror*, written by Big Boss Emma Rios...

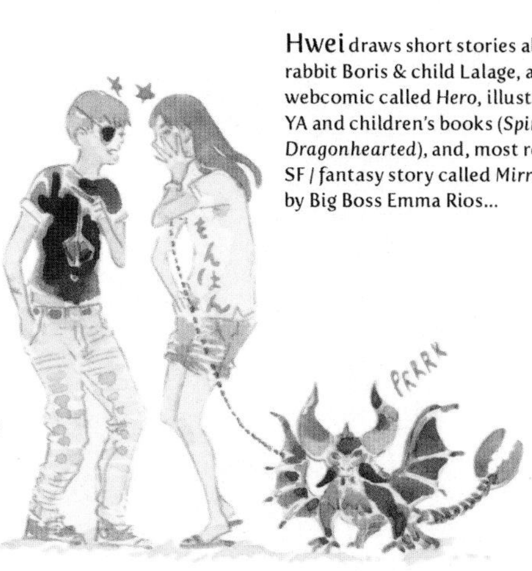
PRRRK

Emma wrote and drew I.D., co-edited *Island* and currently co-creates *Pretty Deadly* with the flawless kraken Kelly Sue DeConnick.
She adores this little book in your hands on which she worked really hard along with her sister-in-arms, Revolver Ocelot Hwei Lim.

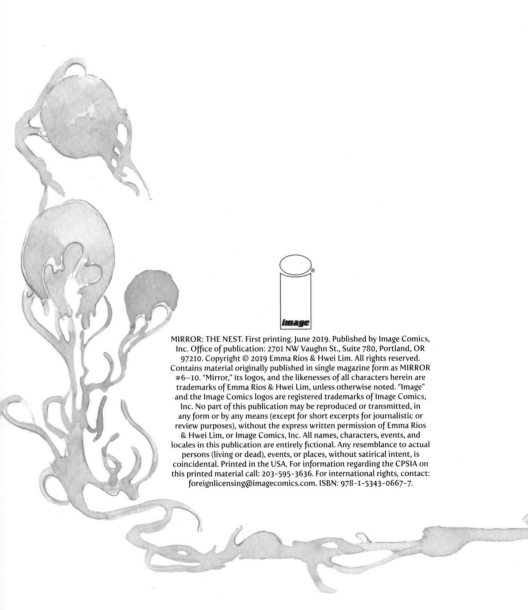

MIRROR: THE NEST. First printing. June 2019. Published by Image Comics,
Inc. Office of publication: 2701 NW Vaughn St., Suite 780, Portland, OR
97210. Copyright © 2019 Emma Ríos & Hwei Lim. All rights reserved.
Contains material originally published in single magazine form as MIRROR
#6–10. "Mirror," its logos, and the likenesses of all characters herein are
trademarks of Emma Ríos & Hwei Lim, unless otherwise noted. "Image"
and the Image Comics logos are registered trademarks of Image Comics,
Inc. No part of this publication may be reproduced or transmitted, in
any form or by any means (except for short excerpts for journalistic or
review purposes), without the express written permission of Emma Ríos
& Hwei Lim, or Image Comics, Inc. All names, characters, events, and
locales in this publication are entirely fictional. Any resemblance to actual
persons (living or dead), events, or places, without satirical intent, is
coincidental. Printed in the USA. For information regarding the CPSIA on
this printed material call: 203-595-3636. For international rights, contact:
foreignlicensing@imagecomics.com. ISBN: 978-1-5343-0667-7.

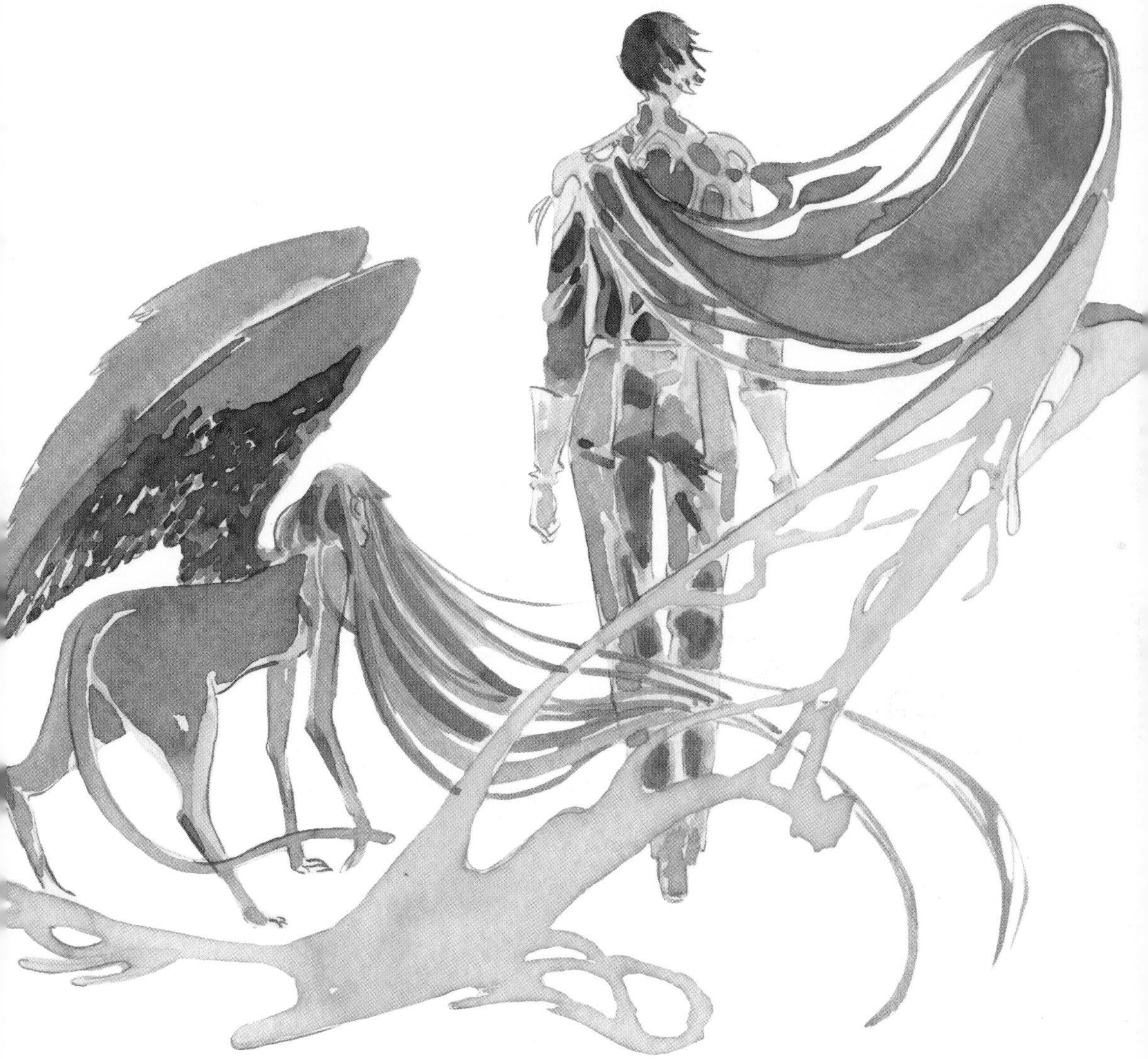

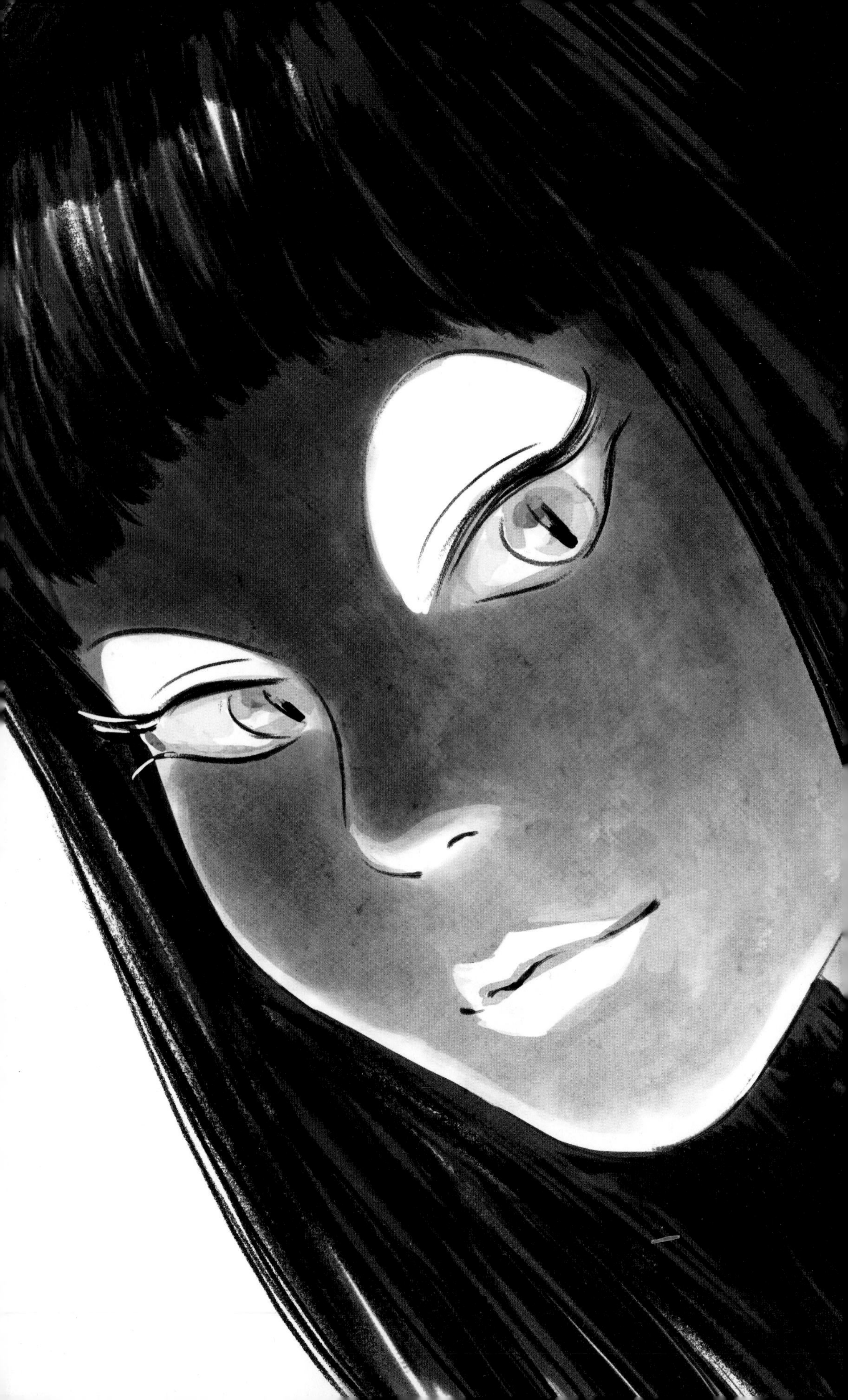